NICOLA ROSE

TASTE THE DARK

ELWOOD LEGACY BOOK I

COVER DESIGN by Deranged Doctor Design

For my Mum - Maggie
The most amazing and wonderful mother that any child could have asked for.
Always positive, strong and thoughtful.
A truly inspirational woman.

I miss you.

"Deep into that darkness peering, long I stood there, wondering, fearing, doubting, dreaming dreams no mortal ever dared to dream before."

— Edgar Allan Poe

1

ZAC

The gathering inside the Great Hall of the de Monsos castle was the very definition of disparity.

Down the left side of the aisle the swelling crowd was beautiful beyond reason; poised, elegant, pale-skinned, striking. They wore their carefully composed masks of calm with an air of superiority, but also a hint of expectation and excitement.

In stark contrast, the other side of the aisle contained a mixed bag of guests who were pitifully ordinary; standing beneath elegant chandeliers, surrounded by grandeur, yet dressed in shabby clothes and, honestly, needing a shower.

Wringing their hands with unease, they whispered to each other, standing in little groups, aware of the way the '*others*' were looking at them with calculating eyes.

I leant back against the wall in a darkened corner, letting out a bored sigh. This could be a long night.

A hush fell over the room as a man entered, dressed in an expensive suit, with a blushing bride on his arm. She giggled when he ushered her through, gathering up the silk train that billowed out in her wake.

His smile was serene, his pace casual. But the buoyant smile on *her* face quickly faded when she took in the room. Her eyebrows scrunched in confusion. To the left of the aisle they grinned and nodded at the groom. The other side shuffled around awkwardly, as if they didn't actually know why they were there. Probably for the best.

"I thought we weren't having any guests?" the bride whispered in the groom's ear. "You told me no family or friends. *Just us.* Who are all these people?" She scanned the crowds, searching for anyone familiar.

"Hush now, everything's fine. We'll talk after the ceremony. Just enjoy this moment, my love."

They arrived before an altar and stopped to face each other. She glanced around again at the watchful, expectant stares from the crowd. I pressed myself further into the wall to stop from walking out. *Why was I even here?*

Emory de Monsos, leader of the Bael, just fucking loved toying with me, that was why. I shifted my gaze and tried to get his attention, but he was standing behind the altar, waiting for the bride and groom to notice him. He was staring at the bride like she was his Christmas present — eager to get on with opening her up.

Her hand went to her chest in worry, a flush creeping up her neck, but then the groom smiled and her shoulders relaxed. She took a deep breath and smiled back, reaching out to stroke his face as if utterly in awe of him.

I would never do this. *Never.* Yet, the excitement from the left of the aisle was a tangible thing in the air, and the wisp of fear beginning to weave through the others... I clutched my fists beside me. *No.* I would not partake.

Emory cleared his throat from behind the altar and the bride finally snapped her attention to him. Within a second she was shaking her head in a daze. No doubt blinded by him, as everyone was, with his pure white hair and skin like bleached bone, smooth as the marble before him. Today he'd dressed himself in some weird, priestly robes.

Part of me wanted to tell her not to look at his blood-red eyes, but it was too late, and I wouldn't actually have done it anyway. Her hands began to tremble.

"Good evening," Emory said, loud enough to carry through the vast hall. "We're gathered here today, at this *sanguine mating*, to celebrate the joining of two souls fated to be together. Their union is demanded by our laws and their fate is binding. This bride will surrender herself wholly to this groom, and he'll take from her until he's had his fill."

She tried to pull her hand free from her beloved, but he held tight. "What is this?" she demanded in a low whisper, as if we couldn't hear. "This is not a vicar. I don't—"

"Quiet, my sweet," he soothed, his grip tightening on her until she was squirming in discomfort.

"Say your vows," Emory commanded.

The groom gazed hungrily at his bride. Her struggling faded as he turned her around to face the audience. So confused. Her watery eyes so wide, but she couldn't speak, couldn't run. Rooted to the spot. Through fear, or mind control. Could be either.

"Blood of my blood, bone of my bone, you will surrender your body, so that we might become one." He smiled at her; a sharp, toothy grin. She stumbled back a step. The guests to the right were out of their seats, eyeing up the 'others', who stood like adders poised to strike.

I folded my arms, resisting the urge to yell at them to hurry up.

"Your life will pass through me, Bethany," his voice dropped. "Your death will bring me new strength, new life. I'm truly blessed to have found my sanguine mate. I claim your essence as mine, for eternity. Sanguis quia aeternum. Mortem erit mea."

3

He moved forward to kiss his bride. Her head shook. A shallow cry came from somewhere in her throat, but faded to a whimper as he pushed her up against the altar.

"No," she pleaded — a whispered word that sent excitement surging through the room. The confused guests tried again to leave their seats, and were pressed back down by the groom's men. His hand hiked up her dress revealing a garter on a delicate thigh. Higher and higher, the material rose until a flash of red panties had him growling with desire.

Had she noticed that the infinity tattoo on his hand was also present on all of the other 'guests' down the left of the aisle? The mark of the Bael was everywhere. Closing tighter around my throat...

"You should feel honored to serve me," he groaned in her ear. "You were born for me. Be grateful the service has been short." His teeth found her neck and a moment later blood flowed down her chest, spreading through the material of the gleaming white dress.

Messy. Wasteful.

Finally.

Maybe now we could get on with this so I could leave. I made a move towards Emory, but one of his guards halted my advance. *Sanguine etiquette.*

So I waited, less than patiently, until the groom had his fill. Then he turned his fated bride around, pushing her down over the altar. She thrashed against him, shying from the bloodied lips and the hands that spread her legs apart. I turned away as he dropped his pants and drove into her. I didn't need to see his white ass jerking back and forth.

Chaos erupted through the hall.

People ran and fought, tugging on locked doors.

Then the screaming began.

4

Elegant guests turned into savages. Such was the way with vampires.

———

SOME PEOPLE BELIEVE THERE'S A MONSTER IN ALL OF US. THAT it sits there, hiding and dormant, and that under certain circumstances it may be released. Sometimes instances out of our control set it raging free, other times we *choose* to let it out. Some of us are better at keeping it locked down. Others fail to contain it at all.

I didn't believe it existed in everyone, but what I did know was that no one could truly understand the meaning of 'the monster within' until they'd battled a darkness so savage, so powerful in its desire to consume, that it shattered your soul into nothing but fragments. Left you clutching at the pieces, pulling them back together, trying to forge them into something of meaning and worth.

I called it the Beast, and testing the Beast was the only way to control it. To release it, just enough that it threatened to break free, then draw it back. Each time releasing it further, taking bigger risks — because with each victory came greater strength. A power almost as strong as that of the Beast; the power of hope.

My monster might have been locked away, but its voice was always there. Pushing, testing, taunting. Trying to be heard and have its words tumble from my lips instead of sitting mute in my head. For now, it was trapped in my carefully erected cage, and not at all happy about it. If it found a foothold, there'd be no putting it back.

And it certainly wasn't in the mood for playing on this day, with little intention of staying locked down. An unusual electric ache scratched down the back of my neck. I'd liked

5

to have blamed the bloodbath unfolding before me, but it wasn't just that.

No. It wasn't dead humans giving me a headache, it was dead *vampires*.

Dead vampires didn't pop up often, you see. We were notoriously hard to kill, and when we did slaughter each other, we were meticulous about hiding the evidence. Yet, I'd lost two men in as many weeks.

Someone was on my island, killing my vampires under my nose, and I had nothing. No scent to pick up on, no trail to follow. It was like the damned invisible man was wandering around my territory, teasing and taunting me with his invincibility.

Speaking of invincibility, or assholes, for now I was keeping a close watch on Emory as he made me wait for his attention. His sole focus was on the groom, who was still fucking his new bride into oblivion, her pure dress drenched in blood.

Such a waste. A sanguine mate should be savored. The evening should have been drawn out over days, weeks, and her essence taken gradually. Not that I approved, but if you were going to go all primal, then at least do it correctly.

However, events were escalating quickly and I supposed at least that meant I wouldn't have to endure much more.

The vampire guests were just as impatient as the groom — they hadn't wasted any time in devouring the humans, who were most likely homeless people, rounded up and brought in for the entertainment. People with nothing, who'd been promised an evening of alcohol and merriment. If any of them ended up being missed, then a Bael goon would go in and clear up the issue. Innocent people in the wrong place at the wrong time. Lured in by the beautiful vampires.

Whilst just down the hallway, in another soundproofed hall, the richest members of society had been invited to an entirely different event. Politicians, the chief of police, lawyers, scientists, megacorp members; they were all there, sipping champagne and nibbling canapés, enraptured by the 'World of Emory' — all of them in his pocket, thriving off the attention and bribes, blissfully unaware of the monsters in their midst. Or even worse, some were well aware, but uncaring. Foolishly believing that because they did his bidding they were safe.

Only Emory would host several events simultaneously, as a clear demonstration of his power and rank. He'd spend the evening casually slipping between the two parties — one minute feasting on the blood of an unfortunate guest in a gruesome, frenzied orgy, and the next minute he'd be schmoozing with those elitist cocksuckers just down the hall.

He finally turned to look at me, wiping bloodied hands down his robes, and I wondered how many outfit changes he needed on a night like this.

I shrugged away from my observation post against the wall, impatient for this bullshit evening to end.

"Biggest party of the year and you didn't invite me?" Leon appeared at my side, resting a hand on my shoulder.

I smiled at him, shaking my head. "Which party are you referring to? Did you come for one of the homeless saps or a business tycoon, because personally, I'd prefer the perky, spring-break tits back on our island?"

He laughed, inching closer. "You're not yourself at the moment. You shouldn't have come here alone."

Emory appeared in the next instant. About time.

"Mr. Elwood," he nodded, red eyes scanning me up and down. "I don't remember putting any other members of your repellent clan on my guest list." He glowered from

Leon to the security guards by the door. Thanks to my best friend, they'd be dead by dawn — if they were lucky.

Leon nudged my ribs and gave Emory a wide grin, knowing that the Bael leader had a taste for blonde, surfer-looking dudes like himself.

"Follow me," Emory sighed, ignoring Leon and turning on his heels. "Alone," he added over his shoulder.

Leon grunted, and I followed Emory to the back of the hall, side-stepping past the pools of blood and mangled bodies. The mayhem seemed to pause as we picked our way through, all eyes drawn to arguably the most powerful vampire on the planet, and myself, arguably the most baffling. The human guests that were still alive made pleading eyes at me. The vampires observed me with disgust, because outcasts didn't belong at such events.

Tension in the air thickened. Leon sent me some thoughts about watching my back, and how he'd 'tear each member of the Bael a new one' if they overstepped. I shook my head at his idiocy. He was a fool for coming. If things went bad here, he'd be joining the doomed security guards, and he knew it. A pang of guilt swept through me at the memories of those I'd already lost, clouding my vision... rattling the cage.

Get a grip, Zac. Do what you were sired for and take them out. The Beast reared its head, whispering into my ears.

Beyond the altar, Emory settled himself into his ridiculous throne; intricately carved, upholstered in red velvet, and sitting atop a marble dais. It might have seemed appropriate hundreds of years ago, but to me it looked gaudy and absurd.

Looking bored now that the bride was lying utterly dead on the altar, he cocked one leg over the arm of the throne, toying with his long ponytail. Albinism robbed every bit of pigment from his skin and hair. Even his eyelashes were the brightest white, their delicate purity tainted by the devil eyes they framed.

Those eyes were a window into hell. Gazing into them for too long had been known to send mortals insane. Though that was really just a trick, it was his mind-control that did that, not the eyes themselves.

Just as I was about to speak, Emory nodded to one of his men and a whimpering woman was thrust at me. I pushed her aside, finding that she was chained up to three others, all naked. They formed a little line before us and Emory shot to his feet like a kid with candy. For fuck's sake, had he not had enough already?

"I do love to eat before conducting important business, don't you, Zac?" he asked.

"I already ate."

Liar. I squeezed my eyes closed for a moment, silencing the Beast.

A smile lingered on Emory's pretty-boy lips before he tore into a woman's throat, deliberately doing so with enough force to splatter blood all over my white button-down shirt. I stepped back, attempting to wipe myself down. The heat from the naked bodies caressed me, their pitter-patter hearts skipping through my head. My fangs threatened to descend.

It was so hard to stay focused with a man being stretched apart on a rack to my right, several chained up to my left, and now these tantalizing treats before me. Fuck knew what was going on behind me, but it sounded fun.

Take them.

"Enough of the show, Emory. Get it over with. Why am I here?" I barked, clenching my teeth together and trying to hold my breath.

"You sure I can't tempt you first?" He smeared the woman's blood over her nipples, licking it off.

I turned to leave. The Bael could 'encourage' me to attend their events when summoned, but they couldn't change who I was and, much to their disappointment, they couldn't make me fulfill the Elwood Legacy either. They remained ever hopeful, however. And patient. They had eternity, after all.

So they just kept me close, a watchful eye always bearing down, keeping the pressure on. It figured that eventually they'd find something to leverage me with, but today was not that day.

"Not one, but two dead vampires," Emory called after me. "Do you need our help?"

I froze, hackles rising. "Your help is the last thing I'll ever need. Besides, I haven't yet ruled *you* out as the perpetrators."

He laughed. "Come now, Zac, you know I gave up killing your men long ago. I'm going with the patient approach these days. Softly, softly."

"Yeah? So why am I here?"

"My dear boy, don't be so hostile. You know I like to check on you every so often, see how my future prodigy is doing. It seems you're not doing so well and I can't have anyone threatening an Elwood. I'm posting agents to help you."

"If you put a single man on my island, I'll kill them. I can take care of this myself."

Emory's eyes narrowed. He placed a finger over the woman's lips to hush her dying cries. "See that you do. I'm returning to England for a while. You have six weeks and then I'm coming personally to deal with it." For emphasis, he plunged his hand into her chest and pulled out her barely-beating heart.

I LEFT THE HALL IN A HURRY, THE BEAST PRESSING AGAINST HIS cage inside me. My head spun with so much aggression that I hardly noticed the screams behind me as Emory tore into the other chained victims.

Leon was at my side in an instant as I exited the building.

"We'll find them. We'll fix this," he said. "Whoever is messing with us, they're on a countdown to the end of days."

"I haven't felt like this for a long time. I'm barely keeping a grip on myself." I pumped my fists to unclench them at my sides.

"Sounds like you need a hit," he mumbled.

We didn't speak again for the journey home. I stole through the living area and attempted to go unnoticed past the men from my Cell, a couple of whom were snorting coke from bouncing tits and getting sucked off. They indulged me by casually ignoring my roiling tension. The women couldn't see that though, and one attached herself to me immediately. I muttered some apology for my lack of interest and broke free from her clutches.

Storming through the hallway, I ripped off my black tie and tore the buttons from my shirt, discarding it behind me. I passed down the basement stairs and pressed my fingertip against a scanning panel until it beeped. Heavy metal doors clunked open. Four men and one woman were playing cards in the corner of the room beyond.

They fell dead silent in my presence, leaping to their feet and lining up against the wall like shuffling sheep; heads hung low, eyes not daring to meet mine. They were starting to look like the undead, too. Black circles under their eyes, and pale, gaunt faces. I fed them well, their diet was something they couldn't complain about, but it wasn't enough to sustain what they lost in here.

I stood in front, willing one of them to look, urging

someone to step out of line and give me an excuse to release the Beast. The smallest of the guys shuffled uncomfortably. He was a skinny little runt, all pointy-nosed like a shrew, with a straggly goatee and yellow teeth.

"Whose turn is it today?" I asked.

All of them. The Beast stirred.

No one replied. I let their scents wash over me, the fear rolling off them and into my core like a drug. Raised pulses tasted so exquisite at the back of my tongue. My body knew this drill; it knew what I was here for. The Beast was aware of the treat it would soon receive and it salivated in anticipation, clawing and scratching inside the cage, desperate for freedom. Tonight I was teetering on the edge, and it knew it.

On the inside, I was burning up with all-consuming need. The dark fever, turmoil and hunger…

On the outside, I was motionless, calculating, and cold as fuck.

"Number 266," I stated, brushing past the dinner line and pausing at the other door. I felt him follow behind me, heard his mind racing with thoughts about who I was, what I would do to him. Yet he couldn't argue, he couldn't fight or refuse to come. He knew too well what the consequences of rebellious behavior brought. Those were some painful memories that I let him keep.

He smelled different today. I mean, he always stank like trash to me; his scent didn't press my buttons even on a good day, but today was worse. He'd been fed from too many times, the blood scent was weakening. I'd been looking forward to his expiry date coming.

I turned to face him, but he didn't flinch. He knew that he'd go into the other room and then he'd come back out, unable to remember what happened. He also knew that, occasionally, they didn't come back.

"Say goodbye," I whispered in his ear.

His eyes flew to mine in panic, heart instantly doubling in pace.

"No... no... please, not yet," he panted. The others kept their heads down, particularly Runt, but their escalated fear surged, along with a mixture of relief that it wasn't them.

Pressing my finger to another security panel, I dragged him through the door.

Number 266 had been in this room many times already, yet he viewed it with fresh, fear-laden eyes. Spinning around in panic and confusion, taking in the bare, tiled walls and floor. There was nothing here except for us, a hose, and the cold, hard tiles. Easy to wash down.

Immediately, he pressed his back against the closed door. He wore a Robocop shirt which read, 'Dead or Alive, you're coming with me.' Funny guy. He'd been wearing it the day I took him and I'd made him wear it every day since; a little reminder about why he was here.

Eva liked him wearing it too, the way it clung to his muscles. She'd be pissed with me for this. She wanted to end him, have some fun and screw him one last time, but the jackass in me was taking over at an alarming rate; 266 was mine.

"W... what is this place?" he asked, pressing harder into the door, like he hoped to melt into it. Beads of sweat multiplied on his forehead, his hands twitching in feverish fear, goose bumps forming on his skin.

"It's your nightmares." The words came out slow and snarly as I ran my tongue over my teeth and embraced the surge of hunger. Shivers ran through me at the sound of his breathing, labored with dread.

"You can't do this," he said, with a sudden burst of bravado. It was at this point they either crumbled in terror, or they fought. My smile widened, hoping he would choose the latter.

I tried so hard to slow my muscles as they bunched in their familiar way, knotting and tensing reflexively. I wanted to *feel* it and make it last, but my head was spinning, I couldn't hold back.

I circled the room and sprang silently to my prey, covering the distance between us in a single, exhilarating move. If only every day, every minute, could be spent hunting.

Pinning him to the door, his eyes fixed on my fangs, then flicked to my eyes, and back again. The stench of urine drifted into my nose, nearly making me gag. So disappointing. I'd hoped for more from him.

Tuning out all the external chatter — his thoughts, the thoughts coming from the other captives, the sounds of sex two floors above, not to mention the din of cars, music and shouting from all over the island – I focussed instead on the only thing that mattered in that moment; the sound of blood rushing through 266's veins. A rhythmic whoosh, over and over, like waves crashing against the shore, drawing me into a gradual trance.

The darkness swirled inside my head, allowing me to see only a singular thing; Life and Death as one. Yanking his head back, my teeth sank straight through his jugular. Blood spurted down my throat in a dizzying rush. He struggled, arms flailing and grabbing at me in surprise. I held tight and drank deeply, until all too soon his legs gave out and I had to hold him upright.

His over diluted blood was odious, but somehow it still sent a sublime energy through my being, purifying and calming. It ran down my chin and warmed my neck. After a final few twitches I had to accept that he was gone. I pulled back and found his eyes wide and frozen from a fleeting moment of terror.

Dropping him to the floor, I immediately needed more.

With my senses in overdrive, the instinct coursed mercilessly through my veins, spreading out of control and burning everything in its wake. Soon, all rational thought would dissolve to embers, all human feeling scorched.

Because their breath slows, their heartbeat fades, their blood stills… but the hunger never ends.

Take them. Drain every last drop from each of their wretched bodies. One by one. Drink them dry and bathe in their blood.

The other captives were still lined up in the adjoining room, waiting to be relieved back to their card game, to live another day. I stalked toward the door, a low hiss escaping my lips.

"No! Zac!" Leon burst into the room, placing a hand to my chest.

"Fuck you," I shoved him aside, slamming his back into the wall, and moved on another step before he jumped me. Grabbing his forearms, I yanked him round into a headlock and squeezed until he relaxed his body into submission.

I released him with a shove and continued to the door, but it was too late, the moment was ruined. The darkness disappeared and snapped me back to reality. The Beast was locked behind bars again before it even had the chance to get going. It would make me remember that with a vicious ache all over my body.

Pussy. It grumbled.

I spun on Leon and he threw his hands up. "Everything's out of whack! You're not yourself. You'll only regret it if you take them all in one go, besides, I'm fucking hungry, you need to save me some."

Snorting a brief laugh, I dragged my fingers through my hair, clicking my neck, trying in vain to ease out the pain that was crawling through my flesh. It was like an army of fire ants had been set loose just under the surface of my skin, stinging and burning. The ecstasy had been too short-lived.

"Get that mess cleaned up," I jerked my head towards the body lying slumped on the floor, a distinct lack of blood anywhere, despite the gaping holes in his neck. At least I was clean, unlike Emory and his animals.

I dropped my head back to sigh at the ceiling and became aware of something different prickling at the back of my neck. Something really did feel messed up. "What *is* that?"

Leon shrugged, giving me an '*I told you so*' look.

Something was coming.

The notion slapped itself into my consciousness and settled there, causing a thrum of anxiety in my core. I stormed off, climbing back up the basement steps, my spine tingling in anticipation.

2

JESS

*M*y therapist once labelled me a *'nymphomaniac with self-destructive tendencies'*. Some shit like that. I just needed a buzz and a bad boy, that wasn't so abnormal, was it?

I refused to believe this was a medical condition that needed writing down in a notebook, by some suited and spectacled bore, to then be typed up and filed on the computer under 'Jessica Layton: Epic Failure'.

I mean, sure, I may have spent my life careening from one disaster to another, but sometimes the world threw that crap your way, and you had to deal with it. Move on.

That was why I was here, riding down the only road access to South Padre Island on the gulf coast of Texas, with the two mile causeway stretching out before me like a glinting road to redemption.

Let's call it my own brand of therapy, since the shrinks' never worked. One last blow out; get it out of my system. Then I'd sort my shit out. I'd grow up and swallow their incessant drivel about how to live a 'normal' life. Really I would.

But I'd read a book once about how to quit smoking — it

encouraged you to keep on puffing the whole time you were reading until you got to the last page. It worked. I hadn't had a cigarette since.

So I reckoned this was the same. Keep on with the reckless living whilst contemplating my new life, with my friend Anna tutoring me on *how* exactly one went about living like a normal person. She'd agreed to take some vacation time and introduce me to the island in style. Once the vacation was over, I'd be cured! Bam! Maybe I'd write a self help book about it afterwards.

Seriously though, it needed to work, because I had a new job lined up ready, and I couldn't let Anna, or myself down.

I glanced down at my jacket, which currently held a distinctive bare spot — the red leather too clean compared to the rest — where I'd removed the patch from my old fire station.

It was a conspicuous reminder that I'd fucked up, and I couldn't wait to get patched in with the Carnage Crew – South Padre Island Fire Department. Cover up that bare patch on my jacket, and maybe the one in my soul.

I skirted round the slowing cars in front of me as the island drew near. It was tempting to rip open the throttle on my brute of a motorbike and blaze my way into town, starting as I meant to continue, but another speeding ticket wouldn't be the best start. I'd lose my license at that rate. Anna told me the police were tough on that around here, unless you were one of 'them'. Who knew what that meant, she'd changed the subject in a flurry of excited babble.

I held off at a steady speed, just a fraction over the limit, since I couldn't bring myself to slow down any further. Then, with the bridge behind me, I hit the boulevard. It went on in an irritatingly straight line, with smaller roads crisscrossing the island in grids.

Thankfully, neat and orderly ended with the roads. Everything else was clearly a carnival of crazy. I rode past bars overflowing with bronzed, half-naked bodies — drinks in hand, dancing, shouting, singing, making out. Neon lights decorated the roadside with an array of color in the fading evening light. The party went on and on, from one bar or hotel to the next. Barely an inch of ground was left free from a gyrating booty. Even through my helmet, and the growl of the engine, I could still make out the constant rhythm of music.

As I began to wonder if I'd missed Anna's turning, a guy stumbled into the road like a deranged version of Bambi, all gangly legs going in opposite directions. I might have seen him sooner had I not been checking my eyeliner in the side mirror. My brakes slammed and the back wheel locked up, rising a foot into the air, very nearly face planting me into the asphalt. I stopped an inch away. He looked up, bug-eyed and confused.

"You fucking shithead!" I yelled, flailing my hands.

He clutched a beer bong, the tube in his mouth and funnel held up high, guzzling the last few drops. His buddies caught up and patted him on the back, putting him into fits of choking laughter and sending beer spraying all over me. I could handle that, but the sticky shit on my baby, dripping over the paintwork and handlebars?

"Not cool, dude." I wiped at the tank with my sleeve, biting back the urge to get off the bike and shove that tube down his throat.

"Holy shit! That's a chick riding that thing!" One of the guys drew closer, staggering and peering into my helmet like I was a circus exhibit. Jeers went up from the gathering crowd as they tried to get a good look.

Lifting my helmet visor, I grabbed his drink and downed the blue poison, before shoving the empty bottle back in his hands. "Come find me later, boys. Maybe one of you'll get lucky and I'll show you what else I can ride."

Jerking back the throttle, I left them eating my dust.

"A OUIJA BOARD?" ANNA ASKED, PICKING OUT THE OLD, WORN board from a growing mountain of stuff on her table, and wafting it at me. "You still believe in that crap?"

"Of course. I thought it would be a blast from the college past. You know, my psychic, Julie, says—"

"Your psychic? You have a psychic now?" She cut me off laughing and dropped the board back in the pile.

"Look, lady, there's a lot of shit out there we don't know about. You need to open your mind a bit. Maybe your gift will help with that." I finally located the bottle of Rebel Yell whiskey at the bottom of my camping backpack and tapped her forehead with it. She poured two glasses, adding some ice.

"Anyway, what did your psychic say?" Anna threatened to burst into giggles again.

"Screw you! I'll tell you later when you're shitfaced, then you can go right ahead and split your sides."

She slurped at her drink to hide her smile and watched me faffing with more belongings. I'd tried, and failed, to pack light for the journey, since the rest of my meagre possessions were being shipped to Anna's in a few days.

"I can't believe you're actually here, Jess!" She clapped her hands in sudden excitement, making her glasses wobble down her nose. "I wish you wouldn't pay for a motel though, you can sleep here while you're looking for a new apartment."

"I'll already be cluttering up your apartment with boxes, you don't need me here, too. It's fine. The motel looks a little run down on the website but, no offense, it does have a bed, which has to be better than your sofa."

"Don't be silly, you'd have my bed." She gave me a pleading look.

"Then have the guilt of being all cosy in your bed while you suffer? Thanks, but no thanks. Anyway, forget that; tell me more about the wild nights we're going to have, and why you never forced me to get my ass here sooner! This place looks amazing." I took a slug of whiskey, the hot, syrupy warmth easing down my throat.

"You ain't seen nothing yet. You don't get two hundred and fifty thousand spring-breakers here every year for no reason."

"That's insane, the island is tiny!"

"Yep. And that many horny, drunk people all together in a small space...?" She waggled her eyebrows playfully. This girl was a walking contradiction; all nerdy looking with her little chubby face, always flushed, and big-rimmed glasses, yet, get some alcohol in her and she was a live wire.

"So let's go!" I downed the rest of my drink. One wouldn't hurt. Okay, two, if you were counting that blue shit. "I hope you've still got that spare helmet and leathers?"

"Nowhere is further than a few minutes away round here. Don't you think we should walk or get a cab?" she frowned.

"Humor me. It's my new baby, I've only had him a week and I want to take every possible opportunity to ride him."

"Him? It's a motorcycle, Jess!"

"Yeah, yeah. I'll fetch him back tomorrow."

She sat in rigid hesitation, fiddling with her glasses.

"Come on! I'm a good rider, you'll be safe."

Begrudgingly, she grabbed her gear from the back of a cupboard and dusted off the cobwebs. Her jaw dropped when she noted the huge, red bike outside.

"I'd like you to meet my Ducati Streetfighter. Isn't he beautiful? I've named him Loki, after the God of Mischief."

"Fitting," she mumbled. "It looks fast... and dangerous. Shouldn't you be more careful with money? Danny said you're only going to be working two shifts a week."

I flapped my hands at her silliness. "They're twenty-four hour shifts, the pay is pretty good. Anyway, I still have a shit tonne in the bank that my parents left me. Benefits of being an only child with rich folks."

"Oh yeah, their deaths were really fortunate for you," she said sarcastically, immediately clasping a hand over her mouth in horror. "Shit, Jess, I'm so sorry, I didn't mean it to come out like that."

"It's fine," I lied, as she cautiously settled herself onto the bike and the engine roared to life.

Truth was, that really was the opinion of most people after the event. Suspicious explosion, daughter suffering amnesia about what happened, *very convenient*. I shouldn't have been here, alive. It was my fault. I didn't know how, but I'd caused that explosion. Somehow.

And that suspicion and guilt still followed me around years later. It wasn't going away. Ever.

I WHEELIED AWAY, CHUCKLING AS ANNA NEARLY FELL OFF THE back, frantically clutching at my jacket. She directed me to the beach with taps on my shoulders — as if it was hard to get lost in this place — and I cruised over to the parking lot. A group of guys hovered around their bikes. One of them watched us approach, no doubt appreciating the thundering machine heading his way.

Pulling up next to him, I dismounted slowly, trying to act casual, even though for some reason his sullen gaze had my heart fluttering. A quick sideways glance told me that he was gorgeous, in the *'is this guy actually real'* kind of way. Dark spiked-up hair, lean and muscled, dressed casual.

I removed my helmet, red hair falling around my shoulders in a dramatic cliché movie moment, and shaking it out before looking up to return his smile.

He wasn't smiling though; he was giving me some sort of twisted, murderous look. I was used to guys being surprised when they figured out it was a woman on the bike, but they loved it, they didn't look at me like *that*. It quickly became awkward. I tried to look away and found I couldn't. So I stood there, gawking at him, his eyes burning through me in weird hatred. Just as I threatened to crumble into ash under the heat of his glare, he screwed his face up in disgust and turned his back to me.

The world snapped back into focus. Noise filled my ears and drowned out the sound of my heart, which had gone from fluttering to all-out thudding. I hesitated with the key in the ignition. Should I approach him? Anna was dithering, trying to undo the strap on her helmet and looking embarrassingly flustered, so I yanked the key and pulled her away down the beach.

"Darn it!" she mumbled beneath the helmet, still fumbling with the release.

"Calm down, would you?" I batted her hands aside and pulled her free.

"Can't breathe in that thing!"

"Not around hotness like that." Curiosity had me glancing back over my shoulder.

"That was Zac Elwood," she said the name with hushed awe, but her face turned sour. "Hotness doesn't even cover it. He's also a complete A-hole."

"Is that why he was looking at me like I'd just insulted his mother?"

"Don't take it personally. His group are always around here, everyone idolizes them. Zac's in his own little world though, he never notices anyone."

"Typical. Always the best looking ones that have issues."

"You should know." She gave me a disapproving look and I shoved her playfully.

"Ta-dah," she said suddenly, sweeping her arm in a grand gesture as we arrived at a beach bar. "This is MoJoe's. Best party on the island!"

"Oh yeah?" I glanced around at the fading paint and a woman puking her guts up into the sand outside the door.

"Danny owns it. His little sideline. That means half price drinks, and that means it's the best!" She slapped my shoulder.

"Shit, Danny? Is he going to be here?"

I wasn't ready to see my new boss. Last time I saw him was about four years ago, when I'd fucked him and then ignored his texts. It didn't escape me that he may have given me this job out of a twisted urge to watch me squirm. Or maybe with the hope of more fucking, which, actually, wouldn't be so bad.

I don't know why I'd ignored him, what's not to like about a fit Fire Chief? Even if he was ten years older. He was aging in total style, his steel-gray hair always spiked-up, and his sharp, bright eyes always full of mischief. At least, that's how he was then. I wondered — half hoped — he was still as I remembered.

Danny's parents were close to Anna's and, as a result, they were close too — right from when Anna was born and he would help look after her, play with her. He was practically her big brother, which meant I'd encountered him numerous times since Anna and I became friends at college. He was impressed when he'd met me and found I was studying fire science.

Anna and I had been studying different things, but hit it off right away, from that first crazy night at the student bar. We all fell into an easy, casual friendship. Anna was the only person in the world to see past my ups and downs, the mood swings, the quirky shit, the weird occurrences. She stuck around when no one else did.

I guessed now I could officially class Danny as a supporter, too. Following a massive fuck-up and suspension at my previous fire department, I'd miraculously landed this job. Either my old chief fluffed up my reference in an eager bid to finally be rid of me, or Anna had done some pleading with Danny to take a chance on me.

We found a table outside on the beach, with the parking lot not far away. Thankfully, Danny wasn't around. I could avoid that first greeting for a little longer. Anna rambled on about what we were going to do over the coming weeks. Should she get her hair cut to celebrate my arrival? Should we try out bungee jumping?

I was only half listening. I kept glancing back toward the motorbikes where Zac sat poised and moody, glowing under the floodlights like a smoldering apparition, whilst his friends laughed and joked around him. He toyed with an airgun and was idly shooting cans across the parking lot with remarkable accuracy. I heard them ping away with each shot fired.

I told myself I was only looking to make sure my Loki was alright. If one of those bullets hit him, he'd be a dead man. But the truth was, he fascinated me. Each time I glanced up, I was sure he'd been watching me, but within a second he wasn't anymore, and he'd shot down another can. Always so quick that I couldn't be sure whether he'd really been looking at all.

I turned to look once more and the hair on my arms sprang up like I'd been dumped in ice. My breath caught in my throat. I coughed to try and cover up the gasp that snuck out. This time he was definitely staring at me, head tilted. In fact, he seemed utterly transfixed. I had to clutch the table as a dizzy wave ran over me.

"Jess... Jess... *Jess!* Are you listening?" Anna poked my arm.

"He's kinda staring at me."

"Huh!" she said with surprise. "I've never seen him show interest in any of the women, but he's certainly interested in you right now." She jabbed another finger into me, harder this time, with a suggestive edge to her tone.

"I don't think it's *that* sort of look. He's not checking me out, it's kind of menacing, don't you think?" I spoke out the side of my mouth, as if he could hear me all the way over there. Alarm bells vibrated through my head, making me feel anxious and excited at the same time.

He looked away and carried on shooting like nothing had happened. Then he laughed at something, but there was still an uneasiness about his posture. With his gaze averted, I was released from a strange pressure inside my head, and immediately longed for more.

"And there you have it," Anna muttered. "Weird A-hole."

JESS

*R*olling over in bed, I was relieved to find an empty space in the crumpled sheets where Mr. Goatee had been snoring a few hours ago. I rubbed my head, trying to remember if I'd even bothered to find out his name. Memories from the night before were vague.

He couldn't have been particularly earth-shattering, given that my most vivid memory was when he'd pulled out of me too far and rammed himself back in with, to his credit, a great deal of force — but had misjudged his aim and went halfway into my ass. After an initial squeal of shock, I tried to reassure him that it was fine, he could stay there if he wanted, but maybe we'd need some lube.

The poor boy was mortified. It had gone downhill pretty fast from there. Thank goodness he'd had the decency to creep out whilst I slept, avoiding all that unnecessary and awkward '*morning after*' talk.

I made my way to the shower, clutching my throbbing head. Leaning my face back into the spray, I closed my eyes with an image of Zac forming behind them. I hadn't seen much more of him, he'd disappeared soon after the glaring incident. His expression had been so intense that it kind of frightened me, and that took some doing. It also made me eager to see him again.

A familiar thrill had me putting my hand between my legs. I stroked and rubbed, thinking of that gorgeous, brooding face and imagining how his body would be all shades of heaven. Delving my fingers inside myself, fantasies danced around me, ideas of that foreboding stare bearing down on me as he pinned me to the ground, hands held up over my head, taking me roughly—

My cell phone rang in the other room. I tried to ignore it, but it was so persistent, and the shrill ringtone went right through my head like a dagger. "Yes, Anna, what's the emergency?"

"Good afternoon to you too, cranky pants."

"Sorry. I was a little busy in the shower, if you know what I mean?"

"Eeeew, too much info!" she groaned, and I imagined her cheeks going red. "It's two o'clock already. We have to hit the town and get drinking. It's the only way to cure our hangovers. We're still celebrating your arrival, right?"

"Hell, yes." I pulled on yesterday's underwear with one hand. All my gear was still at her place. I should have just agreed to stay there. If only I didn't have so many anxious emotions around sharing living space with loved ones. The burn scar on my back itched at the thought.

"I'll meet you at the parking lot," I added. "I need to check my baby's unharmed. If any drunk twat has touched him, I will hunt them down."

ZAC WAS EVERYWHERE. THE BARS, THE BEACHES, THE FAIR, THE grill where I ate most days — though he never ate, just watched me in a psycho-stalker way. He paid extra close

28

attention each time he found me kissing another man, but annoyingly, not enough to make him come and claim me for himself. He was even loitering across the road of the garage in Port Isabel when I took my bike for a service.

He *had* to be following me. It couldn't just be coincidence all the time. But if I tried to go and talk to him, he'd disappear. Anna said I should call the cops before he kidnapped me or something, but I figured he'd already have done that if he wanted to.

Plus, the little dirty and irrational voice in my head (the one that always got me into trouble and should never be listened to), decided that being whipped away by this ridiculously attractive man didn't seem so bad.

My first week on the island disappeared in a blink. A blur of alcohol, laughter and sex, just as planned. Only one more week to go, then I'd have to start working and behaving myself. And I really ought to start looking for an apartment.

"Enjoying the vacation, Jess?" Danny appeared at my side in MoJoe's, taking a barstool next to me. I'd been so lost in my Zac daydreams that I hadn't noticed Anna vacate the seat. She returned from the restroom and gave Danny a hug over his shoulders. A bartender provided him with a beer and, all of a sudden, the staff looked a lot more attentive.

Someone elbowed me in the back as they pushed past. "I sure am, although, I think I'm getting *old*. I don't know how much more of these crowds I can handle." I left my seat and pushed into a bikini-clad woman, attempting to create a little bubble of space where I could actually breathe. The heat and smell from so many alcohol-fueled people in the small bar was overpowering.

"Take it from me, there isn't anything old-looking about you. In fact, you haven't changed a bit from when I last saw you, what... four years ago?" He flashed me an amorous smile.

"Thanks, nor have you." I hoped the heat burning in my cheeks wasn't visible like it always was on Anna. He was certainly a fine specimen of older man, as he stood there rubbing the gray-flecked stubble on his jaw. He had a body that most twenty year olds would kill for, let alone forty-somethings. It was hard not to blush when he gifted you that smile.

He motioned to a barman and spoke in his ear. A moment later I was presented with a cocktail glass full of something bright pink, complete with slices of fruit and the little umbrella thing.

"Happy Birthday, by the way," he grinned, leaning across to kiss my cheek.

"Anna!" I scolded. "You promised you wouldn't tell! You know I don't celebrate."

She shrugged and blew out a whistle, picking at some invisible fluff on her skirt.

"Thank you," I said to Danny, who was still beaming and clearly enjoying my discomfort.

"I'm really excited to start work soon," I added, shifting in my seat. "Thanks for giving me this chance."

"Don't thank him," Anna scoffed. "He made me work for it. I totally had to suck up to him to get you a position."

He coughed and a knowing, suggestive smirk passed between them.

"You didn't?!" I gasped.

"Of course not! I'm just kidding," she laughed. "You got the job square on your own, because you're awesome and deserved it."

"Absolutely. I expect the very best out of my crew," Danny said. "Which reminds me, I have your patches at the station, come get them before you start if you like?"

"I will, thanks. Carnage Crew, right? Where does the department name come from?"

"Look around," he sighed. "On certain days during spring break this island can have up to fifty thousand people on it. All wasted, all looking for a good time. It's carnage. And we have to play a big role in managing that. Like I said to you on email, we don't get many fires round here, it's mostly beach patrols and mopping up the mayhem. You'll be pulled over to Port Isabel Department sometimes, too."

"Sounds great." Limited work on actual fires sounded beyond great, it was perfect. I'd lost my nerve somewhere along the line in the last few years. Less responsibility might help to lift the pressure that weighed me down all the time.

"I look forward to seeing you at the station soon, then. Have a wild birthday, you're in the perfect place." Danny wandered off to join some friends. I watched him leave, admiring his smooth confidence as he approached them, slotting easily into the group.

"I'll be right back," Anna said, scooting off after him.

A girl in leopard-print hot pants flew towards Danny's vacated seat, desperate to grab it before anyone else. She got hold of it, but at the same time as another, larger, girl. They floundered into me, arguing and bitching, and Miss Pert-Cheeks-in-Hotpants spilled her vodka all over the bar.

Lord, help me. I needed air.

———

THE STENCH OF BEER, SWEAT AND TESTOSTERONE ASSAULTED me as I pushed my way through the mass of bodies. A couple of dudes took advantage of the tight squeeze and 'accidentally' grabbed my ass. Whatever. My ass was like a juicy peach, so who could blame them.

I made it to the decking area outside on the beach,

which was relatively calm compared to inside. A laser show from a nearby rave sent purple and blue beacons of light soaring upwards into the night.

From here, I was reminded of the main reason I loved MoJoe's so much, and it wasn't the half price drinks. The sight of Zac pulling into the parking lot, with that engine roaring between his legs, shattered any Danny-fucking thoughts in an instant.

Often, he would just stare at me, although occasionally he'd give me a lazy half-smile that made my heart skip.

Whenever I decided it was getting ridiculous and that I was just going to talk to him, he'd be gone. Was he some weird figment of my imagination? I could have been having that relapse breakdown the shrink warned me about.

But, sweet baby angels, his smoldering vibe left me breathless with desire. Dark hair, shorter on the sides, spiked up on top... faded jeans with a hole in one knee, sculpted around lean legs... tight fitting white tank top skimming his torso, giving a teasing glimpse at the heart-stopping, inked muscles underneath...

He leant against his black chopper like James Dean. I'm pretty sure if you Googled 'stereotypical hot rockabilly guy', he'd come up.

He was never alone. He always had this little following with him, whom I could easily recognize now because I'd been studying him so scrupulously.

There was the surfer dude who he seemed closest to; blonde haired with a friendly, boyish face.

Then, in contrast, there was the giant man; straight, black hair tied in a ponytail, sporting a mustache and wearing the most bizarre, regency clothing. He appeared angry most of the time and always on the edge of the group.

There was a bunch of others too, five or six, who routinely hovered around Zac. All of them too attractive and composed to be hanging around here with the drunk kids and the freaks. They stood out a mile, looking like kings amongst peasants.

Despite my best efforts at parading around, I appeared to be invisible to all of them except Zac. And let's face it, he only paid marginal attention when he seemed to feel like it. I'd tried to explain to Anna that the others were deliberately ignoring me, going out of their way to look away when I was near, but she told me to get over myself and accept that not every guy wanted me.

Then there were the women. Oh, the women. They flocked to him in a constant stream of tits and ass. At first it made me want to loathe him, but Anna was right. Whilst his friends enjoyed the attention they received from the women, he never appeared too bothered. That didn't stop them trying though. And for their persistence he did occasionally participate in some groping and kissing, but it was half-hearted at best. I still wanted to beat those women to a pulp for touching him.

Except one. One of the females wasn't a devotee. She was a clear insider in the group; one of the guys. Anna told me her name was Eva. All porcelain skin, bright red lips and dusky eyes. Long dark hair curled with rollers. Polka dot dresses with corsets and stockings. She was sexy and sassy yet demure, not slutty. I liked her style, but I still kind of hated her, because she was the only woman on the island that could attract his genuine attention. Along with that of every male in her vicinity. *Greedy*.

They looked like a couple, her and Zac. They were beautiful stood next to each other. Yet he never showed any intimacy with her. Yes, he eyed her with adoration, but he didn't touch her.

Anyway, she wasn't there tonight, but Zac and I were busy having another staring match when one admirer followed his gaze to me and made a face as if to say, '*what on earth is he looking at you for?*' She then promptly thrust herself in front of him, huge tits first. Speaking to him with one hand on her hip, the other twirling her hair.

He adjusted his position so that he could continue to watch me, blanking her like she was an irritation. Ha! She shot me the dirtiest look I'd ever received and I couldn't help but give her my smuggest smile in return.

He must have noticed the embarrassing exchange between us, but he showed no sign of it. His face remained expressionless, body rigid, dark eyes pinning me. Totally focussed, like a lion eyeing up a gazelle. Was I a gazelle?! Fuck that. No I wasn't.

What was up with this man? No one on this island bothered playing hard to get. You couldn't move without bumping into someone making out. Was I *that* weird and repellent that he couldn't bring himself to approach me?

But then, why was he watching me all the time? What if he really was some psycho, serial killer stalker? A feeling ran through me, one that shouted out how alarmed I should be by his abnormal attention, yet I couldn't help the excitement fluttering under my skin.

Once again I thought about acting on my excitement and approaching him. And as if reading that thought, he disappeared. As usual. Maybe I'd got him wrong and he kept vanishing to have sex with those women after all. It didn't escape me that Big Tits had gone too.

———————————

SWALLOWING BACK THE PANG OF LOSS FROM HIS disappearance, I distracted myself by finding a man to flirt with. I placed Todd as a little younger than me, probably mid twenties. He was on vacation. It didn't take a genius to work out why he'd picked this place, at this time of year.

The spring break girls were up for anything, but evidently he fancied more experience in his bed tonight. He'd make a good, mindless sex toy for the night. He wore smart chinos and a shirt, his dark hair slicked over to one side, looking out of place amongst the muscled and half-naked frat boys, but in an entirely different way to Zac and his group.

Apparently he worked as a Sales Executive, giving off the impression of company car and big bonuses. I suspected it was more bored guy sitting at the end of an office phone, selling useless items to old ladies and waiting for home time. I dodged his questions about me. He had a dog named Dude and liked my hair. He also liked my outfit and every word I spoke, which wasn't very many. I tried hard to lighten up, but something was missing, an empty space inside that I already knew he couldn't fill.

A few drinks later and his arm had slid around my shoulder. He smelled nice so I didn't remove it. Anna appeared briefly and then disappeared with friends again, scooting away and giving me playful looks. As Todd began edging his face closer to mine, I caught the return of Zac from the corner of my eye. He had a different look about him. More strained. He angrily swatted away the girls that approached him.

Well, now. *Hello, Zac. Are you interested enough to do something now? End the cat and mouse?*

I wondered what he'd do if I let Todd's lips reach mine, so I smirked at him and leant in to my toy. Just as my lips were puckering, I was pushed away and heard a loud slap, only to find a short, angry girl next to us. Todd had a big red mark on his face. Oh dear.

"You bastard," she screeched. "You were only with me last night, LAST NIGHT, telling me you loved me."

Loved her? God bless youngsters and their naivety. He spluttered out some excuses, and then her hand swung up in the air towards my face. I grabbed her wrist, holding her firmly away.

"He's all yours," I sighed, releasing the wriggling bomb who was about to explode on his ass. *Good luck, Todd.*

I walked over to the dance floor as calmly as I could manage, my cheeks burning, shaking my head. Zac was smiling now. Full and radiant. Something I'd not seen on his face before.

Oh yeah, real funny. We'll see how much you laugh later when I find a real man to make you jealous with.

He raised his eyebrows before looking away and resuming the Mr. Cool act.

Twatface.

I wasn't so cool. In fact, I was a wreck. My head spun with need and frustration. Surrounded by men, but the one I was inexplicably drawn to was behaving like a total dick.

As I was dancing, I kept watch on him. He darted his gaze my way a few times, as if he were merely scanning the room. He was so bloody difficult to work out, it was infuriating. I knew if I went over to see him he'd disappear. I'd been trying all week with the same result.

This inexplicable pull toward him was driving me nuts. Sure, he was ridiculously hot, but it wasn't like I'd never encountered attractive guys before. I'd never felt this compulsion to get close, to hunt them down.

Then again, it could have just been the hard-to-get act. I was never one to shy away from a challenge. In fact, I lived for that shit. Guys who came on too strong usually bored me. I preferred having to work a little.

Because I always won in the end, and the victory tasted sweet...

Still. This pull for his attention was getting painful. What kind of asshole was he? To infiltrate my mind so thoroughly that I couldn't think of anyone else, and yet, he'd actually done nothing for me. There'd been no romantic kiss. No playful teasing. No touching.

What the hell was wrong with me? And more importantly, why couldn't he just come on over and claim me? The silent-treatment chase had gone on long enough.

He glowered at me intently. Mr. Fucking Moody. Was he thinking about murdering me? Or was he thinking about fucking me?

Standing abruptly, he walked straight towards me with that beautiful dark, solemn face. Approaching closer and closer, the whole while staring me down. Hours seemed to pass in the time it took him to reach me. I clutched my sweaty hands together, thinking I might faint from nerves.

Grabbing my waist, he turned me round, pulling me flush against himself. Swaying seductively to the music, he squeezed tight around my body with such strength that I struggled to breathe. Stiffness pressed behind me, and I don't just mean his cock, his whole body was strained with tension.

His lips brushed against my ear as he whispered the words, "Yes, ma'am. All the time."

Lifting one of my hands to his lips, he took a fingertip into his mouth. I gasped for air. His grip tightened. His chest heaved into my back with ragged breaths. I struggled to turn around and face him, and then the strength disintegrated entirely. I spun around, but he was already gone. Like, magically gone in a puff of nothing. Nowhere.

How the hell did he do that? What *was* that?!

4

JESS

I had to hand it to him; Zac had the mysterious man routine down to a tee. Try as I might, I couldn't get my heart rate to settle. Anna found me sitting at the bar, willing myself to calm down. Deep breaths.

"You okay?" she shouted over the music.

I gave her a drunken, excited grin. "Better than that. Wishes come true!"

"What wishes?" she asked, knitting her brow down and grabbing a stool.

"Zac-type wishes. He's still trying to mess with my head, but I was dancing and wondering if he wanted to give me some hot lovin' too, when he came over and grabbed me. I'm telling you, his lips on my hand blew me away. Just imagine what those lips would do to me elsewhere?! If he'd let me, I'd have fucked him right there in front of everyone." I drew a deep breath.

"For real?! You're telling me you pulled the most unobtainable, sexiest bachelor on the whole island?! What else happened?"

"Well, then the alcohol got in the way, because I thought

he said, 'All the time', but that wouldn't make sense. How would he know what I was thinking?"

"It's pretty obvious what you're thinking, Jess. You've been obsessed with him since the day you got here."

She had a point. Irritating as it was.

"Seriously though, I wish I knew what he'd actually said, it could be important. But with his damn sexy body so close to mine... and he called me ma'am... in this rumbling cowboy accent. Ugh. I went all light-headed. It felt like I'd had a whole lot more to drink." I instinctively looked at my glass to check how much was left. Damn. I really had drunk a lot. Again.

"I wish I had those sparks," she sighed, looking around in disdain at the sea of sex-crazed animals.

"We best find you someone to scratch the itch then!" I slapped her shoulder.

"Men are like bank accounts," she smiled. "Without a lot of money, they don't generate a lot of interest."

"Anna!" I gasped. "I didn't have you down as a gold-digger!"

She could always be relied upon to crack a joke though, I swear she had them all written down in a little book, ready to be plucked out at appropriate opportunities.

She shrugged. "Not a gold digger per se, just looking for someone different to the broke party-boys around here. I can't believe you've been here a week already. Our vacation time is going so fast."

"Tell me about it. I'm nowhere near ready to sort my shit out." My chest tightened at the prospect. Danny was relying on me. She was relying on me. I couldn't screw up, not this time.

"You'll be fine." She leant forward and put her hand on mine. "You promised; one last blow out, then I'm helping you. We're going to find different hobbies. Ooh, a book club!

Yes! And we'll start exercising together. We'll join a gym. Get focussed. I know you can do it..." she paused, looking away, clamping her plump lips like she wanted to say more but didn't know how.

"What is it?" The dread grew. I always found myself getting told off for something. My father's voice rang in my ears. *'Jessica, when are you going to learn? You'll never make anything of yourself, you're so damn stubborn and impulsive.'*

The burn scar down my back and shoulder itched, in the way it always did when I thought of my father. After the explosion the doctors had said he had a fifty percent chance of surviving. He didn't make it through, but at least he'd had that chance, which was more than my mother got.

"Just try to start choosing the right men and it'll help you," she mumbled.

There it was. The eternal *wrong guy* story.

"Since these weeks don't count, I'll let you off," she continued. "Last blow out on booze and dodgy men." She smiled, but her little, round cheeks didn't dimple the way they did when she meant it.

I gave her a tight smile in return and rolled my eyes in a mock tribute to my bad choices. She was right, of course. I had a habit of flitting from one disastrous relationship to another. The most recent — the cage fighter — or 'Scary Twat' as Anna affectionately called him, had been good for only two things; rough sex and teaching me to fight.

Falling for another bad boy would be a mistake. I *did* need to put myself first for a while, without interruptions from men and indulgence. Straighten shit out. Find new, healthier priorities. Vacation flings were one thing, but *fling* being the operative word. No more deep shit.

We sat in silence for a while and found ourselves sandwiched between several guys, all vying for our attention. I decided to take a stroll down to the shore for air. Anna hit the dance floor with friends and was gyrating like a geeky sex-kitten before I'd even reached the door.

I only got a short way down the beach when I was stopped sharply in my tracks. He was standing with his back to me, watching the surf. Even from behind he was too captivating for words. Something about the way he stood, hands in his pockets, stretching the denim around his tantalizing ass. The slim-fit shirt hugging muscles that did funny things to my insides.

I dithered a few yards away, stepping backwards and forwards, changing my mind about what I should do.

When did I become such a pussy?

"Hey," he said, without turning around.

Sexy. Creepy.

"So, which one of us is the stalker?" He turned to face me and his smile was sly, naughty, breathtaking. His gaze wandered up and down my body.

"I'm not sure," I stuttered, hoping my huge smile was dazzling him in the same way. It was generally a good weapon in my seduction arsenal. At school I was nicknamed Gobby, not for my big-mouth attitude, though that would have been apt; but for the sheer scale of it. My lips half filled my face at the best of times. As I grew older I'd felt awkward about it and as a teenager I tried not to smile too much. But then something happened in adulthood; the teasing stopped, and the guys started queuing up.

"You're British? Here on vacation?" he asked.

I often forgot about my accent until someone reminded me. American guys loved it. Just as I loved theirs, especially the deep, southern drawl that came from his lips.

"No... yes... I mean, originally yes, but I've been here long enough to call it home."

He dug a hole in the sand with the toe of his boot. Military para-boots, laces done loose.

"You're in the army?" I asked hopefully. I loved a man in uniform. Holding a gun, even better.

"Not these days," he shrugged.

A couple of men approached from nearby. They went straight to Zac and pointedly refused to look at me. Before they could even say a word he glowered at them and tipped his head skyward, taking a deep breath.

"Back off, guys, not now," he spoke slowly and quietly, but he looked anything but calm. In fact, he looked like he was barely keeping a hold of himself. The tension between them made me take a step back.

They didn't move.

"Go!" he yelled, his eyes suddenly full of venom, swirling with golden hues, mesmerizing and terrifying.

They sulked away.

"I'm sorry about that," he said stiffly. "Sometimes they forget their place."

"No worries. I love a dominant man," I blurted.

Wait. What?! Wrong words, Jess. Back up.

His smile was brief. "Yes ma'am, I know you do. That's a problem."

Seriously, if he called me ma'am one more time, I might lose control of the last shred of willpower that was stopping me from launching myself at his lips.

"Why? You don't seem like the sort of man to have an issue with taking charge?" I bit my lip, taking a step towards him.

"Exactly." His hungry eyes held mine.

Hardcore BDSM? I could deal with that. I mean, I hadn't before, not the major kinky stuff anyway, but there was a first time for everything.

He laughed, deep and seductive. "Not like that."

"Huh?"

"Not like you're thinking. I'm not going to shove a ball

gag in your mouth and bring out the nipple clamps and butt plugs."

Oh, shit. Those words out of his sexy mouth made me wet.

"What *are* you going to do with me then?" I took another step closer. Almost touching hands. My heart jumped all over the place. There was no need for more words, which was convenient, because it was hard to think of them around him, and I was clearly saying the wrong ones.

I should have been asking him about that angry exchange with his friends. Or why he'd spent so long watching me without speaking. Or why his eyes looked like they were alive with something out of this world.

Instead, I lifted my chin to kiss him.

He took three steps back, looking at me in horror, as if I'd grown a third arm right out of my forehead and turned purple.

"I'm so sorry," he muttered, looking at his feet, eyes wide. "There's something... I need to do..."

Then he turned his back on me and slunk away into the night. Just like that.

Son of a bitch.

This took mortified to a new level for me. I prayed for a giant sinkhole to open up beneath my feet and devour me.

What a prick.

So why did the sight of him walking away make me want to run after him, grab hold and never let go?

Fuck!

RELUCTANTLY, I FOUND MY WAY BACK TO ANNA, SULKING LIKE a baby. Then I spent an hour drowning my embarrassment with copious amounts of alcohol.

"What's going on over there?" I pointed across the beach to a crowd gathered around a bonfire, curbing my instinct to go check it for safety measures.

"That would be your new boyfriend and his crew," Anna replied dryly.

"What?" I yelled, a little too loudly, slamming my shot glass down with finality. That was the last one. No more until after sleep. "Wow. Had something to do, did he? We're *so* gatecrashing that party." I attempted to stand on wobbly legs and had to grab the stool for support.

"You can't exactly gatecrash on an open beach party, Jess."

"What?" again, even louder, possibly sounding shrill this time. "Why aren't we there already? Why didn't you tell me he was there?"

"Now, his twin brother, Alex, on the other hand," Anna rambled on, ignoring my complaint. "He's equally gorgeous, obviously, also equally weird. Lives out on the other end of the island, to the South. You never see the brothers together. There's all sorts of rumors about why they don't get on. So anyway, what was I saying?" she frowned, looking at her drink and pushing her glasses up higher on her nose.

"Oh yeah," she continued. "Alex's parties are different. He owns a couple of bars with strict entry requirements. Namely that you have to be hot. They love spring break, with the influx of young women, all desperate for their attention. It's a little sick actually."

"Hmmm, sounds it," I mumbled, as I began heading towards the party. "Wait, what?! Zac has a *twin*?!"

Now my shouty, shrieky levels were through the roof and I could do nothing to control it.

"Identical... except the hair color, and the eyes... those eyes..." She shook her head. "And we aren't over there because I actively avoid that lot." She hung back and I sat down again, mainly so I could stop wobbling on my feet.

She looked miserable. Probably the sixth shot. She'd better not puke on me.

"Those guys, I love looking at them and dreaming about them, but that's as close as I go. They freak me out, and to be honest I've already been there and done that with the Elwood Brother Obsession. I'm over it. I don't want to get involved in the shit they do. I don't think you should either."

She had my full attention now. "Like what? What shit?"

"I dunno, they're just wild. They don't live like normal people."

"Has someone stolen my best friend and replaced her with an impostor? What are you talking about? They sound like a perfect match for us!"

Okay, maybe not for *us,* but for me. She was the only person who could claim to actually know me, though she still didn't, not really. She knew I was weird, yet she didn't run like everyone else. I had issues, ones that 'normal' people could neither relate to nor understand. I couldn't even understand them myself.

But she tried, and she'd brush off my quirks, telling me to get over myself, pulling my feet back to the ground when I started flying away on my own hype. And she knew how to party, but she rarely crossed the line, no matter how hard I tried to drag her over it.

"They're... creepy. You never see them doing regular stuff. They're up all night and dead to the world all day. They race their motorcycles up and down Ocean Boulevard each week and—" she cut herself off, taking a breath.

"They race their bikes?" My eyes were surely glowing like beacons. "Come on, I thought this was party therapy time, so nothing dodgy counts, right?"

"There are so many rumors about them, Jess. You know,

the police once raided one of Alex's parties and found an actual dead body. They all got away with it. It was reported as an accidental drug overdose." She shook her head as if it were nonsense.

"Maybe it was. Must happen a lot around here?" I gestured wildly at the throng of wasted souls to prove my point.

"Don't say I didn't warn you. I have a bad feeling about this," she moaned, but she stood, and we walked, wobbled, down the beach.

5

JESS

I expected to find Zac sulking somewhere in his moody way, but instead, I found him moving around a clearing in the crowd with precision and confidence. Nunchucks flew effortlessly around his body, the ends ablaze with fire. Golden orbs danced and flew in the dark, skimming past his shirtless torso in arcs of flame. Up and over his head, around and around his body, moving so rapidly they were merely bright blurs that captivated and entranced.

The combination of darkness and fire played tricks on the senses, his whole body joined the nunchucks in becoming nothing more than a blur, as if he himself were moving too fast. So brisk and graceful that I couldn't keep track, couldn't make sense of it. Flashes of bare skin, of glorious muscle, of fire. He created a blazing, magical dance like some sort of sex-god ninja.

He spun up high and the fiery chucks flew so close past my face that the heat briefly kissed my lips. Then he faltered, slowing the pace. His stature changed, his fluid motions stiffened, suddenly looking out of synch with the dance he'd created. Stopping abruptly, he angrily tossed the chucks into the sand, giving me a quick glare over his shoulder.

A 6ft vision of smooth-skinned, fuckable perfection, panting and shaking his head, every exquisite muscle standing taut.

The onlookers shuffled about, confused. He took an awkward bow and they broke into cheering and clapping.

He briskly sat down on a large rock, grabbing his shirt and pulling it back on. Someone came up and handed him a can of beer and a cigarette. He took the beer and declined the smoke.

I didn't know what just happened, but I felt responsible. I waited for him to look over, which he stoically refused.

The flames from the bonfire surged and filled my back with an almost unbearable heat. A weight of anxiety and pain dropped right through my belly. I instinctively looked around for an extinguisher in case of emergency, but of course there was no such thing to be found here. The fire wouldn't spread on the sand, but this many drunken people could not be trusted around such a blaze. Myself included. I'd be in a bucket-load of shit if Danny caught me hanging out here, whilst this wasted.

"Come on, I love this song," I lied to Anna. "Let's go dance over there."

I led her away to a safer distance, pushing the flames out of my mind. A makeshift stage had been set up, wobbling under the weight of the young women dancing on it. A generator and sound system sat next to the stage, pumping out a deafening beat.

Anna and I had attended a few salsa and pole dancing lessons during our college days. Then we'd quit and made up our own sexy routines together.

I swayed my hips provocatively until it caught Zac's attention. His eyes burned into me, brooding and hungry, undressing me on the spot. Until a gigantic man appeared, towering over him, wagging a finger in his face. Zac shoved it away and stood with deliberate slowness. It started almost calm, but escalated fast. He inched closer, until they were in each other's faces, yelling and gesturing.

The giant turned and I found myself with both of them staring me down. Still yelling at each other, the big guy held out his hand in my direction and spat out some angry looking words. I recognized him now, the freak with the black ponytail, always on the edge of the group. He'd also been one of the guys that approached Zac earlier when we were talking. Before the fucktard had disappeared on me to come and play Fire-Nunchuck God.

Mr. Ponytail continued to gesture in my direction, until Zac landed an almighty back fist right on the side of his face. It was swift and brutal, the guy should have been on the floor. Instead, he merely faltered, but didn't retaliate. His hands went up and his eyes went down, backing away. Zac pressed on towards him, fists clenched, seething rage pouring from him. The blonde surfer was at his flanks. I'm not sure if he was getting ready to launch into attack himself, or ready to pull Zac away.

Either way, it dissolved as quickly as it had begun. Mr. Ponytail sulked off, and Zac went back to sitting and watching me like nothing had happened.

I tried to talk to Anna about it, but the music was so loud and she just wanted to dance. So I obliged and carried on with my sultry performance. At least, I hoped it was sultry, though I was aware of how much I wobbled and my head spun. I had his attention more than ever before so I shouldn't waste it, no matter how intimidating it was. *Keep dancing.*

He observed me as if he were a scientist analyzing an experiment — focused, excited, eager, worried. He sat so motionless, it was trance-like. I was pinned by his gaze, making me squirm with a mixture of fear and excitement.

I'd never seen eyes like his before; to call them brown or hazel wasn't enough. They were bright and fierce. A fiery copper, with darkness around. Falling into their depths consumed me with yearning and lust, all other thought lost.

Maybe it was the flames from the fire playing tricks on me, reflecting in his irises, though it felt like something more. Whatever was going on, I couldn't think straight around him.

Time passed in a haunting, slow daze. It seemed like forever that he'd been watching me. People came and went around us. I switched from dancing to fetching more drinks, which was water, at Anna's insistence. The first rays of red light began to peep up over the horizon as morning threatened to break. He never let me out of his sight for a second.

What exactly was he playing at? Was he expecting me to trot over to him like an obedient little lap dog? That if he kept the pressure on me long enough with his crazy, wild eyes I'd eventually give in and crawl to him?

Well, yes, that did sound hot as hell. But, no! He had to earn that first!

"That does it," I announced to Anna. "Enough cat and mouse. This should get his attention. Last chance to make up his mind if he wants me or not."

"Jess, you already have his attention, he hasn't taken his eyes off you for hours. If I were you I'd get out of here, before it's too late," she sighed.

The women on stage had started stripping, to the hooting joy of the crowd. I jumped up with them and motioned for Anna to join me. She rolled her eyes as she climbed up. The water had sobered me somewhat, but I was probably about to make an uncoordinated, un-sexy fool of myself. The thought just made me giggle in Anna's face.

I unclipped my bra and, with a load of awkward wriggling, I managed to pull it out of an arm in my white t-shirt. Always a t-shirt. I never wore pretty, thin-strapped tops. They showed too much skin.

The whooping from the crowd grew louder as they saw what I was doing. I leant forward over the stage and beckoned to a fairly attractive guy, except for his weird mullet hair. I hooked a finger in his shirt collar and whispered in his ear that if threesomes were his thing then he might be in for a good time — if he gave me his cocktail pitcher first. It was three quarters full with something fruity and sweet looking. His eyes bugged out as he handed it to me.

Taking a step back into the middle of the stage, I held the jug up high and ever so slowly poured the sweet liquid into my mouth. After a couple of gulps, I let it dribble down my chin, falling along my neck and down over my front, because, well, what can I say? I like my cliché moves. When on South Padre, join in or go home.

Deafening roars of approval erupted from the crowd as the cool drink soaked right through my top. When it ran empty I tossed the jug back to its owner, giving him a wink, and cast a quick glance down, satisfied that my drenched white shirt was now see through and clinging to every curve.

Taking Anna's hands, grinding myself into her, I whispered in her ear, "This will drive them wild. Come on, we haven't done it for years. For old time's sake?"

She rolled her eyes for the hundredth time. "Since it's your birthday."

With that she reached up to take a fistful of my hair and pulled me in close for a lingering kiss.

WE PERFECTED THE 'DANCING SEDUCTIVELY TOGETHER' ACT IN

college. Back then I could always rely on my little sex-nerd to get on up and grind dirty on me. My nipples tingled at her soft touch, the sticky fabric of my top chaffing against them. The idea of Zac watching us made me even hornier. If I didn't want him so desperately for myself, then I'd have entertained the idea of a threesome with him, instead of just with mullet man.

Zac would not be for sharing though. Not with women, anyway. He could probably bring in a guy without my objections, especially if it was one of his fuckaliscious friends, like surfer-dude. Not the grumpy ponytail prick though, he could fuck right off.

I turned, pressing my ass into Anna, and searched around to find him.

He was gone.

There was only the cute surfer guy left standing where Zac had been, shaking his head at me.

Shit! Great plan, Jess. I really shouldn't be allowed to make decisions for myself, I never made the right ones.

Mullet-man crept forward from the crowd and pulled on my waist, yanking me down from the stage. He laughed playfully as I fell into him, twisting my ankle. Pain shot up my leg.

"What the hell? Get off me!" I pushed him away.

With Zac's sudden absence, I was once again left pining for him. I wasn't in the mood for anyone else. This guy just looked like a little boy compared to Zac. Immature and weak.

"Don't be a tease," Mullet said. "You promised me a good time."

"I changed my mind."

His hands were on me again. "Whatever, baby. Come on, show's over, let's get down to business."

"No!" I yelled. "I told you, it's off. We were messing with you. Fuck off." I pushed him harder.

Anna took my hand, smiling apologetically at him, and we made our way back along the beach, with an uneasy feeling settling in my gut.

OUR SHOES HAD BEEN DISCARDED HOURS AGO, LEFT AT A BAR somewhere, with the foolish hope we'd manage to locate them again at the end of the night. I clung to Anna as I half walked and half hopped with my aching ankle. She was still so drunk that she didn't provide much support, zig-zagging in and out of the water.

We laughed as we strolled further and further out along the shoreline in the dawn glow, escaping the crowds who were back towards the bars, the sounds of their partying still loud in my ears.

Seaweed squished between my toes like cold jello. I tripped, splashing seawater up our legs.

"We haven't done that for so long," Anna squealed. "You're a naughty influence on me, Jess!"

"Yeah," I replied, but I wasn't laughing any longer. I'd glanced back over my shoulder to see the silhouette of two men walking behind us. Walking with purpose, stiff and brisk.

I quickened my pace.

"Hey!" came a shout from behind. From Mullet. "Going somewhere, you little prick tease?"

"Crap," Anna said under her breath. "Should we scream?"

"Don't be daft. He just wants to chew my ass for damaging his ego. Ignore him."

I realized too late that they'd sped up and then he was

right behind me, clutching at my waist like a randy, leg-humping dog that just wouldn't fuck off.

"Come on, baby. You've shown me what you can do, now it's my turn," he grimaced.

Grabbing hold of my throat, he forced me to look at him, leering and sniggering as his other hand groped around, trying to find a way under my top. I hadn't noticed how well built he was, he'd seemed a bit small and inadequate before.

Something kicked at my foot.

It was Anna, lying in the sand with the other guy on top of her, one hand up her skirt and the other over her mouth, muffling the screams.

My Anna, the only friend I'd ever loved, was about to get raped. Heat burned through me. Martial arts defense kicked in, despite it being many years since I'd trained. Once you teach your body to react during sparring, it stays with you. Muscle memory. My body reacted independently of my mind. I twisted myself free.

Stepping back as he came at me again, I lifted my leg and kicked him hard in the stomach. I'd been aiming for the nuts, but that would do. He stumbled backwards momentarily, then came back at me with fury. Okay, maybe it wouldn't do.

I attempted to wrestle the pig that had Anna on the ground, but Mullet yanked me away.

"Listen, bitch, this can go easy or it can go hard, but you need to be taught a lesson," he shouted.

Spinning around, I attempted another kick, this time to his head, but I wavered as the weight bore down on my aching ankle, sending a shooting spasm flying up the entire leg. He dodged and struck me across the face with the back of his hand.

"Son of a fuck maggot!" I hurled myself straight into his chest. He staggered and grabbed my arms, holding me tight as I struggled to get loose. I turned my head to the side and bit his shoulder as hard as I could, causing him to release me with an angry shout.

I didn't have time to comprehend what might happen this time, but I could feel it building inside me, harnessing my rage and gaining power. Just like it had when I was fifteen and my family home exploded. And just like it had done several times since, on smaller scales. Each time different, yet the same.

An energy exploded from my fingertips, sending him sprawling onto his ass.

Gasping for air, I was suddenly more terrified of what *I* might do than what this guy could. A pillar of sand rose next to him, as if being sucked up by a vacuum in the sky, and dropped back down onto his face. It clogged his eyes, his nose, his mouth. Rising and falling, cascading over him in waves. He choked and thrashed, held by an invisible force, drowning in the sand.

Memories flooded me. Crushing pain stabbed through my heart. My mother's screams were deafening. I clutched my ears and in that moment he was back on his feet again; dazed, confused, coughing and spitting. He backed away like I was a rabid dog, stumbling, and landed straight into the arms of Zac.

———

Zac held him with a bored, blank expression; like Mullet-man was just a toddler having a tantrum, not seeming to even register the fact that it was in fact a full grown man thrashing under his steel grip. After a moment, he turned his head to study me. He seemed curious, then angry.

"My turn," he finally said, releasing Mullet and shoving

55

him so hard that he flailed away, crashing into the other douchebag and surfer-dude, who were grappling fiercely. Anna was still lying spread-eagled on the ground.

Mullet shouted obscenities, lurching at Zac, who stood there indifferently, waiting for the attack. As Mullet drew near, Zac stuck out his arm and caught him by the throat, lifting him clear away from the ground.

Mullet dangled there, clutching at the hand cutting off his airway. Spit flew from his mouth. His face went from red to blue. I couldn't imagine how anyone could have enough strength in their one arm to lift a man a foot from the ground like that.

"If I see you on my island again, I won't be so lenient. Understand?" Zac asked.

Mullet tried to speak. Zac dropped him back down, grabbing one of his arms and twisting it behind his back. He shoved him towards me, making me take a step back.

"Say you're sorry," Zac said in his ear.

Mullet looked at me with unbridled hatred. Zac twisted his arm harder. I flinched at the sickening sound of bone crunching. Actually, no, even more sickening was the sound of the agonized yell that followed.

"Sorry, sorry, sorry," Mullet wailed.

"Speak clearly, you fucking inbred, I can't hear you," Zac growled.

He screamed even louder. I don't know what Zac did to him that time; I was too busy looking at the terror on Anna's face.

"Sorry!" he yelled again, choking on his own vomit.

Zac walked a few paces, Mullet dangling like a rag doll, and dropped him into the waves. He came up spluttering onto his knees and was swiftly kicked in the face. His nose splattered, blood streamed everywhere, arm hanging limply at an odd angle.

"Wait!" I shouted, snapping from my immobility. Through the inky fading darkness, hundreds of people were still laughing, drinking and dancing not far away, unaware of the action unfolding. Had they noticed, I should think they'd have formed a chanting circle and whooped the fight on.

"I thought you said you were being lenient? You're going to kill him!"

"Maybe," Zac mused, pausing his assault and finding my eyes. The hateful glare forced me to look away. I took Anna's arm and helped her up. She stood silently, staring into space.

"That was a really dumb thing to do," Zac said.

"What?" I asked, already knowing that he'd witnessed my sand display. He knew I was a freak of nature. He wouldn't come anywhere near me now. What man would? Who'd want to risk getting blown up or choked by Mother Nature if they pissed me off?

"Your little strip display for him." He nodded at Mullet, who was still heaving into the ocean.

"Oh, you did see? It wasn't really for him..."

He was staring hard at my nose. Something tickled. I wiped it, finding blood on my hand. He fixated on it, looking from my nose to my hand and back again, grinding his teeth in anger. His shoulders hunched up and he grabbed hold of his hands in front of him, twisting them together and flexing his fingers. He didn't like seeing a woman hurt by a man, that was for sure.

"It's nothing," I said, hastily wiping the blood onto my jeans. "Probably looks worse than it is. I could have handled it, you know."

He took a huge intake of breath and released it slowly. Grabbing my wrist, he gripped me so tight that searing pain burned through to the bone.

"So I saw. But you're lucky they were the only guys to take a serious interest in what you have to offer. It could have been—" He trailed off, watching Mullet with narrowing eyes.

"You're hurting me," I pried at his fingers with my other hand, but he wouldn't release.

His gaze settled back on my bloody nose and he leant in closer. Jaw clamped tight. Eyes blazing. Was he going to kiss me with that much anger on his face?

"Get out of here," he ordered, letting go abruptly and turning away to follow the pitiful figures scrambling their sorry asses back along the beach.

6

JESS

*T*he bruise on my wrist was fading, having gone from angry purple to greeny-yellow. I was pretty sure it had been caused by Zac, not Mullet, which was confusing. But then, most things from that night were confusing.

Anna struggled for a couple of days; crying, shouting at everything. Then Danny gave her a pep-talk, told her he'd kill the next man that tried to hurt her, or me. Our vacation time was over and she had to return to work, back to the reception desk of a budget hotel.

I think getting back to reality helped her though, because she sent me a cheery message telling me she loved me, and wishing me luck on my induction day at the firehouse.

Ten minutes later, my cell pinged again.

Anna: *What did the fireman say when the church caught fire? ... Holy smoke!*

I chuckled on my way to the firehouse, relieved that she was feeling better.

Danny introduced me to the other guys and ran me through my paces on some training exercises. Twelve hours

59

in and I knew this crew would feel like family in no time. They took the piss out of me without holding back, and I gave them as good as I got. I didn't know whether Danny had told them about any of my problems at my old department, but if he did, they didn't let it show.

We sat down for food and Danny showed me his phone screen with a new message.

Anna: *Why doesn't a fire chief look out the window in the morning? Because then he wouldn't have anything to do in the afternoon.*

"She knows me too well," he laughed.

I was staring hard at his masculine face, the wide strong jaw, covered in that steel-gray stubble, when I noticed the missing persons posters pinned to a noticeboard behind him. Three different pictures; two young women and a guy.

"How long have they been missing?" I asked, nodding at the board.

He rubbed at that scruff on his chin, as if aware that I'd been admiring it. "A few weeks, I guess. The pictures change so often, it's hard to keep track sometimes."

"Seriously?"

"They usually turn up within two days, having passed out somewhere," he shrugged. 'The—"

"This place is riddled with problems, Jess. Keep your nose down, don't make waves," interrupted a firefighter nicknamed Meat, taking a seat opposite with his tray. I hadn't yet asked him where the name came from, I could already imagine his crotch-grabbing response.

"I don't have a great track record with keeping my nose out of trouble," I replied, giving him a devilish grin.

He returned the smirk, pressing his foot into mine under the table. Danny cleared his throat and stood up. "Come on, Firefighter Layton. I have a simulation for you."

"Aye, I bet he does, Jess! Are we all invited to take part,

Chief, or is this a *special* simulation?" Hoots and jeers went up around the table, the crew slapping their hands against the wood and making lewd faces.

"Settle down, idiots," Danny barked, just as the alarm went off, signaling an incoming emergency call.

We hurried off to assemble. A few moments later a firefighter called Clark appeared.

"It's a distress call for a first responder at Emerald Beach," he said. "A girl looks to be in a bad way. An ambulance has been dispatched from Port Isabel, but in the meantime, the beach patrol unit are already dealing with another situation. Want me to go, Chief?"

"No, I'll take Firefighter Layton." Danny grabbed his jacket and had me rushing out the door with him.

We were at the beach in less than two minutes. A hotel worker waved us over and led us to a girl, sitting under a parasol, with her knees pressed into her chest. She was completely naked, her skin bleached of all color, save the bruises on her arms and neck. Her eyes were wild, frantically darting from side to side as she muttered to herself.

"Elwood!" she screamed, her teeth chattering.

Danny heaved a breath.

"Alright, love, it's okay," he said, wrapping a blanket around her shoulders.

"What are these?" I asked, opening the blanket a fraction and pointing at the small, circular scabs over her neck and arms, surrounded by bruising.

"Track marks. Junkies," Danny mouthed.

Bullshit. I knew firsthand what track marks looked like, and that wasn't it.

"No!" she screamed, fighting free of the blanket and launching herself at Danny. "No. Alex? Alex!"

"Hey!" I yelled, trying to get hold of her in a firm, but reassuring way. "You don't like him? It's okay, I'm here." I stroked her hair, easing her down onto a lounger and shooing Danny away.

A crowd had gathered to watch the show. Danny yelled at them until they backed off. I placed the blanket back over her quivering naked form. I'd never seen anyone so skinny in my life. Paper-thin skin stretched tight over bones that poked out everywhere.

She looked up at me, goggle-eyed, the whites of her eyes wide and bloodshot.

My mouth flopped open for a moment before I could form the words, "Shit, Chief! She's from that poster. She's the missing girl."

———

SHE LOOKED DIFFERENT TO THE PICTURE, HAVING LOST ALMOST every bit of plumped-out flesh from her features, but it was definitely her. Her face followed my thoughts around for the rest of that night. So afraid, rambling on about trust and blood. That poor girl had been through something horrific.

"She was talking about Alex Elwood. Have the police arrested him yet?" I asked Danny, as he took down the girl's poster.

He heaved a sigh with his back to me, but didn't answer.

"I bet he's connected to the other missing people, too. This could be a massive case. I dread to think what else they might find when they raid him," I continued, my stomach doing somersaults. If this was Alex's doing, then what did that say about Zac? Was he connected?

Of course he was connected, look at the way he'd been stalking me. He wasn't normal. I knew that. I knew the way he watched me was dangerous, that something lurked underneath, and yet I'd brushed it off because I wanted to fuck him. Like that was more important than listening to the alarm bells. Because, maybe, those alarm bells excited me. The unknown, the thrill. The energy that unleashed under my skin.

Stupid, stupid girl. That could have been me to end up a missing person. Hairs crept up along my arms and neck. The sooner they were arrested the better.

"She was a junkie, nothing more. Lots of kids run away to come here and get wasted on Carnage Island. He might have provided the drugs, but he'll just get a slapped wrist," Danny said.

"No way!" I shouted. "The police won't buy that crap. That girl was terrified, he did something to her."

Danny screwed the poster up into a ball and turned on me, his face full of anger.

"The police are there right now. I give it another twenty-four hours and it'll go silent, as if nothing ever happened. The whole thing will be hushed up."

"Why? How?" My face scrunched up as he shook his head at me.

"Because the Elwoods own the island and everyone in power. They're untouchable. As much as I hate it and would never accept their bribes, they own my ass, too. I'm powerless to do anything. And so are you, so don't go sniffing around." He'd stepped so close to me that he took hold of my arms.

"You're scared of them?"

He snorted, letting go and walking away. "I'm scared for you, if you push them. I mean it, Layton. Stay away from both of them."

7

JESS

*T*elling me to stay away from danger and trouble was as good as handing it to me on a silver platter. I gravitated towards it, with my scalp tingling and my crotch throbbing. As a result, I didn't imagine my life expectancy was particularly long, but at least I'd go out buzzing. Probably.

The tension tore at me inside. I had an overriding need to seek out Alex and find out what the hell was going on around here. Still, a better plan would be to get close to his brother, since Zac had already shown such a keen interest in me. I'd lure him in further and work them out. They were surely working together, taking young women and doing goodness knew what to them.

Danny had gone down in my estimations. He might have been prepared to sit around and ignore it, but I wasn't.

In the meantime, I found myself at the island casino, since one of the best ways to release stress was to play poker. It had helped me through many rocky times, starting out a day feeling low and finishing up on a high. This would definitely be one of those times, I could feel it brewing already — the wave of anxiety. It scratched and tickled at me inside.

These were the days when I got into trouble, when I'd follow the rush wherever it went, chasing it down.

The fact that Anna had once told me how Zac played poker was of course no bearing on my being there.

I should have stayed home. Being out meant I'd likely do something crazy. Vacation was over, I was working now. New life, new rules. I was pretty sure that gambling at the casino whilst looking out for the mysterious bad boy, was not on Anna's list of appropriate hobbies.

Nevertheless, I strolled out of the rest room dressed like some gold-digging bimbo, and stashed my jeans and helmet into a locker. My low cut shirt was pulled as far down as it would go, with a push-up bra trying its best to give me some sort of cleavage. The clingy short skirt chafed my butt cheeks and my long lean legs flowed elegantly beneath me on high heels. Oh, okay, not elegantly, I was awkward in heels, but you get the idea.

I tottered around aimlessly, making out I didn't know where to go, whilst discretely taking in everything, looking for the most promising cash game.

I dismissed several tables with players who clearly knew what they were doing, especially the ones where the obvious pros were already seated, taking money from tourists and college kids who'd blagged in on their false IDs. I guessed this time of year the casino management got sloppy, just like the bars did. All those young things eager to lose their cash would be hard to turn away.

That left two other tables. I settled on one with some British tourists, pretending to be on 'holiday' like them, and we bonded over talk of British cities and weather. I gave them the hustle routine, explaining how I didn't know what I was doing and that they better go easy on me. Piece of piss. So easy to take their money.

I kept up the stream of nervous giggles, asking them

"Was that hand good or bad?... What on earth is the flop?... It sounds funny!... Should I have folded then? Oooops, silly me!"

I'd accidentally win a few hands here and there so I didn't lose too many chips, then gradually win a few more, putting it down to beginner's luck.

I was mid flow in a story about how I lost all my chips the one time I'd played before, when my ears started burning. Someone else was watching me.

Zac had taken a seat at a table nearby and was giving me the usual stink eye. I didn't dare look away in case he'd be gone when I looked back. Instead, I braved the angry expression, took it on the chin, and used the opportunity to fully admire every inch of his face — the rich hazel eyes with a kind of darkness around them, like he wasn't getting enough sleep.

He didn't seem tired or haggard, though. Quite the opposite, his eyes were more alive than anything I could describe. Like an animal. His luscious, full lips pressed together, with 5 o'clock shadow covering a strong jaw. How I longed to feel that stubble on the inside of my thighs. If only he wasn't a psycho.

His lips twitched ever so slightly, almost a smile. The guy sitting next to me gave me a nudge.

"Uh, sorry, I get so easily distracted, what was I saying?" I glanced down at my hand, a pair of tens. Placing the minimum bet, I hoped someone might try to bluff me with a raise. It wasn't an exceptionally strong hand, but it might be enough if they tried to take advantage with a mediocre hand themselves.

Zac watched with quiet amusement on his face. At least some of the animosity had faded, but having him watching made me nervous. I'd die of embarrassment if I stuffed this up.

Three guys folded, except one, called Max. He raised the pot considerably. Bingo. I hadn't seen him raise with a decent hand all night, he preferred to slow play them. He'd been raising all night with nothing though, and this time I was ready to catch him out.

That left one other, Mr. Cowboy Hat, who called the bet. He'd been throwing chips away carelessly, I didn't have much faith in him knowing what the hell he was doing, so that was good, unless the fish got lucky.

I paused with feigned distress, finally agreeing "*what the hell*" and throwing my chips in. Another ten came down with the flop and I knew this was the one. I'd cash the hell out on this and get over to Zac.

Max was oblivious to his tell, reaching instinctively for his drink, but I noticed it. Cowboy Hat was staring at the Ace on the table. He'd probably hit one, too. Great! If the fourth one in the deck came out, they'd each think they had the nuts, when actually it would seal my victory.

The rest of the cards came down in my favor and I made myself look weak with unsure calling and bets, until the final action when I threw everything I had into the middle. Max was excited, thinking he'd won. Cowboy Hat was confused.

"Really?" Max groaned, too melodramatically, "I ought to fold this, I bet you've got me beat." He sighed, but placed the chips in the middle. *Idiot, I can act better than you.*

Victoriously, he revealed his trip Aces and reached out to take the chips.

"Wow," I beamed. "That's a good hand, Max, but I think mine's better?"

I laid the cards down on the table, enjoying their shocked expressions as they registered my full house. His face went from happiness, to confusion, to pain, in an instant.

"Well, gentleman, it's been a real pleasure doing business with you. Particularly you." I blew a kiss at Max. "Some advice, though, you really want to watch that tell of yours, it's a dead giveaway. And you two—" I nodded to the young guys. "You need to do some reading up and start playing the odds better, stop chasing. And you, Cowboy Hat, well, you just need to stop playing, there's no hope."

Their jaws dropped around the table. I finished grabbing the chips and hurried off to the cash-in counter, before they could recover and say another word. Behind me, I could hear Zac laughing, loud and free. Possibly the best noise my ears had ever been blessed with.

THE SECOND I HAD THE MONEY IN MY HANDS I MARCHED straight over to Zac, ignoring the jeers from poor Max and his crew. He gazed up at me quizzically, a hint of a smirk remaining on those delectable lips.

He'd already attracted a group of eager women. They bunched around the table, watching, waiting, hoping they'd get lucky with this inhumanly gorgeous man and his buckets of money. His stack was practically piled up to the roof.

"So it's settled, then. You're the one stalking me," I said, with more confidence than I felt.

"Do you *want* me to be stalking you?" He sucked on something that smelled like a mint, toying lazily with chips in one hand. The tricks were good, flipping them effortlessly around his fingers without even seeming to be concentrating on it.

"As if! Why would I want some creepy guy who keeps giving me psycho glares to be following me? Maybe those guys at the beach weren't the ones to be afraid of?" My voice came out harsher than intended. Heart hammering in my ears.

Gut wrenching silence. *Oh, way to go.* What kind of dick-head would bring that up? I squirmed on the spot.

"Maybe you're right," he said simply.

Of course I was right. This was the habit of my lifetime, wasn't it? I couldn't hide from that string of dodgy men in my past, culminating in The Cage Fighter. He'd been in prison for assault and I'd followed him down some dark paths. It was a slippery slope and somewhat of a miracle I'd managed to step off it. I really needed to stop chasing down these storms.

"However," he continued. "You didn't *accidentally* attract that asshole, you sought out his attention with your games." Glancing at his cards, he absently threw a stack of chips into the middle as the game continued around him.

"MY games?!"

He stared at me flatly for a moment, before turning back to his cards.

"Anyway, I could have handled it myself," I scoffed indignantly.

"You're welcome." He shot me a fierce look this time, the disapproval on his face quickly turning into full blown reprehension. He could go from nice and smiley to weird and serious in a heartbeat. A familiar buzzing started up in my ears; faint, but growing.

No. No. *Not here.* The adrenalin bolted round my body. I could feel myself reaching the peak, I was going to do some-thing stupid and then crash. *I shouldn't be here.*

Zac cocked his head. "You should do what you can to avoid attracting unwanted attention around here, not go seeking it out."

I stared back at the curious faces around the table,

everyone listening to us, the horde of women eyeing me with disgust.

"Well, I can see you're still angry about it." I suddenly felt like a silly little girl. Having a whole table of people watching my telling-off didn't help. "Thank you, but next time, don't bother coming to my rescue. I don't need your help or your fucking cat and mouse stalking. Your games aren't much fun any longer."

———

OUTSIDE, I GULPED DOWN THE FRESH AIR AND TRIED TO steady my shaking hands. Tears welled up, which I hastily wiped away.

Well, that was bullshit, Jess. Way to go. If you don't want or need him in your life, then why are you such an emotional wreck?

It was absurd to be crying. I knew that. But I also knew this was just a dip, a comedown. I'd ridden out enough lows to recognize them for what they were. My life was a series of peaks and troughs. I surfed the highs, buzzing my tits off and searching for the next rush, and when I failed to grab it, I'd crash to the ground in a feeble heap.

I stuck the key in Loki's ignition. Fuck it, my clothes and helmet were still stashed in the lockers. I went to open the casino door, but changed my mind, and sank to the ground. With my back pressed against the wall, I buried my face hard into my knees in a futile attempt to quell the tears.

I always ended up here. Breaking this cycle was going to be harder than I'd anticipated. Had I really thought that I could come to a hedonistic island and actually sort myself out?!

An arm slid around my shoulder. He pressed his nose into my hair, sighing deeply.

"I'm sorry. No games. No more following from a distance. I want to be with you," he said, that deep voice making my brain feel like mush.

"So what's stopping you?" I didn't dare lift my face, to have him see my red, swollen eyes. Or was it that I just couldn't bare the heartache of seeing his beautiful face right then? Knowing that I needed to stay away from him. Knowing that no matter how much I craved his attention, I had to walk away. He was dangerous.

"It's complicated." His words came out low and he shifted sideways, increasing the gap between us. This time, I had to look. Had to check if the man who sent me wild with unsolicited desire had really uttered that lame line.

He was staring straight ahead, eyes hooded with an unknown burden. Popping another mint into his mouth, he shook his head slowly. "I'm trying, I really am. I'll make it work if you give me time."

"That sounds like one of your parting lines. You going to vanish on me in a puff of freaking smoke again?" Those damn brooding eyes made me want him so much. My chest constricted with the need to reach out and grab him, kiss him, fuck him. He frowned, pressing a fist into his forehead.

"You can't resist playing with fire can you? Guys don't like to be hustled by a woman much more than they like to be led on by one. It belittles them, damages their ego."

"That was their tough shit for not knowing how to play poker. I didn't force them to hand me their chips."

His lazy smile made a brief return and my heart fluttered. He had the power to scare me to death in one instant and fill me with wonder the next.

"I admit, that guy's face at the end was priceless. Only played once before, huh?" He rolled his eyes. "Men are so easily and willingly fooled by you."

"Not you. You're different."

71

Pressing his lips together, he looked at his hands, mirroring me by toying with his motorbike key. He flicked it round and round, like he'd done with the poker chips.

"You could tell I was hustling as soon as you walked in, right?" I asked.

"Of course. You're good, but not that good."

"One of the guys on my table spotted you and started spouting off. I hear you're a pretty spectacular player? I could try out my beginner's luck on you sometime?" I edged back closer to him.

He chuckled. "Even a pro hustler like you can't beat me. I don't want your money, save it."

"Oh." I wanted to come back with a remark about how cocky his confidence was, or that we could play for fun, not money — maybe strip poker — but rejection pain pricked behind my eyes at the declined offer. I never said it had to be money, it was just a sociable suggestion.

"Maybe a little friendly competition elsewhere then, away from the poker tables?" Turned out his rejection just made me more determined. I was talking reflexively, before I'd even thought about it. I hated it when that happened. Typical Aries impulsiveness.

"I'm not racing your motorcycle." He folded his arms across his chest, giving me a stern look. He needed to loosen up. For such a wild party guy he was awfully well behaved around me. Whatever his brother was up to with missing girls, I found it impossible to believe he was the same. Yes, he was weird, but in a different way.

"That's not what I was going to ask... I.... I don't...." Wait a minute, was I about to say that? It occurred to me that I probably was. "Why not, are you chicken?"

"Yes, I am," he deadpanned. "I'm not racing you. I'm not racing a—"

"What?" I snapped. "A woman? You won't race a female?"

"Something like that."

"You know, I had you down as being a little more exciting. So what then, dinner? That can't be too scary for you?"

"Dinner," he stated, giving a non-committal grunt and shifting up onto his feet.

"Fuck, Zac! You watch me all the time, you seem interested, but you constantly dodge all my moves towards you. I just don't get you at all. What are you doing?"

"I want to do the right thing," he sighed, returning his attention to me, eyes catching on my bruised wrist.

"Girl meets boy. Girl likes boy. They hook up. This shouldn't require that much thought." I threw my head back in despair, running a hand up and down my neck. When I looked back down he was staring at me, all tense again. As usual, he recomposed himself so fast that I couldn't work out what the expression had been on his face.

"How about a walk along the beach?" he suggested.

"The beach? How very tame. And not at all uncomfortable after our last encounter there." I pouted, but then had an idea. "I know the perfect place right up at the far North end, it's deserted this time of night. Anna showed it to me when I first got here. We'd have it to ourselves."

"What's wrong with the main beach?"

"Well, memories, like I said, and it's too crowded."

Why didn't he want to be alone with me? That had to be a good sign, right? At least, on the psycho front. If he wanted to kidnap me, then he'd surely leap at the chance for isolation.

Irritation made my skin prickle. I was sick of the games. Time to spice things up, whether he liked it or not.

Before I'd even finished thinking about it, I snatched the

key out of his hand and found myself astride *his* bike, fumbling with the ignition.

"Whoa, what are you doing?" He appeared unsure whether he should grab hold of me or if I was joking.

I didn't even know what I was doing myself, but I threw Loki's key at him. The next thing, his Harley roared to life and I was off, front wheel leaving the ground as I sped away.

I shouted back something embarrassingly childish like, "Wooo hoooooooo. You're gonna have to race me now, Mommy's boy, I got your chopper! Want it back? Come get it! Wooooo ha ha ha ha ha."

I had a vague notion of people shouting at me and staring, pointing at the crazy woman tearing up the road in a mini skirt, high heels and not even a helmet.

Yes, that was me, because I was clearly a complete shitweasel.

8

ZAC

"*U*nbelievable! Stupid, crazy, impulsive, fucking siren of a woman!" Grabbing her Ducati, I took off after her. How did I not see that coming? She didn't even think that, she just did it. She was so hard to track, so spontaneous.

Oh, you won't race a woman? Her voice rang in my head. No, I won't race a human... woman... one that I need in my life. "You're far too fragile and breakable, you crazy bitch," I yelled, ripping open the throttle and pulling alongside her.

We sped down the highway, with me yelling at her to stop. She just kept looking at me, shrugging and speeding up. She was afraid of the anger she could see in my face. Frightened that when she stopped I was literally going to kill her for what she'd done. I sincerely hoped she was wrong, but she might very well have been right.

"The road, look at the *road*!" She finally registered my flapping and steered back in the right direction, coming way too close to wrapping herself around a streetlight.

I positioned myself in front of her and hit the brake, but she accelerated and dodged around. She was pretty good. Still, my reactions could outstrip hers easily and I could've re-adjusted myself in front of her before she could get past. She was so crazy though, I knew that with the speed of it all, she'd just crash into me in confusion.

We left the city limits and entered the Strip, where my Cell and I often raced. I never thought I'd be having this kind of race. The road was a continuation of the main highway; it kept going and going, right through the sand dunes, then ending abruptly. There was nothing this far out, just sand and more sand. It was the beach she'd been wanting us to come to, to be alone together. I hadn't realized she was that desperate to get here.

At least I didn't have to worry about her hitting a car or streetlight now that we were so isolated, but we were rapidly approaching the end and it dawned on me that she didn't know it was coming.

The road dead-ended suddenly into the dunes. Maybe she hadn't been this far out with Anna — it was a long strip, she could have stopped earlier on her previous visit. I honked the horn and got in front of her again, but she was oblivious.

We were hurtling towards that end at over a hundred. She finally registered what was coming. *Too late.* At that speed there was no way she could stop in time. I felt the fear smack her in the face like a battering ram. She looked to me in panic , slamming the brakes so hard that the back wheel locked and she lost control of the metal death-trap underneath her.

I decided in that instant that after today I was skipping town for a while. This beautiful tornado of a woman was driving me to limits that I wasn't sure I could handle.

I didn't want to have to do something that might let her see who I was, but she left me no choice.

There was only seconds left, yet it unfolded like slow motion to me, I had plenty of time. I threw my body at Jess, grabbing her with one arm, whilst keeping the Ducati pinned between my legs and grabbing the Harley's handle-bars with my free hand. One foot jolted into the road, nearly breaking my leg as I pushed off and leapt sideways.

I flung us all into the dunes ten feet from the side of the road and took the full force of the landing, slowing and breaking the impact of the crash, my ribs fracturing. We skidded through the sand and came to a stop with her pulled over me, wrapped in my protective embrace. It would all have been over in a flash to her.

Just like her imminent death if she kept provoking the Beast.

SHE LAY COMPLETELY STILL ON TOP OF ME. HER HEART pounded through her chest onto mine, and the smell of her fear, of her blood racing through her veins; *it was unbearable.* Like wafting crack under the nose of an addict.

The darkness lapped at the back of my neck, prickling right down through my spine. Fuck me, who was this woman? With her impulsiveness and blinding aura, unlike any I'd ever seen before. Not to mention her scent, which ripped through every part of me, filling me with more desire than I could take.

Four seconds. The *moment* I saw her. That's how long it took to know that she was trouble. That she'd simultaneously bring heaven and hell to my door.

Deep-rooted need rose from within me, starting at my cock and spreading to my fangs. Or was it the other way around? Maybe it started with the fangs. Fuck knew. It was almost impossible to separate the two. They both throbbed and ached with insatiable desire to have her. To consume her. To take her in every possible way and make her mine.

Taste her. Just a little bit. One small sip of her sweet blood...

My boner pressed into her. My lips skirted along her throat. She groaned, leaning in closer.

Fuck this. Fuck it all.

Clenching my teeth, I shoved her off me, dragging my legs away, fighting against the darkness. Each step was agony, taking me further from the paradise she offered.

She also offered hell, darkness and misery. Once that Beast was loose, there'd be no putting it back in its little box, not without an epic fight.

I went over to the motorcycles, engines still roaring, and stood them up. Hopefully she wouldn't notice the ease with which I lifted them, but that was hardly a big deal now. I silenced the noise with swift turns of the keys. A cracked yellow sign lay on the floor where my leg had knocked it from a pole as we crashed — ironically it read 'Road Ends Ahead'.

The bikes were scraped up, but nothing that couldn't be fixed. They'd crashed into the sand dune, which made for a soft landing.

"Are you okay?" I asked, without turning back to look.

She didn't reply.

"Say something," I urged.

"Are *you* okay?"

"I'm fine." *Get a grip. Turn to face her. Take her.*

"How are you fine? *How* am I fine?" She waved her arms around frantically. "One second I was doing a zillion miles an hour with the end of the road right there, but then instead of getting totaled I was here, on top of you... with the bikes just there... and there's barely more than a scratch on us or them."

Here we go. "Yeah, we were lucky. Must have guardian angels." *Hahahahahaaa.*

She seemed to ponder on that for a while, face in her

hands. I sat back down beside her. I could do this. I'd been acclimatizing. Deep breaths.

"When are you going to yell at me?" she asked.

"I thought I'd save it until I'm sure you're alright."

"Seriously, you must be hurt. We flew pretty far and I landed right on top of you."

"No, I'm fine."

She reached out and I shrank back against my instinct, the two needs fighting each other in an endless inner turmoil.

She was thinking about how I looked a little too fine, with the same calm expression as usual, not even surprised by our good state of health. I should have pretended to be hurt. My ribs would take a few hours to heal, but the pain was insignificant. She got busy probing her body, trying to find some pain of her own somewhere.

"How did we land like that? You must have literally leaped off and pulled us, and the bikes, into the sand? But I landed so softly. I don't understand."

"You're in shock. Moments like that, where you panic, tend to happen in slow motion in your mind. It all feels very surreal. We managed to brake in time and ran ourselves off here, that's all. We had a lucky landing with the road being surrounded by sand."

"No... we were going too fast, and my back wheel had locked. I was *fucked*. I thought I was going to die. One second you were in front of me and then you were leaping and grabbing, so fast."

"Drop it, will you! I told you, you're in shock. Come on, I'll leave my chopper here and ride you home on yours."

"What, my bike that barely has a scratch on it after a high speed crash, much like myself?" she screeched. "You don't even seem fazed by any of it. What if *you're* in shock — you just had an accident too, remember?" She stamped her foot and I nearly laughed. Something which didn't happen often enough these days.

Instead, I let anger take over my outer facade, a good way to distract her from the questioning.

"I did just have an accident, didn't I? And why was that? Oh yes, because you stole my fucking Harley and took off like a maniac. Another one of your games, just trying to have a bit of fun, right?" I moved toward her aggressively. That part wasn't intentional. It was the moonlight radiating off her heaving chest, the silence and darkness around us. The fear. *Helpless prey.*

"I... I'm sorry. I don't know what came over me, it was idiotic." She backed away.

Good girl. Keep going. Turn around and fucking run. I could almost taste her blood. It would be exquisite. I'd never known anything like her scent. Through a century I'd wandered, and nothing had come close. As for her aura; it was like a rainbow galaxy, glinting and fragmenting.

I desired nothing else but her.

The last time I'd been even half this drawn to someone, it was Selena. She was nothing compared to the pull from Jess, and yet, I'd loved her. I loved her, and still I took everything from her. The Beast saw to it that the beautiful, carefree woman was left a haunted woman, trapped in the shell of her feeble body. Weakened and ruined.

Jess was still backing away, and I was still stalking. She found herself up against a palm tree at the edge of the road, fidgeting with her hands. Yet, even through that fear, she still wasn't running. Her thoughts were centered on how she'd messed it all up, how much she wanted me. Uncaring and unseeing of the threatening monster that loomed over her.

Good. Make her see it, make her find her fight. She'll taste so much better when she starts to struggle. Claim her. It's your right... it's our laws. She belongs to you.

I could see clearly how it would go down — her naked body spread before me, bound under my spell. Panting and wanting. I'd fill her with my cock and fuck her until she was crying. As my orgasm approached, I'd sink my aching fangs into her butter-soft skin and drain her dry.

"Look, we've landed near the beach we were talking about earlier," she whispered, with a shy smile and a flutter of hands. "It's nice here. Can we please just stay a while? I don't want to go back to the motel yet. I just want the chance for us to spend some time together being normal. You know, chatting, relaxing. No more games."

I took her hands and pinned them into the small of her back, forcing her chest into mine, our lips poised, so close to touching. Her body slackened and melted against me. Total submission.

Own her.

No.

I was stronger than that. I'd fought through too much pain to let her undo me. Taking the biggest intake of breath, I shoved the depravity back down with all my might. I told it that we should savor the most amazing meal of our lives, not rush through it. The time would come later, *have patience.*

It seemed to work. For now.

I released her, but stayed close. "I don't think you know how to drop the games. You seem to live by them." I breathed in slowly, easing out the pain.

"You can talk, Mr. He Likes Me, He Doesn't Like Me... he wants me, he watches me, but wait, he's disappeared again." She stared me down boldly.

"I don't play games intentionally. I don't want to. I wish I could be normal with you, but it's not that simple. *I'm* not normal."

"No shit." She started walking across the dunes, towards the sea.

"What are you doing? You can't go walking around in the middle of nowhere on your own."

"I'm not on my own, you're going to follow me," she breezed over her shoulder.

"Seriously? The chasing again?!"

Damn woman.

I didn't answer to anyone, except my own dumbass conscience... and occasionally the Bael.

And yet, she was right, wasn't she? I would always follow her.

9

JESS

"*A*t least do one sensible thing and put my jacket around you," Zac offered.

I glanced down at my ridiculously skimpy outfit as he wrapped the leather jacket over my shoulders. It smelled of gasoline and something else I couldn't place. Heavenly. I wanted to wrap that smell around me like a blanket and snuggle up in it.

Taking off my stupid high heels, I spread my toes into the white sand. An animal rustled around in the dune grass and sprinted off into the trees at the edge of the beach. There was no civilization this far up the island; we were in complete darkness, only the bright full moon laying a delicate light over us. Warmth battled with the cool sea breeze, which ultimately won, covering me in goosebumps.

"I don't normally dress like this. It was for the hustle, part of the ga—" I cringed, cutting myself short. No more games. That was the rule. The new life. Sort it out.

"I know you don't, I've been following you, remember? But don't apologize, you look so incredible I'm having difficulty staying focussed."

I believed him. He seemed distracted — had that

weird look in his eyes, lust mixed with anger. The look I usually received right before he'd disappear on me. Luckily he couldn't escape this time, not without me noticing.

"Don't feel you have to stay restrained for my sake. I'm a little unfocused myself." I gave him my best sexy bedroom eyes and he smiled awkwardly.

How could he be so nervous around me? He must have had a million women. When I watched him interacting with others there was always a fluid grace around his movements and demeanor. Easy, never missing a beat. Yet, when he was close to me there was this stiffness and tension. Alongside something else, something heavy and burdened in his expressions.

It didn't fit, didn't belong, and made me feel like I repulsed him or something. That didn't make sense either. If I thought too much on it, tried to look and analyze, he'd change the subject, move away. Then he'd be back to normal, leaving me reeling.

I brushed my hand past his. He sucked in a breath like I'd caused him pain. Then he reached out and took hold, lacing our fingers together. I froze, looking down at our connection in astonishment. My palm tingled and throbbed, shivers erupting along my arm and into my core. Blood rushed to my head making me feel dizzy. I must have been in shock after all.

He cleared his throat and clenched his teeth, tension visibly spreading.

"Oh... this feels weird... nice," I slurred, trying to remember if I was drunk.

"Yes," he mumbled, and we started walking again. "So, let's chat. Start talking now so I don't have to let go."

In my giddy state that sounded weird, but I wasn't sure why. Were my legs actually going weak at the knees? Yes. Yes they were. Like that feeling after a workout at the gym, all heavy and wobbly.

"We could start with the usual. What do you do for a living? And we ought to do names, even though I already know yours. Your reputation precedes you, Mr. Elwood. My name's Jessica Layton, you can call me Jess."

"I know who you are. I wouldn't be much of a stalker otherwise, would I? As for my work... this and that. I earn a lot from poker, so I tend to call myself a professional gambler. What about you?"

"Sounds like you should already know?"

He didn't respond, but offered a faint smile to the ground as we walked.

"I'm a firefighter."

"Figures."

That wasn't the answer I expected. Generally I got a snort of disbelief, accompanied by a comment about how women can't be firemen.

"Danger, thrill-seeking," he said. "Seems like that's your kind of thing. A job to suit you."

The job did suit me. I also hated it at the same time, but I was extremely lucky to still be working, given the suspension following my spell on smack, drinking and late nights. Fortunately, they didn't know about the drugs, but they knew I'd been out on an all night bender when I was called to a fire the next day. If they'd drug tested me, it would have been over. I made a stupid mistake and put my crew in danger. Unfortunately, it wasn't the only time that management had noticed the failings in my performance.

Don't get me wrong, I took saving people's lives very seriously, but taking life itself seriously was an area I struggled in. Which caused a great deal of difficulty with the whole work life / personal life balance thing. It meant I often wasn't as focussed on the job as I should be. And that needed to change. Dammit, it shouldn't be that bloody hard to quit being an idiot and grow up.

"Fuck!" I shrieked. "I'm dead! So many people saw me tonight, tearing down the road on a bike with no helmet and a goddamn skirt and heels! They'll recognize me. Danny is going to kill me. When this gets back to the department I'm fired."

A pit opened up inside my stomach and I wanted to throw up.

"No, you're not," he said.

"Yes, I am. I already had a suspension, I'm in so much shit. One day on the job! ONE! That's all I could manage before screwing up."

"Stop, would you? No one's firing you. I won't allow it." He paused and I noted that we'd circled back round to the bikes.

I eyed him with suspicion, Danny's warnings ringing through me. "Who are you to allow, or not allow, something like that?"

"Just trust me, if I say you don't get fired, then you don't get fired."

"And your brother has that same authority, does he?"

"What do you know about him?"

"Nothing. Except that he's bad news. And clearly, so are you." I tried my hardest to resist the magnetic pull towards his lips. He was so close, my breath kept catching.

The giddiness had eased off, but there was still a tingling flowing from my hand where it joined with his cool skin. I wasn't in any pain from the accident, but wondered again about hitting my head – I certainly wasn't feeling right.

"You're cold, you should have your jacket back," I offered.

"I'm fine. Listen, Jess, you're right about us being bad news. Alex, he's... well... I'm..."

I wasn't even listening anymore. I was gazing into those eyes and thinking filthy things. The next thing I knew, I'd planted my lips on his and the tingling through the joining of our hands paled into insignificance compared to what our mouths did.

The thrill sucked the breath right out of me. His body went rigid, radiating tension, as he let his tongue tentatively enter my mouth, minty and cool.

He didn't stay cautious for long. He kissed me with exhilarating urgency. A hand went behind my neck and the other into my back, holding me tight. He felt so strong and fierce, yet... was he trembling?

I let my fingers roam to his chest, underneath his shirt, seeking out the hard contours of his abs. Groaning, his teeth tugged at my bottom lip. I thought I heard him make a weird noise, like a hiss, but then there was only crashing darkness.

I AWOKE TO THE PLEASURE OF WARMTH BATHING MY BODY, AND then something far more delightful; a whispering tingle along my cheek, where thousands of tiny butterflies fluttered their wings against my skin. Such a nice dream. I hummed in appreciation.

Wait, was this a dream?

Cautiously, I opened my eyes a fraction and found Zac leaning over me, stroking my face. His smile was more relaxed than I'd ever seen. There was no strain in his body. I sat up and threw my lips towards his. The tension returned immediately as he dodged me. I must have been dreaming after all.

"Sorry," I grumbled.

"Why?"

"For throwing myself at you again. I know you don't like

me being too close. Do you have one of those phobias about being touched? Or OCD or something?"

He laughed, taking hold of my hand, and the wonderful zinging returned. "Something like that. I need to take things slowly."

"Sure. Whatever you want. Just don't let go ever again, it feels amazing." I ran my thumb over the back of his hand.

"Yes, ma'am, it sure does."

"You're still so cold. You must have got chilled sleeping out here without your jacket. Why are you sitting in the shade, the sun's baking this morning." He was leaning back against a tree trunk, so I pulled him towards me.

"Would you stop worrying about me, I'm fine," he replied gruffly.

"I don't remember falling asleep. The last thing I remember I was kissing you and... oh... oh! I take back my agreement. Please don't make me wait too long for that again!" I stared at his red lips, remembering how oddly cold they were, but they'd felt so good.

Then something horrible came to me. A terrible vision. Too awful to even contemplate.

"Wait... did I... pass out? Shit the fucking bed! How humiliating. I passed out, didn't I? No wonder you don't want to do it again." I hid my face in my hands.

He chuckled softly. "It was probably just the shock setting in from the accident."

"The accident!" I shot up with a start. "How could I have forgotten all that?"

I was confused and disorientated. I shook myself, noticing there was still no pain, not even a slight after-ache. "Crap, what time is it?"

"About eleven-thirty."

"What?! Why didn't you wake me? Anna is going to be so pissed. I promised we'd go bungee jumping today on her day off. I need to get back. I better ring her." I pulled out my cell and cursed at the No Signal sign. "Dammit. I can't ride Loki in broad daylight dressed like this, I don't even have a helmet with me." I paced a frenzied circle in the sand.

"Calm down, Jess. After you... fell asleep, I had one of my friends go over to the casino and get your gear out the locker. I hope you don't mind. It's all there, next to your Ducati." He waved back to the road.

I stopped pacing. "How did your friend know we were here?"

"I called him."

"On your cell? I don't have a signal."

"Sure. I do." His jaw set in a way that told me the conversation was over. I didn't have time to argue, anyway.

"Well, thanks." I started hurrying off up the beach and then stopped.

Don't ask it, Jess. Don't do it. Keep walking, step away from him. He's trouble with a capital T and you're into Phase Two of the new life plan.

"When will I see you again?" I asked anxiously. *Dammit, girl!*

"When would you like to?"

I thought about being casual, sounding like I wasn't that bothered, but I'd promised no more games. "Tonight?"

"Yes, ma'am," he nodded.

Sitting in MoJoe's that night, my cell vibrated in my pocket. I pulled it out to find I had a message from a 'Hot Stalker'. What the fuck?! My fingers quivered as I pressed the open message button.

Hot Stalker: **Spent the day dreaming about the crazy girl**

89

who stole my Harley. There really should be consequences for such delinquent behavior.

He helped himself to my phone contacts while I was asleep?! I hoped to hell he hadn't scrolled through my old messages. My pulse sped up as I typed the reply.

Jess: *I'm sure I'll have committed more punishable crimes before the night is out.*

His response came back instantly.

Hot Stalker: *My palm is twitching in anticipation.*

Jess: *Go ahead, leave a nice pink handprint on my ass if you think you can handle me. Luckily I'm wearing my best silk pants.*

Hot Stalker: *HaHa. I can hear you saying that in your cute British accent. But surely you mean panties?!*

Jess: *Ew! No! I have managed to adopt most of your Americanisms over the years, but I draw the line at panties. #Shudder.*

Hot Stalker: *You love hearing the word panties in my Southern accent though, right?*

"So, you're telling me that you *stole* his motorcycle?" Anna was scowling at me. I put the phone back in my pocket while I thought of a suitable sassy comeback. He'd never been so candid and relaxed. It made my stomach flutter.

"I didn't just steal it, I crashed it," I corrected.

"Why are you grinning?! You need help, Jess. Your issues are beyond my healing capabilities."

I tried to stop smiling. Honestly, I did.

She rolled her eyes in despair. "Are you hurt? You don't look hurt?"

"I'm fine, that's what doesn't add up. And so are the bikes, and him. We all crashed together in a heap, doing ridiculous speed, but it was like it happened in slow motion

90

and, this is going to sound stupid... but he kind of swept me off the road and shielded me."

"Sit down will you." She scanned the bar for available seating.

"I'm not hurt and I'm not in shock. I'm fine. I'm sorry we didn't do the bungee jump. Next weekend?"

"Did you get checked out at the ER? Why didn't you call me?" she fretted.

"No! I'm FINE! He's fine. We stayed at the beach, and we kissed." The blood ran to my cheeks at the mortifying memory of passing out. I decided to only tell a half truth, "It was so amazing, it took my breath away."

We lingered in semi uncomfortable silence for a beat.

"Have I ever told you how lucky you are? You always got all the best boys at college, too," she said.

"I thought you didn't like Zac? Too weird? Anyway, you had Mark Adamson at college. He was tasty. I was jealous."

"You were jealous of me?" she snorted, fiddling with her glasses as if to prove some point.

"Come on, you know you've got the librarian sex-doll going on. Apart from that one year when you insisted on dressing like your grandma." I teased her with my oversized grin.

"You want to wear this drink?" She thrust her glass forward and hovered it playfully over my head.

Phew. She wasn't angry at me for standing her up on our bungee date. Zac wasn't angry that I stole his bike. Danny hadn't called me in to give me the boot from the department. Life was good.

I was struggling to believe that Zac had anything to do with that missing girl. And he hadn't mentioned the small fact that the sand had risen up of its own accord to choke Mullet-man. Maybe he hadn't seen. I was in the clear. Anna had certainly been too occupied to notice it.

But then, that was how most people dealt with my weirdness if they witnessed it — by shrugging it off as themselves seeing things that weren't real. And that was exactly how I dealt with it, too. I pretended it was nothing, it was a coincidence, I was imagining it. Because what else could I do? I had no idea what it was, or why it happened, or how to control it. Only that when I was mad enough, you probably didn't want to be near me.

That night, after Mullet-man, I'd spent hours online researching magical beings that could summon the elements. If Google was to be believed, then I was a warlock, or a witch, or psychotic — all amusing notions that I should continue to ignore.

I plucked out my cell sneakily whilst I went for a piss and sent Zac a message.

Jess: *Yes, Master. I love every delicious drawl from your lips. So where the hell are you? You best come find me before someone else comes along and takes advantage of how damn horny I am. Come stamp your mark on my ass.*

I SPENT THE NEXT FEW HOURS HUMMING WITH ANTICIPATION and skittering about all over the place. But, always one to disappoint, Zac didn't arrive. He hadn't replied to my last message either. Were we really continuing the cat and mouse? We hadn't said where to meet, but he'd agreed tonight and surely this was the place he'd expect to find me?

My earlier happiness wore off fast. I couldn't stay out too late, I had a 24hr shift coming up in the morning. I wouldn't be going in hungover any more.

Zac was missing his chance. Each ticking minute that went past made me angrier that he wasn't there. Screw him.

I wasn't going to wait the entire night like a lost puppy. It was humiliating. I'd go and sulk somewhere else instead.

"Why don't we try out the bars on the other end of the island?" I asked Anna. "I'm bored of the same old faces here."

She looked at me quizzically. "Except one face?"

"Yes, well that face isn't here, once again, so he can kiss my ass."

We took a cab to the South side, which lasted all of a few minutes. I dusted off potato chip crumbs from a chair, before dropping myself down in between a pack of frat boys and... oh yes, more frat boys. I was surprised by how much they were starting to irritate me. Maybe older, more mature binge drinkers would be nicer. Easier to relate to.

"You think the North is wild?" Anna shouted at me above the din. "It's nothing compared to this side."

She wasn't wrong. It was lingerie party night. If only I'd had the invitation, I would have made the effort to wear matching underwear and stripped off. My silky pants were cute, but... oh, who was I kidding. The scar on my back would always inhibit me from stripping off in public. There was a reason I always wore clingy t-shirts instead of strappy tanks.

No one else seemed to care what their undies looked like, though. They went right ahead and removed the little clothing they were wearing, prancing around in an array of thongs and bras. The guys dutifully performed a few acts on those women that ought to belong in more private places. I could probably have had fun here if a vital piece of the equation wasn't missing.

Or was he? An electric heat flashed behind my eyes and I scanned the crowd to find him watching. That was happening a lot. Finding his penetrating stare bearing down on me out of nowhere. My heart stuttered every time, the way only he could make it.

Except, today it was different.

The same sensual lips, the same high cheeks, damn, it *was* the same face. But his hair was a little longer and darker, almost black — kind of messy, tousled, instead of spiked up. A thin, silver scar ran along his left cheekbone. It didn't detract from his unearthly good looks, it enhanced them. I wanted to study it further, but he was too far away for me to see clearly, and besides, the woman that was glued to his hip was now planting her lips all over his face.

So, this was Alex Elwood.

His hands gripped tight onto the woman's waist, holding her firmly against him, fingers digging into her flesh. She found his lips and their tongues worked furiously at each other. He fisted a handful of her hair and she jumped to pull away, but he mouthed something into her ear and slowly, hesitantly, she leant back into him, head tilted.

He licked along her jaw, ending up below her ear, where he kissed and sucked. Still holding her hair, his other hand rubbed her ass. She visibly melted under his kisses, her body wilting and submitting to him.

I was overcome with a totally irrational and jealous urge to go and slap her away from him. Probably because he was the spitting image of Zac, which was confusing for my heart.

He raised his head to look at me once more. The room wobbled as I clutched at a few ragged breaths in my throat. The side of his mouth turned up in a lopsided, seductive smile. Her lipstick had rubbed off on him; his full lips were a bright, blood red against his pale skin. He let go of her hair and her head slumped limply into his shoulder. Then he snapped his fingers in the air, his gaze never leaving mine, and two men stepped forward from behind him.

One put his arm around the woman and pulled her, so

that she was now leaning limp against him. I guessed the alcohol, or drugs, had kicked in too much for her. They half guided and half carried her away out of a side door.

He held my gaze way beyond the comfort zone. A lazy, amused smile etched permanently across his face. Blood hammered in my ears, making black spots swim in front of me. I'd always thought of myself as pretty confident, but the dizzying mess that these brothers left me in was getting ridiculous.

Memories came to me of the poor missing girl that we'd found, confused and drugged out. My heart pounded heavier. This was my chance to approach him about it.

I somehow managed to break away from his stare to find Anna, to tell her what I was doing. The moment I did, my heart crashed against my chest. I needed to have his gaze on me again. The pull towards him was too great to ignore, like every part of me needed his eyes.

I scanned the corner where he'd been just a second before, but he'd vanished.

Jesus H. Christ. They were too alike.

*a*nna wasn't at all surprised when I told her who I'd seen. I was still looking around anxiously, trying to catch another glimpse, hoping he'd return.

"This is *his* side of the island, he's here all the time," she said, with a casual wave of her arm. How could she dismiss his presence as nothing unusual? Everything about him was exceptional.

"How are you not in awe of him?"

She grunted. "I was, years ago, when I first came here. But after all the times I tried to get his attention, and Zac's." She looked away, fiddling with her glasses. "Well, eventually the spell wore off and I gave up. I started to see them for what they really are. And they're not nice men, Jess. I suggest you stop thinking about the gorgeous brother of your gorgeous, freaky man. Seriously, ditch any ideas of either of them before you get into trouble. Find yourself a decent guy for a change... like Danny."

"You tried it on with Zac?"

She huffed, pushing away the considerable ass of a woman who'd perched on the arm of our sofa.

"I'm not jealous. That's not why I'm saying this. I just

think someone like Danny would make you much happier, and be a more calming influence on you. He's genuine, thoughtful. A fireman! Every girl's dream."

"If he's so perfect, why aren't you with him?" I asked bitterly. Fucking *calming influence*?! How patronizing.

"He's practically my brother. I'm not stupid enough to go down that road."

"He's my chief! That's not a stupid road? But of course, I always make the stupid choices, right?"

"Jess, don't be angry. I only want you to be happy."

"Then quit playing matchmaker and support me being with Zac."

Was I with Zac? And if so, what the hell was I doing on the other side of the island, lusting after his twin brother — who may, or may not, be responsible for a spate of missing persons?

A SCREAM RIPPED THROUGH THE ROOM, COMING FROM DEEP within my core, consuming the space around me with the sound of helplessness. I awoke from the nightmare drenched in sweat, my hair plastered to my face, still hearing their screams in my head. My mother's screaming, mixed with my own.

The usual dream had changed. This time, amongst the flames, there were visions of cascading sand, pouring into open mouths, clogging and overflowing. I could smell the burning flesh as my father barreled out of the door after me, a walking fireball, reaching out to grab me.

The shiny, puckered skin across my back felt extra constrictive and taut over my spine, pulling and itching, wrapping me in a claustrophobic layer of anxiety. I reached round to scratch it.

When the alarm went off, I leapt from bed, showered, and got to the firehouse without allowing myself a moment to think.

I walked in and was immediately summoned to Danny's office, much to the amusement of Meat and the other guys. They all cracked jokes as I walked past, about what happened in the office to naughty girls.

"You must get called in there all the time then, right Meat?" I smiled.

He whooped with laughter, slapping my back.

"Chief," I said, closing the door behind me.

"Firefighter Layton. Take a seat." He nodded, folding his hands on the desk and waiting for me to sit.

We eyed each other cautiously.

"One day, Jess."

Fuck-a-duck. No. Please no. I cast my eyes to the table. "I'm so sorry."

"Look, I get it. I live on the number one party hot spot in Texas. I don't have a problem with you indulging in what this place has to offer. But you have to be careful. I'm worried for you. Can't you see the warning signs with the Elwoods?"

"Yes, I can. That doesn't mean I'll heed them though."

He rubbed his hands over his face in exasperation.

"I can't force you to stay away from them, but I'll keep trying. When you're on my time, I need you one hundred percent on the job. You're my firefighter, with no fuck-ups. Outside that time, well, that's yours. But you need to separate the two parts of your life, draw a line between them. And even off duty, if you get involved in more trouble that reflects badly on this department, then... I'll have to deal with it. Go ahead and do your wild shit if you must, but either off the island, or in private. Understood?"

"Yes, sir." I shifted sheepishly.

I hear you, Chief, really I do. But all the warnings do is make me want to tear up this island and dive headfirst into the Elwood drama...

The firehouse alarm broke the uneasy tension, causing the whole crew to scramble to the truck.

"It's an actual fire," Meat yelled. "Must be the first one in eight months! Over at the Requiem bar."

Danny threw a heated look my way. "Speak of the devils. This will be interesting for you, that's an Elwood property."

11

JESS

*F*aint traces of black smoke wafted into the blue sky, swirling and drifting on the sea breeze. The crowds were going wild, held back by the beach patrol unit who were already there. They'd done an initial assessment, and one of them rushed over to tell Danny that all the doors were locked.

"What the hell? There's no windows on the ground floor?" I scanned the building, watching as several firefighters attempted to kick through the doors. No windows downstairs meant the only indication of a raging fire within that level were the delicate threads of smoke that had escaped through gaps and air vents in the building, and the thick, swirling masses of dark gray that fogged the upper windows.

"They're all locked," the patrol guy repeated himself. "Heavy-duty steel doors. Chief, I can hear people screaming inside, we have to get in quick."

Danny was a machine when he was in action. He launched straight into the chaos and started giving out orders. I watched as they scurried this way and that, following his commands. The police had also arrived and he exchanged a brief, animated conversation with them.

I stood watching, my feet rooted to the sand, my bunker gear suddenly feeling like it was five sizes too small and weighed a ton. I didn't know this crew yet; the routine didn't come naturally to me. I felt paralyzed, unable to contribute. They told me fires rarely happened here. I wasn't prepared for one of this scale.

A window shattered on the second floor and a huge, black plume billowed out. Shadowy figures passed by the glass, moving too fast, blurring with the smoke. Shrieks erupted from the onlookers as another window shattered.

A face came close to that window. It was Alex, I was sure of it. Then he vanished, back into the whirling gloom.

Meat got the ladder out, ready to climb up to the windows. The police attempted to kick down the main door, whilst some of my crew worked on the other one, but they wouldn't budge. Kick after kick... nothing. An officer pulled out his gun and cleared the area, firing several shots to try and breach the door. Still nothing. Others arrived with sledgehammers, hydraulics and disc cutters.

A few moments later they had it open. The second it swung wide the flames surged out. No way through without damping it back first — the fire looked like it had already spread throughout.

The screams were the first thing to hit me, followed closely by the smell. I knew that smell... burning flesh. Terrified shouts, mixed with wails of pain. The open doorway had released those horrific noises to batter my senses and all I wanted to do right then was run away.

"Firefighter Layton!" Danny dragged me from my immo-bility. "Get up that ladder with your crew and find a way down, the doorways are no good."

I cast a glance at the water being pumped through the

open door, before scrambling to join Meat on the ladder. Each step upwards had my chest growing tighter. Meat looked back at me with a reassuring smile as he climbed through the open hole where a window had been.

I burst through after him and was met with a wall of searing heat and thick smoke. It was impossible to see beyond my own hands as I stuck them out in front. Alex was here somewhere, I'd seen him, and others. We yelled out to them, but no one came.

I yanked the hose line along with me and followed Meat through an internal doorway, along a hall and down stairs, always keeping a wall against our left hands so we couldn't get lost. We came to the bottom and Meat started cursing at another locked door.

The sound of banging fists on the wood lined my stomach with ice. People kicking, and screaming. So much screaming.

"Stand back," Meat shouted through the door, bringing his leg up and kicking it.

"Wait," I yelled. "We don't know what we're opening up on to, you should test the door first."

"No time for that." With a couple more kicks, it flew open.

Heat blasted me in the face, and surging flames shot straight over our heads. I dropped to my knees, along with whichever crew members were behind me. Meat cried out as a blazing figure tumbled through the doorway, falling right into him.

"Shit!" he barked, rolling around in the confined space, trying to get them off.

The flames.

The smell.

The screams.

Buzzing exploded through my head, deafening me. Meat

was yelling, I could see his lips moving, but I couldn't hear a word. Someone pushed past from behind me and started spraying them with the second hose line they'd brought.

Beyond the lapping flames, I could see into the main room of the bar. So much fire. People everywhere. But, unless it was my lack of hearing, I thought the screaming had dulled. Most of them were now overcome with smoke inhalation, coughing and whimpering, or completely passed out. The few that still stood, with clothing pressed to their faces, were flailing and trampling the bodies that littered the floor.

If I could just forget that night, forget the sound of the explosion, the sound of my mother's screams. Forget the smell of her burning flesh, of *my* burning flesh. Forget the pain, searing into my back, temporarily blinding me with the agony.

This is not that night. Those are not my mother's screams. That's not the smell of my family's flesh. I don't fear fire. I own it... I don't fear fire. I own it.

I caught my breath and drove the memories from my mind. Blasting water from my hose, I aimed it through that door and began tackling the inferno.

But this was no longer a rescue operation. The screams had completely quieted.

There was no one making it out alive.

AFTER I'D DONE ALL I COULD I LEFT THE BUILDING WITH Meat, and slumped against the fire truck in a heap. The sweat under my bunker gear was literally dripping down me, pooling into my boots. Ripping off my coat, I shoved the suspenders over my shoulders, heaving deep breaths as the air hit my slick skin.

I watched as part of the crew continued pumping water through the front door. They'd made progress, most of the blaze was under control.

We couldn't save them though. We'd been too late. It had spread so fast, and with the doors locked, valuable minutes were lost.

Trapped. They'd been *trapped*. And burnt alive.

"No survivors," Danny said into a phone, standing next to me.

After a brief conversation that I couldn't focus on, he tucked the phone away and dropped down next to me, rubbing his face.

"What about the people that were upstairs?" I asked. "They got out on our ladder, right? So there were some survivors?"

"There was no one upstairs, we searched the whole place."

I twisted round to face him in confusion. "That's not right, I saw them. Alex was there, and others..." Jumping to my feet, I grabbed my coat. "We have to get back up there. They're in there, somewhere."

"Jess, the other team are still up there. Trust me, they've checked everything. There was no one on the upper floor." Danny took my hand to pull me back down.

Then I saw him from the corner of my eye, sauntering towards us without a care in the world. Walking along the beach like it was a normal day, like his bar hadn't just burned out with everyone in it.

I lurched towards him, but stopped short when the police approached. Danny stood beside me, huffing and rubbing his neck. I waited, watching them talk quietly, waiting for the handcuffs to go on. Alex reached out and rested a hand casually over the officer's shoulder like a close friend.

He stared at me whilst he spoke. My skin bristled. Someone shouted Danny's name. He grunted, shifting on his feet, but not leaving me. They called him again, but he was too busy glaring at Alex to notice.

"Someone's calling you," I said.

"Don't talk to him, Jess," he urged, reluctantly following the call of his name.

I debated leaving. Following Danny, since technically he'd given me an order. I should go help the other team. Or go home to wash off the stench of death. Drown away the memories with alcohol.

Alex finished his conversation with the cop and strolled over.

"You," he stated.

"You," I replied.

He squinted his eyes. "What are you?"

I scrunched my own face up, looking down at my bunker gear. "Um... I'm a firefighter. What are you?" *Back at you, Dickwad.*

"I'm everything," he smiled.

"Is that what you told the girls you abducted and abused?"

"Careful, little girl." His voice was low, but his face was alive with curiosity.

"Little girl? Last time someone called me that I was fourteen years old. I responded by breaking his nose."

"You gonna try break mine?" He rubbed a thumb casually down his cheek, along the silver scar, and over his chin.

"I haven't decided yet," I breathed.

He cocked his head, smiling, pressing his tongue into his teeth. Looking me up and down, his face disturbingly the same as Zac's. Different eyes though. Alex's blue eyes shone brightly with amusement, the color like glittering topaz. I clutched my fingers into fists to stop them reaching out, which they seemed to want to do of their own accord.

"What kind of bar doesn't have any windows and needs heavy security doors?" I blurted, shuffling on the spot, the sweat beginning to pour from me again.

He shrugged, "Mine. Let's say it's... gothic. They love all the gloom and mystique."

"Loved. Past tense. You know they're all dead, right? Why were the doors locked? And how did you get out?"

"Are you a cop?"

"I think we already established what I am."

"No. We only established your occupation, not what you actually *are*. You going to cause me trouble, darlin'?"

"Firefighter Layton!" Danny stormed over, placing a hand in the small of my back. "Time to go."

Danny and Alex exchanged icy glares.

"You don't even seem upset by what's happened here? People are dead. In your bar," I yelled.

"Enough," Danny said.

"Yes, that's enough, Miss Layton, leave it to the cops. Right, Danny?" Alex grinned from me to him. "I like your choice of new recruit, by the way, Chief. I hope you'll ensure she's shown all the ropes and made aware of how things work around here?"

Alex didn't wait for a response. He strolled away, hands in his pockets, whistling. Danny gritted his teeth and watched him leave, holding my shoulder to stop me following.

12

JESS

"Holy mother of god!" I stood in awe, gazing up into the pure cobalt sky at the bungee jump platform which seemed to be about ten miles up. Poised, serenely, in the vast expanse of blue, waiting calmly for us to take a leap and break the tranquillity with our screams.

"Do you have to blaspheme so much? It makes me uncomfortable," Anna muttered, as we passed through the ticket gate and began climbing the tower steps.

"Excuse me? Dear Lord, please don't try and tell me you're religious now?"

She stopped, mid step, to glare at me.

"Sorry, that one slipped out. I can't help it, I'm excited!" I grinned.

"You know I'm not anymore, but I was still raised that way and it doesn't sit right hearing it. And if my memory serves then you were raised that way, too. Heathen." She stopped again, but this time with a playful scolding look. We hadn't known each other as children but had spent many college nights comparing stories from our past. *Heathen*. I liked that, it suited.

"Yes, well, it's precisely that upbringing that makes it so much fun to rebel and cuss all I like. It's a 'stuff you in the face' to all those who tried to make me behave like a lady. You should try it, it's liberating. Now stop procrastinating and get up those steps, it's too late to bottle it now." I urged her onwards and upwards, just as a shrieking woman leaped and went down loudly, reaching a crescendo as she pinged back up.

Anna jumped and cursed at the noise. She was becoming more afraid by the minute. This might have been her idea, but it was a damned long way up to the top of those steps, even my heart was struggling.

She'd driven us off the island and into the heart of Texas to find the best jump — according to their website it was one of the biggest bungee towers in the state. The tower itself was on the edge of a large amusement park, the whir and hum of rollercoasters and rides drugging the air with excitement.

We managed to drag ourselves up early in the morning for the long drive, but the afternoon was still getting on by the time we'd arrived. I was relieved the place wasn't too busy now that the main rush had passed. Patience and I didn't get along.

Hopefully this was just the distraction I needed after my run in with Captain Dickface yesterday, and the trauma of what went down. Danny would make me see a counsellor for it. Department rules. We all had to.

Like I needed another shrink in my life. I'd deal with it in my own way, just like everything else. This was no different. I'd seen death before. Even so, the smell still clung to my nostrils. I had a feeling it would stay that way for some time.

Panting hard, we finally arrived onto the platform,

which crept out before us, beckoning down a long walk into nothingness. Just metal railings to our sides and the big open drop at the end. I wiped my clammy palms on my jeans and dared a look down at the dizzying drop. Anna clutched the rails when she did the same.

I smiled as the familiar thrill of adrenalin surged. I always hid inside adrenalin. One rush after another. Craving the power, the thrill, secluding myself in its embrace so as not to deal with reality, then crashing when it was gone.

A small group of people had arrived far below and were paying for their jumps. My skin prickled as one of them caught my eye, staring up at me. But surely, it couldn't be?

Dressed in his usual jeans, white t-shirt and leather jacket. Wearing sunglasses and a cap.

He never wore a hat. It messed too much with this perfectly spiked-up hair.

"Anna, why is Zac wearing a cap?" I asked.

"What?" she gasped, as she followed the line of my finger. She caught sight of him after a second of peering down and her mouth dropped. Then she gaped at me like I was a moron. "Never mind his *hat*, Jess! What about why on Earth is he even here? Did you invite him?!"

That was a good point. Why the hell was he there? We were hundreds of miles from South Padre. This took his stalking to a whole new level.

He stood motionless, giving me that hard glare that I alone seemed to elicit from him. This was not good. This was supposed to be a bonding day with Anna, since things had been tense after our near-miss with Mullet. Now I had my nutjob stalker to deal with.

My delicious, mesmerizing, intriguing, sexy-as-sin stalker.

A YOUNG MAN IN A BRIGHT BLUE GRAVITY FALLS BUNGEE shirt stepped past us with a nod and wink, pulling me from the Zac-induced daze. Another man in the same work shirt stood at the end of the platform and ushered us over. He had an attractive, outdoorsy look. Anna blushed as he eyed us up. I gave her yet another push forward.

"Be right with you," the man smiled as he fiddled with the ropes and harness. "Need to make sure it's safe."

He looked us up and down several more times as he pulled at straps. Anna shuffled around on the spot, clearly unsure about whether it was best to go first and get it over with. A tough decision — whether to take a terrifying, death-defying jump first, or put it off a moment longer, but have to hang out with this guy whilst waiting. He made the decision for her when he took my hand, pulling me forward.

His gaze settled on my tits as he strapped the harness around me, getting his body a little too close to mine. Just as I was trying to decide if he was actually sniffing me — with his nose up against my ear whilst reaching round to tighten a strap — there was a commotion far below and then a yell. Too loud, too close.

"Stop!" Zac's voice boomed.

He got hold of the bungee guy by the neck and pushed him backwards along the platform, back towards the steps. I didn't even know how Zac had got hold of him, since he'd been behind me with the straps just a second ago. Anna looked at me in a daze, her mouth flapping open and closed like a goldfish.

After several moments of my own stuttering, I managed to yell at Zac, who'd now reached the steps and was saying something into Mr. Bungee's ear.

"What the actual fuck, Zac?" were the best words I could manage.

Bungee man disappeared in a bright blue whoosh down

the stairs. Zac stood silent, his back to us. His head dropped, his shoulders slumped, and he turned ever so slowly to face me. Still looking at his feet, he seemed to take a moment to brace himself before finding my gaze.

My mouth hung open like Anna's until I screwed up my face. More commotion and banging on the steps distracted us, then a furious man in yet another blue shirt appeared, with a badge that read 'Manager – Simon Shivings'.

"Time to go," Zac said calmly, removing my harness with ridiculous swiftness.

"Who exactly are you?" asked the red-faced, puffing man. The worker who'd passed us on the steps when we arrived was hiding behind him.

Zac put out a hand to brush aside the manager and pulled me along. I did my best to root my feet to the hard metal beneath them. I wanted answers too.

He let out a long, impatient sigh, followed by a patronizing smile.

"Well, *Simon*," he said, tapping the manager's badge. "The bungee cord is not safe."

"That's absurd—" he began, as Zac grabbed the harness and waved a frayed and broken cord under his nose. It was only held together by a few strands, the rest all split and sticking out. There was no way it would have held.

"I... I... I..." Simon stammered, grabbing the cord and thrusting it at the employee behind him.

"That can't be right," he said. "I just did a safety check five minutes ago, right before I handed over to—" He looked around in confusion. "Where'd the other dude go?"

"Who?" Simon spat, his face swelling out in rage like a pufferfish.

"The new guy? The one you sent to cover me for my break? I left him here with these ladies."

"Fuck me!" shouted Simon. "There is no *new guy*. Cancel

all bookings for today. Get rid of that crowd down below. Miss—" he smiled grimly at me. "Would you please accompany me to the office?"

Zac gripped hard onto my hand and yanked me away. "No, she's fine."

"But, Sir, I need to speak with the lady."

"Fuck off," he growled.

Simon had positioned himself in front of us, blocking the platform. My breath caught because I feared for him. It seemed like a really dumb thing to have put himself in our way. Instinct told me that it wouldn't end pretty if he didn't move. An instinct that came from spending time with a cage fighter boyfriend.

Zac's grip on my hand was now so tight that it hurt. I tried to wriggle free.

Simon put his hands up, like he was trying to calm a child, not the raging, psycho-stalker-crazy-man that I could see.

"One of us could have died," Anna suddenly shrieked, breaking the stand-off. "We want compensation."

"Of course. If you'll just come with me I can sort that out for you. I'll also need you to issue a statement to the police. There's clearly a dangerous person on the loose that I need to report... and then they'll close us down for incompetency," Simon said through gritted teeth to his employee, who'd gone back into hiding behind him.

"No police," Zac insisted. "I'll see you in your office now."

He released my hand and the blood rushed back to my fingers. Taking Simon's shoulder, Zac urged him towards the steps and away. Simon didn't resist, as soon as Zac touched him he just relented and went with him. I stood gawking at Anna, who was staring at the employee.

After our three-way stare out, he opened his mouth to

speak but changed his mind, and we all walked back down the steps in silence.

By the time we reached the bottom the employee had gathered his wits and went into work mode, dealing with the throng of people all talking and shouting at him at the same time, waving their tickets around.

"You do realize how fucked up this is, Jess?" Anna's face was drained completely white, maybe with a tinge of green. So much for her day out, our day of bonding and repairing relations.

Zac burst out the office door and headed straight to his motorcycle, which was parked in the distance, next to Anna's car.

"We're done here," he said over his shoulder, in a tone that was clearly intended to demonstrate how he was not to be messed with.

Screw that, asswipe. I ran after him, tugging his jacket relentlessly until he stopped.

"I'm not leaving here until you give me answers." I sat down on the grass. Anna joined me in our little peaceful protest.

Shaking his head, he took his hat off to run a hand through his hair. He looked cute in the cap, but I preferred him without it. Cocking his eyebrows, he firmly yanked it on backwards. Then he sat opposite us to receive his grilling.

Those honey-drenched amber eyes dared me to sink into them. I could melt and forget everything when he looked at me like that. He ran his tongue along his lips, so full and juicy next to his pale skin, which was only darkened by slight stubble.

"Jess!" Anna shouted, glaring at me. I don't know how long I'd sat in silence staring at his beautiful face, but it suddenly felt like a long time.

"Right," I coughed. "I don't even know where to start,

Zac. You followed me all the way out here? Do I need to tell you how creepy that is?" *And kind of hot.*

"I was concerned for your safety," he shrugged. "Clearly it's a good job I was."

"How did you know the rope was damaged?" Anna joined in. "How could you have known that from all the way down at the bottom?"

"Yes, and in addition to that, how the hell did you get to the top so quick, and past the gates?"

He looked at us with pity, like we were poor imbeciles who had no idea about anything, before putting on a fake, patient voice. "Call it intuition," he said to Anna, who immediately shook her head and replied with, "Bullshit."

I was impressed with her sudden confidence around him, she was usually flustered in his presence, but the adrenalin seemed to have changed her this time. Hooray for adrenalin. She should seek more of it, it suited her.

She shakily wiped at the sweat on her forehead and adjusted her glasses, whilst Zac just smiled at her, remarkably playfully for him. I think he liked her this way too. The smile lingered on his lips and he didn't say anything else. Waiting for one of us to challenge him further.

I found myself mirroring his grin. My heart was still pounding from it all, from the excitement of being about to jump, from the fear and drama that had ensued, from the way he was smiling at me now. His eyes roamed down my body to my hands in my lap. One thumb was stroking the other absently. I wanted to reach out and run them along the stubble on his face, over his lips, along his neck and down his chest.

"Screw you two!" Anna huffed, standing up and dusting down her jeans. "Go ahead and make out right here. Once that's out the way you can talk and call me later with the rational explanation. I'm sure there is one, right?"

She didn't wait for an answer. I stood up to follow her, but my feet wouldn't move. I watched as she stomped away back to her car. Zac stood beside me, his fingers brushing against mine.

I should have called after her. I should have gone with her. I should have shouted and demanded more answers from him. I should still have been raging for what happened with the fire yesterday, question him about his brother. Furthermore, I should still have been angry that he stood me up the other night when he'd told me we'd meet.

Should haves, should haves.

Instead, I kissed him.

———

THE KISS WAS MIND-BLOWING. SOFT, YET SOMEHOW FIRM AND hard at the right moments. Passionate and heated, but through cool, minty breath. I slid my hand around his neck as his tongue swept deeper into my mouth. He tasted unusual underneath the mint flavor, but not in a bad way, something vaguely metallic.

The energy that passed between us sent my thoughts drifting off into space. I couldn't grasp them back again. There was simply no thought, other than that of needing him. Of needing more. Always wanting and needing more.

He found my waist, digging his fingers so tightly into my hips that I gasped. My open mouth was at once smothered by his consuming lips, stealing all the air from me. I let my hands wander down to his ass, pressing myself into him. My head spun as my body melted against his unwavering strength. He was solid, I was putty. Rapidly dissolving into nothing but feeling...

The amusement park crowds flowed and whirled around us, the ebb and fall of a hundred other people. They meant nothing. It was just us. Frozen in time and motion. He groaned and pushed his erection harder into my crotch, breaking the kiss to search deep into my eyes. His lips grazed over mine, featherlight, despite the shocking strength of his grip on me. His breath was heavy, coming fast in excited pants.

He seemed to be physically straining with effort, as if finishing a workout, his face a crumpled picture of anguish, eyes burning with desire. Veins popped out along his forehead, his teeth gritted. My whole body cried out for him. His touch was icy cold, and yet somehow it warmed me, set my body on fire, burning with an aching need.

I began to pray that he would bend me over right there and fuck me. I doubted anyone would even find that shocking back on South Padre, I'd already seen masses of people engaged in public sex acts.

"There's a time and a place for that," he said through a tight smile, breaking the moment.

"For what?" I asked breathlessly, struggling to regain some composure.

"For public fucking. Before that, I'd like to go someplace private and you can give me my own personal show? I've seen what you can do on a stage." He stepped to the side and gave my ass a firm slap, hard enough to make me jump. "And that's just to get you started on the pink ass I owe you."

Zac told me to wait and he disappeared for ten minutes, returning with a helmet for me. He sat astride his bike and waited for me to join him, looking like a retro sex-machine in his leathers and white t-shirt.

By the time we got back to the island, it was late into the

night. He pulled up at my motel. I was about ready to burst with excitement after hours on the bike just thinking about what would happen when he came inside.

I'd just swung my leg off the bike when another pulled up beside us in a blazing hurry, gravel crunching and spraying as it skidded to a stop. The rider wasn't wearing a helmet. He nodded at me, then Zac.

Cute, yet sexy, face. Straggly surfer-esque blonde hair. I'd seen him lots of times before, always at Zac's side, but he'd never acknowledged me.

Zac stared hard at him. Surfer guy stared back. I stared from one to the other, wondering if they were actually going to speak.

"I'm really sorry, Jess," Zac sighed. "I can't stay. There's something I need to deal with."

"You can't be serious? You're going to run off on me again? What's so important? Another beach party? And who the hell is this, anyway?" I stared hatred into the surfer-twat through squinted eyes, and he held out his hand.

"Leon," he declared, smiling, as if the introduction made it all okay.

I shook it half-heartedly and returned my glare to Zac. He didn't say anything, just gave me an apologetic smile of his own. His jaw was set tight, grinding his teeth. As fucking usual. Someone should give him an Oscar for the dramatic expressions.

"There's so much explaining that you owe me. I have so many doubts that I can't even keep track of which ones are the most important. But right now, the biggest issue is that you're a complete asswipe," I said.

"This motel is trash," he replied. "There are much better ones on the North, I'll find you one."

"What?! What the fuck are you on?"

"You're in danger. I need time to think." Shaking his head, he slipped away into the night. *Again*.

Motherfucker.

13

ZAC

"*A*lexander is dead blood. He's crossed a line. I'm taking him down." I slammed my fist clear through a table. The cabinet and chairs were already broken, laying about in pieces, thanks to the rage that I couldn't hold in check. Leon stood in front of the giant TV on the wall, self-assigned protector of it, lest I smash that too and deny him of his stupid racing games.

"Why would he try to kill her like that?" Leon asked.

"Because if he took her personally then I'd find out. He was trying to cover his tracks by making it a random event off the island. Or maybe just to fuck with me, I don't know."

"But why would he want to kill her in the first place?"

Selena's face flashed under my eyelids. Why, indeed. Because he wanted to take everything from me.

"Because of her damned crazy aura," I replied. "He's threatened by her, by not knowing what she is. He thinks she's involved in the attacks on us. Whoever that is, they set fire to his bar too."

"You don't agree she's involved? You must admit, it seems a bit of a coincidence that she's arrived now," Ruben said from across the room.

"*She* doesn't even know what she is. She's not part of it. A simple scan of her thoughts on me can make that clear."

"Not if she's got the ability to control the thoughts she puts out. What if she's stopping you seeing? What if you're too wrapped up in the spell cast by her sweet pussy that you can't see it?" Ruben sneered.

I lunged for him. He sidestepped and spun round, ready for the next attempt. Leon got between us, an impatient look on his face.

"Or," Ruben added over Leon's shoulder. "What if *you* end up being the one that kills her? Alex tried to do you a favor. We all know that if you continue on this road then you're going to lose it and take her out. Then what?"

"You doubt my strength?" I asked Leon, slowly turning to meet the eyes of the other members of my Cell in the room.

They're weak, all of them. They all doubt you. Don't tolerate their insubordination.

"Of course not," Leon replied. "I mean. I don't know. This has never happened before. You've never been challenged this way. You're different."

They all sat around, eyes lowered. The sitting room was vast, yet it felt claustrophobic in that moment. It was hard enough battling the dueling forces inside my own head; I didn't need fights breaking out with my men over it too.

"She's different, but you're going to have to trust me. I admit, I don't know who she is, but I know that I need her. And right now she's not safe. I want one man shadowing her at all times when I'm not with her. Leon, sort that out for me." I held my position and resisted the urge to pace up and down. Or to break something else. Maybe Ruben's face...

Leon nodded in reply, just as a shrill giggle contaminated my ears from the adjoining room. A handful of drunken ladies were shrieking in excitement at being in our mansion, waiting for the boys to come and play. Their mindless chatter threatened to make me explode. I rubbed my temples, concentrating, clearing the external noise.

"Why are there women here? You're partying under our current threat, like nothing's wrong, then you have the nerve to come in here and challenge me?!" I yelled.

Punish them.

Ruben huffed in the corner, itching to let it out. I wished he would go someplace else. Disappear with his ponytail and ridiculous clothes and attitude, away from my Cell. I could banish him, but that would really upset his sister, Eva. And that was a whole other argument for another time.

I stared, waiting for him to acknowledge me. "Come on, Ruben. Don't go shy on me now. For someone who doesn't give a damn about me, or our way of life, you've sure been showing a lot of attention to Jess."

"I care about Eva. What affects her, affects me."

"She can take care of herself."

"You're mistaken."

"Because of the one time she needed you? I was a different person then. She's moved on from it, why can't you?"

"If anything happens to her while she's under your leadership, I'll hold you personally responsible."

"You and me both," I replied through gritted teeth.

"OK, boys, there's only so much of this bullshit I can sit and listen to." Eva rose up and walked over to stand beside me, confirming her allegiance. "We've been here before. If it wasn't Jess, or the recent attacks, it would be something else, Ruben. You'll always find stuff to fight about. Just leave it. Please."

The attacks. The dead vampires. As if Jess's arrival alone didn't give me enough to deal with. I had someone targeting us and the Bael threatening to come deal with it. Now my brother was trying to kill said woman, who'd wandered onto my island, all sweetness and sass, with an aura that made her appear like an angel, and a scent that made me want to set the devil loose to devour her.

My guys were right to be worried. I had no useful information on what was going on, who was killing us. There was a weird, fuzzy energy around the dead vampires, blurring any scents or clues. They thought I was going to screw up and allow more of us to get killed, because my mind was elsewhere and not where it should be.

Or that Jess would undo my restraint and I'd go on a savage island rampage, uprooting our little life we had.

Or that worse still, Alexander would find a way to use all this emotion in me to his advantage and force me to activate the Legacy, which would probably tear me away from the Cell forever.

"I heard Romeo got killed. They're also picking off Alex's Cell," Leon commented.

"No, that was Alexander's own work. Romeo messed up letting that missing girl escape. He paid the price, Alexander made an example of him."

Ruben stormed past. *That's right. Leave before you become one of my examples.*

"Time to get dirty, ladies," he said in the room next door.

"Anyone else want to challenge me? Or you want to go let off steam too?" I asked.

Everyone vacated the room in a split second, and I begrudgingly followed them through to the party. A couple of women glued themselves to me with speed almost as impressive as my own. One of them smelled pretty good. Nothing close to Jess, but enough to make me uneasy with need. She started rubbing my dick which didn't help.

I let them touch me for a while, without reciprocating. What was the point? I didn't want to touch them. I wanted to touch the one woman that I couldn't. After a while they gave up and trotted over to Leon, who was busy making out with another two already.

Leaving them to it, I marched down the hallway. Eva emerged from the basement, wiping blood from her lips. She put a petite hand on my shoulder and pulled me close.

"She doesn't look like Selena, doesn't smell like her, or act like her, and yet Selena is all I can think about when I look at her," I sighed. "What I did to Selena... I can't let that happen again. Not to Jess."

"You're not that man anymore." She rubbed my shoulder.

"If I don't destroy her, then Alexander will. *He's* still the same man. He'll take her from me. History will repeat. I can't keep her safe, there are too many dangers in this world. And I can't take the pain of losing another love, it would push me back into darkness." I took a deep breath. "They're right, this is a mistake. I need to drive her off the island before it's too late."

"Sshhhh," she whispered, running a blood stained finger along my lip until I shuddered. "Don't stress it. You're stronger than you give yourself credit for. You'll handle it... all of it. But you can't go near her without getting a fix first, you're too hungry. Go fill your boots."

She slapped my ass playfully and I continued past her, down the basement steps.

14

JESS

*F*unny how the sight of a mere piece of paper could fill you with instant rage, but that's precisely what happened when I saw the white sheet fluttering on my Ducati. People leaving flyers under your car wipers was one thing, but touching my baby and taping it to the seat?! That was taking the piss.

I ripped it away and went to screw it up, when the writing caught my eye.

YOU'RE PLAYING WITH FIRE... LEAVE BEFORE YOU ARE BURNED

Written in scrawling red letters above an advert for a firefighter vacancy out of state.

What the hell? I mounted the bike and sped up the street, hesitating at the junction before taking the turn towards Anna's apartment. It was Sunday, she should be home, she always had Sunday off and then rotated her other days.

"What do you think this means?" I shoved the paper into her hands as soon as she opened the door.

Before she had a chance to reply I was ranting, "Zac used those words with me the other night after poker. He said I liked playing with fire. Who did this? Was it him trying to be funny? I thought the games were over?"

Anna didn't say anything, she shifted about not looking at me, so I carried on, "He was weird last night. One of his twatty friends pulled him away and he ditched me for the hundredth time, saying he needed to think. Then he does this? Where the fuck are his balls hiding? He couldn't tell me to my face? He blows hot and cold every five fucking minutes—"

"Have you tried talking to him, instead of speculating?" Anna offered.

"I can't. I have such an uneasy feeling about this. I've been feeling sick from the moment I found it."

I marched up and down her apartment and tripped over a pair of massive Doc Martens boots. Muttering further obscenities, I picked them up and noticed they sure as hell were not Anna's. She gestured to the bedroom.

"I have a guest," she said under her breath.

"Right," I replied briskly. "Sorry, I'll leave you guys."

As I was saying the words, a man I vaguely recognized came through and took his boots from my hands. I'd definitely seen him around the island. He had an appearance you didn't forget. Hard face, thick black beard, dressed head-to-toe in black. Attractive, but rough around the edges.

"Don't worry," he said, his voice deep and commanding. "My work here is done... for now." He gave Anna a wink and then returned his gaze to me, smiling for a while until Anna sniffed to break the silence. He turned and kissed her for a long time while I stood waiting, not knowing where to look.

"Thanks, Anna, I'll call you." He finally broke the kiss and left us standing there, contemplating each other in silence.

"I'll put the coffee on, should I?" she asked, ambling into

the kitchen. "Go on, I know you don't want to talk about me and William. Carry on."

"Fuck it!" I yelled instantly. "He thinks *I* like playing games?! At least I don't do stupid shit like this. I should have known, all those bimbos hanging around him. He probably plays with a different woman each week and then gets bored. Well, I have completely run out of fucks. Zero left. I won't give him the satisfaction of seeing me like this. He can go to hell." And with that, I threw myself down on the sofa in protest.

"Did you get any answers about the bungee jump incident, or just suck his face off all night?" she asked, playing with her hair, which had a distinctly ruffled, just-fucked look about it.

"Not really. I have a million unanswered questions."

She raised her eyebrows.

"I know, I know! I should walk away, but there's this magnetism. I can't help it. I can't get him out of my head."

"Well, I'm writing to the bungee company and issuing a formal complaint. Whatever happened, it was messed up. The police need to be involved, regardless of what Zac wants." She cast me a sideways look, as if too afraid to face me full on with this news.

"I understand, you're right. Do what you need to."

We settled into another awkward silence, flicking through TV stations. The hours passed slowly. Evening approached and I was adamant I didn't want to go out and bump into him, so we continued to sit, bored and uneasy.

When the shrill ring of my phone went off we nearly leapt from our skin.

"What?" I snapped.

"I was hoping I'd have seen you at the beach by now. You are coming out tonight?" Zac asked.

"Is this a joke? What is *wrong* with you? Do you have

some sort of multiple personality disorder?" My voice rose with each word.

A quiet pause stretched out.

"I see. I know you think I've done something bad, but I haven't," he said, calm as ever. That was bullshit, I could picture the completely *not-calm* body language he always had going on. He might have had good control over his voice, but his body always told a different story.

"How do you know if you didn't do it, jackass?"

"It's pretty obvious by your mood."

"You can't say you didn't do it, if you don't know what IT is."

He sighed heavily, "Please, Jess, come to the beach and talk to me. I'll explain."

"THANKS FOR COMING," HE OFFERED. HIS FACE WAS SO beautiful, it wasn't fair. My heart threatened to rip open at any moment. If this was the end, before we'd even begun... well, I didn't know how I was supposed to deal with that. How could I have fallen for him so hard? I didn't even know him.

"Anna practically handcuffed me to try and stop me." I focussed on the ground, not daring to get sucked into those eyes, not this time.

"Someone's trying to separate us."

"Really," I replied flatly.

He didn't respond, so in the end I had to look at him. "Who? One of your ex-lovers or dirty groupies jealous of me?"

"I don't know who did it."

"So how do you know what it even is? I haven't told you what happened."

"No."

"No?" Could he ever give a straight answer? Oh hell. It was his wife, wasn't it? I bet he was married and playing me, and now she'd found out.

"I'm not that sort of guy."

"Why do I feel like you answer my thoughts?"

His mouth set in a line and his fingers rapped on the bar. We'd somehow made our way to MoJoe's whilst talking, without me even noticing until then.

Danny was there, watching with a weird mix of disgust and longing on his face. Shit. Had *he* left the note? Or even Anna?

No, no way.

"How open-minded are you?" Zac asked.

"Enough to try anything once." I winked at him automatically, which made me furious at myself. I was supposed to be angry with him and yet, as usual, it was diminishing fast under the scrutiny of that deep, hazel gaze. *Don't look at him.*

He laughed, a soft chuckle with a wry smile, which softened the hard eyes for a moment. "That's not hard to believe. Listen, you've already noticed that I'm a little weird. I have good senses. I can read people really well," he paused, uneasy. "Sometimes, I can get the gist of what people are thinking."

"Like a psychic?" Excitement tickled under my skin.

"Yeah, if you like."

"So, you can read my mind?" I sat forward eagerly, already lost in the thrill of that idea.

"Are you not even a little bit freaked out by this?" he frowned, shaking his head. "I was bracing myself for a big problem convincing you that I'm not mental."

"No way, I love all that supernatural stuff! I go to a psychic back home and... I've had weird experiences myself that I can't explain. I believe in forces outside of what we know. I mean, I don't believe in God as such, but I believe in the soul. There has to be some spark that makes us what we are, right? And that spark can't just disappear?"

His face darkened. I went on, hoping to get the smile back, even if only a half-hearted one. "And I believe that once upon a time we probably all had extra abilities in our minds. The brain has these bits that we don't even use. Some people are probably better at tapping into that than others. Extrasensory Perception."

"Well, I wasn't expecting it to be this easy. I wonder if I should be done with it and tell you all my other secrets, too?" There it was, the half-smile. Even that was dazzling enough to blind me with awe, his full grin would surely be atomic. Maybe I'd get lucky and see that one soon?

"There's more? Don't tell me you can use telekinesis?" I laughed, despite my head telling me to quit giggling like a love-struck schoolgirl and start demanding answers.

"No."

"What then?"

"Nothing. I'm just kidding. This is enough isn't it?"

"It's awesome! Tell me what I'm thinking now."

"It doesn't work like that. I can only usually hear thoughts that concern me. And even then I can't always hear them. They come to me sometimes."

"Oh." My cheeks felt hot, remembering all the dirty fantasies I had about him each day.

"Yeah, those are the ones," he laughed.

"Bloody hell, stop it at once!" I pushed him, expecting him to stumble sideways, but found myself up against a brick wall, his arms wrapped around me.

"You're strong," I whispered. He was hugging me gently, but I had the feeling I could snap at any moment if he tightened his arms.

"Don't be embarrassed, I love those thoughts. You have an extraordinarily imaginative and dirty mind." He leant his head into me as tension dropped over him again. "There is something else we need to speak about, though."

Crap. That didn't sound good. I didn't want to ask him all the questions. Now that his arms were around me, I didn't want the answers. I knew I wouldn't like them. And he felt too good to let go now. I tried to kiss him to shut him up, but he dodged it.

"My brother, Alexander. You need to keep away from him."

Memories from the other night flooded through my mind, like an unwelcome guest that you just can't help warming to. Initial thoughts were of fear and hatred, closely followed by desire. Images swirled of him sucking on that woman's neck, in public, so erotic. His appearance after the fire. The way he made me feel when he looked at me, sparks throbbing between my legs.

I shook my head to clear it and took Zac's hand in mine, because he suddenly looked mad as shit.

"You've spoken with him?" his voice low, threatening.

"Kind of. He acts like you — irritatingly evasive."

"You won't ever find me over the South side. Don't go there again."

"Yes, boss," I said with a mock salute.

"I mean it." He tried to smile as he pulled me back close. "I don't get on too well with my brother."

"So I hear. Who exactly is he? Because it sure looks like he's involved in some bad stuff, like a pimp maybe, I don't know. Do *you* know? Because if you do, what does that say about you? You're hiding so much from me. I wish I could walk away," I blurted. A constant stream of babble, needing to get it all out before I looked into those eyes again and forgot all my worries. Was he drugging me? I looked at my drink and set it down on the table.

"You're right, he's dangerous. That's what I'm trying to tell you."

"And what about you? Are you dangerous?"

"Yes," he said simply.

I caught movement over his shoulder and noticed for the first time that Leon and another follower were loitering nearby.

"Can't you go anywhere without them? What are they? Bodyguards?!"

He scoffed, "I don't need bodyguards. They're pretty adamant *I* need protection from you though."

I laughed. He didn't.

"You're not without your own dangerous secrets," he said. "Since we're opening up here, are you going to tell me about yours?"

I laughed nervously and bit my lip in hesitation. "I don't have any."

His eyebrows went up.

"I don't know what happened on the beach, if that's what you mean. That's the truth. Do you believe me?"

He paused, thinking, rubbing his delicious bottom lip between thumb and forefinger.

"There are things you still haven't told me, but yes, I believe you don't understand it," he shrugged, like we were talking of not understanding a math problem, as opposed to a conjured sand monster.

"Shouldn't you be the one freaking out then? Running from me? That's what usually happens..."

"I don't run. In fact, want to go for a ride?" he asked with sudden happiness. "We need to get away from here, and there's an amazing place I'd love to show you."

"It depends. Will you kiss me there?"

"Yes, ma'am, I do believe I will."

We left the bar holding hands and as we approached the bikes I was filled with dread at the sight of another piece of paper taped to the seat. At least it put him in the clear about doing it.

Zac quickened his pace to get there first, making a funny noise beside me. *Was that a growl?!* He snatched the paper, screwing it into a ball.

"Hey! That was for me, I want to read it."

He reluctantly uncurled his fingers and handed it over.

HE'S NOT WHAT YOU THINK HE IS.

Well, I guessed it ruled out Danny, too. He'd been at the bar the whole time, burning a hole through Zac with the evil eye.

"They're trying to freak me out. They obviously don't know that you've already told me about the psychic thing. Although, we still haven't established who *they* are?"

His face burned with an urgent intensity as he sat himself astride his chopper. "Later. Come on, I still have something to show you."

Well, where's the fun in tall, dark, strange men if you don't allow yourself to be whisked away by them?

15

ZAC

*T*he sound of stones crunching under the wheels as I pulled my Harley into the driveway was not unlike the static rage noise that filled my head when I was struggling to keep cool.

The constant swirl of a hundred different noises in the world around me, stirred up with my anger and my animal. Sometimes those noises threatened to send me crazy, because ironically, that would actually calm it all. The release of the darkness would wash over me and soothe it all away.

That's right. Go ahead, let me out.

Some days it was worse than others. Since she arrived it had mostly been worse. And now this. Whoever they were, they were pushing their luck with those ridiculous notes. I needed to find them and fix the problem, fast. I'd just have to add it to the list of big fucking problems that needed my immediate attention.

"Is this where you live?" Jess asked, dismounting and strolling towards the large sweeping steps of my veranda. "I'm sorry to disappoint you, it's impressive, but I don't generally find houses that exciting."

She gave me a playful look over her shoulder and paused, hand on her hip. My cock twitched. Damn that big seductive smile. "Then again, it depends on what happens *inside* The Bachelor of the Island's pad. I imagine all sorts of mischief could happen in there."

Yeah, best you didn't know. I grabbed her hand and led her around back. "I said we were going for a ride, I didn't say it was on the motorcycle. Come on."

"Are you shitting me?" She stopped dead in her tracks with a hand over her open mouth, staring at the helicopter. I loved that mouth. So big and beautiful, her whole face was all about the mouth. When she smiled it made me forget, just for a moment. I could forget Selena, the Bael, Alexander. I could imagine happiness without fear.

By the time we were settled into the cockpit, she was still jabbering like she'd had a full wrap of speed, with 'ooooohs' and 'aaaaaahs' and pointing at buttons. It was infectious, and thankfully helped to distract me from the inappropriate notions of her mouth on my cock.

It didn't take any effort on my part to impress women, I certainly didn't need a helicopter to do it, but pleasing her was fucking wonderful. I wanted to make an effort. Seeing her eyes alive with excitement, and her juicy lips in that mischievous grin.

Dumb, cock-sucking, dickhead.

Once we were airborne she managed to start stringing together words, even whole sentences.

"Why on earth do you have a helicopter?" was of course the first question she asked.

"Business trips," I replied, leaving out the part about how living in one place meant our hunting choices were limited and so we travelled out of state a lot.

"What sort of business? I thought you played poker?" She looked at me doubtfully.

134

"I do. There are other casinos around the country, you know. They get so suspicious of me I have to move around. Besides, I have my teeth into a few other projects, too." I touched her leg to distract her away from the topic. Turned out no distraction was necessary.

Her response was, "Hey, if your business gets me flights in a chopper, I don't care what it is."

She might change her mind about that. When would that time come, I wondered? When would she find out?

Leon was knocking on the edge of my consciousness, asking to be let in. Now that Jess was absorbed by the twinkling city lights passing below I dropped the barrier without any enthusiasm.

Yes? I asked, my lips not moving.

'With respect, Zac, I wanted to ask if you know what you're doing?' Leon's voice drifted telepathically into my mind.

I have no idea, but I'm going with the flow.

'Do I need to remind you that this could play out really badly?'

No, you don't need to remind me of anything. In fact, with respect, you should watch your step. I already warned you all to stop questioning me.

'I'm here as your friend. Are you asking me to sit back and watch you burn?'

I'm asking you to have faith in me. I can't stop, Leon, not even if I wanted to. I'm too drawn to her. It's agony trying to stay away.

'Which is precisely why you should stay away. She could undo so many years of being clean.'

I raised the barrier back up and blocked him out, ignoring the scratching in my head as he tried to get back in. Jess was still mesmerized by the view and I decided to surprise her with a little more of the thrill that she so craved.

135

"Do you trust me?" I asked.

"Hell no!" she snorted. "I barely know you. You're freaky, and a stalker, and into some dodgy business."

I returned her grin and banked the chopper sharply upwards into a vertical rise before flipping it over several times, then nose-diving towards the earth. I let us drop way lower than a human pilot could before pulling back up from the dive. Not many helicopters can go upside down, but I have the money to buy the best.

She screamed. And screamed some more. My teeth tingled.

"What's up?" I asked, flipping us round again. "I thought you were an adrenalin junkie?"

"Oh... my... fuck... stop it!" she spluttered.

I leveled us out. She looked as white as me, but then a smile crept back on to her face.

"Holy fuckbuckets! Do it again!"

I complied, and the fear and excitement rushed off her, bouncing around the cockpit. The beat of her hammering heart went right through me. Her blood smelled so hot and sweet, surging around that delicate body.

The Beast emerged from the shadows within, silent and predatory, stealthily creeping to my core and testing my resolve. My mind swirled with the torment of one half wanting to touch her and the other half just wanting to rip her throat out and drink her dry. Her jugular was pulsing so loudly, it hammered in my ears like a passing train.

Louder and louder... my vision darkened at the edges. I poked upwards with my tongue to try and stop my fangs from dropping, but they were half out and showing no signs of retreating.

She'll taste so sweet. Sweeter than any other. Drink from her. Savor her. Add her to the basement and feast on her daily until she's an anaemic, withered soul like Selena.

The aerial stunts were clearly a mistake. The last thing I needed was the increased appeal of her pulse racing, as if the temptation wasn't great enough already. We still had a couple of hours of flying and I couldn't afford to lose focus up here. A crash wouldn't likely kill me but it wouldn't do her much good, assuming I hadn't already killed her before even hitting the ground.

"Enough of that," I said, facing away in case she saw my teeth. "Don't want to give you a heart attack."

"Yes, if I'm going to die up here there must be better final moments." She leant over and rubbed my dick. Was she crazy? Had she already worked me out? And if so, why on earth was she doing that?

That was also a terrible idea at any time of day, but especially at five thousand feet in a confined space. My erection was instant and the darkness on my periphery closed in, fangs entirely out, throbbing and aching. I hadn't known I was even holding my phone until I looked down and found it shattered and crushed in my fist.

I hastily dropped it down the side of the seat. In a moment of ludicrous madness I'd been about to call ahead and book us a hotel room.

She looked out the window as she stroked and rubbed at me, playing a game of 'who can act the most casual despite the ridiculously raised tension?' Oblivious to the imminent danger. She was perilously close to either being screwed senseless or sucked dry. Or, let's face it, both at the same time.

Her thoughts swirled with sex. There was a small amount of underlying fear. Unfortunately it wasn't a big enough part to make her act on it and get the hell away from South Padre. The idea alone sent another wave of pain through me.

The Beast snarled in anticipation. I grabbed her hand a

little too roughly and stilled the rubbing. Hurt and rejection swept across her face.

"I'm sorry," I said. "I need to take it slow."

"Sure," she muttered, quickly withdrawing her hand and placing it in her lap. "You must be the first guy to ever say those words to me. What's your story? Messy break up? Are you on the rebound?"

"Messy life. There's a lot to work through."

"Sounds familiar," she sighed, resuming her scrutiny of the view from her window.

She was quiet after that. The silence brought a calmness back over me and I managed to contain myself for the rest of the flight. Still, I must admit, I was taken aback when I landed her safely on the old cracked helipad.

"Where are we?" she asked, rousing herself from a half-sleep.

"Pittsburgh. Have you been before?"

"No."

"Good." I led the short way to a parked car and opened the door for her.

"You have a car waiting? That doesn't look good, you know. Exactly how many ladies do you bring here?"

"You're the first, honestly. I called earlier and had the rental company leave it here."

"Slick," she said, stroking my face as she slid past and climbed in. Ten minutes later we were at the top of Mount Washington.

SHE GAZED OUT AT THE SPECTACULAR NIGHT SKYLINE FROM the viewing platform.

I gazed at the spectacular view of her body. My heart aching and breaking, demons scratching and gnawing.

I was totally unprepared for feelings like this to surface. Where did she come from? Why was she here, tormenting me?

We sat down and drank in the view together. The panorama of downtown was something else. The Golden Triangle skyscrapers lit up, dazzling, where the Monongahela and Allegheny rivers flowed together creating the Ohio. The whole town shimmered and sparkled; glass, steel and concrete, lights, bridges and water.

In the forties it was a different scene; the Smokey City. The heavy industry smog was sometimes so thick that the streetlights were left on during the day. It was one of the few places I could wander in the daytime without that niggling dulling of my senses, the undercurrent of pain, the aching uneasiness.

I returned my attention to Jess, who sat leaning on her hands, so that her back was arched, tits begging to be touched. I couldn't help thinking about how they'd fit so perfectly in the palms of my hands. It was chilly up here, her nipples poked the fabric of her top. I'd have offered her my coat if I'd been chivalrous enough to remember to bring it, but my mind had been preoccupied with other ideas for keeping her warm.

I couldn't do that though.

Then again, I couldn't *not* do that eventually. Catch 22.

The breeze changed direction and her scent caught in my throat, setting it on fire. "You're so beautiful, you take my breath away."

She laughed, her mouth overtaking her whole face. Radiant.

"That wasn't supposed to be funny. Too cheesy?" I was no good at this.

Loser.

"No, it's not that," she said. "It's just that I'm sure you

139

were only speaking romantically, but you literally do take my breath away. I'm frequently dangling on the edge of consciousness around you." She looked away, flushing pink. "As you well know."

"Oh yeah, I promised to kiss you. You won't pass out again?"

She blushed pinker, looking even tastier. "Hey, that was just the one time, and it was because I was in shock that night!"

I leant in and kissed her before she could say another word. Her juicy lips parted eagerly, urging my tongue to enter. She tasted better each time, it was getting harder instead of easier. Her delicate hands reached for the back of my head, grabbing my hair. I hoped that I'd sucked on enough mints to take away any taste or smell of blood from my mouth.

Her heart thumped heavy in my ears with increasing speed. She swayed, even though she was sitting; she really might pass out again. After sliding my tongue languidly across hers once more, I forced myself to back off, with momentous effort. She looked about as pleased as I was for stopping.

"How long do we have to go slow?" she rasped. "It's the middle of the night. There's no one up here except us. It's perfect."

"I don't want to have to carry you down when you lose your faculties. I don't think you can handle any more of me yet. I'd blow your mind." I flashed her a mischievous grin.

That made her smile, as she nudged me playfully with a shoulder. "You know, I'd love to call you an egotistical, deluded prick, but I'm sure you're right."

I caught her and laid us down, pulling her in tight against my chest and burying my nose into the waves of her fiery, red hair.

She stroked her fingers along my arm and paused, circling at a certain spot above the crease of my elbow. Such a gentle touch. If only she knew the feral surges that tore through me, pulsating out from the touch of that finger.

Take that fucking finger and bite it... suck the blood from it as she watches.

"Lux?" she asked suddenly, snapping me from the hunger. "That means light, right?"

Her finger had found a particular tattoo, amongst the many. Skirting past the magical circles and symbols of the Legacy mark, she'd identified the scrawled words *Fiat Lux*. My chest tightened at the stabbing memories associated with those words.

"You speak Latin?" I asked.

"Not much, I remember some from school. What does it mean?"

"Let there be light."

She snickered. "Is that intentionally ironic? I don't think I've ever actually seen you out and about in the daytime! You're like one of the spring-breakers, sleeping in all day. Do you have some sort of sunlight aversion?"

She asked it innocently enough, but there it was. The beginning of the end. It would start to unravel from here.

"It's this place." I faked a smile. "Well, not *this* place, but the island. I've just spent so long living on rave central that my body clock adjusted. It feels natural to me now. I'm not a morning person."

"You don't ever get sick of the constant parties? Not seeing the beauty of the world in daylight, riding your motorbike away into the blue sky?"

"It's who I am now, I live with it."

You don't have to. You could have more. Fulfill the Legacy and walk in the day, you pitiful weasel.

"That doesn't make any sense. Why not just go to bed at a normal time for a change and get out?"

"I don't live entirely by the night, Jess. I do go out in the day. I just choose not to do it very often."

"I still don't understand. I mean, I like to party, but not at the expense of living in the normal world."

How was this ever going to work? There was no way I could have another relationship with a human. Too many questions, too many secrets to hide, too much hunger to suppress. Too much danger to not only her life, but also ours. At least, to our *way* of life. I should listen to my guys more.

"I'm not a normal person."

"Me either," she sighed. "I always seem to be looking for something more. When life gets too familiar I pack up and leave. I don't even know what I'm searching for, but I usually go looking for it where trouble lives."

"Maybe you've found it now?" I asked, immediately regretting it. Encouraging her was positively wrong.

"Maybe," she sighed again, trailing her hand down my chest... and the darkness snapped its jaws in my ears.

16

JESS

*H*e'd taken me to Mount Washington to see the beauty of the night skyline, in his own private helicopter, which, by the way, he could fly himself. I looked to my left to check he was definitely real.

He was riding his bike beside mine as we travelled down the island highway under a sunset glow. The blur of lights and people barely registered on the edge of my vision. Hell, the road ahead barely registered. I couldn't draw my eyes away from him now that I'd looked.

We'd just been on an actual date on Port Isabel. I think he wanted to make an effort with the whole daytime thing, so he'd met me a few hours before sundown. Not that we saw much sun, we spent the evening at the bowling alley.

He'd been tense early on, but once we were inside he loosened up. And man, could he bowl. It seemed there was nothing he couldn't do. He hit a strike almost every other go, and I had a feeling that he could have got more but was trying not to show off.

A group of people had gathered to watch, which left me less than comfortable considering my complete lack of bowling skill. I hurried through my turns so that everyone could coo over his. Obviously most of the admiring group were female. Zac even managed to make bowling shoes look sexy, I felt like a total dork in mine.

A group of guys on the next lane took exception to Zac's attention-stealing and made snide comments to each other in extra loud voices. Zac's face set harder with each one, until he ended up going over and asking if they'd like to say something to him. I don't know what look he gave them, or if he said something else, but I'd never seen a group of lads back down so quickly.

A loud pop brought me back to the moment, and my bike wobbled beneath me. I hit the brakes, easing to a stop at the side of the road. "Damn, my tyre's blown."

"This isn't a good place to stop." Zac cast anxious glances up and down the road.

"I know, right on the highway. Luckily it's not so busy this time of night."

"Climb aboard. I'll send one of the guys over with a spare." He patted the seat behind him impatiently.

"Let's just call the tow truck people, it might not take them too long to get here. We might as well wait." I didn't want to abandon my baby on the road in carnage town.

"We can't hang around."

"Well, let's just call—"

"Jess! You're not listening," he cut me off loudly. "We need to move, get on the back."

He switched his view, staring off up the highway.

"Fuck! Listen to me and don't speak. Just keep your mouth shut," he growled, grabbing my waist and pulling me up close to him.

He seemed to be staring at nothing until, far in the distance, a flashy, yellow sports car came onto the horizon. It was a long way off but in no time it skidded to a dramatic stop at our feet. Three men stepped out of the Chevrolet from behind tinted windows. Their attention immediately settled on me. They gave me déjà vu. So similar to Zac and his friends, all pale and dark eyed and crazily gorgeous.

"Parker," Zac said.

"What's up?" the man at the front of the group replied. He had long, dreadlocked hair and was dressed like a billionaire playboy. His features were sharp and pointy and his eyes quick.

The other two men were standing slightly behind him, one with the biggest muscles I'd ever seen in real life and the other a complete contrast, scrawny and feminine looking. They looked comical standing next to each other. I might have laughed were the whole encounter not so fucking intimidating.

"We're not stopping," Zac said firmly. "Someone will be back later with the spare and be gone quickly."

They didn't respond. They just stood there staring at me. I shifted uncomfortably.

"Are we going to have a problem here, gentlemen?" Zac asked slowly, with a heavy edge to his voice.

He was rigid, his hand tensing around the handlebars. The men looked just as tense, waiting for the fight. Each stood unwavering, feet planted apart and their hands gripped together in front of them. Their eyes were fierce, and they were all trained on me. Yet, over the top of all that, lay an offbeat mask of calm. Their faces expressionless, their voices even and steady. I held on to Zac's protective arm in front of me.

"That depends. Are you leaving this lovely damsel in distress as an offering to us?" Parker licked his lips like he was anticipating something delicious.

"Funny. Real funny," Zac said, pushing me backwards, so that I was now pinned tight against his Harley.

"Who's laughing?" Parker whispered.

"Get on the back, Jess. We're leaving."

I wasted no further time in doing as he said.

"Awww, don't be like that, Zac. What's the hurry? Why don't we wait for the tow truck together and we can get to know your little friend."

"I'll be back later, we can talk then."

Parker raced forward and stood in front of us with a hand on the headlight. "I really think you should stay a while," he said.

"It wouldn't be wise to push me right now. She's not of interest to you," Zac sounded like he was about to lose his shit.

"She is now." Parker tugged his bottom lip, his glare never leaving me.

Zac revved the engine hard. "You going to make me ride right through you?"

Parker laughed as he moved out of the way with deliberate slowness.

"We'll see you around, Zac, but I doubt you'll find anything here if you return." He was smiling as he walked to my Ducati and swung a leg over.

Zac wheelied away, hitting over a hundred in seconds. I tried to look back, but everything was a blur.

HE RAN ALL THE RED LIGHTS AND RODE SO FAST THAT I couldn't understand how we didn't wipe-out on a bend, or into another vehicle. The town passed by in a flurry of light and thumping music, like some surreal dream where I knew I was moving too fast, but it felt like I was sinking, slowing and fading. Whatever just happened, it had left me surging with adrenalin, but I was already losing it, a pit forming in

146

my stomach. I suspected the crash from this one would be severe.

After we tore down the driveway, he led me straight into his huge stately house in a maniacal hurry. He ran through the required pleasantries like offering me a drink, which I declined. He asked if I was okay, I replied with "No." Then we sat in silence. I tried so hard not to be the first to speak. He owed me an explanation without me having to pry it out of him, but it soon became clear that the silence may well go on forever.

"Fine. You win, I'll go first. Even though it's obvious what I'm going to ask," I said.

Silence.

"You're really going to make me ask?"

Silence, followed by a sigh.

"You're a jerk," I mumbled.

Silence.

"Oh, come on, Zac. Why were they looking at me like that? What *was* that?"

A moment more silence before he spoke with another heaved sigh. "That was Ce—" he paused and shook his head. "Gang... rivalry, and because of me you're now bang in the middle of it."

"Gang?"

"Yes."

"You're in a gang?"

"You haven't noticed all the guys I hang around with? I live with. Isn't that odd to you?" His eyebrows knotted, mouth twisting.

"I thought they were friends."

"They are."

"Gang friends."

"Yes."

"*Gangs!* On little South Padre?" No point even trying to hide the incredulity in my voice.

"They have their end, we have ours. We have to pass through theirs to get on and off the island. Your tyre blew on their end."

"So, who are they? Why is this happening?"

He shoved his hands into his pockets and stared at me with a mix of defiance and despair.

"Well?" I pressed.

"The less you know the better."

"You're unbelievable." I stood up and grabbed my purse.

"I can take you back."

"Don't bother." I stomped towards the door and as I opened it he called after me.

"Actually, there is something else. You're moving motel."

"What?!" I spun on my heels and almost tripped over myself.

"You're staying on their side, and now they're going to get interested. More so than they already were."

"I'll take my chances, thanks."

"The fuck you will. This is not a request, Jess. I can't guarantee your safety there."

That made me laugh out loud. "Can you hear yourself? You think you're some sort of mafia don?"

He didn't laugh.

"I won't be dictated to by a guy I barely know, who continues to act like a total dick and expects me to accept it. You're crazy. In fact, that doesn't even cut it, you're fucking certifiable," I bellowed.

"I'm asking you to do this for your own protection."

This was South Padre for goodness sake, were these guys serious? Yes, it did appear that some lunatic tried to kill me at the bungee jump, but that was miles off the island. Totally unrelated. I shook my head before thoughts of missing girls and burning bodies could creep in.

"I'm not scared," I said, hoping it sounded convincing.

"You should be." His face seemed haunted. Okay, so I was a little scared, but I'd be damned if he was going to tell me what to do.

He was fuming. A little vision of smoke coming out his ears popped into my head and I bit my cheeks not to laugh. Laughing was a good defense mechanism in stressful situations, right?

I continued out the door.

"One more thing," he called after me. "You won't be seeing your motorcycle again."

"You'd better be fucking shitting me?!"

He went back to silent mode, staring at me, eyes ablaze. Infuriating.

"That bike cost me fifteen thousand dollars," I screeched.

"I'm sorry. I'll buy you another."

"Bite me," I yelled, slamming the door behind me.

17

ZAC

*H*onestly, I'd just have gone right on over and killed Alexander if it were that simple, but he was incredibly strong, and never alone. Plus, it would trigger a full-scale war with his Cell. My own people would suffer.

He didn't even like being on the island. He stayed to torment me, or at least, that's what he'd have us believe. The real reason was that he was too scared to let me out of his sight, in case he never found me again. I held all the cards in that regard. I was the only one who could activate the Legacy, which would likely grant us both more power than any other vampires in existence, save the other Elwoods, and a few ancient ones.

Unfortunately for him, I had no intention of doing so. Between him and the Bael, the pressure to carry out the bonding ritual was forever around my neck like an albatross. Of course I wanted the power, but it would rip away everything I'd worked so hard for. I'd walk in the light without any pain, and yet I'd be lost to the darkness, dragged down to a blacker place than ever before.

I quit running from the Bael once I realized they couldn't do anything to make me conform. And hell, they tried damned hard. They'd tortured me, tortured Alexander, tortured those I cared about, including Eva. They *killed* some that I cared about. Still, I wouldn't waver. Now they let me be, biding their time, waiting in the shadows like vultures. They'd pounce at the first opportunity.

I'd shamed them, and they wanted me in the fold, where I belonged, bowing and nodding to their commands; their lethal toy to enforce their laws. They let me live for that reason – I was valuable to them. But the truth was, they could take me out any time they wanted.

Now Jess was here. I wasn't ashamed to admit to being terrified. And infuriated, because of the feeling of being powerless to her pull. Needing her. I didn't want to *need* someone. I couldn't afford that. It was too dangerous. It gave me a weakness, one that they'd try to use against me.

Now should have been the time to walk away. Either make her leave the island, or leave myself. Because, what if I couldn't protect her? And what if the one she needed protecting from the most wasn't Alexander, or the Bael... what if it was me? What if I fell backwards?

She smelled like honey-laced ecstasy, like an intoxicating dream. Her aura blinded me with its glittering shine. I wanted to devour her. But one little taste and I'd need to have more. I'd use her, just like I did with Selena.

She'd be the same, giving to me willingly in her foolish belief that it was okay because it was love, but I'd take more and more. Eventually she'd end up a shell, a mere husk, her soul drained away and her blood too diluted, sapping her strength and vibrancy.

Exactly. Right where she belongs. At your feet, begging for mercy.

Maybe after this, she would leave. Maybe I wouldn't need to do anything else.

She was so angry at me, for so many things. So many

fears and doubts. She might leave. Then again, this was Jess, and I'd delved into her thoughts enough to know that she craved danger. Thrived off it.

As soon as her footsteps were far enough away, I let the mask drop and indulged myself in a rage-induced feed. It went some way to calming me, but not nearly enough as I'd hoped.

"He'll love this," I growled, kicking at bits of wood that had splintered off a door when I'd torn through the house.

"They'll just snoop around for a few days, get bored and move on," Leon replied.

"No. He's been silent since she arrived. Too quiet. Now that I've been seen so protective of her, his mood has shifted. I'm going to have to speak to him."

Leon gave me a skeptical look, but I was already casting my mind out to Alexander. I knocked for him at the edge of his consciousness.

'You're asking permission to come in? How domesticated,' he thought.

You've heard what happened today? I locked down as much of my head as I could, only giving him the basics.

'Of course.'

And?

'And it's interesting. What is she?'

She's mine. And I have a problem. She's staying on your side. I clenched my fists. My knuckles stung as splinters of wood worked their way out and the grazes healed over.

'That must be troubling for you.'

I could feel him grinning.

She won't move.

'Don't tell me you are so weak that you can't influence a human?' The disdain floating around his head was palpable. His weak brother was letting a woman — a human woman — do what she wanted.

152

She has her own mind and I'd like to keep messing with it to a minimum.

'How odd,' he replied.

There's something else. Someone's toying with me. They've been leaving her notes, I think they know what we are. It's not a vampire, there's human scent on them, but it's off. I can't place it. It might be linked to the recent attacks on my men.

'Things really aren't going too well for you at the moment, brother.'

The scent is coming from someone on your side. I need you to track them for me, or let me in. There was no way he'd agree to the latter.

'You care enough for this girl that you're prepared to ask me for help?'

Glee. Definite glee in his mood now.

Yes.

'Notes are so impersonal, don't you think? When I want to mess with her head you can bet I'll be making some live appearances.'

The lockdown around my other thoughts slipped as I snarled at him, and his smug whistling made it slide further.

"You know what will happen if you go anywhere near her," I hissed out loud.

I will rip out your eyes and feed them to you. I will tear your head from your body and use it as a footstool. I will drain you to the point of no return...

'Yes! I love it when you let the Beast slip out to play! More, more!' The sound of his clapping hands reverberated through my skull.

I didn't indulge him with any reply, waiting for his happiness to subside.

'Fine,' he sighed. 'I guess I'll see him again soon, anyway. The way your jumbled head feels right now, you don't have long left. So, the question is, what makes you think that I would have *any interest in helping you? This is far too good. Unless, of course, you're ready to help me?'*

Keep dreaming.

'Well, then, this conversation is over.'

Who set fire to your bar, Alexander? I asked quickly. *You let someone get that close without sensing them? Are you losing your touch?*

He paused, I could feel him trying to lock down the rage that I'd invoked. The fact was, if someone could get that close without him sensing it, then he'd be worried, and I knew it. He wasn't that immune to emotion.

You're going to help me, because it serves your own interest. If this person knows who I am, then they know who you are. And they're in your territory, I pressed.

He didn't speak again, but I did hear him growl inwardly.

I'll have someone meet you on Port Isabel with the scent. Oh, and Alexander, if you ever pull another stunt like the bungee jump again, I guarantee I'll set the Beast loose, and you won't live to see through it.

18

JESS

"*I* take it you had a fight?" Anna asked, once I'd stopped pacing and cursing, and sat myself down opposite her and Danny. William sat to my side; imposing, filling out twice the space of a normal man, and sitting a little too close for my liking. Evidently he was now classed as her boyfriend.

I hesitated, acknowledging Danny for the first time since arriving. Was it too awkward to start talking about this in front of the guy I once bedded, who was now my boss?

"Chief," I nodded.

"*Danny*," he smiled. "We're not on duty, relax."

"Well?" Anna asked.

"He expects me to move motel because he snapped his fingers. Oh, and he got my bike stolen."

"For real?" she laughed, until she caught sight of my face. "Back up, lady. What's going on?"

"Did you know there are gangs on the island? Apparently he's in one, and there's a big feud with another."

"I wouldn't have thought to call them gangs, but I guess a bunch of scary guys always hanging out together would constitute it. He must mean his brother's crowd. I told you they didn't get on," Anna said.

"There's squabbling brothers not getting along, and then there's full-scale gang warfare which is what he's implying." I cast furtive glances between Danny and William, who were staring at each other.

"So, you're splitting up with him?" Anna sounded hopeful, darting a glance of her own at Danny, which got my back up even more.

"No!" Just the sound of that made me feel sick. "Look, I know you both don't like him and this is giving you more ammunition for it, but I love... being with him. I can't help it."

They looked at me like I was crazy. I fidgeted in my seat, feeling my anxiety levels rise. My hands were fluttering around and I knew my voice was too high.

"I'm worried, Jess. I feel like your mother, like I have a responsibility to hold you back and sort you out. Have you been taking your meds?"

What the fuck, Anna?! In front of Danny?!

His eyes widened.

"No, because I'm not bipolar. I don't need them," I hissed in reply.

"Doctors don't just hand out a diagnosis like that for nothing."

"They don't? Could have fooled me. I've had just about every label on the planet over the years. I'm done listening to them. I'll find what I need by myself."

"Not by yourself. Together." She reached out to touch my arm. "I'm always here for you, Jess."

I smiled weakly in response.

Danny cleared his throat. "Jess, if this is a thing, I need to know about it."

"It's not a thing," I trilled, a little too quickly. "It's fine,

I'm just... quirky. Sheesh, Anna, have you never heard of time and place?"

"Shit, I'm sorry." She bit her bottom lip, her dimpled cheeks flushing.

"You don't need to worry, I'm fine. I mean, I will be fine."

Who was I trying to kid? Of course I wasn't fine. I was in a whole heap of messed-up shit and veering off down another uncertain road.

"I know you will. You always are. You got through the shit with your parents. You somehow survived all the crazy stuff you got into at college and you came out the other side of the cage fighter boyfriend and drugs episode. I'm sure you'll handle whatever this is," Anna nodded.

I glared at her even harder until she squirmed and blushed more. Danny's brow furrowed in surprise. He opened his mouth to say something, but changed his mind.

"So, William," I said, all sing-song, with another flutter of my hands. Damn, I was definitely on the anxious hyper before the comedown. "What happened to your eye?" I turned to face him, eager to deflect the attention from myself.

He was dressed like the first time I'd seen him, entirely in black military gear. Now he had a whopper of a black eye to match.

"Had a run in with your island mafia," he smiled. "Maybe they didn't like my beard. I'm not pretty-boy enough. Or maybe I was expected to bow down and take their pay-offs like everyone else."

He switched his attention back to Danny, pressing his hands into the table. I eyed the chunky silver rings that covered every finger on his right hand, gothic skulls adorning each one. Further skulls dangled from chains and leather straps around his wrists and neck, along with a myriad of other niceties — daggers, zombies, pentagrams, wolves.

"Are you suggesting something?" Danny asked.

"You never told me it was *them*! You just said it was some loser," Anna spoke, at exactly the same time as Danny.

"It *was* just a loser," William replied to Anna, then, to Danny, "Not at all. You're above all that, I'm sure?"

Danny grunted.

"Zac did this?" I suddenly caught up with the island mafia comment.

"No, I was on the South. One of the others."

Anna stared at me like it was all my fault her boyfriend was beat up. Meanwhile, William glared at Danny like it was his fault. I chose to side with William and joined in eyeballing my boss, since he'd already informed me that nothing would happen to Alex after the fire. How had he known that? Why would he know that?

It should have been big news. A disaster like that with so much loss of life would always be in the headlines, but there was nothing. No reporters snooping around, nothing on the internet, nothing on the news channels. No grieving relatives had arrived to wander around the island in confusion. It was simply as if it never happened. Just like he'd said.

"Talking of being paid off," I said. "What *has* happened to Alex since the missing girl and the fire?"

It was all too convenient. Was he burning the evidence? I'd be willing to bet that some of those bodies would turn out to be other missing people.

"Talking of shrinks and meds," Danny rebuffed, "Have you seen the department counsellor about that fire yet?"

Clutching the table, the sounds and smells came back to me in a rush.

You fucker, Danny.

I let my head drop into my hands, their concerned voices

becoming nothing but muffled sounds as ringing formed in my ears.

Before I could compose myself, a loud roar pierced through the ringing in my head — a roar that went right to my stomach and re-booted me with an adrenaline kick — the sound of a meaty bike arriving at the parking lot. I took a deep breath and shoved away the anxiety.

"Well, this has been interesting. I have to go, Anna. Catch you later." William stood up and brusquely kissed her before hurrying off, barely giving me or Danny another glance.

"What's got into him?" I asked, like I hadn't been the cause of the awkwardness.

Anna shrugged. "You're not the only one with a complicated man. I haven't worked him out yet."

"Isn't he a little... goth, for you?"

Danny snickered and she kicked him under the table.

"You're not one to comment on man choice right now. Anyway, he's not *that* goth," she said, chewing her cheeks.

"He wears guy-liner." I raised my eyebrows.

"Ah, yes, but he offsets it with that big, manly beard. You don't think he's attractive?"

"I didn't say that. He's smoking... if you're into gruff, gothic-lumberjack types." I grinned at her.

Her lips twitched and a part of the tension floated away.

"You're the one always telling me to try new things," she countered.

Further rumbling engines arrived at the lot. I caught myself from turning to see. If it was Zac he could go right to hell. There was no chance that I was ready to even look at him yet, let alone speak.

The noise ceased as the ignitions cut out.

I tried counting.

Nope. I couldn't stop myself from looking any longer. At

least if I knew it was him then I could make my excuses and leave too, before he came over and made this uncomfortable evening even worse.

"Son of a motherfucking whore," I yelled so loud that Anna jumped and knocked her drink everywhere. "That's my damned bike!"

Running in sand was hard, especially as I was so enraged. The short journey seemed to last a lifetime. Danny and Anna were hot on my heels, yelling at me to slow down. The whole while he sat there astride my baby like he owned it. Resting his hands on his thighs, watching me approach with a massive, amused grin on his face.

When I finally hit the asphalt my feet felt cumbersome after being released from the sand. I flew towards him, stumbling, and slammed my fist right into Alex's smug face. A flash of anger passed through his eyes, but he never let the smile drop. In fact, the grin widened as he rubbed his jaw and nodded. I yanked uselessly at his shirt, until it became embarrassing that he was far too strong to be dragged off by me.

"You done yet?" he asked.

"Not until you get the hell off my bike."

He laughed, cocking his head. "You seem to be mistaken, darlin'. This mighty fine monster-machine is all mine." He stroked the gleaming red tank, inked biceps bulging out from his shirt.

I tried to continue my assault, embarrassment be damned, but Anna and Danny pulled me back.

"I'm calling the police," I yelled.

"Let me know how well that goes for you."

"You think you're clever? You're a joke. I've dealt with

scary bullies before and you don't even register on the scale. No doubt you're overcompensating for a serious lack of manhood."

His eyebrows rose so high in amusement they nearly left his face. "That sexy big mouth of yours is gonna get you into trouble if you keep talking like that. Do you want me to show you my lack of manhood?" Alex rubbed absently at his dick. "I bet you give exceptional head, just look at those wicked, juicy lips."

I dragged my gaze away from the straining fabric at the crotch of his jeans, and found the most piercing blue eyes, more turquoise, like opals. They shimmered with rainbow specks, glittering like a galaxy in the abyss of space. There was magnetism in those eyes, pulling me towards him.

"Jess, we need to go." Danny tightened his grip on me.

"Don't be a cockblock, chief. She's coming round to me. I'll take you for a ride on this beauty if you love it so much?" Alex held out his hand, signaling for me to hop on the back. Rage beyond any level I'd ever encountered slammed against my heart. My hands started shaking. My ears thrummed. And yet, my legs began moving towards him. The idea suddenly seemed like a great one.

"Back off," Danny said, stepping forward.

"I don't think so," Alex smiled, taking his sights off me for the first time. I shook my head and stumbled back, confused about why I'd been about to take his hand.

Alex observed Danny and suddenly those eyes had a different look in them. Something animal and alpha. He'd been challenged and his whole body radiated the mistake that had been made. He eyed Danny like pitiful prey.

Alex motioned to the side and from behind him a guy stepped off his bike and grabbed Danny, holding him locked with his arms pinned behind his back. I don't think Danny had realized what was coming, he just stood there and then looked surprised when he found himself captive.

"Never look at me with those defiant eyes again," Alex growled. "Get on your knees."

Danny spat out a laugh and tried to square his shoulders up, fighting against the hold on him. Alex looked delighted. His face lit up brighter, the deadly smile widening. Slowly, he dismounted from the bike and stood before Danny. The man let go of his arm and Danny swung straight for Alex.

I yelled at him not to. He missed and tried again. This time Anna yelled too. Alex toyed with him, shrugging off the attacks with ease. Danny was a big guy, muscled and fit, but after a third failed attempt Alex stopped playing and knocked him to the ground with one swift uppercut.

He stumbled back to his feet. Alex immediately grabbed his hair, slamming Danny's face into his raised knee. He released him and watched for a moment... waiting while Danny staggered on the spot, his head clearly spinning.

"You look like you need to sit down." Alex landed a boot square in Danny's chest with such force that it knocked all the air from him. He dropped to the ground, coughing and wheezing, clutching himself doubled over.

"Stay down if you want to live." Alex loomed over him like the alpha animal amongst his pride of lessers. Like he was marking territory that wasn't his to mark.

"Enough!" I got myself between them before Danny could get up.

Alex reached out, running a finger along my jaw. There was still a dangerous anger on his face, but it was different when focussed on me.

"I'll be seeing you again soon, ma'am," he smiled. His fingers stilled, clutching my chin firmly and making my lips pout. "You might want to help your boss work on his respect issues, he seems to have forgotten. Tell me, do all men lose their minds around you?"

I stared back at him, my chin hurting from his hold. I felt motionless, trapped under his eyes and his touch. As if reading that, he released me and I stepped back.

"Your defiance I can tolerate because it makes my dick hard, but anyone else?" He shook his head and moved back to my bike, whistling as he went.

"Go to hell, shithead." I gave him the middle finger as he gunned the engine on my baby and sped away.

I WAS SO SHAKEN AND ANGRY BY THE ENCOUNTER THAT I behaved like a total bitch and immediately abandoned Danny and Anna to deal with their own anger alone. They had too many questions and words of advice and wisdom — I just couldn't deal with all that. I didn't need to hear any more about what bad news the Elwoods were, or about how I needed to sort myself out. I could figure that out for myself. After huffing around my motel room for hours, I finally fell into a fitful sleep.

THE DOOR BURSTS OPEN AND I SIT BOLT UPRIGHT, CLUTCHING AT the sheets to cover myself. He stands in the doorway, watching as I fumble around — unsure whether it's more important to protect my modesty, since I'm mostly naked, or to grab my phone and call... who? Anna? The police? Find a weapon?

He smiles in amusement. Dark, floppy hair hanging slightly over one eye, a thin scar running along his cheek.

A gun dangles lazily in his hand.

"None of those things," he says, lifting the handgun and gesturing. "Stand up."

My ass is firmly rooted to the bed.

"Now!" he barks, taking two steps forward.

The blue in his eyes seems to shift color as they bear down angrily upon me. I leap to my feet and he casually approaches, whistling a soft melody.

"Better," he says gently. Bringing the gun up to my temple, he traces it down my cheek, along my lips.

"Take off your panties, then my shirt," he commands.

I falter only for a second before following his orders.

He's massive. All hard edges and firm muscles, inked right the way down his arms. Black tribal designs, swirling and enveloping the taut ridges. The angular lines, the blackness of them against his pale skin — it draws me in, making me want to lick them.

"Go ahead."

I regard him in confusion and he nods down to his arm. Carefully, I inch forward and plant a kiss to his shoulder. Gentle, lingering... followed by my teeth in the crook of his neck. He sucks in a sharp breath and I move away, tracing my tongue along one of the black lines, all the way from his shoulder to his wrist.

Grabbing my hair, he shoves further down. With his other hand he unbuttons his Wranglers and lets them fall. He isn't wearing any boxers. His huge, hard cock springs out right into my face.

I try to pull back, but he tightens his grip and presses the gun barrel under my chin. "Open."

My lips part. Slowly, he inserts the head of his cock into my mouth. My tongue instinctively darts forward to glide along the tip. He groans, pushing hard, right the way into my throat; thrusting in and out, holding my head in place.

When I can't breathe any longer he pulls out and leaves me sagging on the floor, gasping for air.

"Get up." His voice deep and steady.

Wetness gathers between my thighs. He pushes me face first into a wall, grabbing my hands and pinning them into the small of my back with just one of his. The back of my head is pressed forward, my cheek grinding into the plaster.

He speaks firmly into my ear, using his foot to spread my legs open. "Who's your master?"

I try to shake my head but I'm met with solid muscle, pinning me tight.

"Who?" he demands.

"You," I say hoarsely, knees weak.

"Say my name."

"Alex."

"Don't ever forget that."

He releases my arms, but I don't move, and I feel him smiling into my neck. Fingers brush along my lips. His other hand roams roughly up my body, grabbing hold of my tits and squeezing them one at a time. Then he spins me around so vigorously that the room wobbles, and throws me onto the bed.

Kneeling over me, he puts the gun against my nipple. It hardens instantly against the cold steel. I shudder as he circles it round the stiff peak, alternating between hard metal and the softness of his tongue.

I reach down to grab his hair, to run my hands through it, but he shrugs me off. Moving down the bed, he drags the gun along my stomach, right down between my legs. He rubs it into my clit before taking the barrel and holding it to my opening.

I gasp and groan for him to stop, but he's already pushing it up inside me. Little by little it roams deeper. I'm so turned on it slides in with ease, but it's too solid, too hard.

He draws in and out slowly as I wriggle and writhe in pain and pleasure.

"Alex!" I scream when I can't take any more.

He crawls back over me, pressing the gun to my mouth. "Lick it. Taste yourself."

I lick until he makes me stop, warm and sticky on my tongue, my eyes burning into his. He watches me with fascination.

"You're not such a bad girl after all, darlin'. Keep doing as you're told and you and me will be just fine. Now on your knees."

I eagerly position myself on all fours, when suddenly a bright light fills the room...

I STRAINED TO SEE, LOOKING AROUND IN PANIC, UNABLE TO comprehend where he'd gone. After blinking a few times it began to make sense. I was still in my motel room, wearing only my undies. No one was there.

The dream left me so horny that it took only a moment to finish myself off with my fingers. Despite now being well and truly awake, it still felt so real. More like a delicious memory than a dream. Like his presence was there, permeating the air around me. I could still smell him, weirdly metallic, with a sporty body wash fragrance.

It made a refreshing change to wake from a dream bathed in pleasure, instead of screaming out from the horrors of burning bodies. I lay there for some time, reliving the fantasy, savoring every erotic detail.

I tried so hard to replace Alex with Zac; to relive the exact same encounter but with Zac as the starring role.

No matter how hard I tried it just wouldn't come together like that. No sooner had I got Zac in my mind than he'd gone again and it was Alex's heated gaze tearing through me.

Eventually I got it worked out by giving Zac a cameo, having him burst into the room and joining in the fun, the two of them taking me at the same time.

19

JESS

he warm fuzzies from the dream didn't last long. The first eager rays of bright morning sun streamed through a gap in the drapes, and instead of basking in it, I found the light irritated me.

Zac's whole *'party boys who'd slipped into their own time zone'* story for their debauched lifestyle still didn't sit right with me, but I was prepared to let it slide. At least, up until then I had been.

He might have been happy sleeping all day, but in my miserable mood I wanted to get out on my wheels. The fact that I no longer *had* my motorbike set my mood to near rage levels. I rolled over, burying my face in the pillow.

I was a failure. I came to the island with the intention of changing. That was supposed to mean choosing different paths, healthier ones. Yet there I sat, sulking and pining over a man who was wrong in every way. He would use me and hurt me, it was obvious. There was no way I could trust him.

And as for his brother? I didn't even dare to allow myself to think about him, or what the warmth between my thighs meant every time I pictured him.

Instead, right then, my body felt numb. A gaping hole in

my stomach, sucking the energy from me. I groaned as I pressed deeper into the pillow, ignoring the alarm clock. I knew this crash would come. I'd been riding a high and now it was time to hit reality. To accept that any idea of being with Zac was madness.

The alarm wouldn't shut up. I lifted my head to yell at it, finding the pillow damp from tears that I didn't even realize I was crying. I threw the pillow at the alarm, then got up and whacked it.

A message came through on my cell phone.

Anna: *Men are like public toilets... they're either taken, or full of shit*

A small smile tugged at the sides of my mouth, before another text arrived, and another, a quick succession of pings.

Anna: *Men are like lava lamps... fun to look at, but not very bright.*

Anna: *If a man speaks in the forest and there is no woman there to hear him... is he still wrong?*

Anna: *Men are like high heels... they're easy to walk on, once you get the hang of it.*

The last one made me snort. I could picture her dimpled laughter.

Anna: *You smiling yet?*

Jess: *All your piss-taking, and you're the psychic one after all?! How did you know I was lying here sulking? And yes, thank you, I feel much better.*

Anna: *Get your ass out of bed, then. Oh, and btw, I googled male celebrities that wear eyeliner. And they're not all gay or goth. AND they're hot. Just sayin'*

Jess: *I wasn't objecting to William's eyeliner, merely pointing it out. You're right, it's hot. I think Zac wears it too. His eyes always look so dark.*

There was a longer pause this time before her reply

came.

Anna: *Men are like mascara... they usually run at the first sign of emotion (couldn't think of one with eyeliner. Anyway - GET UP!)*

I remained snuggled up for a while longer and studied my jacket hanging over a chair, the Carnage Crew patch looking new and fresh.

A fresh start. A new life.

Chasing after an asshole guy might not be starting fresh, but neither was sinking into my usual pit of despair. The cycle needed breaking. No more lows, I was stronger than that.

And so what if this man had issues. Was it okay for me to have them, but no one else? The attraction towards him felt more genuine than anything I'd ever felt before. It seemed like he understood me, like maybe he would accept me for what I was.

Maybe I wouldn't need to do so much explaining with him, or so much hiding, running from the energy within me. When I was with him it felt right, like he could take my crazy and not fix it, but accept it. What if I let myself get swept along by that?

I reached for the nightstand drawer, knowing the meds were lurking there. I never took them, but they were there nonetheless. A thin shaft of light pierced the room, glinting off a key, catching my eye. I trudged over to the side table near the door. The key wasn't mine. After standing puzzled for a while, I opened the door and found my baby in the lot.

Only it wasn't him. This was the 'S' version of the Ducati Streetfighter – the same motorcycle but with higher spec. A giant red ribbon, tied in a bow, adorned the handlebars.

Cheeky son of a bitch. My grin spread wider and wider until my face couldn't take any more.

The face splitting smile didn't mean he was forgiven, but

it went a long way toward it. I tried not to think about how eerie it was that he'd been in the room while I was asleep to leave the key. Or to sulk that he hadn't thought to sneak into my bed whilst there. I was asleep and vulnerable, (and having the most erotic dreams), what better chance to come and take advantage of me?

After showering in record speed, I was out the door and tearing up the highway. I had half an hour before work so I headed straight off the island and rode hard. The bike was familiar but even quicker. I pushed as fast as it would go. I decided to call this new speed devil Anansi, after another mischievous and cunning deity.

The euphoria was golden. Dazzling heat beating down on my back. Buildings, water, trees, people, all flew past in a blur. It cleared out all the worry, irritation, anger; it all got swept out onto the asphalt behind me. By the time I got to the firehouse I was well and truly buzzing.

I walked in and greeted the guys, and was met with an off-putting quietness. No one had any jokes for me, they seemed to look at me with caution, avoiding any close encounters or chatter as we went about the morning duties.

Danny wasn't around. Meat was the deputy and clearly in charge for the day. By lunchtime he still hadn't said more than five words to me. I sat down to eat, awkwardness making my shoulders hunch and ache.

"What's going on?" I finally asked.

"What do you mean?"

The other guys passed glances between each other and tried to act like they weren't there.

"I mean, why are you all behaving like fucktards? Is it because of the fire last week? Because I'm pretty messed up by that too, but—"

"Have you seen the counsellor about that yet?" Meat interrupted.

"No, not yet. Have you?" I huffed, staring him down hard.

He shrugged in response. "I just thought, with your history, you might, you know... you might want to talk it through."

"Fuck you! What do you know about my history? I'm a firefighter just the same as you. If I couldn't deal with fire, I wouldn't be here."

"That's not what—"

"No? So what did you mean?"

"Look, we're all a little tense, okay? That fire was fucked up. And now, with the chief, and you... with the Elwoods. I don't know..." Meat pressed his lips, head dipping.

"What about Danny?"

"He's not here because of the broken ribs. After the *incident* with Alex."

"Alex broke Danny's ribs? Shit!" I pushed my food tray away, suddenly feeling like I was going to vomit.

Meat left the table and immediately issued us all with orders for the afternoon's work, effectively cutting off any more conversation, and leaving me feeling like the shittiest friend ever.

LATER THAT DAY, AS THE EVENING WORE ON AND I SETTLED IN for downtime, I picked up my phone and sent Danny a message.

Jess: *Why didn't you tell me? Are you OK?*

Danny: *I'm fine. I'll be back at work in no time.*

Jess: *I'm sorry.*

Danny: *Not your fault.*

Jess: *Who is he? Why does Alex get away with this? Is Zac the same?*

Danny: *Honestly, I'd love to tell you that Zac's the same, to warn you away. I WILL still warn you away — he's not good enough for you. But no, he's not the same, I don't think. I don't know what they are. Except that you don't want to cross them.*

Jess: *I can't stay away from him. Not until I've figured out what he is. I have no idea if he's right for me, but that's why I need to find out, to know for sure, one way or the other.*

Several minutes passed without any reply.

Jess: *Sorry. I don't know why I'm telling you this.*

Danny: *Just be careful please. And come to me if you need me. Now get some sleep, Firefighter. x*

Jess: *Thank you. x*

I sent an apology text to Anna too. She'd been so good with cheering me up that morning, and I hadn't even said sorry for that shit that had gone down. Lying back in my bed, I tried to read a book, but couldn't stay focussed and kept re-reading the same paragraph over and over. Throwing it down, I curled up and attempted sleep instead.

What Alex had done to Danny was despicable. What he'd done to me, taking my bike, was despicable. I should have reported it to the police, except I knew that he was right — it wouldn't have done any good. These guys had their own rules. I either jumped in and played the game, or I walked away now.

At some point sleep found me and I slept right through to the next day, because no emergencies came in overnight. I got on my bike and rode straight to the counsellor's office on Port Isabel. I knew how these sessions worked. I gave out what they wanted to hear and sat attentively, listening to all their advice, nodding. I let a few tears fall, mainly to show them that I was normal, and a little bit because I actually couldn't stop them flowing when they started asking about the burning bodies.

Afterwards, I went round to some realtors and collected

info on a bunch of apartments available for renting. I couldn't stay in that grotty motel forever. Then I went back to the island, had dinner, showered, and rode to Zac's.

"You think this gets you off the hook?" I asked, dropping the bike key into his hand.

"No. I owed you a motorcycle, so there it is."

"So what *are* you going to do for my forgiveness then?"

"Something romantic for a change," he smiled, and my stomach did a stupid flip.

WE PASSED THROUGH THE HOUSE AND I NODDED AT HIS friends along the way. Gang friends? Ridiculous.

He strolled out through double doors, along a wooden boardwalk, and down onto his own private beach. Of course he had his own beach. This man had everything.

The sun had just set over the ocean. Blazing red glowed along the horizon, turning to orange and yellow before fading into the deep blue.

The sand was warm and comforting as we sat down close together, arms touching, gazes locked. Shivers ran along my skin. There were so many things I needed to say to him, but nothing came out. Try as I might I couldn't find the power of speech when locked into that heated, tense stare.

I had the impression there were many things he wanted to say, too, like he was trying to tell me with his eyes alone. They lulled me into a sense of wonder, of needing and longing, whilst all the while a wisp of fear gathered somewhere within me.

I don't know how much time passed with us sitting that way, but when we lay down in the sand the stars were out overhead. It was a beautiful clear night, the sky awash with thousands of bright specks of light. I picked out a constellation and strained to see if a shooting star might pass.

His hand found mine, locking our fingers together. I allowed my thumb to absently stroke along his. It might have been the most relaxed we'd ever been in each other's company.

At least, it was, until a small spray of sand flew into my face. Scurrying and scuttling right next to my ear sent me jumping back up, swatting at myself. More shuffling noise, and sand hit my bare foot. I hopped around on the spot, shuddering and trying to wipe down anything that might have crawled onto me.

He laughed, loud and free, ringing out into the night and filling my heart.

"Stop flapping," he said through more laughter. "It's time."

Getting down on his hands and knees, he beckoned for me to join him; peering into the sand in darkness, nothing but the moon and stars to light us.

The scratching continued, my eyes adjusted, and I saw there was movement all along the beach.

"Fuck me!" I gasped, continuing to hop around.

"Ssshhhhh," he soothed, pulling my hand until I knelt next to him.

There, emerging from the ground in a flurry of sand and activity, was a tiny turtle. My hand went to my mouth in surprise.

"They're Kemp's Ridley sea turtles, the world's most endangered species," he smiled serenely as he watched hundreds of little vulnerable creatures emerge and struggle down the sand towards the vast, awaiting ocean. One of those near us seemed to be struggling to break free from his egg. Zac lifted him tenderly and peeled back the shell before placing him down with the others.

"It's called a frenzy," he said. "When the hatchlings emerge all at once and scuttle to the shore. They use the moon for navigation. It's fascinating how nature works like that."

Could this man get any more confusing? Feral-looking psycho one minute, nature-loving turtle-rescuer the next? Maybe he was the perfect ratio of bad boy to good boy?

"But look at me!" he said suddenly. "I'm looking after my turtles and have failed to look after you. I haven't even offered you a drink or food yet. I forget, you know? Come with me."

I watched him hurry off up to the house, protesting after him that I was fine, that I had stronger appetites that needed feeding, but it fell on deaf ears.

"You're going to cook for me?" I asked, finding him in the kitchen, turning random dials on the oven and looking confused.

"I'm going to try, if you can call pizza *cooking*." He shot me a quick smile as he opened the fridge.

The kitchen was immaculate, gleaming and sparkling, top of the range appliances. A large island sat proudly in the middle, housing the oven, whilst miles and miles of work-tops and cupboards decked the sides. Yet, when he opened the fridge there couldn't have been less in it! There sat one lonely pizza, a mountain of beer, and not much else.

Had I ever even seen him eat? Anna could have been right about him being on drugs. Something had to keep him running and it sure as hell wasn't steak and fries.

In one of his clever mind reading tricks he replied, "Sorry, the guys got takeout earlier and we've eaten already. But I made sure I got this in for you the other day."

I don't think I'd ever seen any of them eat, come to think of it. They were all real fitness freaks, I supposed. I ought to be able to relate on some level, but I'd spent too many years forgetting that I used to enjoy looking after my body, and treating myself to all the bad shit instead.

The only thing they did consume to excess was alcohol, yet they never appeared drunk. I'd have been on the floor if I drank what they did.

Whatever, they looked shit-hot on it, so who was I to judge them?

I reached around his waist as he slid the pizza into the oven, squeezing him tight. "Thanks, I'm starving."

"You're welcome. I want to take care of you."

Turning around, he swept me up into the air, sitting me down on a worktop. He leant in close, instantly igniting me with that dangerous gaze. His eyes settled on my mouth, followed by his tongue, which passed over my bottom lip in a slow, erotic sweep. My own tongue responded eagerly, lapping back at him, his kiss such a soft, delectable place. Surprisingly soft, given how every other part of him was a solid wall of hard muscle.

Spreading my legs, he stood between them, rocking his erection into me. As he clutched the worktop I stroked up and down his heavily tattooed arms, savoring all that strength, his muscle standing out proud.

His hand slid up my thigh and a gasp escaped me. So cool, even through the denim it made me goosebumpy all over.

The kiss went on for so long that my head spun. Every part of me cried out for more, to have those lips over every inch of my naked skin. I grabbed his head and pushed him downwards, arching my back, urging his mouth to find my nipples...

The timer beeped next to us and he bolted backwards out of my grasp.

"No!" I panted. "The pizza can wait."

He shook his head with a smile. Was that relief on his face? Because I was pretty sure my own face was radiating pure frustration. I pushed myself down from the counter, knowing that the moment was broken and he wouldn't come back to me.

Despite my best efforts at getting him to join me, he only watched as I ate the pizza. Afterwards we went through to a huge sitting room. The latest high tech gadgets were littered around. Tall windows, floor to ceiling, lined one wall, but were covered up with charcoal drapes of a luxurious thick material.

I'd expected us to be alone. I don't know why, given how much his 'gang' followed him everywhere. I was still surprised to walk into the room and find it busy. The chatter died down as I entered, an uncomfortable silence settling. Why did that keep happening? I looked at my feet and tried to shuffle back out the door.

Zac caught my hand and pulled me in, putting an arm around my shoulders. "It's about time you lot got to know each other," he said. "This is Jess."

If I could have accessed one of his magical disappearing tricks then I'd have done so right then. I could have died with the way they all turned to study me.

We walked round and he introduced me to each person, fake smiles all round. Leon, I already knew. He was racing on a video game, the giant flatscreen took up almost the whole wall.

The stunning woman, Eva – the one who I still wasn't sure if I should be jealous of — was the only person to give me what seemed like a genuine smile, as she sat painting her nails. More guys whose names I forgot instantly were chilling in various groups around the room, most of them making out with semi-naked women.

I tried my hardest to act as if that were the sort of thing I saw every day. No big deal. But in truth, it wasn't like the usual scene on the island. These guys were different. The air in the room was heavy with something electric, making the fine hairs on my body stand up. Rubbing at my arms, I suddenly felt freezing.

Zac pulled me over for a final introduction. The big guy who I knew hated me, the one who'd been pointing and fighting with Zac that night of the fire party on the beach. He was called Ruben. He didn't bother to smile, or even look at me, just grunted some sort of response.

With that out the way, Zac and I settled down with drinks in hand. I snuggled in close to him. He hadn't let his touch leave me once since we entered the room. There was always a hand in the small of my back, on my arm, a shoulder. Possessive or protective? I wasn't sure.

The thought that these guys were supposed to be in a gang made me uncomfortable. They were pretty intimidating, and something was way off about them, but they weren't like a street gang or motorcycle gang. Whatever they were, the feeling of danger closed in around my throat.

I downed my whiskey and asked Zac for another. I downed that, too. After a while I started relaxing, and so did the group. We eased up and settled into brief conversations, studded with long pauses.

Leon and Eva had a lot of questions for me; about my hobbies, my job, and everything in between. I didn't like talking about myself, trying instead to throw their questions back at them. Turned out they weren't too keen on opening up either.

Someone started talking about ghosts after one flashed

across the big screen, the racing cars being chased by ghouls and other undead creatures.

"There was a ghost at my old fire station," I said. "Loads of guys saw it. Not many would talk about it though, in case they looked stupid. I'm not afraid of the supernatural. I don't —"

Leon cleared his throat with his hand over his mouth, stifling a laugh.

"Oh, go ahead and let it out, I'm used to it. You should go hang out with my friend Anna. Why do non-believers always find it so funny? Is it really so hard to imagine there's more to life than all... this?" I gestured around the room.

"No. No it isn't. Not at all," Leon hastily left the room, throwing a game controller directly at Zac's head on his way. Zac stuck his arm out and caught it without ever taking his eyes off me. Mr. Cool as usual.

Raising my brows, I waited for his weigh-in on the subject. Daring him to laugh, given his psychic revelation. Did his friends know about that? Surely they must?

Ruben sat forward, focussing on me intently, all suspicion and angst. *Dickhead*. Bristling in his chair, he let out a deliberate, audible sigh. Well, that conversation got awkward.

RUBEN DIDN'T GRACE US WITH ANY FURTHER COMMENT, BUT he did do us the pleasure of leaving the room. The atmosphere lifted further once he was out of the way and the rest of the night passed in a refreshingly normal manner.

In fact, it was definitely the first time we'd had such an ordinary evening. Zac made me food, offered me drinks every half hour, cuddled and gazed at me longingly as I laughed and joked with his friends. I indulged myself with the idea that I'd successfully endeared myself to them — the gang. They were a pretty cool crowd, apart from Captain Dickface, but let's not dwell on him. Zac refused to tell me why he had it in for me, insisting he was just an old loser that hated everyone.

I wasn't worried as I lifted the new note from my bike the next day. They were wasting their time. I wasn't going to let their childish and petty games get in the way. That said, two days in a row without any form of drama would be good.

Zac hadn't spoken to me about the notes again and I hadn't raised the subject, but I suspected his brother was doing it. I was staying on 'their' bit of the island. It was the obvious conclusion and I was none too happy about being caught in the middle of it.

I laughed out loud when I read what this note said. It was clearly only a game to them; not his brother, more like some kids having a laugh. I didn't think I'd been worried, yet I still felt a weight lift off my shoulders as I rushed inside to call Zac and let him know the good news.

Throwing the paper on the bed, I read it again as the phone connected, chuckling to myself and praying he'd answer.

Just one word in careful capital letters stared back at me – *VAMPIRE* – with a few newspaper clippings of missing people in the surrounding areas.

"Hey, I was just daydreaming about you," his drawl came through the phone, soft and silky.

"That sounds nice." Butterflies in my stomach. "What were you thinking?"

"I can't possibly tell you, ma'am, it's far too obscene."

Ma'am... darlin'... seriously, these guys didn't play fair. A little piece of me melted each time I heard those words out of their delicious, Texan mouths. I was going to end up a puddle of goo on the floor if they kept it up.

"Well, if you're too shy to tell me, how are you ever going to pluck up the courage to show me?" I asked.

"I'm sure I'll find it from somewhere, why don't you come over and we can put it to the test?"

Yeah right. All talk and no action. I was starting to wonder if he was actually celibate. Crap, that was a horrifying thought.

"Sounds perfect," I said. "I've got some good news, too. I got another note."

After a long pause he replied, "And it's good news?"

"Yes. You're a vampire."

A strange noise came down the line, like a sudden intake of breath and a deep, chesty groan.

"Are you alright? I know it's funny, but don't choke on it!"

"Funny?" he asked in a tight voice.

"You don't think so? I know its childish stuff, they even went to the trouble to use some ketchup, little blobs of it on the paper for a gruesome bloody effect. They were creative. It must be some kids or something?"

He still didn't speak and an uneasy feeling pressed over me.

"I thought you'd be pleased? At least you don't have to worry about the gang. I mean, you don't think they would have done it, do you? It seems too comical. If they really wanted to get to you then they'd have stuck to serious stuff, wouldn't they?"

"Yeah... yeah... of course. That's great. Listen, about coming over, I've remembered something I'm supposed to be doing. I'll call you later."

I held the dead line to my ear for some time before I put it down.

"*H*ey, Chief, have you seen Anna?" I scanned the room, after seeking out the sanctuary of MoJoe's to quell my pouting mood. "She's not answering my texts."

"She's probably at work. Although, rumor has it that she's called in sick a couple of times lately. Between you and me," he cozied-up to whisper in my ear, wincing from pain in his ribs, "She's getting pretty serious with that William guy, I reckon she's bunking off to be with him."

"No way! That's the sort of thing I'd do, not Anna."

Disapproval crossed his rugged face. "It is, huh? Good to know, Firefighter Layton."

"Crap, no... I mean, the *old* me. Not anymore." I sighed at myself. I was such an idiot.

He studied me for a while. His face coming over with a kind of sadness. He moved to sit down at the bar with slow, tentative motions, one hand always over his pain. Fucking Alex. Who the hell did he think he was?

"So," he said. "You made up with your superhuman boyfriend?"

"Why would you call him that?!" I laughed.

"Come on, you know he has an unnatural effect on everyone round here. I like to imagine he's an alien, it helps my own ego. I can't compete with an alien, right?"

He hobbled off to greet a friend who'd arrived, and left me pondering his words. Visions of Zac flashed through my mind. The things he'd said to me, the first time he kissed me.

I played with my cell, willing it to ring. I hated it when he went freaky on me. Or did I hate it? No, obviously I kind of liked it. The thrill of the unknown.

What I *didn't* like was the constant threat that he would vanish in a puff of smoke and never be seen again.

My mind wandered back to the motorcycle accident, how he'd somehow flung us both from the road and there I was, safe and sound in his strong, cold arms. I flicked back to his eyes, the way he looked at me with such intensity.

Then, the day he'd told me about his psychic abilities and how embarrassed I'd been at him hearing my thoughts. The way he'd followed me out on that bungee jump and reached the top in a second.

My head felt light, as if my brain were floating away out of my skull.

No. I was being dumb.

But the images stayed, flashing backwards and forwards, over and over. His mind reading, his extraordinary speed and strength, his cold, pale skin. His mysterious behavior. The way he reacted to my call.

Oh. My. Fuck.

He avoided going out in the daytime.

He didn't go out in the day.

I laughed out loud at myself.

It couldn't be true. It was ludicrous. Vampires didn't exist.

Yet, no matter how much I told myself that, the idea

wouldn't budge. It almost seemed to make sense. A lot of pieces clicked into place.

Rushing to the restroom, I threw up in the sink.

I contemplated trying to call Anna again, but I couldn't think of how to word it. No matter how I said it, she'd just laugh and tell me to take my meds.

I turned on the faucet with trembling hands to rinse the puke away. When my cell buzzed I practically hit the roof with fright. I was way too terrified to answer it.

Zac kept on calling. In the end I put it on silent to end the horrifying ringing in my ears.

A loud bang on the door sent me lurching backwards into a cubicle, shrieking with terror.

"You okay, Jess? You've been in there ages?" Danny yelled through the door.

I stayed quiet, hoping he'd go away. Instead, he came in and took one look at me before hurriedly grabbing my arm. "Shit, you look terrible, come and sit down."

He guided me to an office, out the back, and sat me in a chair, stroking the hair from my damp cheek. "What happened, Jess? Have you taken drugs?"

"What?! No!"

Stabbing pain ripped into my chest. I clutched at it, pulling my top down, trying to reduce the tightness that was engulfing me. I struggled in gasps for air, but couldn't get enough into my lungs.

"I'm suffocating," I gargled.

"Call 911," Danny yelled out to someone. "Big breaths, Jess, in and out. Time it with mine."

He took long slow gasps, holding my hands. Great monstrous pain wracked right through my heart.

"I'm having a heart attack!" I grabbed at my shirt, pulling it away, trying to release the pressure inside me. The material clung to my skin, drenched in sweat, stubbornly refusing to loosen. My ears buzzed like a swarm of hornets was trapped in them. I shook my head frantically, my fingers prickling with pins and needles.

There was a sudden explosion, a loud thunderous crack, followed by a delicate tinkling as the windows shattered and glass landed like confetti on the floor around us.

"Shit!" Danny yelled, covering my body with his and shielding my face from the shards.

Spasmodic sobs broke through me and I fell to the floor, panting and clutching at my chest. Glass cut into my knees and shins, stabbing and scratching. I kicked my legs out, thrashing them around like a crazed fish out of water, trying to shift away from the sharp little stabs. I was going to die like this. On the floor at Danny's feet, with him brushing glass out of my hair and rubbing my back.

"The windows!" I shrieked. "I'm sorry! It's my fault. It was always my fault. You're not safe near me, Danny. Get away." I shoved against him.

"Stop, Jess! It must have been a tremor, we get loads round here. I think I've seen this before. You're having a panic attack. Focus with me on counting, we'll get that brain distracted."

I listened to his controlled voice, counting up to ten and back again. Suffocating claws scratched down my throat. He pulled me into his arms and held me. The warmth, his steady breathing, his hand stroking my hair; it gradually eased off the pain. I flopped down flat and rolled onto my back, not even caring what the crunching of glass meant for my skin.

Focus. Breathe. In and out. *He's right. You are not dying. This is just panic.*

"It's him, isn't it? *He's* done this to you. Jess, you need to stay away from them," Danny's words broke through the fragile grip on reality that I had left.

I shot to my feet and darted for the door. He grabbed me and I stared him right in the eyes, telling him I needed to go. He wouldn't loosen his grip despite my thrashing around, so I jabbed him as hard as I could in his broken rib. He doubled over in pain.

It was a low move, but I had to escape. I bolted straight back to my motel.

ZAC

"*P*oor brother, she's not answering your calls?" Alexander asked, leaning against the marina sign on Port Isabel, neutral ground for us.

I did my best to ignore him. This was monumentally fucked up. She'd been so relaxed at first, thinking it was a joke. If I hadn't reacted the way I did? Now she wasn't answering and I could hear her. She knew. She'd run through everything and realized it was true.

I should have stopped calling and let her go. I told myself that over and over, but the cell phone was always back in my hands a few minutes later. I didn't know what I was going to say to her. I just knew that I had to say something. I had to try and explain before she left my life forever.

Don't let her go. She mustn't escape.

Left me. Forever. My will began draining away, the darkness moving in, ready to pounce into the empty space where some sort of happiness had been forming. Like a black hole sitting in my core, sucking all other emotions towards it. Consuming, devouring, relentless. I was going to spiral out of control and I didn't even care, it didn't seem to matter. So long as I could hear her voice once more. Tell her I was sorry.

Alexander snorted loudly for my attention. "Are you going to cry?"

"You saw the guy put that note there and you didn't think to go and take it off before she got to it?"

"Are you kidding? This one was the jackpot," he grinned.

"She's freaking out. She's going to leave. Satisfied?"

"I'd be more satisfied if I could see her freaking out with my own eyes. Maybe I'll pay her a little surprise visit before she goes, just to really put the heebie-jeebies up her."

"Stay away." My muscles contracted so hard they hurt.

"I'm starting to like her, you know. She's got some balls at times. If you speak to her, you might even talk her round. Once she realizes what a kitten you are, I mean, there's really nothing to be afraid of where you're concerned, is there? She'll probably be none the wiser as to my dangers."

"You really want to test me on this? I won't tolerate you going anywhere near her."

"You say that as if I haven't already?"

He flashed memories into my mind, projecting images I didn't want to see. My blood just about reached lava state.

"Anyway, enough teasing," he said. "Aren't you going to ask me who the note leaving loser is? Don't you want your revenge on him?"

"Considering he knows what we are, I'm guessing a hunter. The same person that's been targeting us? Is he alone?"

"He had a weird fuzziness in his head, but I'm pretty sure he was alone. And a complete novice. We were his first job, he had no idea how in over his head he was. He thought he was the man, the real Van Helsing. He actually believed he could come in and wipe out not one, but two Cells, all by himself."

"He's doing a pretty good job, he got near us several times, undetected. How did he do that?"

"Witchcraft, I guess. His energy was all over the place," he shrugged.

"Was? Past tense?" I asked, already knowing the answer.

He was grinning that insanely irritating, happy smile. The smirk that made me want to pound his face in.

"Sorry, when I asked if you wanted your revenge, I should have let you know that I'd saved you the job."

"You can't stop yourself, can you? I wanted answers from him first," I spat.

"He burned down my bar. Someone fucks with me like that, they die. Instantly. No trial required."

"It's always that black and white for you, isn't it?"

"It should be for you, too. You're so meek it's depressing. Running around after a human woman like a pussy-whipped bitch. And let's not talk about your denial of the Legacy. You're supposed to be an Elwood. Being related to you should be an honor, instead it's humiliating."

He'd maneuvered himself right in front of me, inches from my face. Provoking my reactions was a favorite game of his.

"Nothing you can say bothers me. It's playground stuff. Go ahead and let it all out, it only amuses me." I pushed him aside.

"Oh yeah? What about your weakness killing our father? Is that amusing?"

My head fogged instantly as his words cut through me. Without a second's hesitation I was on him, pinning him to the ground and smashing his face. Blood poured from his lip and nose. He was still smiling, making no move to protect himself, purely to annoy me further.

I let the rage wash over and consume me, taking its place, settling firmly in my core. From there it could grow and spread its tendrils into every part of me. I would feed off it, embrace it, follow it into the darkest depths of depravity. The release would be so blissful, so pure and primal.

Taking my time about it, I pulverized his face, each crushing blow bringing a fresh surge of relief. He continued to resist the temptation of fighting back, lying limply and laughing wildly as blood splattered around us. He was trying to push me onto the slope, as if I needed any help with that now.

I closed my eyes, the darkness swallowing me entirely, and somewhere from the depths of my tortured soul her big, goofy smile flashed up under my eyelids. Her flushing pink cheeks, her sinful ass. Her witty tongue and lack of fear.

Jumping up, I started my Harley and clutched on to the images, using them as a lifeboat, holding me afloat.

He spat blood onto the floor and called after me, "You know what doesn't add up? Why a vampire slayer would leave lame as shit notes like that in the first place? Why ignore all the women I feed from, but warn the one dating a vegetarian vampire?"

"Vegetarian? If you're going to try and insult me, at least make it factual. And the answer is probably because she's not like any other woman. She's not like your blood whores. She's different."

"You got that right," he grinned.

"I'm going into your territory to see her at the motel. Tell your goons to keep away from us, and you stay away, too. You want to see me in the darkness? Fine. I'll show you exactly how fucked up I can be, after I've seen her and she's safely off the island. Then we can play. Then the war begins."

The sound of his delighted laughter was still ringing in my ears as I hit the highway.

*a*fter shakily stuffing clothes into my backpack, I sat on the bed and stared at my feet. What was I going to tell Anna? I couldn't stick around, I had to go. But how could I leave her here? Knowing what he was? What if he was mad at me for leaving and he killed her? I should warn her, get her to leave, too.

I should do it in person, though. I would go and see her, give her the news. She'd think I was crazy, but when I upped and left maybe she'd think about it and take me more seriously. It was the best I could do.

Zac had given up calling, but Danny had taken up the role. I couldn't answer it. I couldn't tell him before Anna. I'd be letting him down too when I left. Would he understand? He knew Zac wasn't normal. Maybe he even knew what he was already? He'd tried so hard to warn me away.

Sirens wailed outside and the next thing I knew I had paramedics at the door. *Dammit, Danny!* They ran some tests and satisfied themselves that I wasn't having a stroke. Then they pulled out a few fragments of glass and patched me up. They were insistent I should get checked out at hospital. I refused, assuring them I'd go straight there if anything got worse.

If anything got worse. What did that mean now? Puncture wounds in my neck? In a body bag? Turning into a vampire?

I knew as soon as I heard the next tentative knock at the door that it was him. In fact, I knew before the knock because I'd heard the engine as he pulled up outside. The knocking continued when I didn't answer, slow and gentle tapping, like he was trying not to scare me! I stood as far from the door as I could, wishing that I was staying self-catering and would have had a knife on hand.

The patient tapping didn't last long before it turned into banging and thumping.

"Jess, please. I need to talk to you." He sounded like a normal, anguished boyfriend after a fight. Not a blood-curdling monster.

"Stay away," I shrieked. "I'll call the police."

Why hadn't I called them already? Okay, so I couldn't tell them I had a vampire banging on my door, but I could tell them I had a madman out there. I got as far as pressing the 9 before the door flung open with a loud crack and I dropped the phone. He flew into the room, grabbed it, and then backed off with his hands up in the universal '*I mean no harm*' gesture. Calmly, he shut the broken door and put a chair in front to keep it closed.

"Sorry," he muttered, still holding his hands up.

I guessed this was what it felt like when you faced your death and people say your life flashes before your eyes. My mind raced over things that had happened to me in the past, irrelevant things that it didn't make sense for me to think of. I thought of my mother, her beautiful face and the smell of the cookies she baked when I was little. I thought of my father, of his disappointment in me. The explosion. The guilt. I remembered the night that I'd pulled a little boy from a burning room, fire blazing all around me. His mother's face as I handed him to her outside. Then there were some relevant thoughts, like those of Anna and how it would be my fault when he killed her too.

"I'm not going to kill either of you."

"So what are you going to do?" My whole body was shuddering like a maniac on speed.

"Nothing. I just need to apologize."

"For what?"

"For leading you on. For letting you think there could ever have been anything real between us. I knew it would have to end. I was planning on that happening before you found out. I'm sorry."

"Before I found out," my voice sounded distant, my head fuzzy.

"I couldn't keep it hidden forever. If it wasn't the hunter's notes, it would have been something else. You'd have pieced it together eventually."

"Hunter."

"The vampire hunter, he was targeting us," he said matter-of-factly.

That was it then. The word vampire had left his lips and the bile rose in my throat. I wanted to laugh out loud at the silly prank he was playing. Instead, I sank to my knees and cried.

"This isn't real. Please tell me it's a sick joke," I wailed. "You're just one of those sad freaks from the internet who dresses up and pretends to be the undead, right?"

Except I knew you couldn't fake the attributes he had.

His arms wrapped around me. Had I noticed how cold he was before? He definitely seemed colder now. My whole being was screaming at me to run away, defend myself, but his contact sent those little tingles through me and for some unfathomable reason I felt safe. I didn't want him to let go. I buried my face into his shoulder and sobbed.

"I'm so sorry," he whispered, kissing the top of my head. "This should never have happened. I should have left before, disappeared. I kept trying, but I had to keep coming back for more."

Further panic engulfed me. "You were trying to leave me?"

"Of course. I shouldn't have been putting you in danger. But the more I was around you, the more your hold grew on me."

I pulled back. "You said you're not going to hurt me. Why was I in danger? I feel so safe with you, it doesn't make sense."

"I don't *think* I'd ever hurt you, but I can't be certain. It's too risky trying to have such a close relationship. I didn't mean for it to get this far. Once you're gone I promise my stalking will end. I won't follow you. I'll stop myself... somehow."

"But I don't want to be without you."

He pushed me away this time and held me where he could see my face. "What are you saying?"

"I'm... I'm saying I can't be without you."

Was I? How did I let those words leave my lips?

"Yes, you can," he said deliberately. "You have no choice. This is non-negotiable."

"I can't just forget you! I can't go on with my life, go about the normal business of living, knowing that you exist and that I'm not with you."

"What you feel for me isn't real. You only want me because of the power we have over humans. You have no choice but to want me."

"Don't patronize me!" I screeched. "It doesn't matter what the reason for it is. Blame it on your magical powers if it makes you feel better. The fact remains that I can't be without you and nothing will change that."

I'd not realized just how much I needed him, until he was sitting next to me threatening to leave. Buzzing and panic began whirling around me.

"Distance would change it. If you didn't see me for long enough the power would gradually fade and you'd wake up one day wondering why you even liked me."

"No." I swung my head in denial.

"I'm a vampire, Jess. Do you know what that means?"

"You said you won't hurt me and I believe you."

"I said I didn't think I would hurt you, but that I couldn't be sure."

"You'd already have done it by now if you were going to."

"Really? And you're an expert on vampires, are you?"

"I'm... I feel safe when you hold me."

"That's my power, it's not real," he said slowly, like he was talking to a three year old. *There, there, little girl, stop being stupid and come to your senses.* "Deep inside you're terrified, the way you should be. That's why your heart is hammering and your muscles are locked. Vampires are masters at disabling their prey, we're alluring and seductive. We make you want us."

"Prey," I said the word out loud and lurched forward to be sick. Nothing came up, just painful heaving.

"I'm sorry," he said, rubbing my back as if consoling a drunken girlfriend. "I need to make you see reality."

"There is no reality, not since I found out a vampire has been kissing me."

"Look into my eyes and tell me what you see?"

I didn't dare. I held my gaze on the floor until he took my chin gently. "Look at me, Jess."

The tears blurred him. I blinked a few times and

focussed on his eyes. My heart crushed under the weight of their beauty. Golden, glowing, deep.

"What do they say to you?" he asked.

"They say don't come any closer, don't touch me, don't fall for me... *run*." I reached out and cupped his face in the palm of my hands, those beautiful eyes haunting my soul. My lips were so desperate to melt into his. I leaned in and whispered, "Yet my body says to go closer, touch you, fall for you... *stay*."

"I rest my case. Fucked up, right?" He averted his gaze and avoided my kiss.

I let myself slump forward. After a while I found that he was no longer holding me. He'd sat himself back against a chair. My mouth felt clogged with sawdust and fluff, gluing it shut. Words refused to come. Slowly my mind cleared, or at least de-fogged slightly, and my hands trembled again.

He was right, why on earth was I trying to stay with him? He wasn't even human. I could see it now, when I looked in his eyes, that formidable glaring look that I could never work out before. It was evil. It was hunger and lust. They were predator's eyes and they were preying on me.

Without allowing myself another thought, I grabbed my backpack and left. I was half expecting him to stop me, for my life to be ended, but he didn't move. I thought I saw a flicker of despair when I chanced a look back at him on my way out.

I RODE FOR HOURS, TEARS STREAMING DOWN MY FACE, IN NO fit state to be on the road. I kept urging myself to stop at the next motel, but they came and went. I didn't want to have to think.

I narrowly missed a head-on collision when I found

myself on the wrong side of the road, unsure as to how long I'd been there. Eventually, after I realized that my eyes had been closing by themselves, I had to stop. The running was over. My body was still in flight mode, though. It didn't want to stop running. I paced up and down the motel lot, hands shaking. Shaking so much that I couldn't undo the zip on my jacket.

The motel was modern, compared to my last. Nicely painted walls, good furniture, even some fresh flowers dotted around the place. The clerk was a cheery lady in her forties, overweight, with bobbed hair and too much makeup. She was watching a comedy on the television and laughing away to herself when she noticed me at the counter, and her face dropped.

"Oh dear, sweetheart, are you okay? You look like you need to sit down. Come, sit over here while I make you a drink, what would you like, my love?" She removed a Chihuahua puppy from her lap and put it in a basket.

"Nothing, thanks. Just a room." I tried to hold my voice steady and wiped my tear-smeared face with the back of my hand.

"Are you sure you wouldn't like someone to talk to?"

"I'm sure."

She begrudgingly fetched some keys and led me to my room, insisting on carrying my bag for me. Fretting around the place, she found as many things to do as she could — straightening out the already made bed, showing me the coffee pot, showing me how the shower worked. When I just nodded absently at everything she went and hovered in the doorway for a while, before I kicked her out.

My knees buckled under the weight of it all. I collapsed on the bed and something dug into my hip. I reached into my pocket and fished out a syringe, followed by a small bag of heroin. That was a surprise, I didn't remember getting it, but small flashbacks came to me of a dingy bar along the way. I had stopped after all.

I held my hand over my mouth and sniffed my breath. Great. I was drunk. No wonder I'd been on the wrong side of the road. I didn't feel that wasted though, not enough to forget the last few hours like that. What if something more had happened? Last time I had a blackout it was after my family home burnt to the ground.

Something might have happened in one of those bars on my journey. My heightened emotion, it could have caused something. Something inexplicable. Something bad.

Fear clawed over my skin, making me shiver. I sank deeper into the bed and let the silence settle over me, breathing it in, calming the anxiety. I hadn't sat in silence for weeks. Even alone, in your own room on South Padre, there was still always noise from this bar, or that bar, fireworks or pool parties, people fucking or pissing and puking in the street.

Sometimes when I laid awake at night, I'd think about all the bad decisions I'd made in my life. There was so much material to work with, it could keep my mind occupied for hours as the darkness swirled around me.

Was going to South Padre a bad decision?

I'd readily admit to the bad ones. I had no qualms with analyzing my own destructive personality and choices, even if I didn't learn from them. But no matter how hard I told myself that *this* was bad, I couldn't make myself believe it.

For the first time ever it felt totally right.

And wrong.

But right.

THE NEW DAY BROUGHT A FRESH SURGE OF PAIN. I TOOK A

huge lungful of air and slowly released it, repeating the move over and over. I made coffee and gulped it down, burning my throat. I emptied the heroin down the sink. It didn't look like I'd actually had any of it, but I couldn't remember much.

Then I sunk back into the bed and toyed with my phone. Messages had come in from Danny and Anna, asking where I was, if I was okay. What was I supposed to say to them? How could I even look them in the eye? If I told them, Anna would be dragging me to the doctors for more meds before I could get another word out, and Danny? Well, he'd surely suspend me on grounds of mental health issues.

I was supposed to be at work for my next shift tomorrow. Could I walk in there and carry on?

I noticed the social media buttons on my phone's home screen. I hadn't been on to any of them since my arrival at the island. I pressed on one and was greeted with notifications for unread messages.

Message 1: *Jess, what the hell? You changed your number? I want to talk, call me back.*

Message 2: *Where are you? No one knows where you are. Call me.*

Message 3: *Baby, I'm worried. I went to your station, they said you left? Call me. I've been taking that anger therapy you wanted. I'm getting better. Call me!*

Message 4: *Seriously, fucking call me you stupid whore. Who the hell do you think you are?*

I threw the cell phone down like it was poisoned.

Luke.

I thought I loved him once. Turned out it was just the drugs talking. He was just an asshole, cage-fighting machine. A real delight.

Where would I go if I left the island? Back home, to my old town, where Luke would be waiting for me? Would I let him in? In all honesty, I was more afraid at the prospect of getting back together with him, than I was of Zac biting my neck.

Zac wasn't like him. He was *nothing* like him.

There was a ping, as yet another message came up from Anna.

I pondered it all for a while and decided that Zac was not a danger to them. He didn't seem like a revenge-seeking psycho. He wouldn't go after Anna, just to get at me. Besides, he told me to go, didn't he? So that he wouldn't hurt me. He didn't *want* to hurt me, or Anna.

The pain crept back in and I fought to stop the tears. Why did I still want to be with him? What was wrong with me?

Maybe they'd been right about me all along — the teachers, parents and friends. I was messed up and needed fixing. I wasn't capable of making normal, sane choices.

Or maybe it was just that I still couldn't believe vampires were real. That was why I didn't want to leave him, because it was all a big joke that had gone wrong.

I shook my head. I couldn't escape the truth. I knew what he was. When I'd looked at him in the motel it had been clear.

I felt it.

He wasn't human. And that set my core alight.

***

I RODE BACK TO THE ISLAND WITH MY CHIN UP, MARCHING INTO my motel room and noticing that the broken door was still swinging on its hinges. I crept inside, my gaze darting around the room, to the shadows, the closet, half expecting a monster to leap out at me.

It was empty, but ransacked. The furniture was

upturned, the drawers strewn around the room. Opportune burglars? I'd left nothing behind, there was nothing to steal, except the motel's TV, and that was still there. Maybe just opportune fuckwads, then. I pushed aside the idea of Zac doing it in a fit of vampiric rage.

I went over to the desk and told them someone had broken in. They promised to get a replacement door within the hour, and they were right. Once it was all sorted I fell into a fitful sleep, tossing and turning. My regular nightmare morphing once again into something more; the burning bodies now had vampire fangs, and blood... so much blood.

My 24 hour shift at the firehouse passed in a surreal blur, without incident, other than a callout to help the coast-guard search for a guy who'd entered the water on the beach and not been seen since. Danny had supposedly returned to work, but was called over to the Port Isabel department. That left Meat in charge again, which I was grateful for. I couldn't face Danny, not yet.

He did put a call in to check on me though, because I heard Meat confirming that, "Yes, she's come in to work," and, "No, she looks like shit."

Wonderful. I guess Danny had expected me to be absent after my breakdown. He'd send me back to the shrink for that. Story of my life.

Hours drifted by and turned into days. I barely moved from the sofa during my days off, except to buy more alcohol. The vice that was tightening around my chest was becoming so crushing that even breathing was hard.

Anna came to visit. She did the motherly thing and gave me all the best snippets of advice. I nodded through it, barely hearing a word. I decided she didn't know though, and nor did Danny – about the whole vampire thing. If they knew, they'd surely have realized that I did too.

I didn't see Zac at all. I expected him to be watching

from afar, the way he always did, but he wasn't there. He was nowhere. And that left me sinking with depression.

I gradually understood that the underlying panic that had settled so firmly into my core wasn't because of him being a vampire. It was fear of leaving the island, of going back to my old routine. I could go back and slip into an old life that was doomed to a worse fate, or I could dive headfirst into this fucked-up freak show.

Because he was everything.

He was too little and yet too much. Too little when he evaded me and left me panting for more. Too much when he was with me, making me mad with confusion and lust.

He was moody, weird, and kind of an ass. He was so devastatingly attractive that he sucked the breath from me every time our eyes met. I was caught, trapped, under his consuming spell.

And was it really so hard to believe what he was? How could I possibly deny all plausibility of vampires being real, when I myself was far from normal? Had I really believed I was alone, a solitary, isolated freak? What if there were others like me? What if he could help me? If I had finally found someone who could understand and accept me for who I was, should I run from that?

I'd always loved the supernatural. I believed in psychics, in mysterious abilities. Was this any different? Could vampirism be classed merely as an ability? An evolution of the human race?

My heart ached to be close to him. And I needed answers. Many of my original questions seemed to answer themselves now that I knew what he was, but for every answered question, another ten popped up. Leaving the island was not a decision that I could make without informed facts.

I asked myself if I thought he was dangerous? Yes, I did.

He exuded danger. But I didn't really believe that he was a danger to *me*. It was the opposite, he made me feel safe.

Did I think he needed me? Yes, without a doubt.

Did I need him? Obviously.

Was he a killer? I got stuck on that one. Vampires drank blood, they killed people, but I couldn't imagine him wandering around as a murderer.

Was I insane, was there something wrong with me for what I was about to do?

Yep. But I had to go back, and he would damn well talk.

23

___

JESS

*T*he door was open before I'd turned the engine off. He stood staring at me in disbelief, looking a complete mess. And that was hard to accomplish for someone so composed and gorgeous. I dreaded to think how wrecked I must have looked in comparison.

We stared at each other for a long while. I wanted to rush into his arms, but I wasn't sure what the right thing to do was, and another part of me wanted to run away again. He took a step towards me, but wavered and stopped.

"I can't leave without answers," I said.

He nodded solemnly and gestured me through to the living area. Leon disappeared up the stairs. The room stank like a grotty old bar; alcohol mixed with cigarettes and the rotting souls of those who'd hit the bottom. It was usually such a neat and clean place. He hastily cleared up the discarded whiskey bottles, straightened out the furniture and emptied an overflowing ashtray.

I had no idea where to even begin with the things we needed to talk about. How to pick one question out of the swirling mass running riot through my mind?

"So..." I said.

"So..." he replied.

Something occurred to me then. The speed that Leon had gone up the stairs, the way he moved. The way he looked. The way they *all* looked.

"Fuck me. How could I only just have noticed?! You're *all* vampires?"

He stared at me like I was ridiculous. "Of course. My Cell, and... well, we're not the only vampires on earth. Obviously there are others, too."

"Cell?"

"I called it a gang in an attempt to sound more normal to you. Some of us call our groups a clan. We use Cell."

"So, the other... Cell. Alex—"

"They're extremely dangerous, Jess. I fear more for what they might do to you than what I myself could do."

"Why don't you get along with your brother?"

He frowned and lit up a cigarette. I'd never seem him smoke before.

"It's a long story," he said, blowing out smoke. The smell wafted straight towards me and poked at the cravings I thought were long gone.

"I've got as long as it takes," I replied, leaning back in the chair for emphasis.

He exhaled noisily, "Well, it kind of ties in with how we became vampires. And with what I used to be. What I *should* be. Do you really want to hear that?"

"I'm not leaving again until I know everything." I crossed my legs for further insistence.

A foggy glaze settled in his eyes as he stared off into space for a while. Then he thrust his cigarette towards me. "I can hear you thinking about me smoking and how much you want one. Take it would you, tonight doesn't count. It's going to be a long one, so just smoke. You can quit again tomorrow."

The first couple of drags made me cough, but then the heavy smoke sank deep into my lungs in a disgusting and heavenly, tension-releasing wave. I gagged and savored in equal measure.

He watched me with a hint of amusement before starting his story.

"In 1890 our parents died. Alexander and I were orphaned at the age of eleven."

I burst out laughing and spat the whiskey he'd just given me.

He scowled and rolled his eyes.

"What?" I yelled. "That isn't funny? You start a conversation by casually telling me you were a boy in 1890 and I'm supposed to take this seriously?"

"Yes. Our parents were wealthy cotton farm owners in Texas."

Nothing. Not even a hint of amusement on his face. *Fuck this.*

"So, you're telling me you're... wait..." I tried the math, but my muddled brain wouldn't cooperate. "Over a hundred years old?" I couldn't take that in. I didn't want to.

"That's right."

"Over. One. Hundred," I repeated, as if saying each syllable a little slower would help it sink in.

"So, anyway, our parents left a lot of money behind, but we were young and had no other family to take care of us. We were put into an orphanage temporarily while something more permanent was being worked out. But a man called Tobias arrived and took us away. He was wealthy and charismatic. He never really said how he managed to obtain us, but I think he was paying the staff to hand over children.

We weren't the only ones." He rubbed at his arm before continuing.

"He was a vampire, forming his own Cell in New York, after a lot of issues with leaving the Bael. He wasn't too selective about who he chose, mainly adults and a few children. But he needed twins for the Elwood Legacy to pass on, so he sired us, made us into vampires. Vampire children continue to age until they hit around eighteen to mid twenties, then it stops. No one knows why, but it's frowned upon to turn kids these days, so the experiments have all but stopped—"

"Experiments? On kids? That's disgusting."

"Yes. Are you going to keep interrupting?"

"Maybe. If I want to. Do you have a problem with that?" I dared him to get impatient with me right then. And what the hell was an Elwood Legacy? Like, a family fortune to be inherited?

He sighed and went on, "We lived a normal vampire life, killing as we needed. Would you like to make any comment on that before I go on?"

"Not right now." I stubbed out the cigarette and took another. I didn't want to comment on that at all. *Ever*. The use of past tense was encouraging though.

"Alexander took to the lifestyle with joyous enthusiasm, but I was never happy. I mean, I enjoyed the killing, it's impossible not to, and I was good at it. I did awful things. But, well... something happened, and..." he paused, rubbing a palm against his forehead. "I realized that I was hurting innocent people, and I wanted it to stop." He moved to get himself another drink. A haunting ache had flashed in his eyes, clear as day. This story pained him.

I didn't want to push him, despite the thousand things that I wanted to ask right then. I bit my tongue and waited while he rubbed at his head some more.

"It changed me," he said the words with bitterness. "I began trying to control my urges and found that sometimes I could. I practiced and practiced, so much so that the pain of abstaining left me weak and drained. But I kept going.

"We'd grown to think of Tobias as our father. Alexander was particularly close to him. They bullied and tormented me for my weakened condition and *inferior* state of mind. But when Tobias saw me come out the other side and grow strong again, whilst still withholding my instincts, he started questioning himself. He'd never even considered it before, he didn't think it was possible to fight the darkness inside. He just lived true to who he was and accepted it gladly."

I held up my hand, pausing him. My reactions to his words were veering off on so many tangents. One question would come, then another and another. Too fast. Too hard for me to focus on what he was saying. These were the longest speeches he'd ever given.

He waited, less than patiently, tapping his foot and watching me through jaded eyes. I shouldn't have looked at them. They were like bait. I wanted to be pulled into them and get lost there. He blew out his cheeks and released his gaze on me, turning his attention instead to a faded black and white photograph on the mantle. Him, Alex and another man.

"By now, Tobias was amazed, fascinated. He began to see *me* as the stronger brother, not the weaker one. We'd sit for hours talking and I started training him with my techniques in control. Alexander was jealous, pushed out. We tried to educate him too, but he had zero interest in controlling himself and was furious with us. He left home. The rest of the Cell were just as appalled by our actions and left, too. It was just me and him, but we were at a degree of peace. Until the Elwood Legacy and the Bael came to bite us on the ass."

"The what, and the *what*?"

"We'd become complacent about it all. But they found us and I wouldn't listen. I wouldn't do what they wanted. They killed Tobias."

He'd been gazing into nothingness as he cast his mind back all those years. His face was impassive this time, but the hurt showed in his body language. A familiar sight, one I'd seen in my own mirror. Losing a father and not being able to hide the guilt. I wanted to hold him, to ease that pain.

He snapped round to face me. "Don't feel sorry for me. It's my fault. Alexander blames me for changing Tobias, making him weak, for refusing the call of the Legacy; for everything."

"I don't know what this Legacy thing is, but you can't blame yourself for choosing to be a good person."

"That's not what I mean. I know that's not my fault, but I should've been there to help him and I wasn't. Anyway, I've told you enough about that. But, by the way, I'm not a *good person*, Jess. I'm a vampire. I'm bad."

"I don't believe that. Anyone that actually calls himself bad out loud is just a wannabe," I said with a grin, hoping to lighten the mood.

"Would you like me to demonstrate?" He gave me a callous look that made my heart stop dead. His whole face changed, with small veins appearing all around his eyes and popping out in his neck.

A snarling smile twisted his face, allowing the glimpse of two sharp teeth.

"*Shit!* Dammit, Jess, I'm sorry." He pinched the bridge of his nose. "That was out of line."

Mercifully, his face had quickly returned to normal. I

210

didn't ever want to see that other, terrifying face again. How could features so beautiful turn so ghastly? I shook my head, hoping to dislodge the memory.

Despite the feeling that I was standing over a precipice and about to fall, I still struggled with the idea of him being bad. Now would have been a good time to leave, but there was still so much I wanted to know. Besides, I didn't think I *could* leave. I was so caught up with the intensity of the direction my life was taking, the adrenalin was too addictive.

I wasn't a big believer in love. Once I would have laughed at the notion of love at first sight, but now I wasn't so sure. It felt like I loved him. I understood what it was to desire someone so much that they absolutely consumed your whole being. Maybe I was still getting love and lust mixed up. I don't know. All I did know was that I felt as if I would cease to function if I lost him.

And that thought was fucked up enough to make me want to smash my own head into a wall. To wake up and get a grip.

"Why do you and Alex live so close if you hate each other so much? This place is tiny, it doesn't make sense."

"I chose to come here when I started up a new Cell, one that wanted to live the way I do. I picked this island precisely because of its smallness. Less people means less temptation. At least, it did, but of course the spring break craziness has since formed. Still, I rejected the notion of running from the Bael any longer, I was sick of it. Let them come. I loved no one. They had no power over me.

"Alexander took it upon himself to move here to torment me. And to keep me in his sights. He sees it as his duty to make me fulfill the Legacy, and if he can't have that, then he'll settle for making me suffer. It's fun for him, he enjoys trying to fuck me up. Payback for our childhood."

"You could move?"

"I told you, I'm done with running. This is my home. I can handle whatever shit he, or anyone else, throws at me."

"Wait." A cold dread filled my stomach. "That whole thing about me moving out of my motel, because I was in the other gang's territory — that's other *vampires*. Your brother, the badass who doesn't care about anyone but himself and likes to cause you pain? I was in the motel all that time with him around?"

"I tried to get you to move out."

"You didn't try hard enough," I shouted, jumping out of my chair to pace the room.

"Do you not know how obstinate you are? I couldn't force you. I made sure someone was watching you all the time. I'd have been there in an instant if necessary. I won't let anyone hurt you." He put a hand on my arm to halt my pacing. His touch was so wonderful, my heart instantly decided none of this had happened. It begged me to forget all this shit.

"Not even myself," he whispered, his mouth brushing my ear.

"You had me followed? You were spying on me?" I tried to pull back.

"I had you *protected*. That's different." He pressed in closer.

"Sometimes, when we're close like this, you tense up. Is that because..." I didn't want to ask, but it slid out anyway.

He inhaled deeply, right along my neck and his grip tightened on my arm. "I'm hungering for your blood," he said, all husky and aroused.

"Shit on a fucking stick! Go ahead and tell it like it is why don't you!" I shoved him away as hard as I could and he complied, relinquishing his usual strength and backing away, hands held up.

"You don't want the truth? I thought you wanted answers, so I'm giving them to you."

"I know... I do. But you can stop that feeling, the hunger?"

"No, I can't stop it. But so far I've managed to resist it. I won't lie and say it's easy."

"But you're surrounded by people every day."

"I don't want them all. Each vampire is different, only attracted to a certain type of scent. A bit like you not being attracted to every man you see. If I find myself in the proximity of someone that appeals to me then I put distance between us. But with you, your scent, it's much stronger to me than anything I've encountered before. Couple that with how fucking hot you are, how inspiring and exciting I find you, your radiant glow... I can't stay away. Even though the pain of resisting is like acid in my veins."

I shrank back into myself. Was I feeling guilty for the way I smelled?!

"All the times you would see me and I'd disappear, I was gradually acclimatizing myself to you. Getting used to being near you. The night you joined our party on the beach I was starting to think I'd be okay, but then there was your dancing and the fight after. It felt like you were deliberately testing me. I was angry that you came so close to me. *I* wanted to make the decision when that would happen. And angry that you started flaunting it like that in front of me, pushing me to the edge."

"About that... the fighting with Mullet-man. What exactly happened, after?"

"They're still alive, if that's what you're asking. For now."

I shouldn't have asked. I didn't want to know the answer, not with that '*for now*' tagged on the end. I watched his hands for a while, transfixed by them.

"So why *do* you resist? If it's what you are?" I asked.

"I don't want to be what I am. I don't want to kill people. I balance on the fine line between light and dark, blurring the edges of morality, living in the gray."

Relief flooded over me in a delightful wave. I knew he wasn't bad really, I couldn't have fallen for a killer.

"What do you eat then?"

He looked at me in surprise. "People. I'm a vampire."

24

JESS

*T*he '*I eat people*' revelation had me recoiling so hard that I stumbled over a chair and he caught me. He'd been across the room, but it took him a fraction of a second to be at my side. After shoving him away, I made a show of straightening myself up, fighting the churning in my stomach.

"But... you said—"

"I said I didn't want to, and that I don't want to hurt *you*," he replied, as if this clarification was adequate.

"But, all your training, living a different life. What does that mean?"

"I still need to feed," his tone patronizing. "I try to be selective. I pick the bad guys out there."

"Who?"

"Murderers, mostly."

"Oh. Well. That's good." It was good, right? Never mind the fact that, technically, I knew I should be classed a murderer, too. *I'd killed people.* My heart jumped.

He narrowed his eyes at me. "Good? I just told you I kill people." Still squinting at me. Was he inside my head? *What if he knew what I'd done?*

"Yes, but not people that don't deserve it," I ventured.

"I'm a murderer. Just like them."

Don't think it, Jess. Don't think it.

"Not like them. You're not a bad person," I said.

"We've been here. I'm not a *person*."

"Why are you doing this? If you want me so much, why are you still doing all you can to push me away?"

"It's not safe for you to be with me." Regret ebbed across his face.

"We've been through this, too. I know you won't hurt me. You admitted that you only kill bad people. I'm not a murderer. So what's the problem?" The lie left a bitter taste in my mouth. I swallowed hard.

"What's the problem?" he was suddenly shouting. "Jess, you're unbelievable. For one, I did just tell you that your scent drives me wild with hunger. And for another, it's not just me that you have to worry about if you stick around in my world. Alexander, the Bael, the hunters—"

"The hunter." I'd forgotten all about that little gem. "He wants to kill you?"

Fingers of fear reached up and clutched at my throat. This time, not for my safety, but for his.

"You're worrying about *me* again? Seriously?! It's taken care of," he dismissed.

"Taken care of. Like the movies. That means he's dead, right?"

"I didn't do it, though I would have, eventually."

I took a deep breath and quickly ran through the remaining questions that were still plaguing me.

"Who exactly are the Bael?" *Bay-el.* He always dragged out the syllables slowly, bitterly. I presumed they were another gang.

"Not any old gang, the worst one imaginable. The

governing body in our... community. Old, viscous and entirely self-serving," he hissed.

His mood was sullen once more and I predicted it would only get worse if I carried down that line of questioning. How was I supposed to lighten the mood, pep up the atmosphere, whilst learning about the grisly details of vampire life? I sighed to myself.

"So, how much of the movies is right? I mean, all the garlic and holy water stuff?"

He looked pleased by the change of direction at least, his shoulders visibly relaxing. "Forget it, the vast majority of what you think you know about us is crap. Silver weakens us. A stake to the heart hurts. The sunlight thing is half right. It doesn't kill us, but it's uncomfortable. The longer we're exposed to it the harder it gets. It dulls our senses, subdues us gradually. But as we get older, it gets harder and harder. Once we start getting to two hundred years we can't go out in it anymore. I guess it would kill the really old ones..."

I thought about the silver necklace my mother gave me, sitting in my underwear drawer. I would start wearing it again.

"That's why you were sitting in the shade the morning after the accident, on the beach. I was sitting in the baking sun. I knew something had seemed odd about that at the time," I mused.

"You think that was the oddest part? Your miraculous good health didn't escape your notice, either."

"No. Wow. You're so fast, and strong. You did a pretty good job of convincing me it was all in my head."

"That night was the first time I realized you were so different. I should have known what you were going to do with my Harley. If my instincts didn't sense it, then I should at least have heard you thinking it, since it concerned me.

But there was nothing. You're impossible to read sometimes, you act before you think. People say, 'I didn't think before I did it', but actually that's impossible. Not with you though," he was inching back towards me, an urgent gleam in those liquid-copper eyes.

I didn't know what I'd done in the last minute to change his mood, but he was definitely looking at me with that hunger again. Not the scary kind, just the passionate, needing kind, the one that made my heart race. I licked my lower lip as he held out his hands to me.

"I don't understand how you do it. Your thoughts are a second or two behind your actions, but that impulsiveness, it really turns me on. Like when I kiss you, and for once, I can't see what you're going to do. I'm not used to that. It drives me crazy. And scares the fuck out of me."

Pulling me into a sensual embrace, our heaving chests pressed together. My heart was hammering so loud in my ears, heaven knows what it sounded like to him.

"It has nothing to do with my weird mind, it's all down to you. When you kiss me I can't think of anything. It stuns me into a stupor."

"I'm sorry," he whispered.

"Don't be. I'm the luckiest girl alive." His neck was right there, I couldn't resist letting my tongue tentatively glide along it.

His chest stopped heaving as he held his breath.

"Alive being the operative word," he mumbled, withdrawing to safer ground.

I slumped into a chair and closed my eyes. A tidal wave of exhaustion crashed over me.

"You need to sleep," he said.

I didn't argue.

I AWOKE THE NEXT MORNING IN A STRANGE BED, WITH A STIFF neck and a sore head. Memories and ideas rushed at me like a battering ram, pounding away and making it hurt more. I rolled over with a groan and tried to go back to sleep, but it was no use. There was so much to think about, so much I didn't *want* to think about.

He was lying next to me, staring at the ceiling, fingers locked across his chest.

"What are you thinking?" I asked.

"I'm thinking you should do what you are thinking," he replied impassively.

"I don't even know what that is. Enlighten me."

"Go. Spend time by yourself, getting your head around things. Don't be sorry for being afraid of me."

"Is that what you want? For me to go?" My eyes stung.

He refused to look at me. "Yes," he said, without any emotion.

It wasn't true. There was no way he really wanted me to leave. But he'd gone into a meditative-like silence and he wouldn't budge.

Everyone was against us — his gang; their uneasiness around me made more sense now. My best friend, his brother, Danny, the crowds of jealous women that surrounded us daily — no one wanted to see me on his arm. And fuck me, even he was against us in some messed-up way. What exactly was I even fighting for?

There was a plethora of reasons for leaving and I could think of only a handful for staying. After another thirty minutes of nothingness I gave in, took the advice, and left.

I'M NOT TOO SURE WHAT HAPPENED OVER THE NEXT WEEK. I was drunk a lot, no surprise there. Doing things I shouldn't.

I dragged Anna out, telling her I'd had a fight with Zac. But I was a dick. Sulking and behaving like a twat.

I bumped into William one night and started taking the piss out of his heavy-metal jewelry and guy-liner. He took it on the chin with a smile and latched onto me, rambling on about how worried Anna was for me, how I should listen to her and forget Zac. He inched closer, and it suddenly felt weird being alone with him, without Anna, so I ditched him fast.

My shifts at the firehouse were painful. Danny avoided me like I had herpes. The crew flirted and joked, but they were off, they'd distanced themselves. It felt like everyone only put on a front, pretending to be okay with me. Maybe I was just paranoid.

Zac was everywhere I went, always in the background, until I forced him out of hiding. I was sitting on the ground behind a building, in the dark, dirty part where they put the trash out. Broken glass had found its way into my hand and I was running the sharp point along my wrist.

I honestly have no idea why. I didn't want to kill myself. I guess I was thinking about the blood and what would happen if he smelled it. Anyway, I never had the chance to find out because he appeared from the darkness, snatching the glass away. I laughed wildly and declared with smugness that I knew he'd been following me.

"For how long?" I shrieked.

"All the time, every day."

"Why?"

"Why are you doing this to me?"

"I asked first."

"To stop you doing anything stupid. No —," he corrected himself. "Everything you've done so far has been stupid. To stop you doing anything too stupid."

"You're the one that told me to go. I don't need you

protecting me, I need protection *from* you," I spat in a nasty voice that I didn't even recognize. I regretted it instantly because he pretty much vanished into thin air.

Another night or three of spiraling anger and hurt, then I started clearing shit up. I was supposed to be getting better, avoiding the crashing lows after the highs. I had to make a choice, one that didn't involve going back on meds to fix things. This was not the right direction. Either stay and sort myself out, or get off the island and sort myself out. Either way, the overriding decision had to be; Sort. Myself. Out.

———————

THE BEACH WAS HOT AND STICKY. I SAT AND LET THE SAND absently run through my fingers. He was watching, from afar. This had to be one of the sunniest places to live. A beach town?! Come on, weren't vampires supposed to live somewhere more... woody? Rainy and gray?

I used it to my advantage, anyway. I'd been forcing my ass out of bed and into the daylight on purpose. Lazing on the beach under azure skies, knowing damned well it would be hurting him to be out like that. Getting some sick pleasure out of it. Wanting him to hurt as much as me.

I shuddered involuntarily. He was probably thinking about killing me right then, about how good I'd taste.

His chin dropped and his shoulders slumped.

Great, and of course he was still reading my thoughts.

He got up and walked away, round the corner.

His sudden absence left me feeling more frightened than when he was there watching me. I felt so alone in that moment, looking around at the crowded beach. How many of them could be vampires, too? Probably none in that sunshine, but what about in the evenings, when it was even more rammed? Would he protect me from them if they took a liking to me?

And then he was beside me.

"Oh," I gasped.

"Your wish is my command, ma'am." He smiled for the first time in forever and my heart felt like bursting.

"Calling me ma'am is cheating. How can I stay angry with that in my ears?"

"I'll do whatever you want me to. If you don't want me here, I'll go. If you do, then I'm yours. I'm done watching from afar like an angst-ridden teen."

I searched deep into his eyes. I couldn't decipher what I wanted.

"And if you're confused, I'll take the initiative and do what I want." He leant back, sticking his legs out and stretching his hands behind his head in a gesture that mimicked my own from the other night.

"I don't know how you can sit there so smugly, right beside me, knowing that you want to kill me. You've got a nerve."

That sounded a lot better in my head than it did out loud. I meant it to be a playful, teasing remark. Guess it didn't come out right. His face darkened as he gave a bitter laugh.

"Straight in there with the heavy stuff again, then? Have we even had a honeymoon period?" he asked.

"Technically, you need wedding night action first, to have a honeymoon period," I reminded him, digging a finger into the sand and prodding around for shells.

"I don't want to kill you, otherwise I already would have. I just have... instincts."

"I bet that's what all the serial killers say in court."

Ugh. Shut the fuck up, Jess. More stupid words slipping

out that left me wanting to scoop them up and shovel them back down.

"Don't feel sorry," he muttered. "I'm glad you're seeing me for what I really am. Now all you need to do is tell me to leave." He looked pleadingly at me.

"You're not like that. I didn't mean it."

He made some sort of sighing-snort noise.

"What? A second ago you admitted that you want to be here with me and now, once again, you're trying to leave?"

"I'm trying to do the right thing for you. But your thoughts change so frequently, I can't keep up with them. I have no idea what you really want."

"Isn't worrying about what I want my problem? I'll figure it out myself. You just focus on what you want." I froze, realizing what I'd said.

"See, that doesn't work out too well for you either, does it?"

"No... yes... I mean, if you think about what you want, not what that other part of you is saying you need."

"The two are so intricately linked, it's hard to separate them."

"Am I in danger from you right now?"

"No," he said instantly.

"Then you're separating them, and this is what I want."

I jumped into his lap, wrapping my legs behind him, and kissed those sexy lips.

*L*et's face it, if the old me had been told, "Soon, you'll discover that vampires are real and find yourself lusting after their attention, craving the excitement of their life, with little regard for your own safety," what would I have said? Would I have laughed at the ridiculousness of it? Would I have been steadfast in my belief that even *I* would never go that far?

No. My response would have been something like, "Well, duh? Sexy, badass vampires on the loose, craving and wanting me? Of course I'm going to want a piece of that action!"

This was where I belonged. A place I'd spent my life searching for without realizing, always just beyond my reach. Something more, something deeper. Now I'd found it, there was no way in hell was I letting it go.

Which was why I'd let him take me back to his house after kissing me on the beach. It was why I'd spent the evening gazing into his eyes and hoping with all my heart that he would always look at me that way. Like I was his whole world.

His fingers brushed tenderly over my lips, his touch

unlike that of any other man. It was so good that I kept frozen, in feigned sleep, in case he stopped.

"Humans need to breathe," he said softly. "Don't worry, I'm not going to disappear, not until you tell me to."

"I won't ever tell you to." I sat up with a start and took his hand, holding it firmly to my cheek.

He pulled me back down, snuggling me into his chest. His bedroom was sparse. Nothing more than a bed, a chest of drawers and a guitar. I made a mental note to ask him to play for me. But not right then, I didn't want to move from his touch.

"What else do you think is out there?" I asked.

"Not much. A little voodoo. I don't think werewolves and zombies are real, if that's what you mean."

"No, I mean after death. Out there in the rest of the universe. There's loads we don't know about, don't you think?"

"No."

"The vampire, someone not even human, refuses to believe in anything else extraordinary?"

"What would be the point? If there is something there, I'll never reach it."

"Vampires can't ever die, at all?"

"They can, but I don't intend letting that happen to this vampire."

I thought on that for a while. What it meant, having eternity stretched out before you. And thinking of all the ways the movies depict vampire death.

"Those won't kill us," he said. "Only way is decapitation, or by being drained of all blood and not having a chance to feed for a good while after. We might look dead at that point, but a drop of blood and we're back in action. Takes a long time to actually die like that. It's slow and degrading, the worst way to go."

His arms had tightened around me, I think subconsciously.

"So if you ever find yourself in danger and you manage to stake them," he went on. "Don't you give yourself the luxury of collapsing into a ball and thinking it's over. This is one part the movies get right. They're never fucking dead. Even if they seem dead, you run. Even if that vampire is me, right?"

"Yes, sir," I said, without meaning to sound so husky. The strength of his arms had stirred the wanting, stoked the fire. I rubbed his chest, disappointed that he was wearing a shirt. Come to think of it, I was fully clothed, too.

"This is the second time I've slept in your bed. How come we're still dressed?" I pulled at the irritating material that was forming an unwelcome barrier between our skin.

"You fell asleep on the sofa, it's been a busy week."

"What time is it?"

"Evening. You didn't fall asleep until morning."

"I slept all day?! Damn, are you sure you haven't secretly turned me into a vampire?" I laughed.

"Not yet," he smiled, and my stomach flipped.

"So, if I fell asleep on the sofa, how come I'm in your bed?"

"I did the gentlemanly thing and carried you up here. I thought undressing you in your vulnerable state would be wrong though." He'd been looking awkward, but now he gave me a devilish grin. "You're always vulnerable to me anyway, weakened with sleep and confusion just made it way too easy. I wanted you awake before I made my move, so you could at least try and put up a fight against the vampire advancement."

He rolled me onto my back and hovered overhead, pinning my hands down.

226

"I'm sorry to disappoint, but there's no way I'm going to try and stop you, sir."

My nipples tingled, yearning to be free, with his delicious mouth around them.

"Come on, Jess," he said. "It's more fun if you struggle."

Yes. Yes, it was.

Yet, in that moment, with my hands pinned so hard they hurt, and his strained face so close to my neck, I realized that this struggle might not end so fun. Alarmed, I could hear the hammering of my heart thundering in my ears. Fear mixed with wanting. My nipples grew even tighter.

"Perfect," he groaned his approval, kissing me hard. With my hands released, I found myself thrusting them under his shirt, seeking out the smooth contours of his chest, his muscles tight. Somewhere in my mind I was thinking about what a bad thing that was, that he felt so coiled and rigid, but his lips had moved to my neck and it was so sensual.

I pressed closer, digging my nails into his back, dragging them downwards. His neck tasted slightly salty as I kissed and nibbled along his throat.

He grumbled and inched back, straining over me. "What was that?" he asked coldly.

"What? What did I do? You didn't like it?"

I felt stupid, but I didn't know why. Then it hit me. Why would you bite a vampire's neck, one who also had his lips at your own neck, and was so tense with restraint that it appeared he may combust at any moment? Oh dear.

With a long groan he kissed me again, hands roughly groping my curves. I couldn't get enough of that cold, minty tongue. Then his hand was inside my jeans, seeking out my hot core. His ragged breath whispered past my ear. I grabbed his cock through his jeans, stroking and rubbing, and the panting stopped; in fact, I think he stopped breathing altogether.

The next thing I knew, Eva had thrown herself down languidly on the bed beside us. *I shit you not.*

"GREAT," SHE TRILLED. "I SEE YOU TWO HAVE MADE UP. WHAT should we do to celebrate? There's a kite-boarding competition at the beach?" Her tone and body language was over-casual for the awkward situation. Zac stared long and hard at her before silently thrusting himself backwards off the bed with catlike grace. His mouth was clamped shut as he disappeared into the bathroom.

Eva and I observed each other in silence, until she flitted off, leaving Zac to face me alone once he returned from the bathroom. Some of the tension had eased from him.

"Oh my Lord, did you just finish yourself off in there?" I laughed.

His eyebrows rose, but he didn't deny it. Instead, he shrugged and said with a smile, "Eva's right. We should join the others on the beach. I need some time-out from your heat."

He didn't even give me the chance to respond, before sprinting off like he couldn't wait to get away. I trailed after him, my heart still hammering in my ears, the feel of his lips still lingering on my fevered skin.

As was often the case during my time on the beach, the sun was just beginning to set, the sky ablaze in red and orange which reflected in little sparkling jewels over the ocean. The sea itself was relatively calm as it flowed into the shoreline, yet the wind was strong. The opportunity for serenity was there, if the beach had been deserted it would have been beautiful. As it happened, the sand was rammed with several hundred or so young men and women.

Most of the bikini-clad girls sat around on their towels in the sand, catching the last rays for their tans. Sucking in their stomachs and offering themselves up to whichever boy could impress them the most.

And try to impress they did. Loud scuffles broke out along the shore, mostly playful jostling, an occasional real fight. The waves filled with people on their kite-boards, trying to catch the biggest hang time in the air. Some of them were pretty good. I enjoyed watching them fly up into the sky and land back down skillfully.

Until Leon entered the scene, and they suddenly looked like amateur little boys. He rode the waves and sky like a sleek animal, sneaking in a couple of mega loops where he was at least sixty to seventy foot up in the air, level with the kite.

It was fascinating to watch. It looked terrifying being up that high, at the mercy of the wind, waves and a kite. I ought to ask him to teach me.

After a while he left the surf and walked back towards us with water dropping from his tangled blond curls, onto his shoulders and down his broad chest. His charming, boyish face fitted right in with the frat boys, yet he was worlds apart from them in all other ways. Something that every girl on the beach was aware of by now, as we all watched him saunter along.

I wondered how good it would feel to have those huge muscles pinning me to a wall, forcing me to bend to his will...

I fell out of the daydream when I realized that he'd reached our group and was staring at me, eyes wide. As I returned his shocked gaze he gave me a quick wink and a cheeky grin.

Sweet mother. Never mind the blood-sucking vampires, this world was a dangerous place when your own private sexual thoughts were no longer your own!

He pinched his fingers together and brought them across his mouth in a '*my lips are sealed*' gesture, before turning his back to me and grabbing a beer from the cooler box.

Zac grabbed my hand and pulled me down into his lap, lacing his fingers through mine. The tingling pulsing was still there, just like the first time he'd held me. If I was a cat I'd have purred.

"Are you flirting with my men?" he asked.

"It's not flirting if they let themselves into my head. That's cheating."

He laughed, squeezing me.

"Jess?" he said somberly, since we clearly weren't allowed too much light-heartedness.

"Mmmm," was about all I could manage in reply.

"I desperately wanted things to progress further in my room."

"Tell me about it, that was random. What's up with Eva? We could always sneak back up there and carry on?"

He rested his chin on my shoulder with a sigh.

"Oh... you didn't mean progression in that way? What exactly did you want?"

"You want me to say it? Really? Because you won't like it when the sound of those words hits your ears."

"I see."

Did I see though? I kept pushing aside all the thoughts that I ought to be having. Dismissing the danger like it was nothing. That was the only way to deal with it — by *not* dealing with it.

"Eva interrupted because she was worried for where I was about to go. She was right to be worried. We need to set some boundaries," he said. "This is a new journey for me too and it isn't going to be an easy relationship. I'm going to have a hard enough job controlling myself with you as it is, that's without you even doing anything. So doing things that are likely to send me even wilder with desire are not allowed. Calling me sir is borderline. We'll have to see about that. But biting my neck is a hard line. No way."

"I didn't mean to."

"I know. That's why I need you to understand how your scent is so overpowering and irresistible to me. The way your heart beats, you're so alive. It's like you're in a constant state of excitement. It's intoxicating."

"You're drunk on my heartbeat?" I asked dryly.

He nodded gravely, frowning. "Life was a lot simpler when guys only hungered for your tits and ass, right? I'm totally powerless to your lure."

"That's a good dramatic answer. I guess you already know that I feel the same about you. Not so much the smell and heartbeat, but I'm totally addicted to you."

"Yeah, well I cheat. You do it naturally."

"How do you cheat?"

"I told you, enchanting humans is easy for us."

"That must be a crap talent if you can't have sex with those you've ensnared!"

"We have sex." His forehead wrinkled with a look that said, '*You dummy, vampires have a shit-load of sex!*'

"We're a promiscuous species. Scent is pretty closely tied to the more human urges of lust, but they can be differentiated. Each vampire only lusts after a certain type of scent. So long as it isn't too strong for us then we can have sex and control ourselves. If we wanted to. Most vampires don't bother trying with that part."

No description needed for what that meant.

"So," he still had more for me. "The most beautiful

231

woman in the world might only have a mediocre scent to me, but of course I'd still enjoy fucking her."

I didn't care too much for the way he'd switched to first person in this description. Me instead of 'us — the vampires'. The thought of him being intimate with anyone else made me feel nauseous.

"Great. So what you're telling me is that you've fucked loads of gorgeous women, but you don't want to fuck me."

I'd been watching Leon kissing the face off a lucky woman that he'd selected from the beach offerings. As if to prove their point, he took her hand and led her away. Irritation pricked my scalp.

"Personally, I don't bother sleeping around," Zac said, following my gaze to Leon disappearing with his toy. "And I'm saying I want to fuck you more than any other woman in the world, because on top of being shit-hot, you also appeal to every other sense I have. Unfortunately it's also for that reason that I can't. Cruel, isn't it?"

"Let's go back a few minutes. I thought you wanted me to struggle and play the victim, wouldn't that have been too exciting for you? What did you think was going to happen?" I wasn't going to take all the blame for my little neck nibble having upset the balance.

"I knew you wouldn't do it."

"Did you? If you're so good at reading me then you'd know that's precisely the sort of request I *would* follow."

"You're right," he frowned, shaking his head. "It was a dumb move, I got carried away. It won't happen again. Because the truth is, if you struggle and say 'No', I'll enjoy it more. And if I enjoy it too much, there isn't a single safe word that could stop me."

"So, what then? I just have to lie there, not allowed to touch you in case you get too excited. Hoping you don't kill me?"

"To a certain extent, yes. For now."

"That doesn't sound like much of a relationship to me," I huffed.

"If you have a problem, you know where the door is."

Ouch. That one hurt. Where the hell did that come from? I wanted to laugh at the fact that technically there was no door, since we were on the beach, but unfortunately tears began to leak out. A guy pushing me away for being too passionate? That had never happened in my normal life, but was happening way too often with him. And yes, actually, I did have a problem with that.

Fuck him, with his flashy magic eyes and abs of steel.

All the reality of the crazy situation came back to slap me in the face as I traipsed away, finding my way back to my new 'safe' motel on the North side. The bastard didn't try and stop me.

26

JESS

*W*ere we ever going to have a single day that didn't end with him either disappearing or us fighting?

I wondered again how many vampires were out there, lurking in the shadows... no, that wasn't right. They didn't lurk in shadows, they were right there mixing with everyone else. Letting you fall for them.

What was it Zac said to me the other night? "*We don't live on the fringe of society, hiding in the shadows and secretly stealing your blood like vermin. We walk amongst you; seducing you, fucking you, toying with you. All the while you're captivated, enthralled, blissfully unaware of the monsters in your midst.*"

Could it really be true that my need for him was all down to his fucked-up magical vampire powers? That I had no control over my own feelings?

I tore at the beer label in my hand, scrunching the pieces into little balls and flicking them across the room. He had lured me into his arms when he was supposedly so worried about the threat he posed me. What bullshit. I bet he loved playing me.

Still, I couldn't deny the tenderness when we were close. And his haunted eyes. It was rare to see him smile and laugh, at least, to see genuine ones. A heavy burden always hung over him.

There was no question of me leaving. It didn't seem to matter what he was. The idea of being without him sent physical pain through my chest. Luckily, (or not), tempestuous relationships were my speciality. Euphoric highs followed by desperate lows seemed to be as much a part of my nature as my need for a buzz. It wasn't right, or healthy, but it was what I knew.

I tipped the rest of the beer into the sink and tossed the bottle. My motel room seemed different. Something I couldn't put my finger on, but I wasn't comfortable there. Uneasiness settled in my stomach. I'd sooner go and face Zac's weirdness than sit there another second in a room that felt like it was going to consume me.

Waltzing into the night, unfazed and ready for more, I flung the door open with certainty. I wasn't expecting to see him standing rigidly in the parking lot. I blinked and he was beside me, holding my face in his hands.

"I'm so sorry," he whispered, kissing my cheek.

"How long have you been out here?"

"Too long. I was waiting for you to leave, so that it was your decision to see me. It felt like waiting to die, you took so long to come—"

He pressed his forehead to mine and inhaled deeply, groaning with pleasure. After a tentative kiss, we wasted no time in getting ourselves back to his place.

SOMETHING THAT SURPRISED ME WAS THE NUMBER OF GUYS who appeared to live with him in his stately mansion. Ten or fifteen of them. They came and went around us. Clearly part of his *gang*, but not one of the handful of inner circle members who were generally glued to him. I couldn't tell you any of their names, we barely spoke. We encountered each other with cursory nods of the head and awkward smiles.

A few of them passed through the cavernous living room where we were lounging. They asked Zac if he needed anything and off they went. They always checked if he needed anything. Bowed their heads respectfully to him. Like he was their king.

"They treat you differently to the way Leon, Caleb and Eva do," I stated.

He glanced up at me and shrugged. "Pecking order I guess. They're not close friends. They just follow me."

"Are there other vampires here, apart from you and Alex with your gangs?"

"Just us at the moment, that's still too many."

"I can't believe Anna has been living here for years, all this time surrounded by this danger. It's terrifying. She could have been killed. She still could be. How do I live with that knowledge without warning her?"

"I wouldn't worry too much. They don't tend to kill the island residents, only the visitors. Unless their scent is over-whelming, which is rare. If she's been here that long then she'd already be gone if she appealed to them."

That didn't make me feel any better.

"We'll keep an eye on her. If she matters to you, she matters to me," he said.

"Thanks. I don't know how you can live here with them, too. You know what they're doing, but you ignore it? What happened to that missing girl we found? Alex was involved."

"I don't have any choice," a hard edge came into his voice. "It's their business. There are vampires all over the world killing people, it's not my problem. Just because he's my brother, doesn't mean I have to try and stop him. I gave that up a long time ago. He loves to antagonize me, but I try not to rise to it."

"I still don't understand why he hates you so much."

"I hold him back."

"How? He's not part of your gang or lifestyle. He does what he pleases as far as I can tell." I played with the silver necklace that I'd recovered from its hiding place at the bottom of a drawer.

"He could do a lot more with me at his side."

"And hating you, causing you shit, that's going to get you there? That's madness."

"Don't be deceived, he's no fool."

"Oh, I know that. He's on your territory, under your nose, killing the people around you, people you might care about."

He growled, and my throat went tight.

"I don't care about anyone. I mean..." he frowned. "Not before. I guess now it's going to cause problems. He'll somehow try and use you as leverage against me."

"What for?"

"For the Legacy. It's why he does everything he does. It's the cause of most of my problems."

"It sounds very imperial... The Legacy," I mocked, with a posh emphasis on the word.

"It's no joking matter. If I went ahead with my calling and activated the Legacy bond... it would grant us both with unmeasured power and ability."

"And you don't want that, because—?"

"Because Alexander and I would be inextricably linked, bound together in incomprehensible ways. The darkness would run wild. I'd be rampant with power and need, I wouldn't be myself any longer. I might learn to control it again, at some point, but it would take time. I'd be lost in the early stages of transformation."

"And Alex wants nothing more than to have all of that?"

"He thinks it would give us the ultimate freedom. He doesn't see it. We're nothing but slaves to the darkness."

His hands wrapped around my waist, cold and firm. He was darkness. And light. Walking the line in between. And there I sat, following him blindly into the unknown.

"I fear him, Jess. Because he's stronger than me, because he would take everything from me without hesitation if he stood to gain from it, and mostly... because I could become so much worse than him if I fall off this path."

WE DISCARDED THE TENSION FROM OUR HEAVY DISCUSSION BY letting our lips do the talking for a while. His kisses transported me to another world, far away from this one... somewhere I belonged.

I raised my hand and traced the line of a deep vein along his forearm. Why did I find those veins so damned sexy? Maybe it was the indication of muscle and strength?

"You have veins."

"Yes, ma'am," he chuckled, before sucking in his breath. "That feels a little too nice, Jess."

"It does?" I asked hopefully, a dirty smile spreading across my face. I officially couldn't help myself. Being next to him made me constantly rampant.

"Careful," he warned lightly. "That looks like the sort of smile to get us both into trouble. If I didn't know better, I'd say you were going to try and seduce me again."

"Don't be silly."

"Exactly, I mean, what kind of idiot would try to seduce a vampire?"

238

"Not me. I never look for trouble. Little Miss Boring. You sit back and carry on telling me about yourself, don't you mind me and what I'm doing, it's nothing..." I unbuttoned his shirt, willing my fingers to stop shaking. I noted that the entire room had, at some point, emptied of the usual occupants. Had he telepathically told them to go?

"I'll play along for now. You're so ridiculously desperate to see my abs, it would be rude not to comply."

"Oi! Stop reading my mind!"

"When you're thinking about something so much, it kind of shouts out to me like a megaphone."

"Oh yeah, well, how about this one?" I stopped moving and he tilted his head in curiosity.

"Ouch," he said dryly. "If you think I'm going to be that much of a disappointment then why are your fingers on my shirt again?" He lifted his eyebrows, licking his lips, making my stomach flutter.

"So they are," I whispered, undoing the last button and sliding the shirt off his shoulders.

I didn't mean to let my breath catch the way it did at the sight of him, but damn, his lean, inked body was perfection. He watched me with tense concentration, waiting for my next move. I had to kiss him, had to run my tongue over every inch of that body. But would he let me?

He shook his head the slightest amount.

"What about handcuffs? I have some at my motel you know, I like to keep them handy for kinky fun..." I continued to ogle every contour, my fingers itching to touch.

"You think handcuffs could hold me?"

"No. But it sure would be fun to try." I flooded my mind with filthy fantasy.

"You're such a tease, you don't play fair," he moaned. "You're a very naughty girl."

239

"So punish me. We both know your power and my subservience is where it's at. You're my vampire master."

"Well, now, that certainly is more my style." He grabbed my waist and pulled me right into him, as if I weighed no more than a feather. "Although I assume you're only referring to time spent in the bedroom, because you don't take shit from me elsewhere, Miss Layton."

"Well, that's bollocks. I'm totally under your power, and we both know it. It's embarrassing how infatuated I am."

He moved slowly, cautiously, his lips hovering just a hair's breadth away from mine. Dominating not only my mind and body, but the very space around us, stealing the air from my lungs. His tongue ran along my bottom lip and with one blink my mind emptied of all rational thought.

Instinctively, I dug my nails into his back, grinding against him. The kiss lost its gentleness, his tongue roaming forcefully into my mouth, fingers curling around my hair. The feeling of his cool breath against my mouth, vaguely metallic, panting into me...

Need consumed me. The need to have him inside me. To feel him hard and strong, driving into me, filling me, *owning* me. I gasped and wriggled, rubbing myself against him, pushing for more.

His hand still tangled in my hair, he yanked it back, exposing my throat. My lips parted in anticipation of the pleasure, a groan escaping me. Overcome with desire, I closed my eyes and floated away to a different place.

His whole body tensed up and in a second he was away. *Fucking hell.* My life was going round in circles.

"You really are that willing to give yourself over to me completely? Sex is one thing, but you're so eager to offer me your throat, too? You have to help me here, not make it harder!" He gripped the table, his face dark and anxious.

A loud cracking noise snapped me out of my daze,

a little dizzy, like I'd just woken from heavy sleep. "I told you, I can't help it. My body just reacts and I don't even have a chance to think. Anyway, don't you dare blame me. You're the one that decided to *expose* my throat."

Now wasn't the time to tell him that the idea of him munching on my neck also didn't seem so bad to me. At least, the outcome of that seemed like it had possibilities.

"I thought you wanted to practice, and so we did," I snapped. "You can't keep shouting at me every time we try and fail. That's what practicing means."

"Offering me your throat is too much."

"I didn't offer it to you! You pulled my head back and nearly fucking took it, all on your own!"

"Well, at least try and deter me then. Don't conjure up images of me biting you, and you loving it. I'd really appreciate it if you could spend a little less time thinking about sex and a little more time thinking about the danger you're in."

"Oh sure, I'll try real hard to remember that the next time you wipe my mind and body of all rationality with your impossibly intense kisses. But so help me God, if you don't figure out the control soon I'm going to explode."

He clicked his neck from side to side, jaw ticking. "You just have to be good for a while longer, while I figure this shit out."

"I don't want to be good, I want to be bad. I can't suffer this intolerable rejection any longer. For fucks sake, I want you to *fuck* me! I want it so much it hurts."

He snorted, pressing a hand to his forehead. "It *hurts*? Do not talk to me about hurt. What hurts is what I have to go through, every second that I'm fighting the urge to kill you." I cringed and he continued, "And as if that agony isn't enough, you pull shit like that and increase it by the hundreds. Look at the fucking table, I've split the wood. That's pain, Jess."

I went to storm away but he caught me in his arms.

"I swear you have a death wish, Layton" he mumbled. "You should be running a mile from me, not luring me in further like some crazy siren."

Thrumming filled my ears, my head felt distant, away from my body. I pushed out from his grip.

"You know what? I'm a little sick of you making out like you're the only one with problems around here, and worse still, that those are my fault. Seriously? It's *my* fault that you want to kill me?" I stormed around the room, gathering my stuff.

"My therapist taught me a name for that," I went on. "It's called victim-blaming. Maybe you could use some counseling sessions yourself? In fact, yeah... do that. You come find me once you've got your head screwed on, because for once in my life, it's not me with the problem. It's you."

27

JESS

So, the answer was no. We couldn't have a day without fighting.

He was an ass. I had enough problems in my life at the best of times, without having a boyfriend who wanted to kill me, and had the nerve to blame me for that. I might have been the expert in fucked up relationships, but this was a new level, even for me.

I meant what I'd said to him, too. He wasn't the only one with problems. I'd felt it building when I got mad with him. Felt the static tingling through my fingers. Heard the buzzing in my head. He was so wrapped up in the danger he posed to me, but what if *I* was the danger to him? What if I lost control and conjured up something inexplicable, something that could hurt him?

The firehouse alarm dragged me from my melancholy.

I scrambled with the crew as Danny yelled that we were needed on Port Isabel.

When we arrived, there was already one crew in attendance, battling the blaze. It seemed to be an old factory unit. An area out the front had been cordoned off with police tape, a white sheet draped over a body.

The heat bombarded me as I helped Meat with the hose and joined in with the efforts. My second fire since arriving on the island, after Danny had assured me how rare they were around here.

My chest heaved, the breathing apparatus felt too constrictive. From the corner of my eye I noticed the arrival of Zac. And Alex. My immediate reaction was to rush over to them, but I had hold of the hose. I was on duty. I couldn't just walk off and do as I pleased. And this time, I wouldn't let my anxieties distract me from the task in hand.

Even so, I tried to keep watch on them, at the same time as the flames, which were gradually receding. What were they doing here?

Zac kept glancing at me. As did Alex. Body language tight and strained. They stood right next to the police tape, officers and fire crew swarming around, apparently oblivious to their presence; as if they were invisible.

Eva arrived, and Leon, and men that I recognized as part of Alex's entourage. They moved gracefully amongst the chaos — calm, but fast. Touching their hands to shoulders, whispering in ears. Before my eyes the police took on confused expressions, standing and swaying, then, one by one, they shuffled away.

Alex moved under the tape and picked up the body, disappearing with it in a blurred flash. The tape vanished just as quick.

My blood ran cold.

The vampires were doing something to them, to their *minds*. Making them forget, or think differently — to walk away from the scene as if nothing was there.

Danny approached Zac and I tried to scream at him, but the sound of the hose and the fire, the commotion; it sucked the noise from me, drowning it out.

The hose fell from my grip. Meat turned to yell at me.

Picking it back up, I watched as Danny took a swing at Zac. Zac caught his fist, his face full of menace. After a moment, Danny's head dropped and he turned... and walked away.

I threw the hose down, shrugging away from Meat as he tried to grab me. Marching straight to Zac, I took a swing at him myself. He let me make contact, my fist against his temple. My knuckles cracked painfully. He glanced around and pulled me aside, in between two buildings.

I threw a look behind me, spotting Eva talking to Meat.

"You can alter what people think?!" I couldn't get as much anger into my words as the anger I felt buzzing through my head.

"Touch manipulation. Mind manipulation. Some of us are better at it than others." His eyes had a look of remorse. He reached out to put a hand on my hip. I jumped backwards, batting him away.

"Stay away from me."

"I would never use it on you." He stepped back himself, an attempt at reassuring me.

"Am I supposed to thank you for that? It's bullshit. You own me, and you know it. You're a control freak. You hold me like a puppet on strings, dangling me around for your own amusement."

"That hurts, Jess."

"Does it?" I spat. "Boo-fucking-hoo. The immortal man with everything he wants in the palm of his hand is offended at being called out on it. Quit pretending to be Mr. Perfect and own up to the fact that despite all this 'I fight the darkness' bullshit, you still love your power."

"I've never claimed otherwise." His gaze took on a certain ferocity.

My instincts told me to step further away, but I rooted myself firmly to the spot. "Seems to me that at least Alex doesn't lie about what he is."

The growl that flew from his throat made me gasp, his face twisting in rage.

"You know nothing of him," he roared. "And seriously, when have I lied? I've told you repeatedly that I'm not the good guy. That you need to leave."

Despite the continuing assault on my nerve, I remained glued to the spot. He wouldn't make me back up again.

"You're right. I clearly don't know what you are, or what you're capable of." I didn't dare look into his eyes, in case the anger would be forgotten. In case the pull towards him would take over and I'd fall into his lap like a mewing kitten.

But his anger had brought him back close to me, so that I had no choice but to see every fleck in those magical eyes, every fiery spark that made them glow like amber. Lashes so thick and dark, blackness framing the burning brightness. There was a storm brewing in his eyes, and I had the feeling it could be catastrophic if unleashed on me.

"Why were you hiding the body? Which one of you killed that innocent person under the white sheet out there?" I hissed.

Surprise passed his face. "That wasn't a human out there, it was one of Alex's men. Decapitated and drained of every drop of blood. Splayed out in front of the burning building for the world to see. A building they knew *you* would be called to attend... to deliver a message to us."

"What?! Why? Who?" I stuttered.

"I guess the hunter wasn't working alone after all. You must understand, I don't take messing with people's minds lightly. I had to do this, Jess. I couldn't leave a dead vampire lying around."

"They weren't from your gang, what do you care?"

"It's my island."

"Seriously? You're still claiming to own this shit-hole?" A deep, southern drawl made my skin thrum and my heart skip about ten beats in one go. "Nice to see you again, Jess," Alex said, stooping to kiss the back of my hand with a graceful bow.

I went wobbly. As if one gorgeous man and his electric lips wasn't enough, now I had his dazzling twin giving me heart failure too.

He was all shades of bad and yet the memories of all he'd done began fading rapidly, like I had no control. They just slipped away from my body, floating on a breeze, leaving only a lusting sensation where the anger should have been. And what the fuck was the urgent heat burning between my legs?!

Zac snarled like a rabid dog. If I thought he'd looked menacing before, then there were no words for this. He dropped the human facade, his eyes black, lip curled up.

"Calm down, kitten. Can't a gentleman be courteous to a lady these days?" Alex released my hand, smiling sweetly, as Zac stepped protectively between us.

"You? Courteous?! You delusional wanker," I muttered, ignoring my traitorous body which was still singing with delight after the touch of his lips. Alex smiled wider.

"What do you want?" Zac asked. "It's all dealt with here, right?"

I tried to peek out from behind him at beautiful, dangerous, asshole number two. It wasn't fair that they looked so identical. I was angry, at both of them. I knew it, in my head. But I couldn't *feel* it.

Fuck this. Fuck them.

"Zac—" I began.

"Shut up, Jess," he hissed.

Alex shifted to the side to make eye contact. He grinned, easy and carefree, not a single concern in the world. "Evidently not, there's no courtesy to ladies anymore," he muttered under his breath.

His eyes, like Zac's, had an intensity that was clearly beyond human. But where Zac's were deep, golden flames, his were piercing electric blue, almost turquoise. Opalescent, even. The color seemed to switch and change, shimmering blues like tropical waters. They weren't brooding and dark like Zac's, shrouded in angst... no, his eyes sparkled with a seductive playfulness.

Alex took in a noisy lungful of air, nose pointed in my direction, and slid his tongue along his teeth, exhaling with the sound of satisfaction.

"I dare you to do that again," Zac growled. He was seething with so much rage by this point that I thought he might actually transform into a wild animal before my eyes. Was shape shifting a thing?!

Alex let out a long, low whistle as he stepped away. "Okay, Zachariah, whatever you say." Then, to me, he said, "Another time, darlin'," before vanishing in a flurry, a cool breeze sweeping back my hair.

Zac had tried to talk to me more, asked me to go back to his place, but I couldn't. I just couldn't. It didn't matter how much my body cried out for his touch, how whole he made me feel. This was too monumental.

How was I supposed to look Danny in the eye, knowing what they'd done to his mind? How many times had they messed with it already? Zac assured me that Danny didn't know what they were, no one did — they made sure of it.

The mood at the firehouse after the incident had been unbearable. Not because they were distant, or angry, or confused. But because they were normal. Whatever the vampires had done to their minds, they did a thorough job. The crew joked around, throwing joke bullshit at me like I was their best friend, like nothing untoward had ever happened.

I had no doubts that their relaxed attitude towards me was thanks to Zac and his gang. Did they think to just add in a little extra mind-bending whilst they were at it? *Forget all this dead body business and our presence here, but whilst we're at it, go ahead and think of Jess as your best buddy.* Even Danny had lost the anxious look, no longer watching me from afar with anguish, but instead patting me on the back and laughing.

The whole thing made me cringe. It wasn't right. But what other option was there? What would have happened if Zac had gone ahead and left that body there? The coroners would have had a field day with that.

No. They did what they had to. And that made me even angrier. I didn't want to agree with them. Didn't want to accept it as okay. Or maybe I was just terrified. For the idea of what they could do to me.

They could make me think anything, do anything. And of all the possibilities, all the ways they could mess with my head, what made me feel the most nauseous?

The fact that Zac could make me forget he existed.

———

When I arrived at MoJoe's the following night, I found Danny behind the bar, helping himself to drinks. Anna and William sat on the other side, snuggled up close, smooching, passing loving gazes back and forth.

Danny beamed at me, bright and happy, but Anna and William gave me tight smiles. At least Zac hadn't mind-fucked everyone on the island.

Spring break was finally over. Six weeks or so of the constant, incessant, crazed crowds was too much. They grew tiresome with their young, lithe bodies and carefree attitudes. I was thankful to wave goodbye to the last of them. The place was still busy, but at least now you could breathe and get some space. Lord knew, I needed that. If the world around me would calm down just a little, then maybe I could too. My head was such a frantic, emotional wreck.

"Hey there, how's my favorite girl today?" Danny asked, giving me a wink.

"Sulking. But I'm better now, thanks to your gorgeous face." I returned the wink and Anna looked at me agog, eyebrows raised. I cursed myself at feeling thankful for whatever they'd done to Danny, and for suddenly wishing that maybe, just maybe, it would have been helpful to brainwash Anna.

"I aim to please, Miss. Jess. What can I get you?" Danny asked, radiant. It looked to me like his steel-gray hair had managed to turn even grayer since my arrival, but it suited him.

"You look pretty good behind the bar... better in your uniform though. You should stick to the day job," I grinned.

"Oh, don't worry, I am. So you better hurry and choose what you want before I come back round the other side of the bar."

"I don't know, what's on offer?" I hoisted myself onto a stool and leant over, chin resting in my hands. Maybe a little harmless flirting with a normal man was just what I needed.

"Anything you like, baby. I have it all."

Baby? Okay, maybe they'd gone too far.

"I bet you do. You certainly look... well equipped." I nibbled my lip.

"Don't take it on what you can see from that side of the bar, Jess," he moved in closer, wincing from the lingering pain that still haunted his ribs. "I operate a strict 'try before you buy' policy here, you know."

William coughed. Danny's mouth was so close to mine that I could feel his breath on my face. I could reach out and stroke the silver-flecked stubble.

"You do, huh? What exactly does that mean?" I cocked my head to the side as I feasted my sights over his lips.

I shouldn't be doing that.

"It means you can always ask for a sample of anything behind the bar, have a little taste, just to see how much you like it before you come back for more," he paused, his own eyes not leaving my lips. "Trust me. You'll be back for more."

"You know, Chief, you're pretty hot for an old man," I smirked.

"You know, Firefighter Layton, you're not so bad for a cheeky-assed rookie. And anyway, you know what comes with age, right?"

"Erectile dysfunction?"

Anna snorted.

"I was going to say experience!" he laughed. "And, the opposite of your suggestion, actually. I don't get laid enough which makes for a rock hard ride when the opportunity arises. But you know that already, right?"

I inched ever so slightly closer to him, when there was a sudden commotion behind me, giggling and shouting. The tension between us snapped and I turned around to observe Zac and his gang entering the bar, along with hoards of women. Jabbering and squealing, throwing themselves, and their pert little titties, into Zac's face. My blood boiled.

"Wonderful. The carnage begins," Danny pushed himself back off the bar and came round to join us on our side.

I waited for Zac to acknowledge me. There was no way that he wouldn't know I was there, he himself admitted that he could sense my whereabouts from miles around. Yet he didn't look over once.

Anna clicked her tongue, putting a hand over mine. William stiffened in his seat. Danny shook his head and glared at the vampires. I guess they hadn't wiped all reasoning from his mind.

I'd never seen Zac looking so... normal. He let his hands wander over the women, laughed and chatted. Blending right in with the typical South Padre crowd. Even so, there was a flicker of something more, something angry, when another four people entered the bar.

A momentary hush swept through the place, all eyes fixated on the newcomers. Three male and one female. It was immediately obvious that they were vampires, to me at least. Not hard to recognize those startling good looks and the casual-yet-tense posture. The woman was all slender curves, attitude and silky-smooth skin.

The bitch walked right up to my man and started sucking his neck! After a long moment of kissing and lick-ing, during which time I thought the world was going to implode around me, she draped a hand on his shoulder and turned to see what he was glaring at; his expression hard and cold on me as I approached. I hadn't even realized that I was moving towards them, my pulse thrashing in my head.

I stopped in front of them and he gave me a disgusted look that made me flinch.

"Do you want something? I'm a little busy here," Zac snapped in my direction. The air caught in my lungs, like he'd punched me in the guts. I'd never seen that look in his eyes before, but it was venom, and fear.

"Who is this tasty little morsel?" the bitch asked, absently stroking her washboard stomach with long, painted fingernails. An infinity symbol tattooed on the back of her hand.

"I have no idea, another follower I guess. This one's more my type though." Zac pulled one of his adoring fans to himself, groping her. Shocked happiness erupted across her face. I wanted to rip that smug smile right off and shove it down her throat. I couldn't gather my thoughts enough to work out what I wanted to do to Zac, but it wasn't pretty.

"Interesting. She has a type I'm not familiar with." Bitch-tits looked me up and down, sizing me up.

Zac scoffed, "You're just high from the junkie you sucked dry out there. Trust me, she's nothing to get excited about."

I stood there, speechless, while the vampire bombshell laughed at me, along with the woman who was now nibbling at Zac's ear. She got to nibble his ear, but I got yelled at when I attempted it?

Do something, Jess! Shout at him. Hit him. Demand an explanation!

I should have done those things.

If only that look on his face hadn't twisted my guts inside out. I turned and tried to walk away calmly, but I was heaving from trying to catch my breath, and I ended up running to escape the embarrassment.

28

JESS

*I*f vampires could alter people's thoughts, could they do it to each other? Could Alex have made Zac forget me? There I'd been, worrying that they could make me forget them, but what if the opposite had happened? Had Zac forgotten me?

No. He'd seen me, and he'd known me. But the malice, then the longing, they'd flashed across his face so fast. Ambivalence. Why? Why would he treat me like that?

Granted, I always suspected he'd play with me and then throw me out when he was done.

But like that? And so soon?

The pain was soul destroying.

Anna and Danny followed me out, but I ran. I ran and ran, and didn't stop. I cut corners, went through bars, in one end and out another, until I was certain I'd lost them. Then I continued to stumble blindly from one bar to another and proceeded to get shit-faced.

An hour later I was still struggling to breathe. Partly due to the crushing pain in my chest, and partly because of the number of guys I'd kissed without coming up for air.

They were barely older than nineteen, maybe twenty —

the current group of lads that I was sizing up. They'd noticed me, the old woman drinking alone, desperate. I could feel their jokes, their laughing eyes catching mine. I wanted to fuck them. All of them. My body craved it so badly, to have their hands on me. Any one of them would do... all of them together would be better.

They'd take away the worry, the unknown. I knew myself in the bedroom. I knew what to do and how to make it alright, to quiet the voices, the guilt and anxiety. It was my safe place, aside from the number one preference of adrenalin. If I fucked them, there would be no fears or doubts. Simple pleasure and excitement. The way life should be.

Did I feel bad about it? Ashamed for the number of men I fucked in my life?

Well, yes. But only because that was what society made me feel.

On the inside, releasing all that tension, soothing the constant buzzing under my skin with the thrill of sex... well, that felt right.

Or at least, that was the preferable alternative to letting the buzzing grow until I lost control and hurt people. If I didn't soothe it, I might literally explode...

My burn scar itched, reminding me of the pain...

It didn't take long for one of the lads to stalk over. His golden locks dangled loosely around his soft, youthful face as he smiled at me playfully.

With a slight sigh, I turned to smile back at him, letting my lips meet his without having spoken a word. Maybe this one would fill the void, smother the rage...

"That seat's taken," Danny's voice drifted in from somewhere. The guy coughed an apology, making a hasty retreat.

I caught the smell of his woody aftershave as Danny moved in to occupy the space beside me.

"You planning on fucking your way around the whole island?" he asked.

"Have you been following me?" I squinted at him, until his tight lips confirmed it. "That's Zac's role, not yours. You can't be like him. Please don't be like him."

"And what would he think if he'd been following you tonight?"

"He'd have no fucking right to think a single thing. Anyway, yes, I'm considering a fuck-fest. I am nympho, after all. I'm duty-bound to live up to the reputation, right?"

"Yeah, sure, if you're going to listen to the shrink labels when it suits?"

I shrugged.

"I can't bear to keep seeing you like this, Jess, it's killing me," his voice cracked. His muscled body was so close to mine. I leant in and accepted the comfort of his arms. Warm and safe. I looked up and brushed my lips over his.

"Easy there, tiger," he said, pushing away. "I'm taking you home."

"Well, I was considering just using the restroom, but you're probably right. There's a bed at my place..." I laughed, choking on the agony fighting through my chest and into my throat.

He escorted me with few words. Outside the motel, I fiddled around trying to find my keys. I was cursing and crying. He took the purse from me and pulled me in close again. He wasn't trying to get sexy with me; he was trying to stop me crying. That wouldn't do. There was only one way I'd stop and it involved sex, and reeked of payback.

I put my hand straight to his cock and rubbed, swaying on my feet. He didn't stop me, so I kissed him. That's all there was to say about it really. It was an okay kiss, nice and safe.

A stray dog or something was close by. I couldn't see, but

it was growling threateningly, like an animal defending its territory. Something moved on the edge of my vision. Something dark, shadowy... and fast.

"We should hurry up and take this inside?" I slurred.

"Jess, enough. I'm not staying," he said, but his eyes said otherwise.

"Only a few hours ago you suggested I could try your merchandise, no strings attached," I countered. "What's changed?"

"Everything's changed. You're a wreck." His shoulders caved as his forehead leant against mine.

"So fix me. Or are you suddenly afraid that you can't fulfill the role of satisfying me?"

"Cast your mind back four years and you'll answer that question for yourself."

I raised my brows. "I never texted you back. Doesn't look good for you."

"You never texted me because you were afraid that I might actually ground you. Afraid that I could offer you stability and comfort. You weren't ready to settle down."

I laughed, too loud. "I'm still not. I mean, I know I'm supposed to be. New start and all that. But my head is a total shit-storm."

"Which is why, if I come inside, you'll shove me aside again afterwards." His voice so full of need, of conflicting emotions. I knew that turmoil.

I opened the door and stepped inside, urging him to follow.

MORNING CAME WITH A HEAVY THUD, SMASHING MY BRAIN into my skull, squeezing its painful barbs around my insides. I lurched for the bathroom and hurled into the sink.

257

When I returned to the bed, showered and yet still feeling dirty, Danny was propped on his elbows. I dropped down beside him and hid my face into his chest, too afraid to face him.

"It's okay, Jess. You don't have to worry. This won't change anything," he said, his voice too strained.

"I feel like a total dick," I mumbled.

"You're not the only one. I'm sorry... for allowing this."

"You did nothing wrong." I forced myself to look at him, at the rough stubble that had scratched over my most intimate areas.

"And nor did you. You don't owe him anything, Jess. Not one thing. Not after what he did." His arms tightened, fists clenching.

"It doesn't make sense. He wouldn't do something like that."

"Yet, he did."

"Yes. And he won't get another chance to make me feel so low. Starting right now. I'm getting out of this shitty motel and putting my life together. That's what I came here for, that's what I'm doing." I surprised myself with the certainty in my claims.

"You know I'll help you in any way I can."

"Danny, what happened at the fire the other day, on Isabel?" I asked.

I sensed the confusion on his face, even though I couldn't see it, with my cheek resting back against the soft hair on his chest.

"Nothing really. You were there, it was just a factory fire."

"And that missing girl," I pushed. "When I'd just started, what happened with her?"

"What are you talking about, Jess?" He shifted his weight to try and move my face.

I almost didn't want to ask the final question, but I

258

forged ahead since I'd started it. "And the fire at the Requiem bar?"

"What about it?"

"Nothing," I sighed. "Sorry. Guess my brain is on overdrive this morning."

Fucking mind-bending vampire bastards.

He twisted me around, bringing my chin up with his thumb. "Jess, if you need me to get you more counseling sessions, I can? I know—"

"No. No, thank you. I'm fine. But... us? I mean... I don't know how this can work. I'm not..." I took to my feet and grabbed a shirt, suddenly paranoid about the scar on my back, even though he'd seen it before. The buzzing in my skin might have calmed, but I was drenched with the predictable guilt and shame that followed.

"I told you, it's fine. This is what we do, right? You fuck me and then pretend it never happened?"

I winced and thought I might hurl again.

"Honestly, it's fine. I allowed you to use me in the hope of drawing you away from him. And if that fails, I still got a damn good fuck out of it, right?"

"Pig!" I snorted, slapping his chest.

"I'm your chief," he said, not returning my smile. "You can't have a relationship with me, right? That's what I'll remind myself when I'm in my empty bed tonight, and you're already back in his."

THOSE FINAL WORDS FILLED ME WITH MORE FIRE, MORE DRIVE, than he could have ever hoped for. Or maybe that's precisely what Danny *had* hoped for, and intended, when he squashed me under the guilt of my weakness.

Sex. Lust. Adrenalin. Was that really all that ruled me?

Could I not overcome that and become something more? Could I not learn to handle the build up of energy in my core without resorting to that? I made a mental note to look up meditation classes, and then snorted at myself.

As soon as Danny left, I called the realtors and arranged viewings on several apartments. By the time evening descended with its glowing purple sky, I'd chosen the one I wanted. I could move in within a week.

Then I walked myself calmly into the police station and told them I needed to give a statement about Alex Elwood. Zac's name so nearly fell from my lips at the same time, but remained caught in my throat. The man at the desk gave me an irritated sigh, before making me take a seat and wait an eternity to be seen.

In the interview room they went through the motions with the recorder, the introductions, then sat with bland faces as I told them about seeing Alex inside the bar on the night it burned, and about the missing girl who'd repeated his name over and over in her garbled state.

The officers didn't ask me a single question. Just waited, bored, for me to finish speaking and leave. I had no idea why I was there. I knew it was ridiculous. But I had to do something.

Just before I stood to go, I figured I may as well throw in my stolen motorbike, too.

"Do you have a personal vendetta against Mr. Elwood, Miss. Layton?" It was the only question they'd bothered to ask.

Are you going to cause me trouble, darlin'... Alex had asked me

"No. Of course not," I replied tightly, and made my way back to the grotty motel to daydream about the shiny new apartment that would soon be mine.

It was a moderate size, fresh and airy, a dream compared

to the motel. Located right in the center of Port Isabel. *Safety in numbers*. It felt busy enough that I could relax there.

Fuck South Padre Island. Fuck Zac on his North and Alex on his South. I might work on that island, but there was no damn way I was going to live there any longer.

I allowed myself the satisfaction of imagining Zac's rage at me living off the island, away from his protection. But then the image of him with that bitch popped back and blurred all my intentions, thwarted my positivity. Maybe he wouldn't even care that I'd left, given the way he'd treated me.

Maybe he'd even be glad of it. Glad to have distance from my scent, from the weight of me around his neck, clinging on like a desperate, love-struck idiot.

How had I even had the nerve to feel offended by his disinterest? Why did I even care? What business was it of mine? He was a vampire. An immortal being, borne of hatred and selfishness. The things that he must have done…

I shuddered, sitting on the bed, and drew my leather jacket around myself. Soon, this room, and everything that happened in it, would be nothing more than a bad memory.

Zac was a fucking prick. And a dangerous one at that. Complicated.

I needed easy, no ties, no stress, nothing deep. There was no way he would ever give me that. He was more, so much more. A whole package of deep shit, dressed up as a delicious thrill.

Walk away.

Step away from the fuckable freakshow.

One foot in front of the other. Ever onwards.

I'd look for another job, somewhere else, where I wouldn't have to see him. In the meantime, I would carry on with my head held high. I'd play him at his own game.

He didn't exist.

"Help me! Please!" A boy yelled at me as Luna dragged him through my hallway and into the sitting room. His neck was already a mess of bloody, ripped flesh. Eyes wild. Skin pallid from the amount of blood she'd drained.

Leon gritted his teeth when one of Luna's Cell barged past him, dragging a toy of his own to play with. There was only four of them here, but it felt like more.

I couldn't let it continue much longer. They'd invaded my home like a plague of fucking locusts, constantly buzzing in my ears and devouring anything and everything that came close. I was losing count of how many college kids they'd slaughtered. The clean-up process was going to be a bitch.

And of course, my own Cell were starting to lose patience, not only with Luna, but also with me. Because I was allowing it to happen.

I had no choice. Luna had sensed that Jess was different and I couldn't let her get another sniff. Or show any indication that I cared in any way.

So I sat back and let them enjoy their little vacation on

my island. Then they could go ahead and report back to Emory that there was nothing of interest going on with the Elwoods.

Alexander told Luna that he'd killed the hunter and she seemed happy enough with his story. Thankfully, he'd neglected to tell her that the hunter wasn't alone and there was still someone out there — because he enjoyed Luna's invasion on the island about as much as I did. Having the Bael arrive to clean up our hunter shit would be a massive kick to his ego. So at least I could rely on him to play along. It was a rare thing to be able to trust him on anything.

"How long is this going to go on for?" Leon ushered me back down the hallway, into the unused kitchen.

Normally unused. It appeared that now we had a severed head in the sink, unblinking eyes staring up at us.

"For fuck's sake!" Leon hissed, grabbing a handful of blonde curls and throwing it out the side door.

"They'll leave soon. Just let them have their fun and they'll be gone."

"You realize Jess has left the island?"

My fists clenched. "Yes, Leon, I am more than aware of her every movement, being that her presence is so firmly etched into my fucking soul that I can't think about anything else!" I lowered my tone at the end, realizing the error of speaking out loud.

I switched to speaking directly into his head. *Have her watched at all times. I can't leave here and risk leading them to her. I want eyes on her every second, got it?*

He nodded once and left.

I turned on the faucet and watched blood swirl down the drain. Leon was right. I needed to get rid of Luna, sooner rather than later. But every time I thought I might have got myself under enough control to deal with her gentle eviction with minimal fuss, the anger would rise again.

Jess left the damned island! After everything I'd told her, over and over, about how unsafe she was. She saw me with a bunch of dangerous vampires, and what did she do? She fucking left my protection. Was she purposefully trying to destroy me?

'It's a good thing.' Eva appeared, speaking telepathically into my mind. This was the only way we could communicate safely with the Bael scouts around.

What is?

'That she's gone. For once, she's safer away from you. At least Luna won't bump into her.'

I pushed away from the sink and left the house, getting on my bike. Eva meant well, but I couldn't deal with any of them right then.

There was only one thing that might help to calm the boiling rage inside. One thing that needed to be done.

Danny sullied your sanguine mate. He fucked her, and you haven't. He has rammed his cock into her sweet—

I gunned the engine, silencing the Beast. But that didn't mean I wasn't listening to him this time.

I heard him loud and clear.

Danny had to pay.

I watched him for days.

I watched him go to work, go to the store, go to his shitty bar.

He became my new obsession. If I couldn't stalk Jess without putting her in further danger, then I'd follow him and fill up on the thrill of what was to come. I don't know where the patience came from, but for some reason I gained some sick pleasure in letting him live a little longer — watching him go about his business, unaware of the shit

264

that was about to unfold. At least it got me away from the house and the carnage that Luna was causing.

But today was the day. I couldn't wait any longer. Today I was going to drag his sorry ass down to my basement, where I could feed from him every day. And once all this shit had passed with Luna, I was going to get Jess back and kiss her, right after feeding on her Danny-boy.

It felt like a suitable punishment for both of them. Danny would get a long, drawn-out death, and Jess? Well, she wouldn't know she was being punished, but I would. I'd get the satisfaction of knowing who was in my basement whilst she was pawing over me in the room above. She'd be up there, begging me to fuck her, oblivious to Danny getting beaten to shit and drained every day on repeat.

You know what would be a better punishment? Get Jess down in that fucking basement too...

I watched as he emerged from the firehouse, looking as smug and confident as usual. I clearly needed to re-think the way that I dealt with people around here. Pussy-footing around and refusing to use my power had been weakness. It was high time they all got a reminder about who ran this fucking place.

The fact that Danny had the balls to fuck her, to take what clearly belonged to me, was unacceptable. Maybe it was the dent to my ego, maybe it was Luna messing with my balance, whatever it was, the darkness was creeping out and I didn't feel like pushing it back.

Danny got in his truck. I would follow him home and then I'd take him.

"Zac! My main man! The big E! Mr. Elwood himself!" Nyle, one of Luna's men, grabbed my shoulders and gave me a shake.

My answering snarl brought a smile to his face as I

shook him off. Danny pulled on his seatbelt and I swung onto my bike.

"Where you going, golden boy?" Nyle pressed. "What the hell does Emory love you so much for, huh?" He moved to block my bike and I watched as Danny reversed out of his parking space. I revved then engine.

"Oh, wait, I get it... you're going to do that legacy bonding shit one day, and then you'll be all mighty and feisty, right?"

I inched the bike forward, into Nyle's legs, pushing him back.

"I'm sorry, am I keeping you from something?" he asked. "I didn't realize your date with Danny was so important. But then, I suppose fucking your girlfriend has gotta smart, right?"

Fog blurred my vision as Danny drove away down the highway.

"Yeah, we've been busy learning all about your antics, Zac! Did you really think that we've just been hanging around here to take your skanky college kids for fun? Hell, they taste like shit! But, they do talk. Boy, do they fucking talk when you press the right buttons! That's why Luna is on her way back to Emory right now with all the information about your delicious love interest. Oh, and talking of her, I might have sent someone over to Isabel to find—"

Before another second could pass, I'd leapt from my bike and pulled Nyle's head clean off his shoulders. I dropped it to the ground as Leon came tearing over to us.

"Kill them all," I yelled. "Kill every fucking member of Luna's Cell."

THERE WAS ONLY LUNA AND TWO OTHERS FROM HER CELL

who'd come to the island. Well, three others if you counted Nyle, but now he was dead.

I sent Leon and Eva to Port Isabel to find the one who'd gone there for Jess, and ordered the rest of my men to take out the other guy.

I wanted to go and get Jess myself. The last couple of weeks had been living hell. Not being able to explain to her, knowing that she was hurting. I could hear her thoughts sometimes. Every part of her called out to me and it was physical agony staying away.

Just a little longer. We'd be back together soon. First I had to track down Luna before she reached Emory. I needed to deal with her personally.

Racing along the highway, I pushed faster and faster. I could sense that I was gaining on her, but it felt like I'd never get there. Then I rode straight past her. She'd stopped.

I swung back round and found her waiting for me down a deserted road.

"You following me, Zac? I'm sorry I left without a goodbye kiss, I didn't know you cared so much—"

I cut her off with a hand around her throat. "You made a massive error coming here. Do not mistake my way of life for weakness. You and your people can insult me all you like, but when you set foot on my island and you mess with what's mine, don't expect to find the pussycat waiting for you." My grip tightened until the smile dropped from her face.

I should have ripped her head off right then. Or drunk her filthy blood and drained her on the spot. But instead I got distracted listening to the voice in my head — telling me to draw out her suffering, just like with Danny.

My hesitation gave her time to gather her strength and dig her pointed fingernails into my eyeballs until I let go.

Everything went dark. I could feel the blood leaking

down my face. I scrambled around, trying to get my bearings, but I couldn't see shit. I heard her car, though, and was forced to listen helplessly to the sound of it speeding away. *Fuck!*

Stumbling over to my bike, I sank to the ground, clutching my face.

"Come on, fucking heal!" I yelled at myself, willing my vision to return faster. Every passing second felt like an hour. The bitch had done a good job. It took far longer than I'd hoped before I could see again, by which time Luna was long gone.

She should have killed me while she had the chance. Emory would have sentenced her to death of course; no one got to kill an Elwood except him. But death at his hands would be better than what she was going to receive at mine.

She'd better keep running. Fast.

JESS

*I*t was three weeks since I'd moved to Port Isabel. I surveyed the unpacked boxes lining one wall of my sparkly new apartment. They were already gathering dust from sitting there untouched.

So few possessions. How had I reached this age with so little to show for it?

The gleaming kitchen taunted me with its appliances, my gaunt face reflecting back at me from various angles, the cooker spotless due to my inability to eat. No matter what I tried, it was all cardboard in my mouth.

I spent the weeks trudging from one task to the next, without any memory of what happened in between. Swathes of time lost to an empty, aching spiral.

He was nowhere. Not in the bars, not waiting for me outside my door, not watching from afar. Not trying to call me. No messages pleading for the chance to explain. He was simply gone.

And yet he was everywhere, invading my mind and heart as if he owned them for himself. Occupying my dreams and nightmares. Permeating every thought I had throughout the day.

I'd become so accustomed to him following me, always being there. Even when I couldn't see him, I could feel him, and it was strangely comforting. But he wasn't there now, and I was empty.

I forged on, ignoring it all. I would rise above it. Stick to the plan.

———

The bars on Port Isabel were boring. I thought I'd been sick of the spring break frenzy, but it slowly dawned on me over these weeks - I'd missed it. The air charged with sex, dreams, youthful hedonism. Skin slick with desire and smeared with lust. I missed the sea of sweaty, writhing bodies.

Mostly I missed the way his gaze would track me through those crowds. No matter how many people stood between us, his presence was always like a beacon, calling out to me. He could find me no matter where I was with those swirling, honeyed eyes.

The island would buzz and thrum around us, and he would freeze it. The buzzing in my ears and the frantic racing of my heart would bring me to the point of explosion, then he'd kiss me... and it would become still, silent. There was nothing but him. No need greater than that of *him*.

I splashed my face with cold water and stared at myself in the restroom mirror. After searching for a while and not really coming up with any answers, just the usual circling of useless thoughts — *Who are you? What are you doing here? You should be on the island... you should never go back to the island... you need him... you are stronger, you stand alone* — I sighed and made my way back out.

Rounding the corner and lost in my own tormenting inner dialogue, I bumped into someone.

"Excuse me," I mumbled, expecting them to move aside. When they didn't I looked up to find Alex in my way.

"Howdy, darlin'," he drawled, arms folded across his broad chest, leaning lazily against the door frame, filling the space.

"What do you want? Come to gloat again about stealing my bike? Or maybe to boast about the people you get away with killing? Are you going to wipe my mind, too?"

"A little cranky, are we?" he grinned. "Trouble in paradise?"

"What paradise? Turns out vampires are overrated pricks. Who knew, huh? How could the films get it so wrong?"

A soft chuckle. "Oh, you have no idea. You just met the wrong brother first."

"Get out of my way." I leveled my gaze on his, my heart racing so fast that I thought maybe the whole world could hear it.

"You can have your bike back anytime you want, you know. You just have to come get it."

As if Zac would ever entertain that idea. What an ass.

"Does he own you? Make your decisions?" he asked, his face a mask of amused serenity.

"If he did, I wouldn't be here fraternizing with the enemy."

He narrowed his eyes at that. "This encounter is on me. You don't get to claim the victory point in your own bank against him."

I clicked my tongue and moved forward, trying to get past. As my hand pressed into his chest it hit me — his power surrounded my body, cocooning me in raw energy, dark and intoxicating. I could taste it. His grin widened as I stepped back, clutching my hand to my throat.

"Why don't we go for a drink, since we're fraternizing?"

he smiled, bright and carefree. "Don't worry, I can protect you from danger better than those inadequate creatures out there."

"What? Who?" I stumbled.

"Your guards. Leon and another one, whose name I forget."

"What are you talking about?"

"Oh, you didn't realize? They've been watching your every move for weeks. Slipping into their feeble minds to distract them today was as easy as breathing. But the question is, are they here to protect you, in which case they've failed... or are they here to stop you escaping?"

Motherfucker! Zac flicked me off with that bitch vampire in front of everyone and then he didn't even have the decency to come and find me, to at least try and explain... instead he had his minions follow me around?

"I already escaped." I forced a smile. "We're not together. I moved off the island."

"Moving five miles away and spending every minute thinking about us is hardly escaping, ma'am." He cast greedy glances up and down my body until his gaze settled on my lips. At least it wasn't my neck.

"You think that's all we want?" He shrugged away from the doorframe, narrowing the gap between us. I moved back and tried to draw my own gaze away from his lips, but found his mesmerizing eyes instead, which made things worse. The most shocking electric blue, sinister, but with a sparkle of something else I couldn't place. They held me glued to the spot. I found myself wanting to reach out to him, but my scalp prickled with danger.

"Are you afraid of me?" he asked, slowly, quietly, his gaze deliberately wandering down my body again as he inched ever closer. His hand absently rubbed at his groin, his cock clearly straining hard into his jeans.

"Sorry to disappoint, but my fear radar doesn't work like it does on normal people. I like being afraid."

"Indeed you do," he drawled. "Do you love how alive it makes you feel? Or do you just crave the feeling of submission?"

I didn't move back this time, I stood frozen to the spot and he let out a satisfied grin. My hand went to my pocket and I fiddled with my mother's silver necklace. I'd pulled it from my underwear draw weeks ago and taken to carrying it around with me. I couldn't bring myself to wear it. Seeing it in the mirror, feeling it against my skin, brought back too many memories of her, but I carried it around nonetheless.

I scoffed at myself, at the notion that a tiny scrap of silver like the one clutched in my fingers could protect me from a vampire beast.

"I have no intention of killing you, Jess. It's the last thing on my mind. Well, not the last thing, but it's not at the front, and that should mean a lot to you."

My heart rattled like crazy, banging against my chest with deafening beats. Where were all the goddamn wasters when you actually needed them? If I'd been on the island, someone would have needed to relieve themselves by now and broken this meeting on their way through.

"I'm not as bad as he makes me out to be, you know. He thinks he's so pure, but he's still drinking blood. We're the same really," he shrugged, still rubbing at himself, still so close that I could feel his power sliding across my skin, making the hairs stand up.

I gave him an, '*Oh please, you must be kidding*' frown, and he shrugged again.

"So I'm a little unruly. Lucky for me you like the bad boys. He can be so dull at times, don't you think? So... controlled." He said the word like it left a bad taste in his mouth. "I'd have thought an adrenalin junkie like you would crave a little more excitement?"

"He's a vampire! Zac could be sitting in dirty jockies, picking his nose, and just being in the same room would still excite me."

He let out a laugh so deep and loud that I nearly pissed my pants in shock.

"I'll bear that in mind for when we're together. No need to make an effort, the lady ain't fussy." His drawling tone seeped through the flimsy barrier that I was trying to hold in place.

He was only an inch away. His hands went to the wall either side of my head, pinning me in place. He took a long sniff near my neck and hissed in my ear like a damn snake. I tingled from my head to my toes.

"I know he can't fuck you," he said matter-of-factly, a hand suddenly on the inside of my thigh, trailing its way upwards. "Your scent, your aura, not to mention that sassy mouth and cravings for danger... those are *my* reasons for wanting you. His run far deeper, and deadlier."

"Is that right?" I asked, my voice an octave too high.

"Ask him about sanguine mating. Fortunately, I don't have that problem. I can take you all the way and then some. I'll bang your pussy until you're begging me to stop, pounding you into submission..." His hand skirted around my thigh, brushing lightly in between my legs, before settling firmly on my hip.

Shooting sparks of desire careened off around my body. There was no reply to what he had said. I stood like a complete moron, just gawking open-mouthed at him, my lips flapping up and down like a fish, and wondering how bad it was that I felt my underwear sticking to me as I squirmed.

"Or..." he continued. "There's always the other option. It must have occurred to you that you could be like us?"

His words ran up and down my spine. No, it hadn't occurred to me. Well, maybe briefly, but I'd soon shoved it aside. Acid rose in my throat, not because I was disgusted by the idea, but because it suddenly seemed like a great one and I was a horrible person for thinking it. Why hadn't I thought more about it before? If I was like them, then Zac could be with me without needing to be so guarded.

"I know why you're doing this." I stared him down, breathing into his face as his hand crept towards my tits. I noticed that I wasn't pushing him away, and I still didn't...

"You do, huh? Go ahead, enlighten me. Sometimes I have no clue."

"You're jealous."

His hand stilled. "Very astute. I'm afraid it runs a little deeper and more complicated than that though. There's more to Zachariah than meets the eye. He has secrets and they put you in more danger than I do."

He retreated back to lean in the doorway again. "Anyway, there's some food for thought. Meanwhile, your little guards are starting to fight back against me in their heads. I guess it's time for you to go after all."

I waited for him to move, but he didn't.

"Well, excuse me, then," I urged.

He shrugged slightly away from the door, just enough that I would have to squeeze past him, too closely, touching him. He shuddered and gasped sharply as I brushed through. I was sure he'd done it deliberately, it was too theatrical. *Asshole*.

He grabbed hold of my arm and it paralyzed me like a kitten caught by the scruff of its neck.

"If you ever need me for anything, if you need my help, you call for me," he said urgently.

"Get over yourself." I gave him my best derisive look, despite my fear from his face having gone so serious.

He usually looked all happy and playful, but right then he appeared more like a fucking hell hound.

He was every kind of wrong. A cocktail of fucked-up-ness. Defcon 1 on the dangerous, badass guy scale. The more carefree he seemed, the more sinister it made him. *Psychopath.*

Another thrill ran through me, because fear didn't slap me around the way it did most people. I stomped all over its ass and generally went looking for more.

His dazzling smile returned, muttering something under his breath that I didn't catch, but I wasn't about to ask him to repeat himself. He released his grip and I got the hell out of there.

I FLED FROM THE BAR, SCANNING EVERYTHING. EVERY STREET I passed, every doorway, every window, every car. I couldn't see any signs of Leon, or anyone else that looked like a vampire. Maybe that had been bullshit, too — about them guarding me.

Why was I there, running from him? Zac had treated me like shit and I was going to let him get away with it, without explanation? Alex's little visit made it clear that I was going to have to do better than moving to Port Isabel if I wanted to be free of them.

It was all wrong and twisted. Zac was supposed to be the good guy, but he was always so serious and brooding. Moody, even. And yet by contrast, Alex – aka the bad guy — was always cheerful and carefree. Way to mess with a girl's mind.

At my apartment, I grabbed my leathers and helmet, and

jumped onto my bike. I hit the main highway, the one that went away from the island, away from this shitty mind-fuck place.

I raced past the cars, pushing ever faster. The wind howled over me, blinding me, my eyes stinging and leaking. I didn't close the visor on my helmet. I wanted the pain, the blurred vision, the adrenalin-filled rush as it swept through my veins.

I couldn't feel the throttle in my hand as I pulled it further back. The world flashed past me, so fast that my head spun. I had to wipe Alex out of my brain. I was tainted by his power. Lured and tempted like a weak, pitiful creature.

Neither of them deserved a place in my head. Not Zac, and certainly not Alex.

A car swerved and honked its horn as I screamed past. The asphalt gobbled up my emotions — gray and blurred. There was only me and my bike, forged together with the wind.

The front wheel hit a pothole. A fucking pothole on a highway?!

And then I was flying through the air, flipping over and over. Seeing sky, road, sky, road.

Bouncing and sliding. Biting pain eating through my bones.

Skidding, crunching.

A flash of bright, white light.

And nothing.

THE SMELL HIT ME FIRST. STERILE. MEDICAL. *HOSPITAL*.

I hated hospitals.

The rhythmic beep came next, and the whir of machines.

The hideous lighting that made my eyes water when I tried to open them.

His hand tightened around mine. Tingling, and throbbing.

I snatched it away.

His head sunk into his hands, leaning forward over his knees.

I tried to move, get out of bed. My leg was heavy and awkward, trapped in a plaster cast. I sunk back into the pillow with a groan.

"You broke your leg," Zac murmured.

"No shit."

"And collapsed a lung."

I loosed an angry breath, refusing to look at him.

"It's a good job you were wearing your leather pants or you'd have no skin left," he added. "Funny that... you never wear them. It's as if you knew..."

I could feel the demanding, urgent glare on my face. I turned my chin further away.

"I didn't mean for this... I only meant to race. Clear my head. What are you even doing here?"

"What do you mean 'What are you doing here?'" his voiced deepened, louder. "Where the fuck else would I be?"

"I don't know," I said through gritted teeth. "Wherever you've been hiding all these weeks like a coward."

"A coward? Jess... you have no idea."

"No. I don't. Because you haven't deemed me worthy of receiving an explanation."

He took hold of my hand again. I pulled back, but he pulled harder, keeping himself locked onto me. Waiting, until I looked at him.

I shouldn't have looked. His face crushed me. The anger, hurt, anxiety. The pleading.

His energy pulsed through me from the joining of our skin, his immortal presence making my body sing. I closed my eyes and the accident flashed behind my eyelids. The pain. The bouncing and crunching. The white light. Alex swam into my memories, merging with those of the crash. His face, his words.

I couldn't feel any pain. Why wasn't there pain?

Fuck!

I shot upright. "You made me a vampire?"

"*W*hat?!" he yelled, eyes wide. "NO! Never. Why would you think that?"

"I... I... the pain."

"You're on morphine."

"It's..." I stumbled over my own thoughts, Alex's voice in my head.

You could be like us...

Zac stiffened.

There was a knock on the door and Leon walked in.

"Zac," he said, his voice too tight.

Zac's chair screeched as it moved over the floor and crashed behind him. He disappeared from my vision and when I blinked he was at Leon's throat, pinning him to the closed door.

"You were supposed to be keeping her safe. She was with *him*?" Zac growled.

Leon made no move to resist the attack; he let his body relax, like a cat turning away to avoid a fight with another. "I swear, Zac. We were on guard the whole time. But my head, I think he slipped past my barriers. I'm sorry."

Zac loosened his grip, shaking his head. The silence around us prickled at my neck.

"You were supposed to be watching her all the time," Zac said slowly.

"Watch me? Like, spy on me? To keep me safe or to check what I do?" I demanded, remembering more of Alex's words. I wished I could scrub them away. "You made it clear you didn't want me, so I moved on. *Away*. Can I not have a life of my own without your guards?"

Zac rubbed his fingers harder over his head. "When will you understand how dangerous he is? You're in my world now, the one you insisted you wanted to stay in, remember? What did Alexander want?"

How dare he lord it over me like that. Irritation bubbled under my skin. "Nothing really, he just asked me to have a drink with him."

"And?"

"And nothing. I refused and that was that."

"That was that," he repeated, frustrated. "Fine. Whatever you say. A little reminder though — Alexander thinks it's our right to take whoever we want to feed on. To him it's no different to a lion eating a wildebeest, a fox eating a rabbit, a human eating a cow. We eat humans and *that's that*. I doubt you'll be feeling so defensive about him when he decides that you're his dinner."

After a bout of awkward tension, Zac excused Leon and the nurses came to check me over. They gave me more drugs. Then I waited for him to talk.

He knew what I needed from him. What he needed to explain. The way he'd been with that bitch, it cut so deep into my heart that the image alone made my throat close up.

"Her name was Luna. She was a scout, an agent, for the Bael. I couldn't let them know that you meant anything to me. It took me forever to get rid of them that night. And then, when I found you..." His beautiful face crumpled with anguish. "You were kissing Danny outside your motel. And I got thinking that maybe if you really did want to be with someone else then I should leave you alone. It would be good for you. So I hung back in the shadows... I..."

A tear trickled down my cheek. Why was I crying for him? There was a certain deep-rooted pain that went along with rejection. Even knowing that he wanted me, that it had been a lie, the act of rejection itself had left a gnawing pit in my stomach. I should have been crying for me, not him.

But the guilt was there, eating at me. He'd been pretending, with her. It was a show. Yet, I'd slept with Danny. It might have felt like my only option to halt the growing energy under my skin, but I'd betrayed him. In the worst way.

"I couldn't come to you. They decided to stick around and I was terrified of them following me and taking you. And after, there was so much fallout, so much shit I had to clear up. But I made... I *tried*... to make sure you were safe." His words barely more than a guilt-ridden whisper.

I believed him. I'd always known it, really. I'd known that bitch was a vampire and I'd seen the fear on his face as he'd brushed me aside. I knew it was all done for the right reasons. That didn't stop the cutting pain in my heart, though. Or the lead lining my stomach every time I thought he might disappear.

He stood over me and leant in. I opened my mouth to speak and he kissed me. Passionately. For a long time.

This was the kiss I'd wanted, that Danny didn't provide. The kind that made my knees go weak and my mind go blank. No human could kiss like that. By the time he stopped I could barely fathom what I was upset about. Wisps of worry went through me in a fleeting moment, thinking that maybe he was draining my anger with his mind control.

"This," he said, taking hold of my chin and biting my bottom lip. "This big, dirty mouth is all mine. Your lips belong to me. Understand?"

I nodded.

"Don't put me through that again, Jess," he spoke against my mouth so that I couldn't breathe. "My hold over the Beast is only so strong. If another man touches you again, do you think I'll falter before snapping his neck?"

A DAY PASSED, BUT STILL I COULDN'T STOP THINKING ABOUT IT. That bitch. *Luna*. Her hands on him. I was a hypocrite. What must he have thought about Danny's hands doing far more to me?

"The infinity tattoo on her hand," Zac said, leaning back in the plastic hospital chair and stretching his neck.

"Huh?"

"I should have told you about it before, then you might have realized. Every Bael member has a brand on the back of their hand, so they never forget who owns them, and everyone else knows, too."

"Yeah, that might have been useful info!" I snorted. "Why the infinity symbol?"

He shrugged. "It represents many things. The ever-lasting reign of the Bael, immortality, and the fact that once you commit to them, you're there forever. No one gets to leave the Bael unless they choose to release you. And that only happens if you've pissed them off or outlived your usefulness. Release generally equals death."

"What a nice bunch they are..."

Nodding, he scrubbed his chin. "If I act weird sometimes, you just have to trust me that it's for a reason."

"You always act weird," I murmured. "That wasn't weird, that was gut-wrenchingly nasty. You could have done things differently."

"It crushed me to hurt you like that, but I had to play a convincing role to them."

"But *who* are they? Why are they so important?"

He shook his head. "Emory promised to come in six weeks, but he got held up with other business. He sent her to check what was happening with the hunter situation. Alexander told her he'd killed him. He kept his mouth shut about the recent attack. As far as they knew it was over. But I fucked up..."

There was that look in his eyes again. I'd seen it briefly that night. Definitely fear.

I waited for him to continue.

"They know I never indulge in their activities or their games. Acting the way I did with Luna, it showed them I was hiding something. Then they saw you, your aura, they knew—"

"You can see my aura?" Alex had mentioned the same thing.

"All vampires can see auras. People have varying shades depending on their character, their nature, but yours... it's this pure, hyper-energy, unlike anything I've ever seen. And they knew you were different, too. They stuck around. I thought they were just messing with me, but they were gathering information. They found out that you meant something to me. I had to neutralize that threat." He flicked his gaze to mine.

"Neutralize? You killed them?" Was that satisfaction that rippled through me?

284

"Luna proved tougher than anticipated, but she eventually got what she deserved. Then I had to fix things with the Bael, explaining that Luna had encroached on my territory and made waves. That I was within my rights to take them out after they'd killed people on my island. My people. Ones I'd claimed. And it's true, they did kill people, lots of them. I didn't really care though."

That wasn't true. He cared a great deal about the people on South Padre not getting killed.

"Emory is still away. He might be for some time, but I don't think for one moment that this is over. They'll return..." He blew out a long breath before continuing. "I was trying to keep you safe. I stayed away because it's too dangerous to be around me. But then this happens..."

He gestured to me, lying in the hospital bed. "And it's nothing to do with me, or vampires, it's just you... your recklessness. Maybe you're safer with me after all."

32

JESS

*M*y bedroom at Zac's mansion was the size of my whole apartment on Port Isabel. The plush bed, covered in throws and cushions of deep red and gold, had become my prison and my freedom at the same time.

He wouldn't allow me to sleep in his bedroom with him, for fear of *losing control* with me. It felt totally wrong to be sleeping in a different room. Every night, or day, whatever the hell time it was when I tried to sleep; I lay awake, longing for him to come and join me, calling out to him. I knew he'd be able to hear my thoughts. He never came, though.

He insisted that I couldn't stay in my apartment with a broken leg, so I would stay with him. Where he could look after me. *Protect me,* said the unspoken words between us.

There were too many questions that I knew needed answers, but honestly, I didn't want them. It was easier to stumble blindly along and deal with those answers if and when they came.

Being there, in his home, was where he was the most relaxed. A great weight lifted from my shoulders. The feeling that maybe we'd be okay. That we could work through the ridiculous number of issues, one step at a time.

Danny and Anna had visited me before I left the hospital. Worry and anger seeping out from every pore, all directed at Zac. I thanked them for their concern and eventually convinced them there would be no changing my mind. I'd be living with Zac whilst my leg healed, and I would take things from there. *One day at a time.*

There was a gentle tap on the door. "Room service," the voice called.

I grinned as Zac came through, carrying a tray of toast, pastries, fruit and fresh juice.

"Careful," I warned. "I could get used to this."

"I hope so," he smiled, sinking down onto the bed.

I picked at the food — eating breakfast in the afternoon. We always stayed up talking through the night. My stomach growled with relief and appreciation as I ate.

When had *he* last... fed? Had he fed from anyone since I'd known him? Killed someone? It had been months since we met, he must surely have needed to... in all that time...

"I rarely go longer than a few days without feeding," he answered my hideous thoughts. "Since you arrived, it's daily. I have to in order to maintain some semblance of control around you."

Daily. My insides recoiled.

"But, how? Who?"

"I can't answer that right now." I think I found his evasiveness a relief for once.

"Can't, or won't?"

He rubbed the back of his neck. "I'm not ready to lose you again. Not yet."

"You say that like one day you will?" My stomach lurched again.

"Nothing lasts forever. Not even for a vampire."

We sat in quiet contemplation for some time after that statement. As his fingers brushed over mine, I began to forget what we were talking about.

The window was open and the delicate scent of honeysuckle petals swept through on the breeze, the plants growing around the sweeping veranda, clinging and climbing ever upwards in their pursuit of grander heights.

Beyond that, the grounds of Zac's estate stretched out. Ornamental gardens, fountains and swimming pools. The steady thump of music from the island bars attempted to destroy the tranquillity of his home. But it failed. There was a stillness here. Calming.

I wondered what it would be like at Alex's house. What went on inside those walls? What he did to the people that ended up there...

"You know why his eyes taunt you the way they do, right?" Zac asked suddenly.

"What?"

"It's because they're not human. Same reason my eyes have the effect they do on you. Still, that doesn't make me any less jealous about the fact you're sitting right next to me and still thinking of my brother."

"Oh, fuckflaps! I'm so sorry!" I gasped.

No matter how hard I tried, I hadn't been able to get Alex out of my mind. The same face as Zac, but with swirling blue eyes — heavy with intensity, whilst sparkling with mischief. I found myself wondering constantly about what made him so different to Zac.

"Fuckflaps?" The corner of his mouth twitched.

"I kinda have a thing for cussing. You have to be inventive when you do it all the time," I muttered.

He laughed softly, but the heaviness of his thoughts still seemed to shroud around him. Taking my breakfast tray, he set it down on the nightstand to avoid meeting my eyes.

"You know, this mind-reading thing is starting to wear thin," I said.

"I can't help it, it's part of who I am."

"You once told me that it gets distracting with all the voices, like when you have twenty groupies all drooling over you, so you tune them out and just focus on what you want to. Surely you can tune me out?"

"Why would I do that?" he asked, bemused.

"Because I asked you to."

"It's not that simple. There's something about you I don't understand myself. You consume me."

I huffed, toying with a cushion in my hands.

"Fine, I promise I'll try to tune you out a bit more. But if you could try to stop thinking about me for five minutes of the day it would really help."

And my brother, said the words that I knew floated around his head.

I tried to whack him with the cushion, but he predictably dodged it in one of his flashy vampire moves. I threw myself at him instead; a whole body would be harder for him to dodge than a cushion. A sharp stab ran through my plastered leg as I awkwardly lunged.

He didn't try to dodge this attack, catching me in his powerful arms and squeezing. I rested my ear against his chest and tried to listen for a heartbeat. There seemed to be a faint sound, but it could have been my own pulse in my ears.

"Alex told me something. Or rather, said I should ask you something..." I felt him immediately stiffen against me. He waited for me to continue. "He said to ask you about sanguine mating."

His heaved breath came, as predicted.

"Let me guess, something you don't want to talk about?"

"A sanguine mate is vampire folklore horseshit," he growled.

"If it's horseshit, why have you tensed up so much you're squeezing the air out of me?"

He startled and released the locked muscles in his arms. "Sometimes, a vampire is so drawn to a human, they can't escape the bond. They crave that person's blood so much that resisting is impossible. At least, that's the theory."

"Why didn't you tell me this before? I mean, I know you've told me how drawn you are to me, but why not tell me this? It might have helped me understand more."

"I've not even allowed myself to think about it, let alone say it out loud. That label comes with expectations. In fact, I'd just been at a Bael sanguine wedding the day you arrived on the island. I won't acknowledge my feelings for you in that way; in a vampire, ritualistic way. I want to embrace my need as your lover above all else. That nonsense about the sanguine mating would have us believe that we're fated for only one kind of relationship. One that I won't allow."

"What if you have no choice? What if you can't control it?"

"That's what I've been trying to get you worrying about this whole time, but it's a little late to start now."

A COUPLE OF DAYS LATER, HE BROUGHT ME MY AFTERNOON breakfast tray and I had a sudden urge to throw it in his face. Pent up frustration clawed behind my eyes. I'd spent the whole day tossing and turning in bed, sleep evading me, reaching out to him with my mind... pleading with him to come to me. Yet... nothing.

He eyed me wearily, as if he already knew what was coming.

"I already know how ridiculous and selfish I'm being," I groaned. "But every time I see you, or even think about you, my body cries out for your touch. I need intimacy with you. Can't we try to practice again?"

He set the tray down on a table in the corner, knowing I had no intention of eating it.

"I'm scared, Jess. In case I can't control myself. I can't let you be like—" he cut himself off and moved to the window.

"Be like what?"

He shook his head slowly.

"Did you fuck her?" I bit out.

"Who?" he asked, spinning round to face me. He looked innocent enough, but I also knew that he could compose the mask on his face without any effort.

"That vampire bitch, Luna. She was clinging onto you like you'd just made her come."

"That's nice talk, Jess, real nice. No, I didn't."

I did believe him. Really, I did. I didn't even know why I'd asked. Trying to start another argument, when things had been... calm, normal. Classic Jess move.

"I was just wondering how far your acting went to try and convince them I meant nothing. She wanted to fuck you though, right?" I pushed.

"Of course." He was so matter-of-fact it made my blood boil.

"Well, that's wonderful. Not only do I have to contend with all your followers, I now have to try and fend off the advances of female vampires, too. As if I have a chance."

He smiled then, which irritated me more. "If you didn't stand a chance then I would have fucked her, wouldn't I? But I didn't, because you're all I need. You fend them off without even realizing."

"For how long? You *can't* actually fuck me, can you? Or won't. If you vampires are as promiscuous as you say, how long is it really going to be before you jump into bed with someone else?"

That shut him up. The silence that followed made it all too clear that what I said was true and I wished I hadn't said it. What a horrible reality to face up to.

Eventually he spoke, "Firstly, let me remind you that you were the one fucking another man that night. I have women throwing themselves at me constantly and I've resisted, but you glued yourself to him the moment things got rocky."

He spoke the truth, of course. If only I could explain how I needed the sex. I needed it to calm the... weirdness. To feel in control...

"Secondly, and most importantly, I just need time and practice. Once upon a time I never thought it would be possible to resist feeding on whoever I wanted, but I learnt how to control myself. You're different, but I just need to keep working at the control and I'll get better at it. I promise that I will be fucking you senseless soon. You have no idea how much I'm looking forward to that."

"So you *do* want to practice still?"

"Very intuitive," he said, crushing his lips into mine, and making me lose my mind.

33

ZAC

*T*he warmth from the morning sun poured in through the open window, spreading across my skin. I lay next to her, the empty breakfast tray discarded on the floor. Today, I'd made an effort to adjust our patterns whilst we weren't leaving the house. She'd been exhausted last night and fallen asleep late in the evening — as she should. So I'd roused her with an actual breakfast-time breakfast.

It had been weeks since the accident, since... since I'd let this happen to her. And it had been weeks of hell, listening to her every time she was supposed to be sleeping, feeling her calling me. The battle against the urge to go to her was slowly destroying me. I wasn't sure if it had been worse when she was away in another town, or when she was right there in my house, within reach but untouchable.

Not to mention the building rage at having a hunter still taunting us, and evading every daily scan of the island. All we could find was a slight trace, an energy that didn't fit, but couldn't be narrowed down.

I was feeding way more than normal, trying to keep a

hold on all the darkness that seemed to be slipping. Tensions were too high. Having Danny still out there, carrying on with his life, didn't help. But he'd got away when Nyle distracted me, and since then I'd been so busy with Jess. The longer it went on, the harder it was to go out there and take him. With Jess back by my side I wasn't sure I could deal with the guilt of having him in my basement. Could I really look into her eyes after doing that to her friend?

He fucked her.

Yeah. I could. I would...

My cell phone buzzed, which caused both of us to glance at each other in surprise. No one called me via technology, except the woman who was sitting next to me.

I read the message and stuffed the phone back in my pocket. She tried to look like she didn't care, like she wasn't desperate to know what it said.

"Are you bipolar?" I asked.

"Fuck off! Seriously?" she glared. "I've come to expect that kind of labelling from most people, but not you. You can't be like them, you're different—"

"Relax, Jess. I'm not saying I think you are. But this text message from Anna says, 'please make Jess take her bipolar meds'. You gave Anna my number?"

"Shit-on-a-stick! Dammit, Anna, she's so dead for this." Pinkness flushed across her face and for a rare moment I wanted to smile, for real instead of pretend. "She insisted. In case of emergency. Part of her 'keeping my friends safe policy — especially the ones dating weird assholes'."

I laughed. "Very sensible, I'm glad you complied."

"So, what do you think? Are you going to tell me to take them?"

"No."

"Why?" she countered.

"Because it's not my place to."

Because people on meds taste like piss.

"Thank you," she whispered, and her hot lips swept against mine, parting eagerly for my tongue.

Had she groaned his name when he'd fucked her? When Danny had been able to do for her what I couldn't. The thought sent dark waves crashing through me.

You should have killed him already. He sullied your possession.

She panted eagerly for me, her tight little body quivering against my kisses, desperate for more. My cock hurt so badly it made me wonder if I should have jerked off earlier to ease some tension.

"I can't take this," I groaned. "I need to be inside you."

"Do it."

"I'll hurt you."

"Why can't you get it? I *want* you to hurt me." She pressed harder against me in a lusting daze. "You know I can handle a bit of bedroom roughing-up, right? I'm not scared of you, it excites me."

Fucking hell, why did she have to say stuff like that?

The Beast salivated. My cock pulsed harder against my jeans, straining into the fabric. "We both know that your fear radar doesn't work, Jess. You don't run even with the biggest threat right in front of you."

She wants you to take her. Are you not man enough to give her what she needs?

I shifted to escape the hideous light from the window, its sickening warmth making me sleepy. Then the idea hit me. Could it work?

There was one way to find out, and anything was worth a shot at this point.

"The sun," I said, standing up eagerly and taking her hand.

She looked at me like I was insane.

"Come with me. Outside." I put one arm under her legs, the other around her back, and scooped her up, careful not to knock her leg too much.

"Zac! Put me down, you can't go out there," she giggled sleepily.

"It won't kill me, but it'll weaken me. Maybe enough that I can—"

Her smile transcended the darkness, squashing it and taunting it in one move. I carried her down the stairs and outside to the pool, both of us laughing freely like young lovers.

The foolish girl and the beastly vampire who would feast on her.

THE SUN NEARLY BLINDED ME, MY PERFECT VISION BECOMING tainted. The burning buried itself into my skin, dulling my senses and slowing my mind. It felt fucking horrific; a vile brightness contaminating my core.

I carefully placed her onto a cushioned sun lounger. She laughed, spirited and free, as she hobbled up to standing and suddenly half hopped, half ran... straight into the pool. Clothes and all.

"Jess! I didn't mean—"

She surfaced, shrieking and giggling.

"Your cast, Jess!"

"Fuck the cast," she yelled, splashing water playfully over my feet.

Her body, with her wet shirt clinging to it, was a sight that threatened to devour me. Tall and lean, perfect curves.

She attempted to swim a width, her plastered leg floundering behind her, and her rounded ass bobbed below the surface in her little shorts. I needed to spank that ass, bite it, fuck it.

I whipped off my clothes and leapt in to join her, finding some relief from the sun under the water. I grabbed her as she sank under and was, I think, drowning from the weight of the cast. Pulling her back to the shallows, I stopped to stare at her.

Water dripped from her flaming hair, into her eyes. Her cheeks flushed with excitement. She looked more alive in that moment than I could ever remember. Throbbing pain hammered behind my eyes, but I could still see the vein in her neck, hear it calling me. This wasn't going to work.

She put her arms over my shoulders and kissed me. In a split second I ripped all the clothes from her body, discarding the scraps of fabric to float around on the surface. For the first time, we were both naked.

My cock pressed into her, fitting perfectly in the gap between her thighs. She floated up, wrapping her good leg around me tightly, the other poking out behind me.

I pushed against her opening and a thousand shards of darkness broke loose. I couldn't get my thoughts together. Urges to take her battled with the primal need to escape the sun and find safety. Everything tore at me. Everything hurt. But her pussy pressing urgently into me was such intense pleasure that I lost it. My fangs descended.

I couldn't let her see. She mustn't see me looking like that, strained and depraved. I darted back to the sloping pool steps, dragging her mercilessly with me, like an animal with its kill. I had hold of her neck, choking her, forcing her face downwards, away from my eyes, from my fangs.

I shoved her mouth onto my cock. She took me in whole, then drew back, licking the tip, circling her tongue around and down the shaft. She lapped and sucked at me with such enthusiasm, like she was tasting the most delicious thing ever.

Snarling darkness clawed at me.

Burning sun consumed me.

Exquisite pleasure ripped through me.

Combined, they obliterated my mind. I was lost. Buried somewhere beneath it all.

Her hot mouth wrapped around me, drawing my cock all the way in. The tip pressed against the back of her throat. I took her hair and pressed deeper. She gargled and gagged. I was vaguely aware that my grip was too tight and I managed to release her head, but she didn't withdraw. She sucked harder, faster. I grabbed my own head, fingers clawing at my scalp, growling like a demon.

Taste her... let go... feed...

I was laid bare to her. Every piece of me belonged to her. My heart, my body, my mind. Except the darkness. That was not hers to control. The Beast wanted to control *her*. To devour her.

And it would succeed. It would take over and claim her. Right now.

Let me free. Stop fighting.

I pulled on her hair, but she resisted, sucking me tight. She thought I wanted to stop her, to pull away as usual.

I wasn't trying to stop her. I just wanted her neck up higher, where I could suck on it.

Her fingers dug into my hips. My eyes widened when I tore them from her bobbing head and witnessed the full extent of the scar tissue covering her back. The scar she tried to hide. Her soft, pale skin — puckered and tight, creased and shiny. All down the right hand side of her back, across the top of her shoulder. What had happened to her? I snarled louder, wanting to take away whatever pain she'd endured.

Then she swirled her tongue around as she sucked, finding the perfect angle, suddenly hitting a spot that made me yell with rage and desire. Nothing else mattered.

Except claiming your sanguine mate. That matters most.

"Fuck, Jess!" I lifted myself upwards and she repeated the same motion as before, over and over until my balls tightened.

I needed her blood.

I needed to escape the sun.

Fuck it, I needed to come.

Pressing into the back of her throat, I climaxed loudly with a carnal growl. She didn't stop, wouldn't stop sucking, swallowing me down.

I spurted into her warmth as my own blood surged into my mouth. Disgust and pain filled me, my fangs buried into my own wrist to give them somewhere to go. Such sweet pleasure and agony, burning torture, all mixed together.

Slumping back, I pressed my palms over my eyes.

The release went some way to quelling the darkness. My fangs retracted, aching and disappointed that they hadn't tasted her, but I was more overtaken with the urgency to escape the light.

"Shit, Zac! Your skin is smoking! You're burning, you didn't tell me that would happen." She was suddenly scrambling to get up, her leg heavy and useless, weighed down with water.

"It's because I'm naked... too much skin out... less skin is okay," I garbled.

She threw my shirt over my head while I sat there, dazed and confused. Then she scrambled around, trying to fish remnants of her own clothing from the edge of the pool.

"No, don't get dressed. I haven't given you anything yet." I reached for her pussy.

"Are you joking? You just gave me something I've spent weeks dreaming about!" She gave up on the clothes and shuffled back into the house, ushering my burning body along with her.

*T*he nurses at the hospital greeted me with heavy tutting and eye rolls as they took in the sodden plaster cast on my leg. I could feel Zac's stifled laughter beside me. I bit my cheeks and tried my hardest to keep a straight face.

"Don't tell me, you *accidentally* fell into the pool, did you?" the pointy-nosed nurse asked.

"Nope, I jumped in," I beamed at her.

She huffed and fretted, muttering to herself as she replaced the cast and informed me I'd receive the bill.

Plaster cast or not, I think I could have skipped out of that hospital if Zac hadn't insisted on carrying me. I couldn't stop grinning. At least, now that his skin had stopped smoking. For a while I'd not smiled at all, watching him groan and writhe in pain. Thankfully, once we'd got back inside the house he'd recovered quickly.

It had worked. We'd been more intimate than ever. I knew this was positive. It was a good sign.

"It wasn't a victory. I mean, it was amazing, but—" he huffed, almost as loudly as that shrew-faced nurse.

"It was a huge step in the right direction."

"Really? Having a boyfriend that needs to go and burn himself in the sun just to keep a grip on the darkness while you touch him. That's good, is it?"

"Don't. Please."

"I nearly lost it. I had to bite my own fucking arm." He looked away in disgust.

"You were happy and laughing twenty minutes ago. What changed?"

"Being back here. This place. Back to reality."

"Right then, Jess. Time for a girly night." Eva appeared in the doorway, her cheery voice making Zac squirm.

She stared at him. Warning him just to try and tell her to leave. I swear silent words passed right through to each other.

He glared a while longer before conceding, "I do have stuff that needs my attention. I won't be long." He kissed me and sulked away, leaving Eva to bounce into the room.

Considering how bitchy women can be, she could have been totally pissed at the introduction of another woman to the group, but she never showed that.

She plucked red nail polish from a box and motioned for me to give her a hand. She loved red. She always had this awesome style going on; cute little corsets and dresses that accentuated her perfect hourglass figure, heaving bust, high heels, and black hair curled up with rollers and ruby lipstick.

"I take it you're from the fifties era?" I asked, as she began painting.

"I sure am," she laughed. "But probably not the century you're thinking of. Try seventeen-fifty."

"Holy shit! You look good for your age!"

I'd been floored by Zac's true age, this seemed inconceivable.

"You must have seen and done so many amazing things.

What's it like? To have seen the world change around you so much?"

"To be honest, I'm a bit blasé about all that. Yes, things have changed and I've experienced much, but at the end of the day I'm still the same person after all that time. Still just a vampire doing my thing." She gave me back my hand, already complete with perfectly painted nails.

"That can't be entirely true. You must have started out as a vampire... like, more like... you *know*? Before you got with Zac...?" It sounded offensive no matter how I tried to put it.

"You mean I must have been an evil bloodsucker once, with no regard for who I took? Sure. But just because I control it now, doesn't make me different. Not really. I am to you, on the outside, but I still have the same desires inside. Zac must have told you that already. We can't change what we are, we can only manage it better."

"So he keeps saying, but I still don't get it. I don't get why he brushes off being told that he's good. I know I can't comprehend what's inside you, but it's your actions that define who you are and he subdues the darkness, so he's good. I wish he'd stop trying to push me away."

Daily. He told me he fed daily. He wasn't lying. He wasn't *good*. When was I going to wake up to that?

"He doesn't want to, Jess. He wants to be with you more than anything. But he worries for you, and he worries for himself. And for all of us. Being involved with humans is a big deal, it rarely ends well." She gave me back my second hand.

"There's always a risk of a relationship not working and people getting hurt. But you can't choose who you fall for, you just have to go with it and hope for the best. No point worrying about shit that might not even happen," I said, surprising myself by my faith after so many miserable failed relationships.

"Hmmm." She located a hair brush from her box and sat behind me, combing through the tangles. I didn't dare point out that her pampering of me was getting a bit weird. "And the problem is, he knows that, too. I'm afraid he's been there and done that. I don't suppose he's told you that he was in love with a human before?"

"What?" I flipped round as she was mid brush and it yanked on my hair. She clucked her tongue and shoved me back around.

"Don't get your panties in a twist. Everyone has past relationships and you're no different."

"But this kind of relationship *is* different. What happened?" My stomach felt like it was caving in on itself. I wasn't sure I wanted to hear what happened. He'd surely killed her.

"That's a story for him to tell when he's ready. But it tore him apart. And that's when we met. I gave him a shoulder to cry on. He came to me on the rebound; we attempted a relationship of our own while he taught me his ways, but it was never going to work. I stayed by his side though. He changed my life and I'll always love him."

I sat quietly while she continued to brush. I couldn't hide how anxious I was feeling, my body must have given her plenty of signals, but she kindly pretended not to notice.

"You and Zac. You were together." Of course they were. It was obvious. He doted on her.

"I'm pleased you're here, Jess. He's never been happy the whole time I've known him, not really. Then he found you and over the top of all the fights and trauma, he *is* happy. He needs you. So please try and understand the difficulties that you present to him. He's working so hard to overcome them. He needs your help to make it work." She pulled harder on a knot in my hair. It made it feel like her last statement was a threat - I better not fuck him up.

304

"I WONDER HOW MANY OTHER THINGS HE HASN'T TOLD ME?" I mused, as we lounged around on a pretty polka dot blanket Eva had brought into the living room. "He must have a million secrets and know so many things that I still don't understand."

Was I pouting? Yes. I think I was.

"Has he told you about his special ability?"

"Everything he can do is special."

"I adore how love-struck you are!" she laughed. "Most of us have certain things that we excel at. Leon has a more sensitive radar for darkness; he helps us, with our food choices. Zac's is speed. We're all fast, but he's extra fast. When he wants to be, anyway. He doesn't get much chance to demonstrate it without drawing attention."

"That's cool. What about you?"

"I can manipulate people through contact with them. I mean, we all can, to a degree, but I do it best," she grinned. "If I touch them I can sway their thoughts and instincts and make them do what I want. Sometimes my persuasion is so strong I don't even need to touch them."

I'd gathered as much from watching Zac and Alex after that fire. The way they'd waltzed around leaving a bunch of confused people in their wake.

"That's not fair on the human population." I tried to think about all the times she might have touched me. Had she made me do things?

"I would never influence you. That would cross a line that Zac wouldn't forgive. We're all forbidden from messing with you."

That offered some relief, in a messed-up way. He had promised me too, that he'd never do it to me. "What about Alex?"

"He's extra powerful with his mind. He can project thoughts easier than most and get through barriers. There's a faction of the Bael that went rogue, called the Unaligned. They have a huge array of extraordinary abilities. They take on new members occasionally, training them to unearth and harness greater hidden powers. Alex has always been desperate to get in with them, since he doesn't have access to the Legacy power. One day he'll succeed, and then Zac really will be in trouble."

"It's hard to see him as someone so bad. He doesn't seem—"

"Don't judge a book and all that. Alex is an expert at appearing playful and harmless, but the depths of his depravity knows no bounds. He's a demon disguised as a man. The predator that no one sees coming."

You could be like us... Alex's voice sounded, clear as day, through my head.

"Zac's always so evasive about all this Legacy and Bael stuff," I said, suddenly not wanting to talk about Alex because my pulse had doubled in a second.

"I'm sure he'll tell you more when he's ready. It's probably safer if you know less."

"What are you doing with *her*, Eva? Come join us," came an irritated voice through the doorway.

"I'm having a girly night, Ruben. Lord knows I've earned it after all my years in this house."

He scowled at me. "Eva, seriously, come on. We're going to the dunes."

"Ruben, seriously, no."

His clothing choice continued to astound me. This big, bad giant, with his black ponytail and mustache; wearing what could only be described as breeches, waistcoat and velvet tailored coat.

He sped away on his heels, coat tails fluttering, talking to himself.

"I apologize for my brother," Eva said.

"Why does he do that?"

"He's not a people person."

"No, I mean, dress like that."

"Because he refuses to come and join us in the present day. And to wind Zac up, to act as a constant reminder that he's older than him. Basically because he's an idiot."

"He doesn't like me."

"No."

"Thanks," I laughed. "I thought girlfriends were supposed to sugar-coat it?"

"Sorry, I don't understand human interaction like that. Anyway, don't sweat it. Just avoid him where you can. I know he's my brother, but he can be a total jerk."

"I thought that was a normal trait for all vampire males?"

She paused, straight faced, before bursting into laughter with me.

BY THE TIME ZAC RETURNED IT WAS WELL INTO THE EARLY hours of the morning. I'd not long been in bed. Eva had given me an evening that far exceeded my expectations of any relationship with her. She'd opened up to me, not just about herself, but about Zac. Told me things he probably wouldn't be happy about.

She trusted me. The others in the gang... I knew they didn't. But the fact that she did, for some reason, it meant a lot to me. Women standing together I guess.

She'd apologized for the tameness of our night together and promised that once I was out of a plaster cast, she'd show me how a vampire woman did a real wild night on the island. I'd nodded enthusiastically, despite the voice in my head telling me I shouldn't know. I still didn't exactly understand the logistics of how they... sustained themselves. Chalk it up to another fact I was happy to keep in the dark.

The invisible boat upon which I stood was rocking; swaying on a swell tide of unanswered questions, fear and excitement. One little rock in the wrong direction and I was going to fall off.

Zac entered the room in complete silence; an unnatural quiet. It shouldn't have been possible to move without any noise, as if the sound itself was absorbed by his being. He crossed by the window where the moonlight illuminated that haunted face. So beautiful, so strained. He pulled his shirt off and slid into bed, tucking me into his cool body.

His chest rose and fell with shallow breaths. My fingers grazed over the tattoos on his arm. It was one of my favorite things to do — to trace those lines, feeling the hard contours of his muscles beneath my fingertips.

In the darkness, I could just make out the shapes and swirls as my eyes tracked the lines I was tracing. Such vibrant colored art, burning brightly against the utter whiteness of his skin.

The patterns began to clear and I started to pick out individual pieces from the swirling mass. A clock, a dragon, a soaring bird, and... a woman's face. Staring back at me through the gloom. I pulled my finger away sharply and he hissed a breath.

"That's her. The love of your life." My throat bobbed.

"I knew I should never have left you alone with Eva," he gritted.

"What happened to her?"

I felt every muscle in his body stiffen.

"Please don't ask me that question. Not yet."

And I could feel it. His pain. The torment. Whatever had happened with her, it meant a lot to him. His whole body radiated the suffering.

"Do not think of my suffering," he growled. "It's insignificant."

I put my hand on his chest, letting my fingers stroke across him again, until I felt him begin to soften.

"Just answer me one thing. Do you want me, because... because I remind you of her?"

"No," he said instantly. "You're nothing like her. You're so much more than she ever was, Jess. That's what terrifies me."

JESS

"I wish you'd let me do that," Zac said. "Or get one of my men to do it. You should be relaxing."

"Why?" I laughed. "Because I've become a lady of leisure? Don't be ridiculous, I love polishing my baby."

My internal body clock was now so well accustomed to the unsociable hours we kept that it didn't even seem weird to be outside tinkering with my Ducati at 3a.m, under the security light of Zac's driveway.

The gravel stretched out a long way from the high security gates near the road, passing through trees and flower beds before curving round to the front of the house. He sat on the veranda steps, leaning back against the railing, watching me work.

This was actually my third 'baby' since arriving on the island. That was probably a sign, an omen, about the crazy wreck of my life. The first one stolen by shit-for-brains, and the second completely destroyed at the same time as my leg — also partially due to the shithead twin brother. The one whose name I should never think of again, let alone speak out loud...

The insurance company would pay out, especially since

there should never have been a pot hole so big in that road, so I'd ordered a new toy which had just been delivered. I'd have to think of another name.

"I was thinking more because of the fact you have a broken leg," Zac sighed.

"Don't remind me, it's starting to drive me batshit crazy. One more week to go before I can ditch this horrendous cast."

I couldn't wait. It had been nice staying at Zac's all these weeks, having some sense of normality, but seriously? Calling this normal was a joke in itself. The time had passed in a mix of happy, loved-up playing, chatting, getting to know each other better — interspersed with awkward periods of heavy talk about how wrong it all was, about the danger, the hardship of it all.

His gang had an uncanny ability to disappear at the right times. No doubt thanks to him planting that message firmly in their minds without even speaking. One minute they'd be relaxing in the living room with me, the next there would be a moment of tension and they'd vanish.

I needed to get back outside, into the real world. It didn't *feel* real out there any longer, not when I studied every face on the street wondering if they were human, but still... I had to get on with it. Make life happen around this new world. Blend the two together. Danny had been sending me regular messages with updates on the crew. They were looking forward to my return to work.

"Fine. I won't argue any longer because the view of you trying to bend over is impeccable." Zac tilted his head to the side and ran those brooding eyes up and down my body.

I wiggled my ass at him playfully, if only to soften the blow of what I was about to say to him.

"So, Anna called earlier." I continued moving the cloth over the tank in a slow, sultry manner. "There's this party event thing over at Port Isabel tomorrow night. She wants me to go along and meet this new guy she's dating. I'm going to limp along on my crutches. Want to come?"

I'd asked as nonchalantly as I could, but really, the thought of a double-date; Zac having to sit and make small talk with some guy, whilst I tried to prevent anything vampire related slipping out of my mouth — well, it didn't sound like huge fun, but this wasn't about me. I was curious to find out why Anna had ditched William - and slightly relieved, he creeped me out — and I'd been dodging her for far too long. I couldn't keep hiding. I needed to show my face, put her fears to rest, and hope that she'd forgive me for being such a shit friend.

"Off the island?" he asked.

"Yes."

"There's not enough parties here for you?"

"Yes, but she wants to go to *this* one."

I set the polish down, ready for the battle.

"Then she can go," he stated.

"Excuse me?"

"You aren't going."

"The hell I'm not."

"Jess," he sighed. "It's not safe. There's still a hunter out there. Not to mention that Port Isabel is neutral ground. I can't stop Alexander's gang from going, and I guarantee that if he gets wind of you being there, *he* will be there."

"Why?"

"Because messing with me is his favorite hobby."

"Grow up, Zac! You guys can play your little games if you like, but I'm going. I already promised Anna and I wasn't asking your permission. I haven't been the greatest friend lately. I need to do this. If you're that worried then come along and protect me."

"Games? This is no game, Jess. Have you not figured out who had that bungee cord damaged?"

His words caused my legs to instantly buckle. I caught the handlebar of my bike to steady myself.

"What did you say?" I panted.

"Shit, Jess, I don't want you knowing this stuff."

"Alex tried to kill me? That's... it can't be. We were miles off the island. It was just some nutjob."

"Why are you so quick to defend him? To deny what he is?"

I shook my head. The Alex that had spoken to me, he was dangerous, yes. But his eyes always held something else for me. He wouldn't have done that. If he wanted me dead, he could easily have done it by now. Why would he resort to something like a dodgy bungee cord? Surely he'd sooner take me himself.

"You're analyzing the reasoning behind why my brother would like to kill you?" He raised his eyebrows.

"I'm just going on the information you've given me; that all vampires, particularly the bad ones, are blood-crazed lunatics with no self-control. And that doesn't match the man who found me alone on Isabel and could clearly have killed me. I'm going to the party."

"Please don't make me force you to stay," he whispered, as if the fight had gone from him, even though the words suggested far from it.

"If you do that, I will leave this place for good. I won't be a prisoner here. I'm not your pet that you can keep under your command. That shit stays in the bedroom, not outside."

"You wouldn't," he said with confidence, his eyes narrowing nonetheless.

"Try me."

WE DROVE TO THE PARTY IN THE BACK OF ANNA'S CAR IN stony silence. Damn, I missed riding my bike so much. The second this cast was off I'd be tearing up the asphalt. I shifted, totally uncomfortable. There wasn't room for my leg in the foot well, so I was sitting sideways across the back seat, my leg stretched across Zac's lap. He refused to touch it, to touch me. Anger pouring from him.

I felt bad for Anna. It was supposed to be fun and she had a couple of sulking teenagers in the back. James, the new boyfriend, sat in the front passenger seat fiddling with his fingers. What must he have thought of us? He seemed nice enough. A little quiet, but that could be forgiven considering the awkward tension in the car.

I resolved that we — myself, Anna and James - were going to enjoy ourselves, and Zac could mope all he wanted on his own. His gang were already there when we arrived, he wasn't taking any chances. He stormed over to them and I ushered Anna and James off in the opposite direction.

Zac refused to let me out of his sight, but at least he stayed a small distance away and let us chat on our own. Mind you, I supposed he could still hear us. Bloody vampires.

"You've had another fight then?" Anna asked.

"I'm so sorry. I don't want to spoil our night. Just ignore him like I am," I said as jokily as I could, waving a hand dismissively in Zac's direction.

"Why on earth are all his roomies here as well? Can't he go anywhere without them?"

How was I supposed to answer that? It certainly did look crazy. Thankfully, James came to the rescue by changing the subject, enquiring about my line of work. We talked for a while and I found out all about his life. Gradually Anna turned the conversation more and more onto me and James gave up, sitting back in his chair and taking an interest in the surroundings whilst we caught up.

She had a lot of questions about what sort of things Zac and I had been up to over the last month. It was hard to know what to tell her when so much of it revolved around him being a vampire. I dodged and skirted as best I could. It must have been so convenient for the vampires. You didn't like the questions someone was asking? Just pop into their head and make them change. Would the human feel it, I wondered? Since I knew they were vampires, would I feel it if one of them tried to change my thoughts?

Tonight's obvious issues weren't helping to ease Anna's mind. She delicately tried warning me to keep out of trouble. I spent a while assuring her that we were just working through some relationship kinks, but that he was a lovely guy normally. She looked over at him, scowling.

Sure. He didn't look too nice and normal right then, the way he and his gang were watching over us like freakish bodyguards.

When James got up to fetch more drinks I took the opportunity to change the subject. "What happened to William? I got the impression you had a serious thing going on with him?"

"Sssh," she whispered, glancing to check where James was. "Why do you think I set this date up off the island?! I can't have them bumping into each other."

"You're fucking two guys?" I squeaked, causing even Zac to raise his eyebrows from afar.

"Just until I can decide which is the right one," she grinned, and a bubble of tension popped. "William has issues of his own. He has some warped ideas, but I can't help wanting him, despite it."

I cocked my head. Anna the Hypocrite. She acknowl-

315

edged my thoughts with a small shrug, a blush spreading over her cheeks. Laughing, I patted her knee.

Zac soon brought me back down with a bump, staring at me in glum concentration. I was returning his cold stare when he bristled and looked away. I was almost too scared to turn, but when I did, I found the eager, amused watch of Alex.

I threw my head back down before Anna could notice what was going on. During the course of our conversation I kept glancing up to check what was happening, but it was always the same; Zac and his gang poised and tense, watching me and watching him. And when I had the guts to look at Alex, he was always staring at me intently, not dissimilar to the way Zac watched me, but with more humor on his face.

Then a memory popped into my head out of nowhere, so blindingly real that for a moment I couldn't breathe — Alex bursting into my room armed with a seductive smile and a gun. A gun that he used to claim me. To own me in the most erotic way.

Did he...? Had we...?

I felt the color drain from my face. I sought out his gaze and found it burning holes through me. He could manipulate memories. He could get into my head. It had felt so real. *Was* it real? My stomach churned with horror and thrill.

The edges of his mouth lifted in amusement. The images flickered on repeat through my mind. His cock down my throat... his body straining over me, trailing the gun between my legs... my total submission as I cried out his name...

Anna slipped off to dance with James and I felt like bait, sitting there helplessly waiting for one of the Elwoods to come and snap me up before the other could. Shivers wandered down my spine.

Alex was like a pimp; women draped all over him, unnaturally close to them. I tried to imagine how I would have viewed the picture before I knew — it was creepy and lecherous. But I did know what he was and it made it even worse. He was pulling them in so close because he was smelling them. Would he kill them? Would one of those women die tonight?

My chest tightened, a sudden bout of panic threatening to break free. Despite Zac regularly drumming it into me, I hadn't allowed myself much thought about that side of things. I just couldn't imagine him actually killing anyone. But seeing Alex like that, it was bringing home some truths. I had to start facing up to what he was, to what they all were.

Alex never took his eyes off me as a woman licked his neck. And the memories wouldn't fuck off. I tried to think about something else, but all I could see was him in my room. All I could feel was his hands on me, rough and controlling.

I had to find out whether it was real, or whether he was just screwing with me. I also had to warn those women to get away from him. I couldn't just sit there and let them get killed.

Zac appeared in a blink - I'm talking an irritating magical puff — sitting next to me before I'd taken another breath. I hoped to hell he hadn't just crossed the room with his vampire speed, but no one seemed alarmed.

"Don't even think it, Jess, you're not going over there."

"I have to warn them. How can you sit here and let him do this?"

Daily. Zac feeds daily. Push him on it, Jess. Fuck Alex, grow some balls and ask him to explain his own feeding habits!

"Do what? Has he killed anyone? His only crime so far is projecting your thoughts on to me. You've been obsessing

317

over him all night. Are you purposely trying to drive me insane?"

"Shit. I don't mean to. What thoughts?" I scanned the crowd, checking that Anna was still safe and hadn't been snatched off by a vampire. It also allowed me to avoid Zac's eyes, since he was surely about to blow-up at the notions of me and Alex in some kinky edgeplay.

"Thoughts you have about wanting him."

"Oh." I waited for the big revelation, but it didn't come, and I blew out a breath I'd been holding.

There was no use trying to hide it anyway. My heart was racing and they could see it as clearly as I felt it. I was so drawn to Alex at that moment, the very air around us seemed thick, suffocating, pulling me towards him. It was seriously unfair to have them both knowing my thoughts before I could even fully decipher them myself.

"With age a vampire can learn to keep his thoughts hidden from other vampires. We can lock ourselves down," Zac said.

"How nice for you. How does a human go about creating that lockdown?"

"They can't," he smiled apologetically. "We can all get into heads and alter a train of thought, wipe some memories, but Alex is stronger. He can take whole thoughts, memories, and project them on to someone else. You have to be careful doing that with a human though, it can easily frazzle a mortal mind. I knew someone once who used to love projecting and watching the human fall apart and go mad. That was back when mental asylums were places full of torture. He worked there, carrying on the suffering. He stopped finding it so much fun when they became just padded cells."

"That's a lovely anecdote, Zac, you should tell it at every party you go to!" My stomach flipped, because on cue my mind was bombarded with more visions of Alex with his gun. I could even remember the way it tasted when he'd ordered me to lick the barrel—

"What the fuck?!" Zac disappeared from the seat beside me, moving towards Alex, this time definitely too fast for public viewing. He practically teleported there. They collided, and tumbled backwards out of the side door.

I HURRIED OUTSIDE AFTER THEM BUT ONLY FOUND A BUNCH OF people, no vampires anywhere. Spinning around, I marched up and down the area, calling Zac's name, fear increasing the weight in my steps with every passing minute.

This was very fucking bad.

I didn't know why I felt guilty, it was just a dream, right? And if it was more, well, it was still on Alex and not me—

Zac re-appeared with a bloody nose and a torn shirt.

"Zac!" I rushed to his side and stopped short when he gave me an icy glare.

Taking a deep breath, he leant over the railing. I followed suit and we watched the leisurely comings and goings of the town — twice the size of South Padre, yet half the madness. A smartly-dressed couple walked past, arm in arm, on their way to dinner maybe?

"Dare I ask what that was about?"

"Nothing," Zac replied.

"Nothing?"

"That's right, nothing. Just like you told me when I asked what he'd said to you."

"Zac—"

"What?" he snapped, whirling on me. "Why are you even asking? What do you *think* that was about? He's made a direct play for something that's mine."

"It was just a dream, a head-fuck—"

"Was it?"

I tried to talk. Stuttered. And tried again. "Wasn't it?"

He dragged a hand through his hair. "I don't fucking know!"

I stared out at the town, willing my stupid heart to calm down.

"Have I not told you enough times how dangerous he is, Jess? I don't want him anywhere near you. Don't ever approach him. And for fuck's sake, tell me if he messes with your head again. Right?"

I wondered if now was a good time to remind him that warning me away from danger usually sent me right into its awaiting arms.

His answering glare and snort told me that I didn't need to tell him, because he'd just read it in my mind.

I should have told him to stuff his orders up his ass, but found myself nodding instead.

"There are certain protocols that we're supposed to follow, you know," he mumbled.

"Who, twins or vampires?"

His lips twitched in the smallest smile. "Vampires. The Bael is the governing body that enforce them. Most of the older vampires still live by the rules. But the younger ones, they often don't care for them. And nor does Alexander."

"Where do you fall?"

"Somewhere in the middle, I guess. We're relatively young, but I still have a certain amount of respect for the way things should be. That said, I have zero tolerance for the Bael, and I don't follow my instinct to feed on who I want which is frowned upon. So under some laws I guess it makes Alexander the good guy and me the rebel," he laughed bitterly.

"What are the other rules?"

320

"We're not supposed to kill our own kind, but that gets broken all the time. I've no doubt it will be broken between me and him at some point. Soon."

"Don't say that."

He shrugged dismissively. "We must not expose our true identities to a human and let them live, or remember. Oh, crap..." He looked at me intently. "Seems I'm more of a rebel than I thought."

Before I could say anything, he continued, "What else... a vampire must never take a mortal that has already been claimed by another, meaning Alexander should stay away from you, but he won't."

These rules were making me feel more and more like throwing up. I think he noticed because he stopped talking for a while. I watched diners through windows at a restaurant across the street. Chatting, eating their meals, laughing. So normal.

"You asked," he said, once the quiet got uncomfortable.

Looking at him and trying to comprehend the years he'd been alive and the things he'd seen and done was impossible. He didn't look like a monster, he was too damn sexy for starters.

"That's our weapon against you, remember? Even now, as I'm telling you how I'm supposed to kill you, or that my brother might, you're thinking about my body instead of the danger you're in."

"You promised you'd never mess with my thoughts, but you're happy to keep letting yourself in to read them? You said you'd stop that," I scowled.

"I'm trying, but I'm too tuned in to you. I don't come snooping for them, they just come to me."

I grunted in response.

"Long ago, vampires could read all minds and all thoughts, but over time the genetic trait changed," he went on. "We believe it's because hearing all those thoughts was so distracting, and with us being such a narcissistic species, vampires began filtering out anything that didn't concern them. I suppose in the end, the part of the brain that picked up on other stuff just stopped working. Mostly."

"Mostly?"

"Some of us can tap into it better than others. I can hear bits of other thoughts sometimes, but it's not consistent and I have to work at it, so it's not usually worth the effort. Like some humans are good at certain things, maybe sport or math, or dancing..." he smiled appreciatively at my hips, "some vampires excel at controlling different areas of their mind. Leon has a unique ability for sensing darkness and evil."

"That must be pleasant."

Didn't he ever have anything nice to talk about? What were those couples in the restaurant discussing? Their days at work, how nice the food was, vacation plans, bills...

"It's useful," he said. "It's like he has a built-in radar, he can feel the darkness from miles away. We follow his radar and when he's close enough to the person he can not only feel their thoughts, he can see them. If that's all they are, just thoughts, then we leave. But we keep watch on them, waiting to see if they ever decide to act on their desires. If he can see that they've already acted and killed before, then we take them. That's how we find our food."

Oh jeez, this conversation was getting out of hand. My legs wavered as I leant into my crutches.

"You need to know this stuff. You want to start getting back on with normal life, melding our worlds together? This is who I am."

"It's fine," I lied. He was right, I did need to know and I couldn't show any doubts or he'd use it as an excuse to try and separate us again.

"It must get confusing, what with all the other vampires on his radar," I said.

"He can feel the difference between human and vampire thoughts. No human can even comprehend the depravity that a vampire can feel—"

"Fuck, Zac! I'm trying here, but do you have to keep pushing the point? I get it! You're bad, you're evil, you're a vampire. Enough already."

He stared at me, hard. Fine, back on with the pleasantries of vampire education then. "So, with the way you guys live, Leon is really central to your gang? Without him you couldn't find the murderers?"

"We can do it without him, but it takes more work. I can still sense darkness in people, in their aura. I can pick up a vibe and tail them to see what they're up to. But I can't be as selective. Despite what the media depict there actually aren't that many murderers running around. So if I'm on my own I'll take rapists, wife beaters, pedophiles."

"So... you told me you feed daily. There can't be that many bad people running around the island?"

There. I did it. The question was out again and he was going to have to answer.

"I told you I used my chopper for business," he shrugged. "It gets us around when necessary."

"But, every day?" I scrunched my face.

"You don't need to know those details, Jess. Enough," he warned, the threat in his voice enough to let me know that I really didn't want to know. His hand brushed over mine and an alarm went off somewhere in the back of my mind, telling me to push him on the issue, whilst another voice urged me to let it go.

"Why limit yourselves to murderers? Why not always take those other bad guys out, too."

"My Cell isn't here to help humans. We don't care what

humans do to other humans. We try to live some sort of moral life to make ourselves feel... something. So we select the top rung of scum on the ladder. But it's hard to reconcile taking out people who have committed less crime than you have and still take a moral high ground about it."

"That depends how you look at it. I don't see pedophiles as committing less of a crime than murder."

"This is a dodgy area for us to get into. I don't want to discuss the rights and wrongs of who I kill. Focus on the word kill. I do that, because I'm a dark, evil, self-centered being."

"Yes," I sighed. *And ever-dramatic.* "You've told me once or twice. Except you're describing *them*, other vampires, but you and your gang aren't like that."

"How do you know? I could be lying to you. I could be just as bad as the rest of them," he paused. "I *am* just as dark as them, I am *them*. I do a good job of hiding it and keeping it locked down, but I don't know when it might surface again. Anything could trigger it. I've slipped up a number of times."

"Slipped up? As in—"

"As in killed people I shouldn't have. Innocent people."

"But that was before you changed, right?"

I struggled to maintain the casual façade that everything he said was fine.

"Finally, you're afraid," he sighed.

"I like being afraid. That's why I do all the crazy things I do."

"Fear when you're racing your motorcycle, or jumping out of a plane, that's one thing. But being afraid of your boyfriend because of what he is, what he can do, that's not right."

*F*ear; An unpleasant emotion caused by the threat of danger, pain, or harm.

Unpleasant.

It was supposed to feel horrible, to keep us safe. Our body's way of keeping us away from danger, forcing us to retreat to safety.

And yet, my pull toward it ensured I flitted from one fearful event to the next, bounding along like a sick little lamb in the spring grass. It didn't matter if the result left me crashing down in an anxiety-riddled low. I'd still pick myself up and carry on, treading the same paths, looking for something more.

Which was probably why I found myself, once again, lounging around in the vampire's lair, persuading myself not to have a shred of regret.

I hated to admit that anything to come from my father's lips could be accurate, but maybe when he'd told me for the thousandth time that I wasn't wired right... he was onto something.

Fear and anger released that buzzing in my head, the

thrumming under my fingertips. Did I seek that out? The release of that energy?

I drew my arms around myself. That energy was not something I should go looking for. It caused pain. Even death.

We kill murderers... Zac had said.

He killed murderers.

I was a murderer. I shouldn't be around. I should've died too.

My dad was an asshole. I was never good enough, he always expected more from me. The amnesia after the explosion was true. I didn't know what we'd been fighting about that day. But I did know that the explosion wasn't some random, freak incident. Well, it *was* a freak incident, but one I'd somehow caused.

Such painful memories. Keeping them suppressed had been essential. I couldn't bear having them on the surface, creeping around my conscience, breaking me down.

I reached to scratch the itching scar on my back. Zac's contemplative gaze slid across to follow my fingers where they rubbed and clawed.

Please don't ask me. Don't ask...

The smallest, almost imperceptible nod from him.

"Have you always been obsessed with danger?" he asked.

"I'm not obsessed." *Lies.*

He smirked at me. "No? Fast motorcycles, poker hustling, firefighter, hanging out with vampires?"

I smirked back. "You're not dangerous, you just like to think you are." I stretched out my leg, basking in the freedom now that my cast had finally been removed.

He shook his head, dismissing my joke. "You're in a perpetual state of excitement, your body forever on the cusp of fight or flight. Heightened adrenalin. When the hormone levels dip, you start craving more. You're so hyped-up all the time, you make a vampire giddy," he drawled, trailing a finger lazily around my stomach.

I wondered why he didn't allow himself to taste more of the wine if he was such an alcoholic.

"Well, since you have me all worked out, I'll admit — do you know why I took my job at the fire department here?" I mused, daring to lift a hand and stroke idly at the top of his chest.

"Because it's the number one hotspot for nubile young things looking for a good time?"

"Well... yes, obviously. But mostly because my psychic said *not* to come. That something dangerous was going to happen. So I made up my mind instantly that I'd come. I had to know what this dangerous thing was. How crazy is that?"

"I think it's more crazy to live your life based on what a phony psychic tells you."

"She's not fake. She always gets stuff right and she got this right, didn't she?"

"You could put just about anything that happens here into the dangerous bracket, even without meeting me. You see what you want to see. There's plenty of action around here that could be considered dangerous. And with you, since you radiate towards peril, she was bound to hit something."

"Wow. The mind-reading supernatural being is a sceptic about someone else's psychic abilities."

"Humans don't have powers. They're just human. Well, most of them..." He tightened underneath me.

The issue we never talked about.

He knew. He knew that I wasn't normal. How long would he let it go before he started pushing me on it?

"Maybe she isn't human." I said. "Maybe she's a vampire and I never knew."

"A vampire would not cheapen themselves with a career as a fortune teller," he scoffed. "But, talking of dangerous things, I've been meaning to show you something."

We passed down the hallway and I paused outside a door. Up until the other night, I'd never seen any of them use it and had assumed it was just a storage cupboard or something. But I'd seen Leon come through it, and I'd been meaning to ask every time I went past, but always got distracted.

"What's with this—" I began. Zac turned and rested a hand on my shoulder, kissing my lips softly.

"Come, Jess, I need to show you this," he murmured in my ear. My hand fell from the door and I followed him through to the garage.

I knew it was big from what I'd seen outside, but he'd never taken me inside before. When he opened the door and flicked the lights I couldn't believe how massive it was, more like a barn. The smell of gasoline and polish shot up my nose, which I stuck in the air, inhaling noisily. Damn, I loved that smell.

A row of motorcycles stood along one wall, there must have been twenty of them, alongside several extremely expensive-looking sports cars.

"These aren't all yours?" I began walking towards a set of sleek yellow wheels, when he pulled me over to a tarpaulin in one corner.

"Yeah, but that's not the surprise. This is."

With a lightning flurry he pulled the cover away to reveal the most sublime machine imaginable. I glanced at him incredulously, his face full of pride and wonder, before I was drawn back to the other sexy thing in the room.

"Fuck me sideways! That's a Dodge Tomahawk?" I gasped, darting my hand towards it before pulling back, too afraid to do so.

"Go on, you can touch. Sit on it."

Before he could change his mind, I swung my leg over and caressed the dazzling silver metal. It was beautiful, a work of art. Technically, not really a motorcycle since it had four wheels, but they were so close together that it was still motorcycle shaped — a huge, monstrous machine. *A piece of automotive sculpture*, as I'd heard it described before.

It was like something out of a movie, a vision of futuristic transport. The sort of machine that sent grown men weak at the knees and made them talk bhp and torque. I was no exception, I just happened to be female.

"But I thought it was a concept bike, that they never made any more?"

"It is. They didn't. I had to spend a lot of money."

I let out a long whistle under my breath. I could only imagine how much a *lot* was, but I guessed at least half a million.

"It's not even road legal," he went on. "They didn't intend for it to be ridden much, it was never tested fully at speed. You can barely turn the thing round a corner and the tank only holds just over three gallons."

"But you didn't buy it for cruising round town, huh?"

He flashed an enormous smile. "Exactly. That's a V10 engine in there. Nought to sixty in two point five seconds. Top speed of nearly four hundred. The strip isn't long enough to get any more than a fleeting glimpse at that speed, but it's good enough. It's the only thing fast enough to give me a decent buzz."

"And you call *me* crazy?" My head shook in disbelief.

I wondered how much money they spent on bribing the police to turn a blind eye to their activities, to ignore a

Dodge Tomahawk tearing up the strip. Anna had hinted before about the amount of money the Elwoods had, of the rumors about how vast the sum was. Unless, they used other methods...

"They're not even close. It's more money than they dream about," he said simply, cutting off any thoughts of other vampire persuasions.

"So why do you live *here*?"

"You don't like it here?"

"Well, yes, but if I could choose anywhere in the world I think it would be somewhere else."

I'd had so many dreams as a college student, all the places I would go – Australia, Africa, Tokyo...

"It suits us here. The smallness. The atmosphere."

"How long have you lived here?"

"A while."

"Don't people notice... the not aging thing?"

"This island might be rammed to capacity, but the number of people who actually reside here long term is very small. We—" he paused. "Keep them from noticing."

The mind-fucking. The money didn't work for everything, then.

"Besides—" he suddenly seemed distracted and trailed off, staring at me intently. His eyes focussed on my hands which were absently caressing the shiny metal. He looked back up to my face and I saw the hunger, the dark lusting. Fear and arousal battled with each other inside my chest.

"Time for you to get off the Dodge now," he said sternly.

Disturbed by the sudden change of mood I said, "Don't panic, tempting as it is, I'm not going to steal this one from you."

"Seriously, you have to get off. Seeing you astride it, stroking it like that..."

In the next breath I was pinned over the hood of a blue car.

MY HEAD SPUN FROM HIS HUNGRY, ROUGH KISSES, SENDING fuzzy sparks through my vision. One hand held me down, while the other found its way under my top, and I whimpered as he found my nipple.

He pushed my legs up so that I was fully laying across the hood, eagerly spread for him, his urgent hands yanking my jeans down.

"I believe I owe you a sexual favor," his deep voice rumbled over me, and I felt him everywhere — the need, the ache. I didn't understand what had caused him to lose his usual restraint, but I groaned his name in the hopes of keeping him going.

He started at my ankle, planting kisses and nibbles up my calf and inside my thigh. My hips wriggled, squirming with too much pleasure, his lips tickling and teasing.

Licking upwards, he continued ever higher until his tongue brushed past the sensitive bundle of nerves between my legs, before continuing the teasing assault down my other leg, nuzzling my inner thigh. His tongue was so cold it felt like ice trailing over my skin. My toes curled, my legs pressing together against his head. It was too much...

"Zac! Please!" I cried.

He pushed against my knees, opening me back up. In an instant his tongue was there, licking right where I needed him the most. I screamed out at the pleasure and grabbed his hair, eager to keep him in place. He obliged, sliding a finger inside as his tongue continued to flick over my clit.

Slowly, so slowly, he added another cool finger, delving deep inside me, making me feel like I needed to pee and explode with ecstasy at the same time. The rhythm increased, harder and faster. His tongue lapped at me with unrelenting rhythm, along my opening, and then inside, roaming where his fingers had been.

I was a slippery mess, writhing around on the metal hood. I struggled to keep myself from kicking him away and demanding his cock. It wasn't enough. Because it was *too* much. Too intense. Too patient. Too fucking amazing. I needed release...

He found my clit again and sucked. My body arched upwards, yearning to be whole with him. Images flashed behind my eyelids, all the things that I wanted him to do to me. The hard fucking I needed.

"Jess," he groaned against my opening, my name leaving his lips with heated urgency.

He bit me. *There*. I didn't know if it involved fangs. I didn't even care.

I screamed his name and it seemed to echo back to us through the garage.

"Come for me," he growled, nipping, sucking, licking. His movements swift, precise, brutal in their assault on my most sensitive spots.

The submissive in me just loved being ordered to come. That authority, the masculinity, owning me...

Another few moments of screaming his name and I climaxed loudly against his mouth, my whole body bucking and quivering.

He rose, looming over me, and yanked me to the edge of the hood, grinding into me. I wrapped my legs around him, wriggling my wet core all over the straining bulge in his jeans.

Through his panting, he was groaning and growling, all at the same time. A carnal noise. He didn't look like a beast;

he looked so fucking hot that I could think of nothing other than having him inside me.

Bending down, his tongue roamed every part of my mouth, giving me a taste of my own flavors.

I gripped his biceps, bulging and solid. He was huge, as if he'd somehow grown even bigger in that moment, advancing on me and dwarfing my small frame. Fisting a handful of my hair, he growled in my ear, his cock pressing between my legs with ever increasing need.

Shoving my top up, he sucked mercilessly on my nipples.

"Zac!" I groaned.

He knew what I needed. He stepped back and unbuckled his belt. The look on his face froze my heart. Angry and needing. Was he going to hurt me? My pulse quickened.

His forehead crumpled and he stopped himself. Instead of filling me with his cock, fulfilling my every need, he stepped back.

No! No...

I reached forward desperately, pulling him back to me, burying my face into his shoulder.

"I need you," I whispered, grabbing his ass.

He pressed his lips to the soft spot between my neck and shoulder, and my body sung with satisfaction. His tense posture said that he wanted to retreat, but his lips told a different story.

Suck it. Please. Suck me.

I drifted further away on the ecstasy, when I was rudely brought round by a raging shout and the sound of crunching metal.

My eyes opened cautiously to find that he was standing beside the car, his body convulsing in gasping breaths. I tried to take in all the little bits of information that my brain didn't want to read; the huge dent in the car next to me, his bleeding knuckles and, holy shit, his fangs.

"Did you just punch the car?" I squeaked, my voice nearly leaving me.

His face was so sombre that I didn't know what else to say. He'd taken me to heaven, but now he was scaring me. Not because I didn't feel safe, but because I knew what this meant. He thought he was losing control and he was going to pull away.

"I'm sorry," he muttered.

"Why? I was having the time of my life before you decided to trash your very expensive car. Please continue. How do you want me? Like this?" My thoughts stopped coming in the right order, the way they did when I was exhilarated. I was still lying over the car with my jeans at my ankles, fully exposed.

"Or like this?" I scrambled around onto my knees and wiggled my backside at him, giving him full access. I peeked under my arm to look back, and heard him groaning as he left the garage.

"Both," he moaned, not looking back.

"Before you open your mouth, would you please try thinking about it first for a change? *Really* think about it before you let those words come out. This isn't a game, Jess." Zac was so full of angry tension that little veins had risen around his temples.

I paused, playing along, even though we both knew I wouldn't. It was all I could think about.

You could be one of us...

"I know it's not a game," I said. "You've obviously heard me thinking it, so is there any point in me even saying it?" I

334

only hoped he hadn't managed to pick up on anything in my head that would remind him it was Alex who'd suggested it.

"No, there isn't, so don't do it. Once you say it out loud, it's real. I'm begging you not to. We can forget about this and you can say something else, like *let's go for a ride* or *did you see that thing on the news today about blah blah*. I don't care, just make it anything but that."

I studied his face hard. The perfect angles, strong jaw, dark piercing eyes that were pleading with me for the impossible. Desperation.

How could I change my mind about what I suddenly wanted more than anything in the world? Sure, I knew he was right and that I *ought* to change my mind, but how could I? I needed to be with him more than I'd ever imagined possible. It was simply incomprehensible to imagine life without him, and yet I was sure that he would soon slip away from me.

And how could I explain that there was something inside me that craved the dark and dangerous? That fantasized about things no normal person should want. That maybe he wasn't the only one with darkness inside him, because I felt it beckoning me every day... and I couldn't blame that on being a vampire.

I'd thought about this over and over. I tried not to, I tried to forget the whole idea, but those words kept ringing through my head. So loud, so clear, as if Alex was right beside me, whispering them into the heart of my consciousness.

I wasn't afraid of what I was going to ask him. I was only afraid of his answer.

I took a deep breath and took the plunge. "Make me a vampire."

*H*e cracked his knuckles in exasperation and marched to the sofa, where he perched on the edge, head held in his hands.

"You're insane," he said quietly, after an eon of silence.

"I know," I replied, sitting next to him. "That's why you like me, right?"

He didn't answer, so I waited patiently until he was ready. Well, I say patiently, really I think I was just too scared to say anything more. The gap between us was widening when I so desperately intended for it to get smaller. It was too late now, he knew what I wanted and he was going to have to deal with it, one way or another.

"You can't ask me to do this." He took my hands into his.

"Why? Are you afraid of something so permanent and committed? You're used to being a bachelor after all." I tried to laugh.

"Don't be ridiculous, this isn't like marriage. I wish it was, that would be easy. I'm bound to you in ways not even human. Saying yes to this would be selfish. I'd be taking away your humanity because of my own desires to have you."

"How can it be selfish if it's what I want? I've chosen this. Me. I need to be with you, but I feel I'm losing you. We fight every day over the same thing. Something that can be fixed."

"You don't understand what you're asking for. It's not glamorous, it's not fun."

"Unrivaled good looks, immortality, strength and power? What's not to like about that?" I slapped myself as the words came out. It hadn't sounded that naive in my head.

"Burning hunger, eating through your veins every day like acid. The darkest monster inside you, tearing to be let out." His hands had tightened around mine and I shifted uncomfortably. He released me with a start and sat back.

How could I explain that I still wanted it, after what he'd just said?

"Myself, my Cell, we hide that part of ourselves really well. You think I'm perfect and that I have it all. Please understand, what I am on the inside is not pretty. I'm only good at keeping it under control because I've had so many years of practice. You'd be raw and new and wild. The hunger would drive you to things that you can't comprehend."

"But you'll be there for me. You'll help me to become like you. I don't care about the pain, it cannot be as bad as the pain of losing you."

"That's absurd."

"Losing me won't cause *you* pain?" I retorted.

He wrinkled his face, "More than I could handle."

"Well, then. We both agree that we can't stand to be apart, so let's be together. We'll be together, so we'll be alright. More than alright... we'll be happy."

"We're not having this discussion any longer. I just need to get a better grip on myself so that I can stay in control, and you can stay human and alive. Give me more patience and time, I have to keep pushing back at the demons."

"It won't work. And even if it does, let's say we do manage to be fully intimate without any risks, I'm still going to grow old and ugly and you'll stay beautiful. You'll leave me, eventually."

"That's what this is about? You think I won't still want you when you're old?" His saddened eyes burrowed into my soul.

"Partly. Don't patronize me by telling me differently. I can't see you — a gorgeous twenty something year old — making out with a haggard fifty year old woman."

He stroked my face, wiping away the tear that had slipped out. "You could never be haggard. And I'm not twenty-something, I'm a hundred and something, so actually you're the one dating an old man."

THIS SHIT WAS GETTING TOO MUCH FOR ONE GIRL TO DEAL with. I needed to talk it through, let it out, cry, shout, I don't know. *Something.* I needed to vent it somehow.

Eva appeared to be my new girlfriend, but she'd side with Zac in an instant. Could I go to Anna with it? Could I tell her?

My heavy legs carried me up the steps at the firehouse for my first shift in well over a month. Danny had insisted there would be no going out to attend calls, and nothing too strenuous whilst my leg was regaining strength.

I plastered a grin on my face to hide the anxiety and breezed through the doors, instantly relaxing as the crew rushed over to make jokes at me. Meat gave me a bear hug, lifting me off my feet, until the guys told him to watch it with my 'twatty leg' and put me down.

Dumping my helmet and leathers in my locker, I turned to find Meat back in my face again.

"Straight back in the saddle, like a badass bitch!" He clapped my shoulder. "I think I'm falling in love with you, Jess."

"No, you're in love with the junk between your legs and eager to stick it wherever you can," I smiled sweetly.

"Shit! That's why you asked me to come over to your place last night?" Clark bellowed, before doubling over and pretending to retch.

"Nah, I just wanted you out the way so I could sneak in and fuck your wife," Meat deadpanned.

Clark lunged for him and a wrestling match commenced in the apparatus bay.

I picked my way past them. "Where's the chief?" I asked, to anyone listening.

"In his office... with Anna," Johnny answered, passing me a suggestive look and making a crude gesture.

I passed down the corridor and found the door to Danny's office closed. I hadn't paid any attention to the crew's lewd suggestions, but standing before that door, it suddenly seemed like they might be right.

Were they in there screwing each other? I paused, listening behind the door. Talking? How disappointing. Unless they were about to get going...? I pressed my ear harder to the wood. If I caught them in the act I could taunt them over it for weeks.

"I haven't seen her since we went to Port Isabel. Those guys were acting extra creepy. I think she's in some serious shit," Anna said.

"You didn't see the state of her all those weeks ago when she turned up at MoJoe's and broke down in the restroom. She was a total wreck. I'll fucking kill them if they hurt her any more," came Danny's reply.

"William saw her one night too, said she was a mess. I should have been there for her."

Guilt slammed down onto me. I should have made more effort to see my friends, to put their minds at rest. Here they were, worrying about me, while all I cared about was getting into Zac's pants. *And possibly becoming immortal.*

"It was a mistake encouraging her to come here, with all the indulgence. I should have known she'd fall right into the arms of an Elwood, they're right up her alley. I just thought if she was closer to me, then I could help her," Anna said, so softly I almost couldn't hear.

"So did I. And look how well that's going. She needs help. They've brainwashed her."

Fuck you! They have not done anything to my mind. You're the one who's been brainwashed!

The absurdity of that thought made me clutch my head. I was taking the piss out of him, because they'd messed with him? Like I stood on some higher platform?

"I know. But how do we get her to leave now?" Anna asked.

"I don't know. I don't *want* her to leave. I need—"

"She can't stay," Anna cut him off, and then added, in a softer tone, "You don't stand a chance with her here."

"You don't say?! I feel like I'm being watched, too. Shit is going to go down, I can feel it."

They didn't know the half of the shit that had been going down. I should have thought of them instead of running to Port Isabel. What if Luna had hurt them?

But what was this crap that they *'should have known he'd be right up my alley?'*

That shit might have been true, but it still hurt that they thought so little of me. I wasn't a fucking child that needed looking after. Why couldn't everyone stop telling me what to do? It started with my teachers, then my Dad, now my friends. They all tried to fix me. But what if I wasn't broken, they were?

They were only mad because Danny wanted me and Anna thought he was the perfect match. They'd love that, wouldn't they? *The happy MoJoe's crew.*

Well, fuck them and their little matchmaking plans.

I avoided talking to Danny as much as I could during that shift. When Anna left his office and saw me she instantly flushed, looking startled at me being there. I gave her a tight greeting and carried on with my work.

When the shift had almost finished and I was dead on my feet, Danny pulled me into his office.

"Chief," I said.

He ran a hand over his stubbled chin. He looked tired. "You've joked with the crew all day, but barely even granted me eye contact."

"Stay out of my personal life."

"What? I'm talking about here, today—"

"I know. And I'm just warning you to keep your opinions on Zac and my fucked-up head to yourself. I suppose you'll want to keep venting them to Anna, though."

He scrunched his face up before realization dawned across it and he blew out a long breath.

"We're not allowed to worry for you?" he asked.

"I don't need your worry."

"I've found you in a wrecked state several times. Panic attacks. You slept with me, then left the island without a word. Crashed your bike. Then went and holed yourself up at his place for weeks on end. We barely heard a word from you..." he threw it all out in a rush, like the words might not come unless he did it quick. But I'd picked up on the nuance, on how the words 'slept with me' had come out harder, with more force.

"You told me it was okay... that we would be okay, after-wards... if I didn't want..." I shook my head.

"Yeah, well maybe I lied. Or maybe I just hadn't antici-pated your actions and behavior after."

"Yes, you did. You're the one that said I'd be back in his bed."

He stood angrily and opened the door, an invitation for me to leave. "Don't forget who your real friends are, Jess. The ones who'll be there to pick you up again."

FOR ONCE THE ATMOSPHERE AT ZAC'S PLACE WAS ACTUALLY more pleasant than anywhere else I could want to be. These guys were starting to accept me. *They* were becoming my friends.

Something I didn't have many of, because I didn't tend to let anyone get close. For one thing, people generally couldn't take my up-and-down mood swings, but mainly because I was afraid of something happening. That they'd see I wasn't normal, they'd sense the weird energy... or worse, they'd discover that when it blew up and I hurt them

But these guys – Zac, and his gang — they could be friends. Maybe I didn't need to worry about hiding anything from them.

Anna and Danny would have to deal with that or move along. I knew they meant well, I knew I was being too hard on them. They worried for me, with every good reason. But that didn't erase the reflexive irritation under my skin from all the years of people telling me what to do, how to change, how to be a better person.

Zac was playing the perfect, if slightly sombre, host; providing me with drinks, food (well, cookies and crap)... normality. Maybe trying a little too hard on the normal front. His efforts reeked of *'let's make Jess forget about that whole vampire discussion by completely ignoring it and pretending I'm a normal boyfriend.'*

"I'm pleased you're more relaxed here now, Jess. Sorry if things were awkward for a while." Leon scooted himself in between me and Zac on the sofa, putting an arm around each of us and squeezing. "Happy families, right?"

"Right," said Zac flatly.

"Don't be mistaken by the moodiness of His Lordship, Jess," Leon groaned. "All he ever bangs on about is how soulless his existence is, all these women and none that matter. Then he met you and now he's all poetry and rainbows." He ruffled Zac's hair and they jostled with each other.

"Wow, if this is the happy, light version then I daren't think about what he was like before!" I laughed.

"Someone's got to be serious around here to run this motley crew." Zac shoved Leon off the chair and scooped me into his lap.

"And how did this gang come together? I mean, I know how Zac came to be a freak vampire by not following his nature and all that, but what about the rest of you guys?" I asked.

"Did she just call us freaks?" Eva sat forward.

"She's one to talk," smiled Leon, giving me a wink and settling on another armchair. Zac gave me a sidelong glance and my throat bobbed involuntarily. Leon acknowledged the nerve he'd hit by clearing his throat with a tight smile.

"She's right about you, Leon, you're the biggest freak going," Ruben piped up, which took me by surprise. He rarely spoke.

"Why don't we tell Jess about your little fetish, then we'll see who the biggest freak is?" Leon snorted.

"Shut up, prick." This wasn't messing, Ruben meant it. Anger twisted his face.

Leon just rolled his eyes. "Me, Jess? I didn't choose this life, it chose me when Zac crossed my path. We share some common ground in our history, some painful experiences that drew us together—"

Ruben scoffed. "And of course those painful memories involve pussy. You two are the kings of failed human relationships—"

Leon leapt across the room and pinned Ruben to his seat. They snarled in each other's faces until Zac ordered them to stop. Leon shrugged away, a rage simmering under his skin that I'd never seen on him before.

Zac had tensed, too, but then I blinked and when I looked again, the room was back to normal. Leon was draped casually in his seat as if nothing had happened. How the hell did they do that?!

"Anyway, Jess," he continued. "Aside from dickface there, you'll find that most of the other guys here were people who were turned into vampires in a violent way, torn away from a good life too soon, they never came to terms with it and so rejected the normal way of life once they learned of this great leader who could teach them some self-respect."

He made a mock bow to Zac, who nodded in return.

"I wish you could teach *them* to bow to me like that." Zac made a sweeping gesture around the room. "Bunch of ungrateful cocks."

"Fuck off," came the loud shouts from at least five other guys around the house, who'd heard despite their distance from the conversation.

"Gathering followers when I live this way is no easy task," Zac said. "So I stopped chasing and let them come to me. The ones that understand will always find their way."

"So what's your backstory, Jess?" Ruben sneered. "Why

344

would a nice lady decide to come hang out with a bunch of vampires? Didn't Mommy and Daddy give you enough attention when you were little? Or maybe the opposite, maybe you were the spoilt rich kid with too much attention?"

"Get a life," Eva huffed.

"Careful," Zac warned with a piercing glare. Did Ruben have a death wish?

"Soooo," I continued, resolving to ignore his hatred towards me. "Was it really hard for you all, learning to live this way?"

I wondered if Zac could see through my questioning or if it was innocent enough. Gauging the hardship they'd encountered, weighing up whether it was something I could put myself through.

"For some of us more than others," Leon said, shooting a look to Ruben, who simply stood and left the room coldly.

I gave Eva a questioning look and she crossed her arms, mouthing the word, "Later."

"Right, who's up for an ass-whooping at Zombie Road Racer?" Zac moved me off him and leapt up like a sleek, silent cat, grabbing a control pad. He sat back down and kissed my cheek. "Not you, my sweet. I'll tire of having to deliberately crash to give you even the minutest of chances at winning."

I dug him in the ribs and winced as my finger met his unwavering, tight muscle. Leon picked up the other pad and tyre screeching filled the room from a giant soundbar.

"Hey, I wasn't ready," Zac shouted as his car tore after Leon's.

"Snooze you lose, brother."

Zac's lightning reactions meant his car was still roaring off only a fraction behind Leon's, nothing to the human eye, but behind to him. They shouted at each other as they wrestled their way around the track side by side. Zac won with Leon 0.3 seconds behind him.

As mesmerizing as it was to witness their perfection, it got pretty tedious as far as computer games were concerned. I left them to it and strolled off to the kitchen to see if Zac had got any decent food in for me. He'd been trying, really hard, to remember my human needs, but food wasn't his forte.

I opened and closed a few cupboards, finding the usual emptiness. As I closed the final one, Ruben materialized from behind it.

"You're a silly little girl," he whispered, right up against my ear. I shuddered at the contact, his hands on my shoulders. "You think you can walk into the middle of a vampire lair and just chill with us? Everything's peachy and no one gets hurt? I'll be laughing when it all goes tits-up for you. Unless you cause problems for me or Eva in the process. Then I won't be laughing, and nor will you."

———

MY STOMACH SWELLED IN APPRECIATION AS I DEVOURED A steak, sitting in one of the fancier restaurants on the North side. The little encounter with Ruben had left me shaken. I should have gone to Zac I suppose, but I didn't want to give Ruben the satisfaction of knowing he'd got to me. And Zac had enough to deal with already.

My hunt in the kitchen had come up empty, so I'd left them with their game and popped out to eat. It took a great deal of persuasion to convince Zac to let me go anywhere alone. But he was friends with the owner of this place and finally conceded that I'd be safe. Even so, I wouldn't have put it past him to have someone following me.

I'd eaten here a couple of times before. I resolved to

make 'sometimes eat here' into an 'always eat here' because I was already slim, but starting to look skeletal from all the nights I'd spent *not* eating enough. He'd noticed it too. Zac couldn't argue that sometimes a girl needed *meat*.

As for him in the kitchen?! Ha, bless him, he'd tried before without much success. I knew he hated the smell, too.

An unrecognized number flashed up on my cell phone and I answered it absently, pushing the plate away.

"Hey, darlin'. Guess who?" came a husky drawl into my ear.

I choked on the food in my mouth. People turned to gawk as I coughed like a maniac, before regaining composure with a gulp of water.

"I'll give you a clue. I'm tall, dark, irresistible, and I'm your favorite kind of guy — the wrong one."

"How did you get my number?"

"I was thinking, you ought to swing by my place tonight."

After struggling to find words for a while I eventually asked, "What are you talking about?" and finished with, "No, thanks."

Creative, I know.

"Don't be like that," he said.

"What do you want this time, Alex?" I pretended to sound bored, despite the hammering in my chest.

"Did I not make myself clear enough? I told you to get over here." The tone in his voice dropped.

"No." This time I intended to sound assertive, but my voice got caught somewhere in my throat.

"Well, excuse the fuck out of me. I guess I'm still not speaking clearly enough. I suppose that friend of yours, what's her name, Anna? She's cute. I could focus my attentions on her, if—"

"Keep her out of this!" I jumped from of my seat and caught the plate, knocking it to the floor with a crash. Nodding a brisk apology to the waiter, I hurried out the door with the phone to my ear.

"Right now she's singing and dancing around the kitchen, blissfully unaware that a predator has locked her in his sights. I can get into that apartment in a heartbeat."

"NO! Please, don't do anything." I charged down the sidewalk, tripped over my own feet, and shoved a teenage boy out the way as I went.

"I'll see you soon then, darlin'. You know where my place is, right? The big house Southside that my brother has pointed out to you — with a stern warning to stay away? Oh, and talking of Zachariah, it wouldn't be wise to mention any of this to him. I'll know if you tell him, I'll be able to feel his rage from miles away. You wouldn't want anything to happen to sweet little Anna, would you?"

He hung up and my mind raced furiously ahead, I couldn't keep up with any of it. Terrified about what would happen to Anna if I didn't go, and terrified of what would happen to me if I did. Bottom line, I'd sooner take my own chances than risk hers. I couldn't let her get caught up in this too.

I entertained the idea of going straight to Zac, but Alex's warning rang heavy in my ears. I didn't doubt what he'd said about knowing, and I couldn't take the chance when my best friend's life was on the line.

I typed out a message to Zac.

Jess: *Hi, was thinking, I've neglected Anna since you stole my heart, I ought to spend tonight with her. Hope you don't mind. J x*

The ping of a return message was instant.

Hot Stalker: *You OK?*

Jess: *Of course. Thank you! See you soon.*

Hot Stalker: *I don't mind at all, but are you sure you're alright? You would tell me if you weren't?*

For fuck's sake. Could he hear my heart getting ready to explode from wherever he was? No, I suppose he could hear my thoughts.

The shrill ring came abruptly... Hot Stalker calling.

For actual fuck's sake! I couldn't talk to him in this state. My throat felt as dry and scratchy as sandpaper. He'd be sure to sense it in my voice. He picked up on everything. Any slight nuance in voice, body language, even my own damned heartbeat. I had no control over the messages that my body would send him.

I stuffed the phone away.

Better haul ass before he comes looking.

38

JESS

I paused, hovering my trembling finger over the call button on the security gates, but before I could gather the strength to push it they were already opening. The sweeping driveway was edged by huge, spindly pine trees. To the side of the house was a swimming pool, the size of an average house on its own, surrounded by rows of loungers, tables and chairs. The place was eerily deserted, only a slight rippling on the surface of the pool. Colored lights made the water glow a bright, sparkling crimson.

Alex's home couldn't have been more different from his brother's. Instead of the vast, timeless grandeur of Zac's place, this mansion was a modern architectural dream. All crisp, angular lines and shining metal, illuminated by swathes of spotlights. One whole side of the house was mostly window, blacked out with shutters.

I clutched at the churning in my stomach. It was entirely possible my heart would go ahead and beat right out of my chest. Wonderful. That was going to get a houseful of bad vampires really excited. Nothing I did had any effect at slowing the beat.

This depth of fear should have had me turning round

and heading for the safety of Zac's arms, but there was something else going on inside me. A curiosity. An *excitement*. I couldn't help wanting to find out what Alex was actually like. Surely if he'd wanted to kill me, he could have done so by now?

I parked my bike next to the only other vehicle in sight — my original Ducati, my Loki. Left there to stand lonely and isolated, mocking me. Straightening out my leather jacket, I swept my hair back and rang the door buzzer. It swung wide instantly.

There he was.

A less-troubled version of Zac's face. Those cool blue eyes, fierce and predatory, gazing down at me.

He wore only a pair of faded, torn Wranglers that hung low off his hips. No shoes or socks. I tried, but I couldn't look at his feet for long — his ludicrously muscled torso was like some sort of magnet. I felt so compelled to reach out and touch it that I had to grab my hands together behind my back.

Taut and chiseled to perfection. Dark, tribal-looking ink ran from his shoulders, down the whole length of his arms. Just like Zac, except no color, only black swirls.

A shining barbell was pierced through his left nipple, calling out to me to lick it. I'd had a lot of kinky dreams about him recently, and he'd always had his nipple pierced in them, with the same tattoos... but I could swear this was the first time I'd actually seen him without a shirt.

"When you're done assessing me, would you like to come in, darlin'?" He graciously swung his arm to gesture me through, power rippling from his every pore. My head snapped back up to look at his face, ablaze with the brightness of his seductive, smug smile.

"After me then?" He turned, leaving me to follow inside. The whole of his back was also tattooed, thick black swirling lines and patterns that danced like tribal visions as he moved, walking with the speed and grace of a predatory animal. Zac attempted to hide his un-human traits from me, always trying to move and behave normally. Alex would not be the same. He'd clearly get more pleasure from showing me exactly how vampire he was.

We passed through a vast living space, and I caught up with him in a hallway once he stopped. I'd been so consumed by his presence that I only now took in the surroundings, and immediately wished I hadn't.

Through an open doorway was a deathly dark room, with only patches of soft illumination from a few scattered lamps, their light stretching out but swallowed up by black before it got very far. I felt like there were things happening in that blackness, the corners and shadows hiding their secrets. Peering into the gloom only revealed flashes of skin, glimpses of movement.

It was too quiet... but I could feel them. Feel the presence of many bodies, yet no noise, aside from some shuffling and... wet sounds.

A naked man lay sprawled out in a patch of lamplight to my left. Another man straddled him, pouring something thick and oozing into his mouth, only the gentle slurping providing any indication that the spread-eagled man was even alive, he lay so limp.

My breathing came so rapidly, such short, shallow pants, that it began to be the only sound I could hear — the rattled gasping of my own fear.

A hand touched my shoulder and I screamed. The room exploded with hisses and growls, the shadows seeming to move and close in on me. Groaning and snarling, sniffing...

"Quiet," Alex commanded, squeezing my shoulder. The eerie silence slammed right back down in an instant, the shadows retreating back to the corners. "Maybe we should go somewhere a little more inviting," he whispered in my ear.

I felt him disappear from my side and the sudden absence of his demanding energy left my skin cold. I went to follow him, but my feet wouldn't move. Literally, they were rooted to the spot. I pulled and strained at myself, my body paralyzed from the waist down.

A low, evil chuckle whooshed past my ear on a breath. Then a roar, full of rage.

A vampire, still chuckling, swam into view from the shadows, pulled forward as if by an invisible force. His feet walked him toward me, but he seemed to be fighting it. The smile slid from his face and the laughter stopped as I once again felt Alex beside me.

"Sit," Alex said.

The man shook his head, but slumped to his knees.

"You will stay here until I'm ready to deal with that mistake you just made." Alex turned, and this time he took my hand, leading me down the hall with him.

STAMMERING FOR WORDS, I TRIED TO SWING AROUND AND head back for the front door, but Alex's fingers were closed around mine and the tingling shot right to my head, dizzying and confusing.

He paused by another doorway, releasing my hand. I became aware of a new noise; a rhythmic squeaking. A man approached us, pushing a wheelchair; the wheels scratching as they came down the wooden floor. He was the size of a house, towering over the frail, wraithlike woman seated in the chair. Greasy, dark hair hung limply over her face. Her body as white as the delicate lace slip that she wore, barely covering her. So thin, so gaunt. Bruises and puncture marks dotted along her bony arms, hands limp in her lap. A saline bag hung from a pole attached to the chair, the tube running down and into a needle taped to the back of her hand.

The man breezed past us, giving me a sly smile and a little wave with his fingers, like he was waving at a child. I sucked in a breath as he passed.

The woman's face, half hidden by that lank hair, swam past me like an apparition. Haunted, lost, broken. I knew her face. I could see the articles, the social media links that had continually popped up for a few weeks about the B-list celebrity who'd fallen off the wagon and into a mess of drugs and public brawls. I never read that shit, but the headlines had flitted by me enough times. Then, as is the case with celebrity gossip, it went quiet just as quickly as it had come.

I whirled back round to Alex, "That... that was—"

I didn't bother to finish the sentence once I noted that several women had attached themselves to him whilst I'd been gawking at the wheelchair-bound ghost.

Alex raised an interested eyebrow, urging me to continue, as one of the women leant back with a line of white powder spread across the top of her breast. It gleamed in the dim light against her smooth, umber skin. She was slender, but in the right way, curves in the right places. She stood in complete contrast to the wan figure who'd been wheeled past. Her lips were full, her eyes bright and eager, her afro hair styled and preened.

When Alex realized that I'd gone back to staring without speaking, he snorted the powder from her skin. She eased up and pawed at his chest, nuzzling his shoulder.

Another woman to his right... no, a girl — she barely looked legal — had her hand running up and down his thigh, inching ever closer to the goods. Three more ladies stood right behind, in the room off the hallway, eyes to the floor, hands clasped in front. All buck naked. And beyond them, deeper into the room... I couldn't even look. There were writhing bodies in all manner of sexual encounters.

Alex gently brushed aside powder-girl's afro and whispered into her ear. Her face took on a hazy, wistful look as she held an upturned hand out to him. He locked his gaze onto mine, a wicked smile plastered on his lips. His tongue snaked out to run along her wrist. Something in his face changed, flickered for a moment, more sinister. The usually piercing blue eyes darkened.

Holding carefully, he sucked at her delicate wrist and she let out a whimper. A trickle of blood crept slowly down her arm as he took visible gulps, swallowing it down, staring at me. I clamped a hand over my mouth to muffle the gasp. She groaned, her head rolling back, eyes closing.

He drew back slowly, so that I saw his fangs withdraw from the flesh. Two small holes remained, blood seeping out, which he lapped at seductively. One of her hands went between her legs and started rubbing.

She wasn't in pain. She wasn't engulfed by fear or trying to escape. She proffered herself up to him with eager need. The others stood in line behind, presumably waiting their turn. Zac told me they didn't just feed and let people live. This was nothing like the image he'd painted. But then, the other room, the wheelchair...

Alex continued lapping and drinking and not once did his eyes falter from their assault on me. Piercing right through me with their amused, sadistic spell. A pool of heat spread between my thighs and throbbed in time with my thundering heart.

When he'd finished, he dropped her arm, and she grumbled, moving it back up towards his face. He pushed it away in annoyance, so she dropped to her knees, scrambling to pull down his zipper. She wasn't going to? *Surely not...*

He kept his stare firmly leveled on me, some of the intensity gone, resuming the usual sexual smile, slowly licking at the blood pooled on his bottom lip.

She took his cock out and sucked it.

I turned and marched away.

I got a few paces before he called out, "It could be Anna on her knees here."

I stilled, blood rushing in my ears — fear, loathing and lust all crawling up my spine in a fucked-up ménage à trois.

"There we are, good girl. Come join me for a drink," he said casually, as if we were alone and he didn't have bitches rubbing him in all the right places.

I stared daggers into those women, until he glanced down at the one busy sucking his considerable cock. "Well, shit me, where are my manners?" he laughed.

"Maybe up your own ass, along with your head?" I suggested.

He bit his bottom lip, grinning. "Enough," he said, and just like that they all sulked away, blending into the vampire-filled room beyond, finding other cocks to gobble.

He stood alone, adjusting his zipper and gathering himself back together. After considering me for a while, he said, "For the record, my authority is not based on ego, darlin'. It's hard fact. I give orders and people obey. If I decide I want you, then you better be ready to fall in line."

He sauntered off down yet another hall, leaving me to follow his perfectly sculpted ass, which — annoyingly — looked extra enticing in that low-slung denim.

We passed several rooms, each one had a similar scene

inside; sex, drinking, vampires feeding. I hurried past one with a woman chained up naked to a wall. I couldn't tell if she was pleased or not, but I had my own shit to worry about right then. There were bigger problems first, like figuring out how I was going to get back out of this house.

Another male vampire crossed the hallway with a naked woman, attached to a chain via a collar. She was almost as ghost-like as the wheelchair woman. Pale, withdrawn. She crawled on all fours behind him as he pulled her along on the leash.

I was already working out how I could get the cops in here to shut this shit down. Maybe ones from out of state somehow, who hadn't been bribed or head-fucked yet.

Alex stopped in another doorway and I nearly walked right into him.

"Grand ideas like that get people hurt, Jess," he said, dipping through the open door.

Compared to the darkness of the rest of the house, this room seemed as bright as a sunny day. I squinted in at the brushed metal furniture, the sleek leather corner sofa, and weird tube lighting built into the walls.

Two men sat at a metal and glass table, one of whom I recognized as the fucktard called Parker, who'd taken my bike that night. I hated that dreadlocked asshole. Seated with them was a pretty blonde and a prettier brunette. The vampires laughed and encouraged the girls as they drank shots.

A gun sat in the middle of the table. I couldn't work out what was going on at first. I watched in slow motion as Parker handed it to the blonde, saying it was her turn now. She took hold of the gun and, with a little giggle, gingerly turned it on herself, her tiny nose twitching like a mouse.

"NO!" I shouted, trying to run to her, but Alex's arm had shot out. "What are you doing?"

She looked at me with a startled expression and then laughed. "Russian roulette. Want to join us? No? Thought not. Get lost you frigid cow or I'll aim it at you?"

This made them all laugh harder than before, whooping with encouragement as she waggled the gun in my direction. Her ego swelled visibly from their praise. She planted the muzzle in her mouth and pulled the trigger.

Click.

Laughing hysterically, she began shouting about how she was a "bad ass bitch".

"Parker, we're not to be disturbed under any circumstances," Alex said. "Zachariah will try to get in soon, keep him busy for a while."

Dreadlocked twat-face nodded in reply. My stomach churned.

Alex stepped forward and strolled over to the dumb mouse, who sat wide-eyed and open-mouthed at his advancement. He took her chin delicately in his fingers and lifted her face up to his. Her lips pouted to kiss him, that little nose flaring.

"You ever point a gun at my guest again and I will fuck you up," he whispered.

She winced and nodded, or tried to.

Dropping her chin, he grabbed my arm and ushered my lagging feet up a shining, spiral staircase. Polished marble floors, lots of windows, all shuttered up. We passed many closed doors on the second floor, the groans from within could have been pleasure or pain, I couldn't be sure. Then up more curved steps, and into a vast suite.

A massive, modern bed sat in the center, with enough space to sleep an army. The sleek, silver canopy rose from the headboard, sweeping overhead, with built in lights and speakers. Luxurious sofas and chairs decked the edges of the room.

Hanging on one wall was a framed movie poster — a vampire in a white shirt and collared coat, the word *Dracula* written in dripping red letters.

"Is that supposed to be funny?" I pointed to the print. He just grinned in response.

"Did you choreograph everything that's happened here tonight, from the moment I got through the door? *The vampire freakshow!* Put on to... what? Scare me? Seduce me?"

"Considering both of those emotions are running rampant through your body right now, had that been my plan I'd say it was a success." He ambled towards me and for a moment I got distracted by the way his abs flowed as he moved.

Until the sound of a gun echoed through my head, swiftly followed by a high-pitched shriek.

The scream was abruptly cut short, ending no sooner than it had begun. I whirled around in panic.

"Relax," he said. "Parker will have stopped her at the last second and shot it at the wall. Crazy bitches these college kids."

"No, that was a real scream. It didn't miss. What are you doing with them?" I urged.

"Playing," he shrugged.

"Like cats with mice?"

"I thought you liked guns?" The edges of his mouth lifted in a suggestive smile.

"No."

"This isn't the place to start playing coy, darlin'. Didn't you like it when I took my gun and fucked you with it like a little whore?" He took another step and pressed me down onto the bed. I thought he was going to make a move, but instead he sat down on the floor in front of my legs. It was disarming to suddenly have the predator sitting subservient at my feet. I didn't like it.

"That wasn't real."

"No? Maybe you're right, maybe you're wrong, maybe one day I'll tell you. But either way, you fucking loved it."

"Why am I here?" I spat out, straining against the flash-backs from that encounter — memories that suddenly pressed so hard against my core that my body cried out for more.

"Good question. Why *are* you here?" He leant back and the visions faded.

A loaded question. It felt like there was an answer to that, one that I must never voice.

"I... you... if you touch Anna..."

"Oh, yes! Anna! You need to choose. Her or Danny-boy-with-the-misplaced-confidence? Which one's going to join me for dinner?"

"No! You said if I came—"

"Tick tock. Choose quickly, or I'll go with gluttony and take both. Restraint isn't a quality of mine."

39

JESS

"*Y*ou can't... I don't..." Dammit, I couldn't speak.

He broke out into deep laughter, slapping his thigh.

"Lighten up, sweetcheeks, I'm shitting with you. I just want to get to know you better. Don't you think if I'm going to be your brother-in-law one day then you ought to make the effort to get along with me?"

"No."

"I can play nice too, you know. So nice that you won't walk straight for a week."

"Well, be still my beating heart, the master of romance is upon me." I rolled my eyes.

The galloping of my pulse threatened to make me pass out. It was unlikely any amount of sarcasm could hide that, but it was worth a try. Had I really believed I was only there to save Anna? It felt like there was another reason, looming behind a door inside me. I was leaning hard on that door, trying to keep it shut.

"Has Zachariah told you about his secret, yet? Sorry, secrets, plural." He absently rubbed a finger over the scar on his cheek.

His sharp conversation changes left me dizzy. I stared resolutely ahead of me.

"You're too scared to ask him?! Why don't you ask me instead?" he suggested.

"Why don't you go fuck yourself?"

He laughed and we sat in silence for a beat.

"So many questions in your head, Jess. I dare you to ask me them. I won't be as evasive with the answers as he is."

"He told me about sanguine mating. He played it down as just folklore, but I think if we're fated to be together, our souls destined to meet, then that's about as romantic as it gets. Are you jealous of that?"

"Oh, he's your soulmate, alright. The one you're destined to be with. But not as lovers, or even as equals. He's fated to kill you. That's what he desires above all else," he paused. "Still think that's sweet?"

"You *all* want to kill me. I'm over it."

Biting his lip, he shook his head. It was the most hesitant I'd ever seen him look.

"If a vampire finds that human, their sanguine mate, they're expected to keep them. As a blood slave, to feed from when they desire, or to kill when they choose," he paused again, weighing up the blank expression I was struggling to maintain.

"They often draw out the pleasure as long as they possibly can, feeding frequently, little and often. Then they'll indulge in the best night of their lives, by killing them. Usually at a big organized event in front of everyone. Like a fucking wedding. Other vampires will come to watch, congratulate them, celebrate with them. Is this the wedding you've dreamed of?"

"No, but it sounds like you have?" I fake smiled, wondering if this new information was actually going to have me vomiting all over him.

It was fine. Zac told me it was ritual bullshit that he wouldn't acknowledge... but did he want it, deep down? Is that what he really desired? Would turning me into a vampire change it? Maybe he'd get the best of both that way? Presumably he'd need to feed from me to make the latter happen?

"You asked him to make you a vampire?!" Alex beamed.

"Yeah, that went down well." One big argument amongst the daily rotation of other arguments.

His eyes reached for the ceiling. "Have you never had a single day without fighting him?"

"Get out of my head."

"I don't need to be in your head to know that. He's all about free will and not messing with minds. But *that's* the horseshit. He wants to change you."

"And I suppose you don't, right?"

"Congratulations on fucking the chief, by the way," he said with sudden airiness. "Damn, I wish I could have seen Zachariah's face when he found out. Did he cry?"

"Are we done here, yet?"

"Not even close. And before we continue, my little nympho head-case, here's another one for the record – I wouldn't be mad at you for fucking other guys. In fact, I'd encourage it. We'd do it together."

I took a deep breath to say something, although I hadn't worked out what, when he put a hand up to stop me.

"We don't have much time left for the bullshittin', so save the retorts. Don't miss this chance to ask the questions that matter," he urged.

He was right; there was a shit-ton of questions I wanted to ask him. But all I could think about right then was all the humans in that house. How many of them would end up dead. And if my knowledge of them being there made me an accessory to murder?

363

But then, aside from wheelchair woman... and maybe that missing girl from the beach... everyone I'd seen looked healthy. Willing. Happy, even. Then again, no doubt Alex could influence that with his mind control games. Could he make them look happy, when they weren't? Or were they genuinely eager to give themselves over? Was that what *I* was like?

"Is that your question? Because that seems like one you should ask yourself."

I huffed at the invasion into my mind. At least that answered the first questions. He could get inside their heads and warp them any way he wanted. How long before he did that to me? Again...

"The missing girl," I said.

"I picked her up from an event. A vampire one, where the organizers spend months rounding up a load of home-less people, or those who are isolated and alone, ones nobody will miss. Once they've done their research and found enough, they're invited to a party, free booze all night. The vampires arrive and mingle as guests for a while, get some fun out of playing with their food before the main entertainment."

"That's disgusting."

He grinned. "It's fun. But mistakes were made. She was missed enough for someone to put out a missing persons notice. And one of my men let her off the leash, that was a mistake that didn't go unpunished. Anyway, I'd chosen her and brought her home from that event. But believe me, she was treated like a princess here compared to what could have befallen her. Despite my brother's opinions, I'm not the worst monster out there."

"You think you did her a favor?" I scoffed.

"I know I did. Next question, different subject, please."

"The fire—"

"I didn't kill them," he cut in. "I didn't start that fire, you know this."

"The doors were locked."

"The doors are always locked. I can't have anyone just wandering into my club when they feel like it. Now, are you seriously going to keep asking questions about other, irrelevant people?"

"You tried to kill me with a dodgy bungee cord."

"Better," he smiled. "It was an impulsive first response. One of my men was trailing you and it seemed an opportune moment to fuck with Zachariah. Apologies."

"Apologies? That's it? You prick!" I made a move to stand up, but he pressed his palms into my thighs and pushed me back down.

"You know what I am, Jess. But I still don't understand exactly what you are, which puts you ahead of me."

"I'm just a girl. A crazy one." I drew my arms around my chest, as if that might help protect my mind from the thoughts about myself, ones I didn't want him seeing.

"You're far from just a girl, that was established long ago."

I shifted, pulling my legs up and away from the vampire still sitting at my feet.

"When will you accept that you need to fear him just as much as me, if not more?" His face lost the usual mischievous sparkle, eyes turning serious.

"Are you going to elaborate on that or make me ask?"

"He wasn't always all sweetness and 'I am the light' crap. His need for power and control goes back way before he even became a vampire." Alex absently ran a finger down the scar on his cheek. "This was a little gift from him when we were only eight years old. Didn't get what he wanted, so he slashed me. If this was the work of a child, imagine what he's capable of now."

"Is there a point to all this? You're all killers, you're all capable of terrible things, I'm not hiding from that. Why do you care what he does? I thought you wanted him to activate this Legacy shit, yet now you sound like you don't want him to let go?"

"You came along and complicated things. The Legacy is, and always will be, my primary concern, but I'd probably like it if he didn't kill you in the process. I think I could enjoy having you around."

"Legacy schmegacy," I snorted.

"You're mocking it?" His eyebrows shot up, the familiar smile pulling at his lips.

"I'm a little sick of the vampire dramatics."

"You're right. Damn, my manners are shot to fucking shit tonight. Whiskey, right?" He suddenly leapt up and moved to a futuristic-looking desk in the corner, all glass and steel.

"No, thanks."

"No? Smack, then? You like that too, right?"

I pressed my lips together.

"I guess it's all tame compared to the high from making out with a vampire," he sighed, dumping a syringe back on the table and sitting down, next to me this time. "If we're done with question time, should we get straight to the hard-core stuff?"

Taking hold of my hand, he turned it over, his fingers tracing the vein along my wrist. I tried to wrench myself away, but my body didn't move a single muscle.

I could barely even breathe as he pulled my wrist up and kissed it tenderly. The idea of his teeth sinking in like a hot knife on butter made me shiver. What would it be like? Would it hurt? It didn't look like it hurt...

Unfortunately, his lips continued slowly up my arm, leaving tingling patches where the kisses fell. Across my collarbone, finding my throat. He sucked at the skin below

366

my ear. Fuck, would he drink from my neck? He still had hold of my wrist in one hand and I was aware of a dull pain as the grip tightened.

"I know what you want, Jess. You want me to fuck you so rough that you're begging me to stop, knowing full well it'll only make me go at it harder. You need an animal to plunder you," he whispered the words straight in my ear.

Pulling back a fraction, he stared at me, running his tongue along his bottom lip. His eyes narrowed as his tongue moved to probe something else — two sharp, white teeth. This time I did find the power to move and launched myself away from him. I did it with such force that I began toppling backwards off the bed, but he still had hold of my wrist and yanked me back.

Deep amusement spread over his face. "Zachariah never showed you his fangs before?"

I'd caught sight of them on occasion when he'd nearly lost it, but not up close like that. Not bearing down on me with primal intention.

"You know, my brother might think I can't control myself, but he's wrong. I just choose not to most of the time. There's a difference. But look, see..." He bared his normal teeth at me. "Just in the nick of time, too."

Leaping to his feet, he leant into a feral, crouching position facing the door.

It flew open in an explosion of shattering wood. A large splintered piece flew past me and caught my cheek with a sting. Warm blood trickled down.

I couldn't see what happened next, it was too fast. Zac tore into the room like a tornado, with a flurry of motion and growling. Then he was standing helplessly before me in a headlock, Alex snarling at his throat.

"So rude to storm into someone's private room like that, Zachariah," Alex hissed.

A bunch of his men stood just inside the room, Parker at the front, all hissing and snarling at Zac's back. Too many fangs in one place.

No, no, no, this couldn't be happening.

I forced myself to look at Zac's face. There was only pain and rage, directed right at me.

"I'm so sorry." I swear my lungs collapsed as the words left. Another panic attack threatened to rip through me, great spasming sobs causing me to choke as the reality of the situation hit me.

Alex's teeth were at Zac's throat, threatening to close in.

"Don't hurt him," I wailed, punching Alex's back. He shoved me away and I hit the floor hard, cracking my temple on the edge of the bed frame. More blood rushed down my face.

Zac let out a thunderous snarl and lurched forward, flinging Alex over his shoulder and onto the floor. He hoisted me to my feet and held me behind him, adopting a defensive stance. Alex was back on his feet, but all the aggression had left his body.

He stood relaxed, hands in his pockets, eyeballing us, taunting us with his nonchalance. "You think having murderers holed-up in your basement makes you stronger, Zachariah? Somehow more worthy of her attention? News-flash, brother, there's nothing special about you. It just makes you a psycho—"

Zac cut him off with a snarl.

And what? What *basement*?!

I gaped at Zac, who glared pure venom at Alex.

"They're hungering for this fight," Alex shrugged, nodding to the pack of animals in the doorway. Obedient creatures, waiting for their orders. "Leave."

"This isn't over," Zac growled.

"I'm counting on that."

Zac marched me over to the window, smashed it with the back of his hand, and leapt out — with me pressed to his back. It happened so quickly that I could hardly register it. One second I was standing there, then I was on his back and landing gracefully onto the driveway three floors down.

He dropped me to my feet a lot less gently than he could have, and pushed me towards my bike.

"Ride. Straight to mine. I'll be right behind you," he ordered.

I gunned it down the crunching, gravel driveway, wheels spinning out and sliding.

The redness of the water in the pool seemed to have intensified as I passed.

Darker, thicker.

A naked man sank into the depths and shot from one end to the other in a heartbeat. He emerged from the water, *red* clinging to every curve, glossy and slick, sliding down his body.

It wasn't lights making that pool red.

40

JESS

*E*va mopped delicately at my bloody face with a wet cloth. I was sure the blood was making her uncomfortable. That, or it was the overall mood in the room. Both, I supposed.

She hurriedly applied some gauze and taped me up, declaring I was almost good as new, then retreated upstairs. Before she left, she placed a hand on Zac's shoulder and whispered something in his ear. His face remained impassive to whatever she'd said.

His furious eyes burned through me. What had I been thinking? Why on earth had I gone over there and on top of that, why had I been so attracted to Alex whilst there? My conscience swam with guilt, excitement and fear.

Zac had followed me closely on the ride back, his front wheel practically touching my rear one. Even just looking at him from my mirror had terrified me. I'd contemplated just riding, getting on the highway and out of town, keep going until he got the picture and left me. Once he'd had time to cool down, I could go back and explain.

But the voice inside assured me he would never back off, and that when I eventually stopped he'd be even angrier. So

I'd followed my orders and now here we sat in edged silence. At least all the gang were there. Surely he wouldn't rip me apart too much with other people around?

My heart sank when he flicked his head and they all disappeared in the blink of an eye.

He stared at me. His jaw clamped so tightly shut it looked like it could implode any moment under the pressure. I turned my back and dithered with some books on a shelf, but I could feel his rage boring through me. I couldn't will my mouth to open. I think I was even more scared than I'd been on my way to Alex's.

"I can't believe you just let that thought go through your mind," he said, suddenly right behind me. "You're more afraid of me than you are of him?"

"Afraid of losing you," I cried. "I don't know what I was thinking, I was so terrified that he was going to hurt Anna. He said if I didn't go, he was going to hurt her. I didn't know what else to do."

"You should have come to me. I'd have dealt with it. What were you hoping to achieve? What exactly did you think he wanted to see you for?"

"I don't know. I couldn't risk Anna getting caught up in this."

"I wouldn't have let anything happen to her. I told you I'd keep her safe. I can't believe you actually just went along and handed yourself over to the butcher."

I scrunched up my face, shaking my head. It didn't seem right.

"He didn't want to kill me." As I said it, I remembered the fangs, so close to me, but he *had* stopped himself. "He's more controlled than you give him credit for."

That did it.

He swiped his fist along the shelf, sending books flying. "This isn't the time to be defending him, Jess!"

371

"I'm just saying, I don't think that's what he wanted." I sidestepped away, aware of him following me, fists clenched.

"So what did he want?" he barked.

"To stroke his ego. To cause trouble between us." I stopped backing up. Did weakness fuel his darkness? It certainly seemed to. I stuck a hand out to his chest.

"Antagonizing me is his favorite game," he said, frowning, an edge of rage dissipating. "You see this ink?" He turned his arm over and showed me some Latin words amidst the sprawl of colorful tattoos.

"*Aut viam inveniam aut faciam.*" The words rolled from his lips with ease. "It means '*I will either find a way or make one.*' One of several reminders I have on my body. Reminders to keep me on this road. Alexander immediately had a tattoo of his own done in the same place. '*Esto quod es — be what you are.*' Gives him his own reminder to never give me peace. You're the perfect game piece to him."

"What did he mean about murderers in the basement?"

Zac took hold of my hands, twining his fingers into mine. I met his eyes and something flushed through my core. I knew I wanted to demand something... what was it?

"Did he kiss you?" he asked.

"No! Well, not exactly."

Stupid girl. A simple 'No' would have sufficed.

He licked his lips, eyes darkening. Too late for me to backtrack now.

"It was nothing," I added hastily. "He kissed my wrist a bit. I tried to push him away, but... I couldn't."

Had I tried to push him away? I couldn't remember that either.

"Please don't let him have this satisfaction." I cautiously moved my lips towards his. "I should have told you. I'm sorry. I know you can protect me and anyone else I ask you to. I just panicked."

372

He exhaled, wrapping his arms around me, though not as lovingly as usual.

"You're hard work, Jessica Layton," he said, kissing my forehead.

I KNEW.

I *knew* that he was back on with the victim blaming. I knew that raging at me for having gone to Alex was totally unfair. This was their game and I was caught in the middle with little choices. I shouldn't have been so apologetic. I'd only done what I needed to do.

And yet, I *had* said sorry. I'd done anything I could to placate him, thanks to the lead in my gut that threatened to break me every time he got mad. The thought of losing him wiped out any logical thinking on my part.

And even with those lame apologies, Zac hadn't been able to keep the rage in check. We'd bickered over stupid stuff, irritation grating on both of us.

In the end I'd left him to it and gone back to my apartment, despite his insistence that Port Isabel wasn't safe. There was no doubt that he had someone outside watching over me. Maybe even himself.

I slept damn hard for twelve hours straight. My body yearned for more, to escape everything in slumber. I was suddenly full of aches and pains, in body and mind. It had crept up on me. Exhaustion.

Inching slowly into a steaming bath, my skin pinked up on contact. Pins and needles burrowed into my hands and feet.

My phone sat beside me and a message pinged up from Zac.

Hot Stalker: *This isn't me. I don't know where the anger is* coming from. *You fill me with so much raw emotion. I'm strug-gling to hold on to myself. Forgive me?*

Jess: *You already know I'm going to forgive you, what's the point in asking?*

Hot Stalker: *To be polite. A gentleman. Because I'm a grumpy prick.*

Jess: *Gentlemen are overrated. A badass son of a bitch who's going to show me how sorry he is — that's more my type.*

Thoughts of him earning my forgiveness made me immediately horny. Taking a shampoo bottle, I rubbed it over my nipple, peaking under the coldness.

I took a photo of my rosy body amidst the bubbles, one hand between my legs, and hit Send.

Jess: *I'm in the bath remembering your tongue on me. I'm hot, wet, steamy. I need more. I want your hands tracing every line of my body. I want your lips on my nipples, sucking firmly. I want your tongue... everywhere. But most of all I want your throbbing cock inside me, driving in and out until I'm scream-ing. I need you. Hard and fast. My tight pussy clenched around you... If you're such a bad boy, you should come fuck me. NOW.*

I sank deeper into the water. He'd never do it, of course, but it sure was fun to imagine how hot and wound up that would have got him. I let my fingers roam my body and not two minutes had passed when he arrived, looking like he was about to explode.

Without speaking a word, he plucked me from the bath and dropped me onto the bed, discarding his shirt and doing everything I'd asked with careful slowness.

Licking, sucking, kissing.

I squirmed and whimpered, clutching at him in a feeble attempt to make him stay this time.

The aching between my legs was unbearable, so wet and ready for him. I'd been ready from the moment I saw him, months ago. Now I felt like I'd crumple into nothingness if I couldn't get more. Desire shot through every single nerve, teasing and taunting.

"Fuck me," I panted against his bare chest, biting his nipple. "Please."

He finished undressing, never breaking eye contact. His boxers fell to the floor and boy, he was hard. And big. I tried my best not to ogle, but I'd had that thing in my mouth and I wanted it there again. But first, I needed it somewhere else.

He knelt over me, searching into my eyes, hard and fierce. One second he looked like he didn't want to be there, then like he was pleading with me and then, well, like he wanted me for dinner.

Pressing the head of his erection to my opening, he rubbed it up and down. "You're so wet for me, Jess, I want you so fucking much."

"Take me," I begged, digging my nails into his hips and urging him forward. The tip pressed inside and I cried out with a mixture of relief and frustration, needing more. He eased in further with unbelievable gentleness and caution, like he was afraid I might break if he went deeper.

Or maybe he was more afraid that *he* would break.

The slowness made it even more thrilling, feeling each millimeter, escalating pleasure rising like a wave ready to wash over me. It was almost too intense, I couldn't handle the patience of it. I felt like I was going to burst into a thousand pieces.

His whole body trembled with restraint. I knew he wanted it harder and faster, too. I also knew that he wanted my neck — his eyes were fixated on it.

I took hold of his face and pulled his mouth to mine. He kissed me tenderly, lovingly. His hard chest heaving against my soft breasts, so cold against my hot skin. I was still wet from the bath, making us slide and stick. He inched further and then it happened — he was completely inside me, all the way.

Groaning, he immediately pulled out, coming back slow and controlled. All the way in and right back out. The urge to wriggle and increase his pace was torturous.

"Wait!" I tore myself from the moment and reached to the nightstand to take a condom from the drawer.

"You can't get pregnant by me." His eyes hardened as if that was a bad thing. "And I don't have any diseases. None that a condom can protect you from, anyway."

I dropped my hand away from the drawer and grasped the back of his head, moaning deeply into his eager mouth, until he broke the kiss, pressing his forehead to mine.

He dared to push back into me harder. My lips instinctively sought to kiss the soft skin below his ear, nibbling and sucking. I brought my hips upwards to meet him, circling and pressing, quickening the pace. I couldn't hold it back any longer. He followed suit and pumped into me with more force, thrusting hard and deep.

"Fuck!" I cried out as he flipped us round and had me straddling him.

I couldn't help noticing his eyes burn as he turned me and caught sight of the scar down my back. Was this the first time I'd let him see, in all its glory? Maybe he'd been too blinded by sun to see it when we were at the pool. Or maybe I'd been too distracted by his cock, and his smoking skin, to notice his reaction to it.

Either way, I immediately wanted to cover up. My hands instinctively went up to wrap around my own shoulders, but he took them and brought them down to his chest.

"You're everything, Jess. So beautiful," he panted. "You

can't see it, but you're glowing. Like the sunset over the ocean... sparkling and clear."

I rode him slow and sensual, despite my body crying out for more. Grinding my slickness against him, leaning back to hit the deepest spot. He palmed my breasts, squeezing them, pinching my nipples.

Coming forward, I leant over him, taking hold of the headboard, and dipped lower so that my nipple brushed over his mouth, letting him suck on it.

When I returned to an upright position, I gazed into those eyes and felt my mind swim away. His face was unrivaled; no other man could stir the same desire in me.

Finally... finally, I had him inside me and I would never let go. There was nothing in the world that could compare. No one that could make me feel so alive, so elated and terrified at the same time. My heart was heavy, with need, with the fear that this would end, that at some point his body would move away from mine, and I would be empty once more.

I dropped my hands either side of his head and slowed my pace, lifting clear away from his cock and gently sliding back down. Bringing one hand back up, I started rubbing my clit. He growled in appreciation, revealing his fangs — which turned me on even more. I rubbed at myself furiously, throwing my head back and moaning his name.

Then, he lost it.

He sprung up and pinned me back beneath him, ramming into me with force. Drawing one of my legs up over his shoulder, he stretched me out and drove in deeper. His grip tightened on my arms, and with the pain came the knowledge that the bruises would be severe.

He pounded into me with such power that I couldn't catch my breath through the groans. His rhythm never faltered. Each time his cock filled me, it was more delicious than the moment before.

Over and over and over for an eternity.

Hard enough that the bed creaked and shifted beneath us. I screamed out in ecstasy, wanting more, wanting it to never end, whilst at the same time feeling like I couldn't take it. The climax built inside me, spiraling and sprinting towards its desire.

"Fuck! Zac!" I wailed.

The pain had started out small, barely more than a niggle, but it grew, and it grew fast. Ultimately blasting through me like molten lead under my skin. It hurt, everywhere. Such a sweet, exquisite pain.

This was it. He was going to consume me, take me, fulfill my every desire, and kill me in the process. The urgent need in his face was crushing. It dissolved any scrap of will I had left. He needed me, as I needed him. I'd give him anything. Everything.

"Come for me, Jess. Do it now," he growled.

I was rubbing at myself as he drove into me, and that was all it took to set my orgasm free. Those commanding words pushed me over the edge. With a final scream, the warm, juicy pulses spread out from below as I came.

"Fucking hell, Jess." He gave a final thrust and matched my release, growling and shuddering. My body bucked and arched underneath him.

Then he was off me in an instant to shut himself in the bathroom, where I could hear him grunting and panting and breaking stuff. So much for the warm afterglow and snuggles.

*W*hen he came back out from the bathroom he had a calm, resigned look on his face.

It irritated me. I was on a different planet, far away, my body swelling with satisfaction. He could at least make the effort to look a little happy.

"I can't do that again," he said.

"No! Don't you fucking dare. You don't get to finally fuck me, take me to heaven and beyond, and then disappear."

"I'm not disappearing, I just..." He sank onto the bed beside me, war raging behind his eyes.

"It was incredible, beyond anything I've ever felt before." I leant into his chest. I'd get that damned snuggle whether he liked it or not.

"Do you have any idea how close I came?" he asked, an arm wrapping around me obligingly.

"Close enough to get my hopes up." I was pretty sure my bottom lip was sticking out like a baby.

"Not close to making you a vampire, you idiot! Close to killing you. I *need* your blood. I want to drink from you until there's none left."

"Don't be so melodramatic."

His incredulous look forced me to shrink back at my own ridiculous words.

"You won't kill me," I added. "You can't. At worst you'll convert me, or best, depending on whose viewpoint you take. It's win, win. We either have sex and you control yourself and everyone's happy, or we have sex and you don't control it, and you make me like you. I'm still good with that."

Huffing, he stood up and got dressed. Such a waste to cover up that remarkable body with clothing every day. I copied him, though, because it seemed appropriate given that the daily argument was brewing.

"Don't you want some part of your normal life back, in the real world?" he asked, already fully clothed in the speed it had taken me to get one leg into my jeans.

"There is no normal life or real world anymore."

"What about your work? Won't you miss that?"

The long suppressed pain associated with my job swelled up in my chest. "I became a firefighter after I killed my parents in an explosion. This scar on my back? I don't hide it because I'm ashamed of the way it looks, I hide it because I'm ashamed of the story behind it. I want to hide from the reminders, hide from the prying questions. But I have a responsibility to make amends. It's not an enjoyable career, it's a burden to carry. I've resorted to drugs and alcohol to try and shift that load on my shoulders. So no, I don't think I'd miss it that much."

He thought that through for a while.

"You don't realize what you'd be missing out on. Save more people before you have to start killing them."

That almost got through to me, but I chose to disregard the killing people thing. For some reason that part just wouldn't sink in and sway me. Best way to avoid dealing with stuff? Don't dwell on it.

"If I feel the need, can't I still be a firefighter? You guys mix with humans all the time. Think about it, I'd be the best there is. I'd save everyone with speed and strength, not to mention my immortality—"

"But why the rush to do this? I'll never find anyone else like you. I'll wait, longer…"

"If we can't be together during that time, then what's the point?"

"We *are* together. You finally broke my willpower and I fucked you. Or did you not notice?"

"It was mind-blowingly amazing," I tutted at him. "But then you told me you can't do it again. That's cruelty at its worst. You haven't even told me how good it was for you. You just launched into the usual angry *'we can't do this'* speech." Yanking my shirt over my head, I dropped back onto the bed.

"There's a gap in our relationship, Jess. A glaring difference in the way we feel about each other," he said grimly. "It's all backwards. You behave like a vampire and me a human. You see, I *love* you and I can prove it by the fact that my body burns for your blood and I resist. But also, I'm prepared to forego taking you sexually — if it means we can just have time together. But you? You're so obsessed with fucking me, to the point that you'll do anything to get it, even if it actually wrecks us and pushes us further apart. That's not love, Jess, that's just lust."

I LOVE YOU… I LOVE YOU… I LOVE YOU. HIS WORDS WENT ROUND and round my head on repeat. I knew he'd be able to hear me obsessing over those three words, but I couldn't help it. It was hard to stay angry with each other after such momentous words had been sent forth into the world, even if it was kind of by accident. Not to mention the fact that I was still bathing in sexual glow and couldn't feel anything other than love for him, even if I'd wanted to.

He chuckled softly. I raised my eyes wearily to his.

"If I'd known it was going to have this effect on you, I'd have said it a lot sooner," he smirked.

I tried not to rise to the bait and scowled at him.

"I *should* have said it sooner. It just seemed obvious. I don't have much practice at this dating thing, I guess I forgot I actually needed to say it."

"You still didn't, really, not the right way," I pouted.

"I love you," he replied instantly.

I jumped into his lap, wrapping my arms around him tightly. "You know I love you too, right? That it's way more than lust?"

"I shouldn't have said that. Yes, I do know."

"Of course you do," I groaned. "I bet you hear that going round my head all the time, too."

"Once or twice."

Scarlet heat flushed over my face. I'd behaved like a schoolgirl, obsessing over a boy I didn't even know, falling head over heels and thinking my whole existence revolved around him. I had no chance of changing that now, either.

I was falling ever deeper, spiraling into a world where nothing mattered except him. He'd given me his body, made me feel like I was on fire, burning with need. The way he'd entered me so slowly and cautiously, driving me insane with ecstasy, before fucking me so hard I couldn't breathe...

His cock jerked beneath my ass and his hands slid up to caress my breasts.

"It was the most exquisite feeling I've had in all my years," he groaned into my neck.

I leant back, whimpering at his touch, my nipples taut and eager for his lips. Not patient, gentle kisses this time, but greedy and rampant ones, owning my body, dominating every part of me. I writhed down into his lap and his body stiffened beneath me.

"What's wrong?" I hardly dare ask.

"Alexander. The thoughts you have about him."

"Don't start fighting again, not now. You know I love you. He messes with my head, but I can handle it."

"I don't doubt that. What I doubt is whether *I* can handle it."

His hands had found a safe place back on my waist, away from my tingling nipples.

"He'll get bored and move on to a new game soon," I urged.

"No chance. This is the end game. He's going to push through to the finale."

Despite my wriggling and groaning, my desperate attempts at arousing him again fell flat. He'd left the moment, dragging me back, too. I slumped against him with a sigh.

"Since you've successfully dodged any further sex, can I ask something about last night, without you getting worked up?"

"I don't know. You can try, if you really want to risk it."

He was right, it was a risk to bring it all up again. This day had come around with less hostility and I should have been building on that. But it had been bothering me for the last hour.

"Twice now, Alex has mentioned that you have secrets. Dangerous ones."

383

He ground his teeth. "You already know that. I told you. The sanguine shit and the Legacy."

"But you haven't told me though, have you? I still have no clue what it all means."

"You do understand the definition of the word secret, right? Everyone has them."

"I don't."

He sniffed, frowning. "You expect me to believe that Jessica Leyton doesn't have some dark demons hidden away?"

"None that I wouldn't reveal if you asked me to. Anyway, you generally help yourself to my thoughts, so it's hardly fair." Not true. I had plenty of secrets around my mysterious bursts of energy...

"You know that I can't keep skirting round your deception forever, right? Whatever you are, if you keep trying to hide from it, it's going to bite your ass."

"Stop turning this around, I asked about you first."

He sighed and stared ahead for a while. I don't think he was avoiding answering, just thinking about stuff he didn't enjoy talking about. Bracing himself for the inner turmoil.

"It's supposed to be a great honor, a blessing," he finally said. "The Legacy bond has been passed down through many generations in the Elwood bloodline. But only in twins. When Alexander and me were sired by an Elwood – Tobias – the Legacy bond was passed to us. If we were sired as adults then the mark probably would have appeared immediately on one twin, but since we were sired as children it manifested once we'd reached full strength."

He lifted his shirt sleeve and pointed to a bright tattoo, almost glowing, depicting concentric circles with symbols around the edges.

"It's not a tattoo, though it looks like one. The twin that bears the mark is the one destined to protect the Legacy...

they're the keeper, the one that can activate the power. It only forms on a few Elwoods, most never receive the mark, or the power. But it was always taken for granted that, should we be blessed with the mark one day, it would fall on Alexander. He was deemed stronger, more in tune with his *inner vampire*. You can imagine his shock and rage when I stepped out one day with this on my arm." He attempted a smile.

I ran my fingers over the markings. It blended right in with the tattoos and I wondered if that was intentional on his part. Hiding it.

"You skirted past it with your fingers once before," he smiled, genuine this time. "On our date at Mount Washington. You settled on the words underneath. *'Fiat Lux – let there be light'*. Those words have dual meaning. Primarily, to remind me of the lighter path I choose to walk. But also a reminder of the daylight walking capabilities that the bonding would bring. You see, it's not that I don't want to activate the Legacy. I want it a great deal. I want to walk in the sun without pain and of course I want the strength, too. I just don't want the associated dark shit that goes with it."

"How does it work?"

"The original Elwood fell in love with a witch, with the family name Morena. He turned her to darkness and torment. She'd fallen for both him and his twin, and she wanted to keep them both. She was twisted, with a ravenous desire for power. She created the Legacy magic to increase the Elwood brothers' abilities, and to pass down the blood-line indefinitely. I guess she planned to create an army of us to serve her."

"It didn't work? How many of you are there?"

"Not many. Magic can be fickle. It seems to decide by itself exactly how a spell will work, what the side effects may be, what requirements must be met. Sometimes it listens to the witch and behaves as expected. Sometimes it says fuck you and does as it pleases." He absently rubbed a hand over my shoulder. "They've tried and failed to understand what makes it choose. For a while they sired hundreds of twins, all that they could find. They were desperate for their Elwood army, but no further marks came. Emory came along though, and took them into the Bael. So, you see, I'm a rare asset to their council."

"They joined forces?"

"Yes, the original Elwoods sit with him. Others have rebelled. Some, like Tobias, were exiled when they were no longer useful, and then murdered. But they want me and Alexander as their soldiers."

"But you can choose? I mean, you have this mark, but you don't have to become what they want?"

"Only the keeper, the one with the mark, can activate the Legacy through a blood bonding ritual. Only then will both twins surge with unmeasured power and ability."

"But you wouldn't be yourself any longer?"

He shook his head slowly.

This was probably the most open he'd ever been with me. He finally trusted me, let me in. Maybe getting laid had loosened his lips. I wondered what else he'd spill if I could get him to put out again.

He let out a soft snort.

"What?! It's true, isn't it? Don't clam up now, why don't you go ahead and enlighten me on the sanguine attraction shit, too? Has it warped your view of me?"

"Undoubtedly, but I still won't give that notion a voice. It's too dangerous. If I put it out there then the Beast will feed on the instincts, and the Bael... they'd expect the ceremony to be performed."

Conflict around every corner. It was no wonder he was so tense all the time.

But there had been another woman in his life once. Had she caused him as much confusion and distress as me?

"What happened to Selena?" I asked, whilst the going was good.

His jaw ticked. "She fell under my spell, offered everything to me. I fed from her regularly, becoming greedier and more consumed. I believed I was entitled to that blood. She gave it freely and I needed it. But she became weaker, anaemic, frail. One day I looked into her eyes and realized what I'd done to her." He paused to rub a hand over his forehead.

"The vibrant woman I fell in love with had withered away, yet still she offered herself to me completely. I vowed to change. That was when I started practicing restraint, wanting to live a different way. Alexander was furious by my behavior. Selena gradually regained vibrancy as I abstained. Then she went missing. I could never prove it, but I know Alexander took her. Probably believing that with her out of the way I'd revert to my usual self. If anything, it had the opposite effect and firmly rooted me on the lighter side. Then the mark appeared, on me... and pushed Alexander into an unending hatred for me."

"He... he killed Selena?" I gasped.

"I tried to kill him in return. Many times."

"I'm so sorry."

"It was a long time ago," he sighed.

I shifted uncomfortably. They were playing a bigger game than any that I could ever dream up.

"He told me that he hears you calling out to him. He's trying to convince me how much you want him. He wants to shove my nose in it, make me eat that shit right out of his hands." His fists clenched.

"Oh."

Stupidly, I felt hurt and betrayed that Alex was merely

using me to get at Zac. It had seemed more real, like he really did want me. Was I another Selena? A pawn to be played with in their rivalry?

Zac gave me a grim look and it slowly dawned on me that my response of '*Oh*' wasn't satisfactory. Where was the denial?

"That's bull and you know it. I went to his house because I was scared for Anna."

He shook his head.

"I mean... it's not like that... it's just..." Fuck, how could I tell him? I wasn't even sure what I felt myself.

"He's using his power on you. Forget it."

"He told me that *you're* the most dangerous one," I said quickly, before I could change my mind.

He thought on that, licking his lips. "He's right. I've always been a monster. Not because I'm a vampire, but long before that. A troubled child with issues of power. I caused people pain and I liked it. Becoming a vampire exacerbated that. If I slip up and go back, I'd become your worst nightmares. I fear Alexander, not because he's stronger than me, but because of what I could become if he pushed me there."

I fiddled with the silver chain in my pocket. What was I supposed to say to that?

"You know, Selena was everything to me. She made me what I am today. But that came after I gave her pain and fear, and death." His eyes hazed over, so I let go of the chain and took hold of his hand. "I can't let that happen with you."

"You were a different person back then, but you fixed it, you changed. That's what matters," I whispered.

"I'm only ever one step away from ending up back there. Walking the tightrope, balancing between the two worlds. If I mess up and take blood from you, even if I somehow managed to stop myself from killing you on the spot, I'd need more. I would want it every day, more and more, addicted. I'd drain you, weaken you. You couldn't sustain what I'd need, what I would take."

And then he was gone. The vampire who told me he loved me with a sparkle in his eye went back into hiding, and the brooding one returned.

42

JESS

a week later, I stood with the masses on Independence Day. The sky flashed above; orange, red, purple. Whizzing and popping of fireworks exploding in bright bursts. We watched from the deck of a tourist boat, waiting for it to set sail around the island.

I was to be wined and dined. Zac's insistence on more dates, more normalcy. Anything to try and convince me that we could function like a regular couple.

He vanished into the heart of the boat to reserve us a dining table. What would he do while I ate?! The thought amused me and I bit my bottom lip, excited and nervous, as if this really was a first date.

When he returned, he slid his hands around my waist from behind and pulled me into his stiffness. He licked the edge of my ear. Brushed his lips over my neck. My knees threatened to buckle. He made me relentlessly horny, my body could barely handle it.

I closed my eyes and turned, grabbing behind his head, pulling his lips to mine.

He was different, less cautious. His tongue thrust into my mouth and I wobbled. Shit, surely the days of passing out to his electric kisses were behind me? Was the threat of losing my mind over those dizzying sparks ever going to pass? I hoped not, even if it was embarrassing.

His hand cupped my breast with an urgent squeeze. I grabbed his ass to feel that delicious erection pressing harder against me. Let the whole damned boat watch us, I needed him so much. The ease of his hands on my body drove me wild, roaming freely over my curves, his kiss demanding and uncaring. No tension, no threat of him retreating, he submitted to me.

This is how it should always be. Free to explore each other, free to touch and taste without fear and tension. Only the desperate aching need, surging free—

He was suddenly torn away, and there was snarling.

Lots of snarling.

It took a moment for everything to stop spinning. And when it did, none of it made sense anyway.

Zac had pinned Alex to the deck and the whole gathering on the boat fell silent, watching. Alex was grinning, and Zac? Well, he looked like Satan himself.

"I'll fucking kill you," Zac growled, his hand tight on Alex's throat.

"All these years of trying and all it took to put a fire under your ass was a woman," Alex laughed, tight and strained as his throat was crushed.

It was like I was in one of those bad dreams where you needed to run, or speak or something, but you just couldn't make anything happen. I stood like a useless fool.

Where did Alex come from? Why were they fighting like that?

Alex made eye contact with me and winked, all playful and charming, like that hand around his throat wasn't about to crush it entirely.

From the corner of my eye, I noticed Eva and Leon

tearing down the boardwalk and onto the boat, flanked by Alex's guys. Didn't they have lives of their own? Other places to be?

Zac stood, grabbing the shirt at Alex's shoulders, and lifted him up. Then he launched him onto a table, which practically disintegrated at the contact. Glass and wood flew around them. A woman who'd been sitting at the table screamed as she pulled herself from underneath the mangled wreck, blood gushing down her leg. Just fantastic. Now all the vampires were probably struggling to keep their fangs up.

Staff from the boat started shouting and trying to order the fighting animals off the deck. Then other people joined in with the shouting and gesturing, myself included.

Alex had got back to his feet in a second, still grinning and moving with lazy ease, managing to somehow look even scarier than Zac, which was some accomplishment.

Zac hurled himself forwards again and crashed into Alex, who stumbled backwards. He tipped over the railing, pulling Zac with him, and landing in the water with barely a splash. They sank beneath the waves and all I could see was water.

Someone shrieked and threw a life ring over. I laughed, high pitched and a little hysterical. Mainly because the water was hardly more than a couple of meters deep, but also because of the absurdity of two vampires needing buoyancy aids.

Even so, a wisp of fear started to creep into my lungs when an eternity passed and they still hadn't resurfaced. Eva and Leon weren't paying attention to the water, they were too busy standing their ground against Alex's guys.

A whoosh of relieved sighs erupted in unison around me as a drenched man appeared on the surface. He approached the boardwalk and did some sort of un-human leap, landing himself quietly on the wooden planks. Dripping wet, frozen with rage.

The other crazed man copied. Now there were two deranged psychopaths blocking the only exit from the boat. Eyes ablaze with a fire that couldn't be explained.

Panic swirled amongst the crowd. Mutterings about, *how did they do that? How did they get out of the water like that?*

I moved toward them, willing my feet not to fail me in the face of this chaos. They stood, side by side, shoulder to shoulder, chests heaving — watching me advance. Alex smirked.

A flash of realization passed through me. The reason the kiss had felt so different.

Fucking hell! It was his lips that had been on me! *He* was the one kissing me? How had I not realized?

I think my stomach dropped right through my feet and into the sea below, washing away on the tide. I had nothing inside but anxiety.

Every shred of the human façade had crumbled from Zac. I was torn between the fascination of watching Alex, the way he looked at me like he'd won and owned me — it made my heart do weird things.

But I couldn't take my eyes off Zac either; the man I loved, dissolving into a monster before me. That made my heart tear into pieces.

I looked backwards and forwards between them.

"Maybe we should take this somewhere more private," Alex said in a low voice. "Where we can behave *normally* without people noticing."

Zac nodded to Eva and she wandered into the crowd. I turned to watch as she ran a hand serenely over every person that she passed, the lightest of touches. The buzz in the air began to quieten.

Zac shot me a look of pure disgust before telling Alex, "The Strip," and turning away.

He walked down those wooden planks like a ticking bomb, leaving a trail of wet footprints behind him. I wasn't prepared for that fierce look. Rage and loathing, boiling over and spewing out of his tormented eyes.

I watched him go. He didn't grab me and pull me away. He didn't even look back. He just left me there, speechless and motionless.

He left me with Alex?! What the actual fuck?

The devil himself cocked his head in my direction, holding out a hand.

Eva knocked it aside with a growl.

At that moment, it took every shred of energy left in my body to walk away from him, away from the gravitational pull into his dark and twisted arms.

43

ZAC

I paced up and down the road, the oppressive night choking and seeping into me. The whooshing in the air indicated how close the sea was, just over the dunes on both sides. I kicked at the yellow 'road ending' sign — still lying there, cracked and broken in the sand, after Jess's little joyride on my motorcycle. That felt so long ago. How naive she was then. Not that she was much more enlightened now.

And how ironic now. *Road ending.* This was it. The long-awaited end to a painful journey with my brother. Brewing for years and pushed into place by Jess.

Finally! Let go... the release will be exquisite.

But what did I expect? Nothing. Truth be told, I'd always known it would come down to something like this. Something fucked-up. It was never going to work.

I tried to use the rhythmic rise and fall of the tide to calm myself. Fucking useless plan that was. I'd never felt this unhinged before. *Ever.* Not even before I changed. In my darkest days I'd felt more restrained than I did right now.

The need for Jess was so deep in my core that I was barely able to hide it on the outside; holding that shit together on the inside was destroying me. How long could I keep pushing back the Beast before it broke free? I was living on borrowed time.

Eva arrived with Jess in tow. I listened to them talking further down the road.

"Listen," Eva said. "I don't want you to see this, but I have to be here in case he needs me and I can't leave you alone anywhere."

Jess made a move towards me, but Eva stopped her. "No. Do not say one word, no matter what happens here. Don't try to reason with him while he's like this. You'll make things worse."

Too fucking right she would. Why the hell was she even here? I stormed over to them in a second.

"I told you to take her to our place," I said, refusing to let my eyes land on Jess.

It didn't matter that none of this was her fault, that she was helpless against our lure. I hated her. I hated her for being everything, for calling out to my darkest desires with her whole being. For pushing and taunting me, for making me feel like an eternity in hell would be less painful than loving her.

Because I did... love her.

I hated her and I loved her.

It's time. Claim her. Wed her. She's only fit for one purpose...

"I'm not leaving you like this," Eva said to me.

"I've got the other guys. Get her the hell out of my sight, Eva, I'm not fucking around here. I don't want to hurt her."

Jess's pulse jumped. She clutched her stomach like she was going to be sick.

Time ran out to argue about it because Alexander arrived with his men. They strolled towards us, the cheery sound of his fucking whistling drifting along on the ocean breeze. I went forward to meet them halfway, my guys at my back.

"Let's cut the crap," Alexander said. "She wants me."

"Fuck you."

"That's right, she does want to fuck me. You not giving her enough fulfillment in that department?"

His ever present grin tested me. I surged forward. His men moved in front and blocked the way. He wouldn't let me get to him again until he'd finished with the verbal diarrhea.

"You don't even want her," I spat.

"Wrong again, brother. On the contrary. I have feelings for her almost as strong as your sanguine bonding. Tell me, how does that feel to find the woman you're fated to kill, but your own miserable conscience stops you?"

I paced back and forth in front of his battle line, his men smirking at me.

"Don't beat yourself up, Zachariah," he continued. "It wouldn't be the first time she's chosen the bad guy. She has a history of picking them. Ex cons, cage fighters, drug addicts. She's a pretty bad judge of character."

"You don't know shit about her."

Alexander laughed, "Oh, but I do. A little nudge against old contacts, some digging here and there. If you weren't such a pussy you'd have done the same thing for yourself."

"Why would *you* do it?"

"The bigger question is why you *wouldn't*, given that she's not an average human? But Zachariah, I'm offended. I'm only looking out for you. If this vixen is getting her hands on my brother, I want to make sure she's suitable material for you. Unfortunately, she isn't. She's a nasty bitch and you deserve better. She's more my type. We both know I don't deserve any better."

He glanced in her direction and drifted closer.

"If you take one more step towards her, I swear I'll rip you apart."

"Your threats to kill me are becoming tedious. I see I'm still standing," he shrugged.

I hissed and spat at the fucktards standing in my way, surging into them, trying to break through. Alexander was like the eye of the storm, walking calmly and composed, smiling from ear to ear, in the middle of a wave of violence. My men were at it, too, raging beside me, teeth grinding.

"Call your fucking goons out of the way and deal with this one on one, Alexander. I dare you," I yelled.

And just like that he gestured his arms wide and the men before him cleared, swiftly retiring to the sidelines. I snapped my head and my Cell followed suit. They wouldn't attack until I told them to.

I flew through the air and his nose shattered as my forehead met his face. He wiped at the blood, letting his grin grow wider. It was infuriating. No amount of physical damage I could do would even come close to hurting him the way he hurt me.

Emotional hurt was out of the question with someone who genuinely didn't care about anything. Which left only that one option I'd been analyzing and threatening.

Killing him wasn't going to cause enough hurt, but at least I wouldn't ever have to see him again. That was some small consolation.

You'll lose the Legacy if you kill him. Set me free, but do not end him... do not...

He took advantage of my distraction and launched, pushing me down into the road. Towering over me, he stomped hard on my chest. I heard my ribs cracking, but didn't feel a thing. He aimed his boot at my face. I rolled out of the way and caught his leg, dragging him down with me.

We struggled, each gaining the upper hand and then

losing it. Bone crunching blows rained down, over and over. A deluge of blood, swearing and snarling. I had a slight advantage on speed, but he was stronger. When it came to the crunch though, we were too damned evenly matched.

Regaining upright positions, I circled, waiting for him to come back at me. Instead, he reached out, grabbing the person who'd been thrust at him. Jess screamed my name, struggling in his grasp. He pulled her in tight, his hand squeezing around her throat, fangs at her neck.

I whirled around to see Eva on her knees, clutching her chest.

Fuck! Fucking assholes.

"Nope," Alexander warned, as I turned back to face him. "Stay there. Don't make me destroy her, Zachariah, it would be a terrible waste."

Jess was gasping, her eyes bulging, his grip on her neck too tight. I took a step back and he loosened off a fraction.

He started whistling again. Smiling. Pressing his nose into her neck and breathing deep. His fingers tightened as I considered attacking.

I held my hands up.

"Checkmate," he smirked. "I will give you two choices, Zachariah. You give her to me, or you give the Legacy to me. But know that I'm taking one of them. I'm not leaving this round empty handed."

Snarling rage circled my mind, rattling against the cage. This was it. His big game plan. Only two things in this whole world that I wasn't prepared to give up and he was going to make me pick one.

"Get over yourselves, you fucking idiots," Jess suddenly spat, taking us both by surprise. "I'm not a fucking pawn for you to play with. I choose where I go, not you."

He laughed in her ear. "You can be so damned cute, darlin'."

"Oh yeah?" She reached into her pocket and pulled out a silver pendant necklace. Before he could register what it was, she'd pressed it against the hand holding her throat. He pulled away sharply, cursing. It wasn't enough to cause him any major pain, but it had been enough to shock him. And a split second was all I needed.

She ducked away and before he could grab her I charged, knocking him off balance. I got hold of him and lifted his body into the air. Launching with whirlwind speed, I dropped him onto the metal pole of that broken road sign with such force that even his fortified skin couldn't defend him.

The pole pierced straight through his back and out his chest. Shock plastered his face as he looked down at the bloody metal sticking through him, and then up at me. I moved eagerly onwards, knowing what I had to do.

The frenzy of his men behind was deafening. I didn't need to look back to know that the scuffling and snarling was from my own Cell, blocking and preventing them from getting close. They wouldn't be able to hold them back long. The power of a Cell whose leader was in mortal peril was unmatched.

"Wait," Alexander yelled, blood spluttering from his lips and choking his words. "Just wait... think this through. You know it'll cause more problems. You can have the whore. You win."

I paused, some distant part of my conscience pleading with me not to kill my own brother.

Jess wrapped herself around my body, melting into me, sobbing uncontrollably. "Please don't," she cried.

My resolve fizzled, the darkness fuming behind the bars. It was almost there, so close to breaking free. One little nudge.

Killing my brother would be that push. I'd lose it if I did that shit. No turning back.

She quivered into my chest, dissolving the rage further. *Fuck!*

Stepping away from her, I raised my fist, smashing it into Alexander's already broken nose. My fangs slid out, bringing with them a surge of instinctual hunger. I licked the blood from his face, tracing the thin, silvery line of his scar to belittle him.

Grabbing hold of his shirt, I pulled his face up to mine, so that the pole slowly tore out of his body. "Call her a whore again, I'll kill you. Come anywhere near us again, I'll kill you. If you so much as *think* her name, I will fucking kill you."

I let go and the pole crunched back through him. Walking past his snarling men, held back by my own animals, I reveled at the sounds of him struggling to free himself.

44

JESS

*E*va took me under her wing, as usual. Zac wouldn't look at me in the immediate aftermath, he stormed off and disappeared. When we got back to the house I found him in the living area, blood trickling from his lips, down his chin, dripping onto his bare chest. The buttons on his shirt were torn open. I watched, mesmerized, as a line of blood gently ebbed down towards his nipple.

Before I could allow the confusing and inappropriate thought of licking it off to develop further, I sought out his face again; the pain in his eyes, the fury still resonating. Small veins had spread around them, etching little blue spiderwebs across the normally perfect, smooth skin.

He wiped his mouth with the back of a hand, smearing blood across his cheek.

"W... what...?" I began.

"What do you think it is?" He turned the full force of his malevolent stare onto me.

"It's cool," Eva said. "He needed to feed. Better them than you."

Better *who* than me? What the fuck? He couldn't have

just happened across a murderer on his way back from the Strip.

"We can tell you about the basement a different day," Eva said softly, Zac's angry glare shifting to her.

She guided me upstairs and left me in her room. I sat on the silk bedspread and tried to cry. Maybe it was the shock setting in, but the tears wouldn't come. I don't know how long I stayed like that, with the dry, silent crying. This was monumentally fucked up.

Eventually, Zac arrived, and I shrank away, trying to sink deeper into the mattress. I'd never seen him look so terrifying, his shirt still hanging open revealing a bloodied chest, slashed and bruised, just like his face.

I wanted him to fuck me right then.

Yes, I know. Ridiculous.

Having a feral monster before you should make you squirm in fear, not squirm in desire.

But that weird buzzing under my skin was screaming out to be touched.

It would make it okay though, wouldn't it? To have that connection. To touch and be loved, to ease away the anger. To feel him inside me again, making me whole. I needed it. It would fix things.

"I'm not going to say I'm sorry, because it's all we ever do," I said. "And this wasn't my fault. He came up from behind and put his hands on me. I thought it was you. He tricked me."

"You couldn't tell you were kissing someone else?" he asked, slowly and clearly, but deep with rage.

"No. Well... it did feel different, but the point is, I wasn't *expecting* anyone else. My head was swimming, like it does with you."

"You want him."

"No, I don't."

"Then what *do* you want?"

"You know the answer to that."

"Yeah, I do," he said with fierceness.

Pulling me to my feet, he stroked my face, a look of pleading and regret in his eyes. Then his fingers snaked around my throat, pushing my chin up. They tightened, enough that alarm rang through me. I stuttered and he gripped tighter.

"Tell me to stop," he said.

I couldn't.

I was slammed over the edge of the bed. One arm went under my stomach and pulled me up onto all fours, his other hand grabbing a handful of my hair. He pulled me up higher, onto my knees, my back flush with his chest.

His icy tongue ran along my ear. "If you keep pushing me, Jess, I'll kill you. I'll drain every last fucking drop of your blood and I'll keep fucking you while your life slips away."

Letting go, he dropped me back onto all fours. I heard his zipper and he pulled off my jeans, before tearing my underwear clear away. His solid shaft pressed into my backside.

"Tell me to stop," he said again, this time shouting. "*Beg* me not to."

I shook my head and he thrust himself into my ass. I was mortified by my scream. It wasn't the pain, although it did hurt like fuckery. I think it was more the shock, that I hadn't anticipated him behaving like that, or the overwhelming pleasure it would give me.

"He's right, you are a nasty little bitch." He pounded harder and harder into me. "Is this what you want? You want me to be more like him and rough you up? Were the bruises not enough last time?"

My ass cheek stung as he brought his hand down with a

loud thwack. The noise of my satisfaction was drowned out by the whip of further smacks. Sweet pain. Arousal escalated through me, bringing me closer to the edge. My legs trembled...

"No fucking way, you don't get to come this time," he spat. Flipping me around, he lifted me onto a desk, spreading my legs wide apart with rough hands. His grip tightened around my neck once more.

"Did you like it when my demented brother had his hands around your throat?" he yelled, thrusting inside me and continuing to drive with such force that the desk shook.

Yes.

I slammed my hand down to steady myself, right onto a shot glass, which broke and sliced into my skin. Shoving it into my mouth, I sucked on the blood.

He bared his fangs, his devilish eyes claiming me.

I saw it then, for the first time, in all its satanic glory — the darkness he talked of. Right there in those eyes, burning fiercely. He would kill me. I could practically taste the darkness that lurked there.

Suddenly whimpering, I tried to move away. This wasn't right. It wasn't him. I wasn't ready to die. My breath caught and I choked, crying and groaning.

"Finally, you're afraid," he hissed. "That's it, baby, fucking struggle for me."

He fucked me with such ferocity that I screamed. One of the legs on the table cracked and broke, the whole thing lurching down at an angle. His hold on me was so tight that I stayed up in the air, my ass no longer even touching the wood, as he continued to pound me.

His mouth was perilously close to my neck, top lip curled up, fangs eager for me. With a final surge, he yelled like a maniac and his cock pulsed and throbbed, driving his cum deep inside me.

He let go of my ass, shoving me away.

As I toppled backwards over the broken desk, I caught sight of him sticking an arm under his chin and biting down into himself.

There was something entirely fucked up about being brutalized and enjoying it. I couldn't even fathom whether what he'd done was an acceptable act for a woman who liked it rough, or whether he'd crossed a line.

I'd told him I liked to be dominated, and I had been feeling inappropriately horny at the time, which he would have felt. I really *did* like rough sex. There was nothing wrong with that. Many people did. BDSM was a thing. Consensual non-consent was a thing. Edgeplay was a thing — *my* thing. Why should I be made to feel so bad for that?

But that — what just happened, that wasn't him. I battled with my emotions, unsure why I'd enjoyed it when he'd been so callous. Though to be honest, the real cruelness was not the act itself, it was the way he behaved afterwards that cut me so deep.

"Happy now?" he asked spitefully. "You got what you wanted. Well, almost, I'm sorry I didn't kill you or convert you. But you did get the nasty fucking you were after."

"Sex and being a vampire isn't all I want."

"No? Could have fooled me." He glared so hard that I almost forgot how to breathe.

"I want us to be content. I want to show you how much I love you, but sex always gets in the way and twists it." I reached out to touch him, but he shifted away.

"Because that *is* all you want. I've worked, *tortured myself*, for longer than you've even been alive. All that time, training myself to be stronger, to stay in control. I have

406

people that believe in me, who've followed me down the same agonizing road. And you threaten to undo all that. You taunt me for sex over and over, even if it involves risking your life, and with no regard for what it could do to *my* life. This is so much more than lust, or love... it's everything. And yet you're so desperate for more that if I can't give it to you, you'll go to him? And let me tell you, what I just did was fucking romantic compared to what he'd do. But then, that's what you want, right?"

Something imploded inside my chest. My heart crushed under the weight of those hurtful words. He fucked me like that because he thought he had to, in order to stop me going to Alex? To make himself more attractive to me, by being more like him? Way to make a girl feel cheap and dirty.

I couldn't deny it, though. Had I ever thought about what my actions did to him? I was quick to call the victim blaming card, but was I really that desperate for sex that I stumbled blindly along with nothing else in my mind?

No. That still didn't make him right. *He* was the one that kept putting me in danger, who was rough with me, and hurtful, and yet I was supposed to feel sorry?

"You know what? Maybe you're right. Maybe Alex is more of a man than you."

He slammed his fist into the wall beside my head, leaving a hole.

I didn't know why I said it, except that I wanted to hurt him. Spite him. Throw it back in his face. Fuck him for making me feel like this, for crushing my heart and stealing my soul. I would never be the same again.

"Good luck to you. He's all fucking yours," he said slowly, dusting off his knuckles. He turned to leave and I barged past him into the doorway.

"Fuck you! You don't get to fuck me like that and then

fuck off," I screamed in his face and slapped him hard across the cheek. His eyes narrowed, but he stood immobile.

His hands hung down by his sides as I shook him, frantic and raw. I hit him again. And again.

The third time he caught my wrist and pinned it against the wall. "You want him. You can't hide from it and nor can I. I can't give you what you need."

"Bullshit, you can give me everything and you know it. You hold back to torture yourself more. Stop playing the martyr and let go. You are everything. *He* is lust. But you? *You* are love and lust, and everything in between." I pressed my face forward, closer to his, my words hitting him straight on.

"You don't get it. It doesn't matter what I do. Even if I figure this shit out and learn intimacy without the crippling fear that I'm going to murder you, he'll still be there. His vendetta against me won't cease."

"So you're on your brother's shit-list. Whoop-de-fucking-doo. Grow a pair and fuck him off," I spat.

"Grow a pair?" he raged, releasing me and marching round the room, hands dragging through his hair. "I was about to kill him until you stopped me! Why did you stop me? I could have taken him out, once and for all."

"Killing him isn't the answer."

"Then what is? He'll never leave. He'll stay in the background, taunting and pushing until I break. Until he's taken the most important things from me."

He found me again, taking solace in the connection of our bodies, our foreheads together, both of us panting and heaving. Anguish clutched around my heart.

"Let him stay," I whispered. "Let him try. We're stronger. He's jealous and envy will only weaken him."

His embrace tightened, but it felt like I'd lost him.

408

ANNA WAS CALLING. SHE'D TRIED SEVERAL TIMES OVER THE last few days, but I couldn't face answering. I'd called in sick to work and was avoiding Zac too, believing foolishly that a little time-out would calm us all down.

It was insignificant on the scale of my problems, but I was still hurt about the conversation I'd overheard between Anna and Danny. What made it worse was how right they were. How I was sitting in the middle of a messed up shit-storm and now I couldn't talk to them about it, because it was precisely everything they'd tried to warn me about. No way in hell was I running crying to them now.

She'd left messages, sounding upset, insisting she needed to talk to me. I let it ring through to voicemail again as I lay back on my sun lounger and took a swig of vodka.

A new text message came through.

Anna: *I know something important about the Elwoods. You have to meet me asap. Where are you? You're not safe. Please let me know you're OK?*

Wonderful. How the hell did she find out about them? Oh hell, had she got herself involved with a vampire, too? But maybe that would be good, if she knew? At least then we could talk and I could explain. She might understand.

I hid the cell phone under my towel and closed my eyes. She'd have so many questions. She'd be angry that I kept it from her for so long. I had to prepare myself for that conversation. She'd no doubt chew my ass more than ever about needing to leave Zac and get away from the island. I couldn't face that right then. It was hard enough battling the current issues with Zac, getting her involved at this stage would be more than I could take.

I focussed on breathing, counting to ten and back down. A group of lads were cooking on a grill nearby, the smell of burgers wafting around us. They turned up the music, roughhousing in the sand. The familiar island sounds washed over me. For a tiny second everything felt normal.

"Hey, lady, answer your cell would you?" I startled awake to find a skinny guy in a baseball cap looming over me, shaking my cell phone in my face.

"Shit!" I sat up, grabbing it from him.

"It's been ringing over and over for the last ten minutes, you were totally out of it. Someone really wants to get hold of you." He stumbled back to his friends. The grill coals had turned to gray ash, a few wisps of smoke snaking upwards. The sky had darkened, a purple glow on the horizon.

Fuck me, how long had I been asleep?

Bringing up my messages, I listened to Anna's urgent voice.

Jess, please, you have to help me. Please, get help, bring Zac, I need help. Oh shit, Jess. Hurry. I'm at an old outbuilding on the North nature reserve, past that turtle rehabilitation place.

What? *Fucking Alex!* This had to be him. My heart leapt into my throat as I whirled around.

"What's going on, what's the matter, Jess?" Zac grabbed my elbow and pulled me to face him.

"Where the fudge did you come from?" I gasped.

"I felt you getting anxious. What is it?"

"It's Anna - she's in trouble. It's Alex, he's got her. You said you'd keep her safe!" I spun around again, panicking, not knowing which way to turn.

"No, he wouldn't."

"Yes, he would. He's threatened her before and now he's furious at us two. Think about it, this is his payback. He said he'd stay away from me, but not her. I'm scared, Zac, what's he going to do to her?"

*T*he thudding of my feet thundered through my ears as I sprinted down the wooden boardwalk, past the turtle center and out across boggy marshland. An Egret flew up from underneath the planks, with a great thrashing of wings and splashing of water, causing me to shriek to high heaven.

I pressed on through the blinding darkness, one hand on the railing as my only guide. The purple sky seemed to have vanished into inky blackness in the minutes since I'd listened to that message. There was no neon lighting out on the reserve, nothing but the moon to guide me.

Zac was silent as he charged ahead. I was slowing him down, but he wouldn't leave me. Wouldn't go too far ahead despite my protests that he should.

He drew me to a stop, putting a finger to my lips.

We listened.

I couldn't hear a thing other than my own heart. No familiar shouting and music out here. Just us and the birds of the marsh, making an occasional plop as they went to and from the water.

I moved onwards, but was blocked by a wooden rail. The end of the boardwalk.

"What now?" I asked. "I can't see a damned thing out here."

"There's an outbuilding a little further along, the boardwalk doesn't lead there any more, it's not in use."

I swung a leg over the railing, ready to drop down.

"Jess, what the hell?!" Zac grabbed hold of my arm. "There's alligators in these waters."

"I'll have to take my chances." I tried in vain to shrug him off.

"We can't go charging in. I can't even tell what the hell's there. Something's off. I can't sense Anna or anyone else, it's all foggy."

"We can't just stand around here, can we?"

Dropping into the marsh with a squelch, he reached up and I climbed over so he could lift me into his arms. He looked confused, anxious. I wrapped myself around his neck.

He carried me through the marsh, stealthy and fast. Animals hurried away from us, birds taking off in noisy commotions. I thought I might have seen an alligator on the bank but I didn't dwell on that. It would be a dumbass alligator if it attacked a vampire.

"This is fucked up," he whispered, as we drew close to a building. I could just make out the cracked windows and looming stone walls through the gloom. "Something isn't right here. I should take you back to safety first. Fuck! I don't understand where my Cell are. I called out to them, they should be here. I need to get you to them."

"No way. Every minute could be a minute too late. It's only Alex, you can deal with his shit," I urged.

"It's not him. It's—" He suddenly let go of me and I fell into the cold marsh. Landing on my ass, a plume of water shot up into my face, making me splutter. I clapped a hand over my mouth, but I'd already let out an alarmed cry.

Zac clutched his head, moaning in pain. I leapt to my feet, sodden clothes weighing me down.

"Zac, what's happening?"

He shook his head from side to side, growling and shouting.

"Zac!" I screamed, pressing into his face, trying to get him to look at me.

He shoved me away hard, an instant reaction. I stumbled backwards onto hard ground and against the building. He was snarling now, his face twisted in rage and agony. He trained his eyes on me, wild and furious. His top lip curled upwards and his fangs descended.

With a ferocious snarl, he pounced. My head cracked backwards, straight into the stone. Shooting barbs of pain shot through my skull, the blackness of the night engulfing me.

I WAS DIMLY AWARE OF BEING DRAGGED BY MY HAIR OVER HARD stone, which bumped and bashed into my hips, but I couldn't seem to snap myself awake. Chains rattled and chinked together.

Hazy darkness. The pain in the back of my skull stabbed right through to my eyes.

More scuffling sounds, something heavy being dragged. More clanking. My shoulders hurt, the muscle twisting, straining and biting. I wriggled to try and ease the ache, but it wouldn't shift.

Then a different sharp and stinging pain whipped across my cheek.

"Wake up, fang-banger. Sleep time's over," came a deep

voice.

Another slapping pain, and my chin rolled over my shoulder.

"I said wake the fuck up. You don't want to miss the show."

Loud, angry growling. Roaring and gnashing, more clanking of chains. A terrifying feral noise, full of demonic rage.

My eyes flew open to see Zac, stripped naked and bound, his hands chained up overhead. He was writhing around like a wild creature, thrashing and straining at the restraints, foaming at the mouth.

I had to help him. How could Alex do this?

I stepped forward and the pain in my shoulders made me scream. I couldn't take another step. I looked up and found that I, too, was bound; strung up like a pig in an abattoir. My clothes lay discarded in a wet heap.

"There we go, that's better. Everyone present and correct, ready to play." A man swam into my vision. Muscles bulging through his tight, black shirt. Buzz cut hair, thick beard. He carried a long metal pole in one hand, tapping it in rhythm against his other.

Zac stopped thrashing and went completely still and silent, only his eyes moving as they tracked the man. Deadly eyes, watching their prey, analyzing every movement. He was taut and focussed, calculating, suddenly far from wild and crazy.

The man looked familiar, but it was dark and my vision was blurred. I thought my eye was swollen. This fucking lunatic man, who the hell was he to do this? He didn't look like a vampire with the heavy way in which he moved.

Zac would kill him. Those chains couldn't hold him.

Mr. Crazy stepped back towards me, smiling, banging the pole into the floor.

Clunk... clunk... clunk.

He stopped an inch from my face, Zac's stare burning holes into his back; ready to pounce, ready to break free.

I knew this man. I definitely knew him. Why was my head so damn jumbled?

"Oh my, fuck! William?!" I choked.

"You know him?" Zac growled, speaking for the first time. Why hadn't he busted out of those chains yet?

"He's one of Anna's boyfriends."

"*One* of?" William cocked an eyebrow at me.

"He doubles as a fucking vampire hunter," Zac groaned, white froth dropping from his chin.

Tendrils of fear crawled along my flesh, leaving a trail of goosebumps in their wake.

"What the hell? What have you done to Anna? Where is she, you bastard?" I yelled.

"Why would I have done anything to my sweet Anna?" William said. "She's not a vampire. Or a vampire whore."

Zac let out an almighty growl. Surely those chains couldn't hold much longer. He yanked and pulled. Blood appeared around his wrists where he was bound, along with angry, red burn marks.

William followed my gaze.

"Struggling with those chains, Zac? Do you know how hard it is to get hold of silver plated chains like that? Still, we best get on with the show before you start recovering some strength. It's fucking draining keeping up these cloaking and disorientation spells. It's a shame to start without Alex, but maybe this will help draw his attention."

I watched William advancing purposefully towards Zac, and was overcome with the fear of being stuck in a horror movie.

William lifted the metal stake and thrust it straight through Zac's chest with a sickening crunch.

Zac howled as his head slumped forward, blood flowing freely down his chest, and a gargled scream escaped me.

"Silver stakes are easier to source, pretty damned effective, too," William mused, giving it a sharp jiggle from side to side and causing Zac to cry out again. The smell of burning flesh stuffed itself up my nostrils. Red and black welts gathered at the edges of the wound where the stake sat.

"Did he ever tell you, Jess? The most humiliating and painful way for a vampire to die is through bleeding them dry. Let's speed that up..." William took a knife from his pocket and dragged it deftly over Zac's wrist. More blood spurted out and streamed down his arm.

"No! NO!" I screamed, agony surging through every part of my being. This couldn't be happening. *Vampires don't get fucked like this.*

"Now then, for the big, bad wolf. Tell me, Jess, what do you think will get Alex's attention most?" He took a photo of me on his phone, then one of Zac. "The threat of losing you? Or his precious Legacy bond?"

He paused, waiting for me to answer.

"If in doubt go with both," he said with a shrug, tapping the screen.

"William! Why is Jess tied up like that? Why is she half-naked? You promised you wouldn't hurt her!" Another voice I knew came singing through the air to slap me around. A door had opened and there she stood, all agog.

But it couldn't be her. She was in danger, she'd called me for help.

"For effect, Anna-doll. All part of the plan. Relax." William moved over to a far wall and my surroundings suddenly swam into vision. A crude pentagram was painted in red on the damp brick wall, from floor to ceiling, as big as

416

a man. Beneath it appeared to be a wooden altar, upon which a variety of tools, goblets and trinkets sat.

William removed one of the heavy silver necklaces from around his neck and placed it on the altar, whilst muttering chanted words.

"I'm so sorry, Jess. It'll be over soon. This had to happen, to get them here. But soon it will be done and you'll be safe," Anna pleaded, stroking my cheek with the palm of her hand as if soothing a child.

My brain couldn't compute… it just wouldn't. It stuttered and locked itself down. The power of speech left me… fucked off somewhere along with my power of comprehension.

"Well, well, that was quick." William ran to the other end of the room, grabbing a silver chain on the way.

Alex careened into the room, his fingers pressed into his head, just as Zac had done. I tried to yell, to warn him, but I don't think it would have done any good, even if the words had come.

William leapt onto Alex and they grappled in the shadows. William took a punch to the face and blood pooled on his lip. He chanted incantations, frenzied and loud, the words a messed-up jumble of nonsense to my own ears.

Alex's movements slowed and moments later, with cursing and clanking, William had him trussed up like a tame kitty, not a raging monster. Alex's head shook from side to side in confusion and pain as he allowed himself to be manhandled across the room and strung up like the rest of us.

"Fight, Alex! What are you doing? *Alex?!*" I found my voice, but as predicted it fell on deaf ears. He was completely overcome with confusion and weakness.

"Fuck me, I'm getting too old for this shit," William

gasped, doubling over to catch his breath. He snapped his fingers in the air and muttered further foreign words.

Like a fog-inducing bubble had burst, Alex regained composure. He didn't thrash, he didn't yell, but he calmly eyed his surroundings.

"The hunter you killed was a novice rookie, huh? Pity the same can't be said for this one," Zac groaned, and Alex growled.

Zac's head was still flopped forward, blood steadily trickling and forming a slick puddle beneath him. His chest heaved, the pole stuck rigidly right through him.

"I've seen you before, on the island. How did I not sense what you are?" Alex asked, his eyes sizing up William, tracking his movements like the predator he was.

"I'll take that as a compliment," William said, regaining an upright composure. "Especially when your men kicked the shit out of me one night that I pushed my luck at your club, and you still didn't see me for what I was. It was risky staying in such close proximity for an extended period, but it takes a great deal of planning and energy to prepare wards that are strong enough to hold you two, whilst simultaneously masking our whereabouts from your clans. The spells to keep me hidden during preparation were nothing compared to this."

William strolled over to Anna and put an arm over her shoulder. She flinched, darting yet another apologetic look my way. "The *rookie* that you took out served as a good distraction. Leaving those notes gave you his scent to chase around for a while," he went on.

"You're a Wiccan hunter," Zac tried to lift his head in William's direction, but it hardly moved.

"You never told me witches were an actual thing?" I shrieked.

William laughed, hearty and excited. "Oh, dirty little Jess, the irony of those words from your lips. How have you not figured out your lineage for yourself? I could feel it in you the moment we met. So could they," he nodded to the Elwoods. "There's ancient witchcraft in your blood, Jess."

46

___

JESS

"*W*hat?!" we all said together – Zac, Alex, myself, even Anna.

William spun round, smirking at us all, proud of his big, ridiculous lie. "You haven't even heard the best bit, yet," he grinned, his fingers toying with that bushy, black beard. "I did some digging on you, Jess. You have quite the potent family tree if you go back far enough. Your ancestors were of the Morena coven."

Zac and Alex both snapped their heads round to me. I gave them a wide-eyed questioning look. I'd have shrugged if I wasn't chained up.

Then everything fell into place in that foggy bit at the back of my brain.

Witch.

I was a motherfucking *witch*.

"That's not possible. That whole bloodline was wiped out," Zac said, in a voice so quiet that I started worrying about the amount of blood pooled at his feet. Surely he could get free if he fought harder?

"A delicious twist of fate, isn't it? And all true, I assure you. I've checked and triple checked. Seems some witches

420

sneaked through the net and stopped practicing, but continued to breed. Until, here stands Jess. Descended from the very witch who created your Elwood Legacy bond."

This time it was my head that whipped round, so hard it made my eyes throb.

"I checked her history," Alex said. "I never found anything pointing in that direction."

"You didn't look in the right places. The covens are exceptionally adept at keeping our particulars hidden from those who have no business knowing them."

Zac let out a snarl and pulled so hard on his chains that one of them snapped. My heart leapt with excitement. He was still stuck though, it looked like two sets of chains had been used. He yanked again, and Alex followed suit. Anna shrieked, jumping back into a corner.

"Whoops, power's running down," William said, calmly drawing a blade across his palm. He clenched and released his fist, squeezing out further blood until it was dripping down his arm. Then he pressed his hand to the center of the pentagram on the wall. As the blood smeared into the rough brick, he bellowed magical words.

And then they were gone again. The vampires were subdued, heads slumping with a glazed look.

"Enough talking," William grunted.

Without pause for thought, he grabbed a stake and pressed it over Alex's heart. He didn't flinch. Not even as William stared him in the eyes, pulled his arm back, and drove it straight through him.

"Tough boy, Alex. Who's going to get the double-staking?" He picked up another pole. Where the fuck did he get so much silver from?

"Jess? I asked a question? Which one?" He pressed his knuckles into Alex's forehead. The chunky, gothic rings he wore hissed and smoked as the silver skulls burnt flesh, leaving angry red welts. He held them there, the smell of burning skin making me gag, and this time Alex flinched. Satisfied, William walked over to Zac and did the same thing.

Anna whimpered from the shadows.

"Come on, Jess. How many times have I got to burn them? I can keep going all day..." He took the stake and pressed the shaft against Zac's forehead, causing him to shudder — his head forced up by the burning bar, eyes half-closed.

Witch. I was a fucking witch. *Do something, Jess.*

The buzzing thrummed through my ears. I closed my eyes and focused on it, willing it to take form, for something to happen. I'd conjured fire, sand, I could surely hurt William if I tried.

I opened my eyes and directed all my rage towards him, all the buzzing, and the pain in my head. A flimsy layer of static seemed to ebb over my skin, but... nothing. There was nothing.

William took that stake and forced the tip into Zac's mouth. He gargled and choked, head thrashing, as threads of smoke traced up his face.

"Alex! I choose Alex!" I cried.

"Of course you do. Poor old Zac isn't looking too healthy, is he? I guess that slit wrist really did speed it up. Good idea to even things up," William said, all sing-song and cheery, as he plowed another stake into Alex's stomach.

"You can't take us all on, you'll never get off this island alive," Alex coughed.

"I don't need you all. Your clans are confused and unable to trace us thanks to my spells. I'm satisfied with you two, since you're the big guns. Your men will disband. You must be stopped before you succumb to the lure of your damned Legacy."

"Ha!" Alex spat blood straight into William's face with an amused grin. Did he even care that he was chained up by some psychopath who was going to drain all his blood and kill him? Zac managed to raise his chin an inch to give him an exasperated look. "Trust me, there is no threat there. Trying to break Zachariah on the Legacy is about as effective as trying to mine gold out of your ass. Although... that would be a brutal experiment. One I might just try out later."

"Sorry, I should have said I'm happy to take out the *three* of you, not two," William dismissed Alex and allowed his glare to rake over my body, his face a vision of disgust.

Zac and Alex growled simultaneously.

"She's not a vampire," Zac mumbled.

"Yet. But she's as good as. Vampire whores always end up dead, or turned. I'd like to ensure it's the former."

This time the growling from the vampires was drowned up by the yelling of Anna as she marched across the room. "You promised, not Jess... you can't."

William produced the bloody knife from his back pocket and ran it across my collar bone, pressing hard enough to make a sharp sting. Zac yanked at his chains, albeit with a lot less gusto than ten minutes ago. He barely had the energy to speak let alone break free.

You're a witch. Do something.

I felt the power behind my eyelids, sweeping through my core. I focussed everything I had onto the bearded-goth-witch-man in front of me.

"I gave you a chance, Jess," he said. "I told you to leave."

"Those useless bits of paper taped to my bike?" I almost laughed. "Why didn't you just sit me down and talk? How long have you known, Anna?" I turned my glare onto my ashen-faced best friend.

"I... not long... how long did *you* know?" she whispered,

tears welling in her eyes. I should have told her long ago, before this lunatic worked his warped charms on her.

"I couldn't risk revealing my identity before I was ready." William dragged the blade over my chest, drawing blood. "The notes served two purposes. One, to distract my boys here, and two, because when I found you were a witch I owed it to your coven to try and protect you."

"This is protecting me?" I looked down at the knife, which was still trailing lazy paths across my skin. Zac and Alex were too quiet. Their chests didn't even seem to be moving with breath.

"Well," he smiled. "Then I dug deeper and found out you were Morena. Now I owe it to *my* coven to destroy you. You better not have vampire blood in your system... you been doing any kinky bloodletting with your boys? If so, I guess I'll just have the pleasure of killing you twice."

William dragged the blade back across my breast and circled it on my stomach. "I think you should join them in the same death. I'm going to watch you bleed out, you filthy, fang-loving whore."

The knife dug deeper, the point almost breaking through. The buzzing built in my head and surged across my skin.

Anna launched herself onto William's back and he swung around, grabbing her by the throat and throwing her across the room. She skidded on the increasing puddle of blood underneath Zac, crashing into him and landing in a heap next to his dangling body, his blood all over her.

"Don't disappoint me, Anna-doll. You knew the plan. Get your shit together," William spat in her direction, crinkling his face as she tried to wipe the blood away, only smearing it further.

"Not this... this isn't right..." she stumbled over her words, and over the blood, falling back on her ass.

I stared at Zac for help, willing him to look at me and give me a fucking clue. William already had his attention focussed back on me, playing with the knife over my skin. But Zac was staring at Anna, saying something to her. She stood shakily and tried to reach up to his chains.

We'd all been strung from some sort of hooks, hanging down from the ceiling beams. She was on her tiptoes, slipping around in the slick, red gloop; chains clanking.

Seriously, was this how I was going to die? It was hardly surprising, given my penchant for chasing down danger. But it sucked. If anyone in this room was going to have the pleasure of killing me, it should at least be an Elwood. Not this bearded fuckwad.

And yes, I was aware how fucked up that was. But it was the truth.

No one is killing you! Do something!

I had to keep William distracted, which didn't seem like it was going to be a problem. He was banging on about what a whore I was, about what a waste it was to kill a part-witch. The diatribe spewed forth relentlessly. The whole while, the knife nicked and cut across my body, searing and stinging pain accompanying his words.

A tide of rage built inside me. It seemed to blast out into a wall before me, thickening the air, turning it into something more tangible. Growing and consuming.

A flicker of confusion passed over William's face, but I was too lost in his torrent of abuse to focus on it. However, I was shocked back to the present when sudden pain erupted like fire in my core. I looked down and watched, like I was no longer inside my own body, as he slowly drew the blade back from my abdomen, crimson spilling down my legs.

ZAC LET OUT THE LOUDEST ROAR AND THE BRICKS THEMSELVES seemed to tremble. The walls groaned and shifted, dust filling the air as cracks split upwards towards the roof. Was that me? Did I shake the very foundations? It felt like an energy from my core had churned the earth, but then it was gone...

William's eyes grew wider, analyzing me... fearing me?

He turned round, only to find a silver stake swinging through the air, straight into the side of his head. Anna dropped it immediately with a sharp clang on the dirty floor and William slumped to the ground unconscious.

Standing over him, Anna stared at his head.

"Anna!" Alex yelled.

She snapped herself into focus and grabbed a stool from near the wooden altar. With a skittering of nervous mumbles, she climbed onto the stool and began working on my chains.

I looked hard into her eyes, but she refused to look back at me. Instead, she continued her twittering, this time clear enough to be understood. "What's a vampire's favorite holiday?" she squealed.

Her hands were shaking so hard that she couldn't get a decent grip on the chains. My weight bore down and prevented her from getting the leverage she needed to free them from the hook. The ends around my wrists were fastened with a padlock.

"You need the key, Anna," I urged.

She looked down at William and he twitched.

"Check his pockets," Alex called out.

A small groan escaped William's lips. Anna jumped, shaking her head violently from side to side.

"Fangsgiving," she shrieked.

I swear I heard Zac snort, but when I looked there was no sign of acknowledgement.

"You need the keys, Anna."

She stepped down from the stool and cautiously moved towards William. He groaned again, kicking out a leg. She yelped in fright and backed away.

"Now, Anna," Alex ordered.

"Please," I said. "Hurry, Anna. But release Zac first, before William wakes up."

She jolted at the sound of William's name and finally looked into my eyes. Her face crumpled. The normally rosy-red cheeks were deathly white, teeth chattering.

"It's okay," I said gently, the pain in my belly begging to differ. It didn't seem to have gone too deep, and I was pretty sure I'd have bled out already if it had hit anything major. But still, the blood trickled away. "Quickly."

She took a deep breath and thrust a delicate hand into William's pocket. He grunted.

Alex watched her like a lion, ready to pounce. Zac was practically unconscious. She should release Alex first, he was more able-bodied, but I couldn't go along with that notion. I needed Zac free from those hideous chains that were sizzling into his perfect skin.

"Why does Dracula have no friends?" she trilled, her hand fumbling deeper into his pocket. She drew out a set of keys and made back towards me. William mumbled, rolling over.

I shook my head frantically at her and she looked from me, to William, and back again... before grabbing the stool and hurrying over to Zac. He lifted his chin to re-assure her as she climbed up and fumbled with the lock.

Before I could comprehend it, William was back on his feet and lurching towards her. Alex growled, yanking on his restraints.

William grabbed Anna and dragged her down from the stool, pressing the blade against her throat.

"I warned you not to let me down, Anna-doll," he moaned into her ear.

"Because he's a pain in the neck," she screamed, as he threw her against the altar.

"Let's use your blood for this next spell," William hissed, raising the blade above Anna's trembling body.

THE STATIC NOISE INSIDE MY HEAD EXPLODED... ALONG WITH the small window at the back of the room, and the chains around Zac's wrists. Fragments of the metal flew through the air, some of which embedded into my skin with a brief, searing pain.

"Fucking cunt!" Zac scrambled across the room, the silver stake still protruding from his chest.

William slashed out with the knife and shouted random magical words that didn't make sense to me. They came out in a desperate chant, but they didn't help him.

Zac got hold of his throat and snapped his neck without a moment's hesitation. Quick and easy like he was a rag doll. William lay face down, except his head was twisted the wrong way on his body, staring up at me.

Then Zac fell to the floor at my feet, gasping for air. I yelled at Anna to get me down. My blood dripped onto Zac's leg.

He was a mess. I was a mess. Fucking hell, everyone was covered in blood.

"Thank fuck he's dead, that magic suppression was a bitch," Alex growled, staring at Anna. She took a step towards me, but he called her name and she faltered. Even my own stomach dropped at the low, icy voice he used.

He cocked his head and she hesitantly walked over to him with the stool. She was shaking her head, like she didn't want to do this, but one foot kept going in front of the other. The zombie-shuffle step continued, her glazed eyes locked onto his, even with me shouting at her to stop and let me free first.

She wobbled around on the stool, trying to release Alex from his shackles, and all the while he stared forward; serene, patient, a lazy smile on his lips. Double-skewered. One stake through his heart, the other through his stomach. He hadn't lost so much blood, the puddle beneath him was meagre compared to that where Zac had been.

With a final clank, he was free. Anna jumped back and cowered in a corner, sobbing. Deep, red stickiness covered the whole of her right side where she'd landed beneath Zac. She was the only one of us without any major injury, and yet the most covered in blood.

I expected Alex to release me right away, since Zac was still slumped and gasping in shallow half-breaths at my feet.

Instead, he stalked silently towards Anna. My blood turned to ice at the predatory way he moved.

"Alex," I called, but his slow approach in her direction didn't halt. After the momentary relief from William's death, fear once again clawed back up my throat.

"Run, Anna!" I screamed, but instead of fleeing she pressed her back to the wall like a mouse trapped by the cat. Nowhere to run or hide.

"ALEX, GET ME DOWN, I'M BLEEDING OUT," I YELLED, MY HEAD spinning. The pain and seeping sensation from my stomach was nauseating. At least my arms had gone numb, I couldn't feel anything other than pins and needles there, which was some consolation.

"Alex!" I screamed again. "*Zac?!*"

Standing right before Anna, Alex slowly and deliberately pulled the stake from his heart, and tossed it aside. As it left his body a powerful red stream spurted out onto Anna's chest. She finally tried to make a run for it, but it was too late.

He pulled her back into an embrace, and in doing so, the bloodied stake that was sticking out of his stomach went straight through her back and out her front. Her mouth opened in a silent and strangled cry.

"No!" The yell got lost somewhere in my constricted throat, coming out as a gargled whisper.

Alex glanced at me, before his teeth clamped into her neck. She carried on screaming in silence as he drank from her. The sound found its way out this time, my own screams echoing around the damp room and making up for her lack of noise. Her terrified and remorseful eyes locked onto mine, begging me to help her. Yet, I could do nothing other than watch.

I couldn't even muster any of the buzzing energy in my head. There was just helplessness. Emptiness.

He drank, and drank, and drank some more. It felt like the nightmare would never end. I kicked my feet at Zac, shouting at him to do something, but he didn't show any sign of life.

When Alex finished, he pushed Anna forward so that she came away from the stake with a disgusting tearing sound. Then he dropped her to the floor like she was trash. Her body hit the ground with a strange thunk. Dead meat on a hard surface.

He drew the remaining stake from his stomach and moved to stand before me, pressing a hand to my own abdomen.

"You're right, he missed vital organs or you'd be dead already," he said, removing his blood drenched t-shirt and tearing it into strips. He knotted them together and then around me, stemming the blood flow.

Fucking asshole could have done that after unchaining me. Why was I still tethered up?

He was waiting. He cocked his head and wriggled his fingers in a 'come at me' gesture.

"She was my best friend," I sobbed.

"She was a traitorous bitch. She colluded with a hunter to set us up in a trap and have us killed. And nearly got you killed in the process. There's no version of events where I'd have let her live." His shining, blue eyes had never looked so dark.

Zac groaned at my feet and tried to move. Thank fuck, he was alive. But holy shit, he did not look good. Never mind me, we needed to get him fixed right away.

"He's dying." Alex nodded casually at him. He reached up and grabbed my chains, snapping them with his bare hands. Guess mine weren't silver. The numbness left my arms in a vicious barrage of agony. It raced from my shoulders, down my biceps and erupted out of my hands. Alex took hold of me to steady my feet.

"He's going to die unless he feeds," he said.

I stared at him blankly. Anna's blood was smeared all over his lips.

A devilish grin crept over his face as he took my chin in his fingers and pressed those lips into mine, forcing them apart with his tongue. The metallic taste of blood made my skin crawl. Not because of his lips, or his tongue, but from the taste of her blood.

Then something even more unsettling happened. A surge of excitement swept through my core and settled between my legs.

He heaved a satisfied sigh and withdrew. "Welcome to the dark side, darlin'."

431

The moment his touch left me, the world hammered back in to view with force. The bubble popped. The haze cleared. And I wanted to vomit.

Zac groaned and tried to stand. He half charged and half fell into Alex, but ultimately ended up gasping on the floor again.

"Chill out, brother, I won't run off with your girl yet. I made a promise, I should at least keep it for longer than a few days," Alex crooned.

I dropped down, the stone floor biting into my knees, and wrapped myself around Zac. Taking hold of the stake, I was about to start pulling it out, but Alex stopped me.

"Not yet," he said. "He has little more than an ounce of blood left, you pull that out now and he'll lose it all."

I felt him hovering over us while I tried to cradle the slippery, bloody mess of Zac's body, tears blinding me. I let the sobs drown me, choke me. All of our dumb fights seemed so insignificant in that moment. There was no life without this man.

"Fucking hell, Jess! Do I have to go out there and grab a random woman off the beach to fulfill his need?" Alex stormed.

It finally clicked what he was waiting for. Ugh. How stupid was I?

I moved my wrist in front of Zac's face. He made a feeble effort at pushing it away, but his head lifted and his eyes changed, darkening with hunger. A low hiss came from somewhere deep inside him. I pressed my wrist to his lips again.

A sharp pang shot through me when his teeth sank into the delicate skin, immediately followed by a pleasing sensation. It ebbed throughout my being, this bewildering mix of sensual pain, as if it were me being healed. His body began

432

to straighten, his muscles tightened. Strength eased its way back into him.

I watched, fascinated by the sight of him drinking from me, but his face became more blurred as humming filled my ears.

"Alright, Zachariah, stop. She's already lost too much blood herself," Alex said, placing a hand on Zac's shoulders.

Zac gave an angry shrug and grabbed hold of my arm tighter. He buried his fangs in deeper and growled like a fucking lion. I pulled my arm back, but his grip was too tight. He yanked me closer. Shit. He wasn't going to let go. The room spun, the whooshing in my ears intensified.

I kicked and wriggled, bucking my whole body away from him. The pleasure diminished and left a burning ache through my arm as tightness closed in around my chest.

"Enough," Alex bellowed, this time landing a fist into the back of Zac's skull and pulling him away. He stood over him, a foot pressed into his ribs, and a hand on the stake. They stayed like that for a while, neither moving, a silent conversation passing between them.

"You got your shit together?" Alex still had a foot pressed firmly over Zac's chest.

Zac nodded, wiping a hand across his mouth.

"Good, because our men are arriving and they are confused as fuck about what they're suddenly sensing. William was fucking powerful if his other spells only just dropped. I'm out."

And with that he was gone.

Alex fled from one door, as Eva and Leon burst in through the other.

47

JESS

Zac ran his fingers tenderly over red marks where the chains had cut into my wrists. Of course, he'd healed now, back to full vitality in a matter of hours, and there I was a week later; still struggling with the stab wound to my abdomen, and covered in cuts and bruises. If only I had some of that magical regeneration power for myself. I was sure I could take a little of his blood and be healed, that's what happened in the books, right?

But instead of offering me his vamp juice, he just apologized for my pain and refused to try it. What was it William had said? About kinky blood-letting and having to kill me again? I knew that was the reason he wouldn't do it — too risky, too possible that he could make me a vampire if he did.

At least I was out of the horrific hospital bed and back to the comfort of Zac's mansion. His round-the-clock care was nothing short of doting.

I didn't know what to make of William's 'witchcraft in my ancestry' revelation, so I decided to file that away for now. It made a little too much sense and brought back terrible memories of the fire that killed my parents.

Remorse, uncertainty, anguish. I'd spent long enough trying to convince myself that maybe my unnatural outbursts were coincidental, nothing more than freakish events in nature.

Sure, deep down I'd always known. It was obvious that I was far from normal, and that I was dangerous to be around. But now William had cemented it into some sort of reality and it delivered me a fresh wave of soul-crushing guilt.

Don't even get me started on the Morena coven thing. I'd mentioned it once and Zac tensed up so much I thought he might combust. I didn't know if I wanted to hear it, anyway, because if I really was related to someone important to his past, then maybe the whole 'fated to be together' thing was a little too real. And twisted. Another notion to keep locked away for a while. At least until these damn wounds healed. Jeez, if I really was a witch, shouldn't I have been able to speed up that process by myself?

It was harder to put my emotions from Anna's death into a box. Her loss left a raw, gaping hole inside me. The loss of her life was my fault too, and I couldn't hide from that one.

Of course, William would have carried out his plan, with or without her help. He used her. Planted fear into her. I had no doubt that she believed she was doing the right thing to protect me. She proved that when she tried so hard to back-track and stop the shit-storm.

My sweet, funny Anna, with her flushed and dimpled cheeks, always pushing her glasses up her nose. The walking contradiction. The librarian lookalike who could switch to looking like a coked-up go-go girl in the space of two shots of tequila. She shouldn't be dead. I should have told her about Zac, about all of them. I could have made her understand before William worked his way into her head.

I taunted myself daily, running through every encounter, trying to work out if I could have picked up on what William was. I felt so stupid remembering all the clipped conversa-

435

tions and encounters. All that time he knew what Zac was, damn, he knew what *I* was.

He played us all. Biding his time, knowing what he was going to do and worming his way under Anna's skin, confusing her and warping her.

Zac would never have killed Anna, or let Alex, if he'd had any strength to step in. I'd pleaded with him to save her, to make her a vampire so that she'd be back in my life, but he insisted it was too late. She hadn't died with vampire blood in her system, so he couldn't help. As if he would have, anyway. Could you imagine trying to deal with that baggage? When he turned my friend into a vampire, but still refused to turn me?!

Instead, he'd been left to deal with the aftermath. He wanted to 'dispose' of the body, but I point-blank refused. I couldn't bear the thought of him handling her lifeless form like nothing more than a problem to be solved. She deserved a decent burial, with respect. If the police and pathologists started digging too deep on cause of death, well, then the vampires would just have to go and put their powers of persuasion to use.

I rolled painfully onto my side and snuggled into his chest. We lay in silence for hours, holding each other, sweltering heat making us stick together wherever our skin touched. My heat against his smooth coolness. Despite everything, he still felt safe. He filled up my whole being with more passion and desire than it could hold. It spilled out of me; in the way I looked at him, touched him, needed him. I'd finally found what I'd been chasing my whole life.

It was madness and chaos and heat, yet underneath all that, when he held me in silence, it was so much more. A calmness. At last I was satiated. I would never let go of that. Not ever.

I'd spent my life drowning in a sea of boys, barely

staying afloat, their weakness dragging me under... but here stood a man, ready to show me how to swim.

"Or die trying," Zac mumbled, reading my thoughts.

I squeezed him tighter. My life was light and heat. Fire had dominated me from way before I even became a firefighter. The torture of my parents' death, the visions of burning, the scar on my back. He was the opposite — darkness, and coldness. But together, maybe we could balance each other out.

As long as there was honesty. No more games, no more fighting.

———

"Did you know, before all this... that I was a witch?" I asked, stretching out my still aching body on his bed.

His bed. I'd been promoted from the guest bedroom and finally trusted with sleeping in his vicinity.

"No. I mean, yes and no. I suspected, but couldn't find any link to a coven, and your aura is so different. I couldn't be sure."

He'd never pushed me on it. He knew I was different, but he also knew how uncomfortable I was with that, how much guilt and anxiety it brought me. So he'd never chased me for answers, not directly.

I reached up and stroked his neck, pausing to rub the skin under his ear. He turned his head to the side and kissed my wrist. I felt his chest heave as he sucked in a breath and held it there.

His lips had brushed against the two little scabbed holes in my wrist. I didn't know what that meant, but neither of us had managed to talk about it yet. He'd fed from me, and I'd survived. Admittedly, Alex had to stop him, but still... it was promising, right?

He'd tasted my blood and he *had* stopped. He hadn't fought all wild and crazy once Alex pushed him away. This darkness that he thought would break loose hadn't appeared. Not as far as I could tell, anyway.

"Exactly," he murmured, burying his nose back into my hair. "You can't tell."

I cautiously crept on top of him, lying against his chest. "You'll never believe in yourself. But look at how much you've achieved already, not just with me, but with everything you've been through. You can control yourself through anything."

"You think you're safer now because I've drunk from you and didn't kill you?" His head shook. "You're so mistaken. The truth is, you're in more danger than ever before. The Beast knows exactly how good you taste... and fuck me, if you don't taste divine."

I kissed his collarbone, sliding a hand down his side, lower... lower. He shifted uncomfortably beneath me, abs tightening. "If it gets so much as a single drop of your blood again, it'll unleash seven shades of hell to break free and take more. But you know what? Fuck it. Fuck the darkness. I want to be inside you," he groaned, roaming his hands along my back and over my ass. "Now and always."

He rolled us over and pinned me beneath him, pressing between my legs. In a flurry of movement he removed his pants and my nightshirt. He crawled back over me, strained, eyes darkening with need, battling with light and dark.

My hips moved up to meet him and he slid into my eager opening. I cried out, grabbing his ass, pulling him all the way into me.

Moving with the utmost caution and care, his glorious shaft took me to heaven on a wave of gentle thrusts. Passionate, tense, bursting with need. But slow. Over and over... his whole body rigid and trembling, gripping the pillow beneath my head... he made love to me.

I kissed his cool lips, I sucked on his neck, I dragged my nails over his solid muscles, and not once did he retreat. Not once did any doubt flicker through his amber eyes. Locked in our heated stare, we sank into each other.

I disappeared into the wild energy that vibrated between us, drowning in the erotic, slow grinding of his hips. Lost to him. Lost *in* him. I could stay that way for eternity. Forever on the cusp of orgasm, every nerve in my body aching for release, handing myself over completely to his control.

"Jess," he breathed my name into the humid night like I was salvation, hope, life. I kissed him deeply and his tongue echoed the dance of his fingers, moving to the beat of my heart.

"Right here is where I belong," he groaned, lips grazing over my ear. "I'll take the pain... the burning in my veins... the aching need. I'll take that, every minute of the day, and I'll fucking slay it so I can stay here."

48

ZAC

$\mathcal{S}$omething was coming, closing in on us. Something huge. Leon's radar was going nuts... off the charts. It seemed like déjà vu, but Jess's arrival, whilst unsettling, had been a mere pinprick on the radar compared to this.

"It's bigger than anything I've ever experienced," Leon said, pacing the room.

"That's because it's the Bael. They're coming for me. Jess is in danger. *Fuck*, everything's in fucking danger." I slammed my fist into my own forehead.

I thought I was done running from them. After they killed Tobias I vowed no more. Fuck them, let them come and try to make me bond, try to make me one of their soldiers. I cared for nothing, no one. They could torture me, do whatever the hell they wanted, I wouldn't break.

But now a girl had my heart. How could I sit and let them come? They'd destroy her, they'd destroy me. I wasn't fucking strong enough to take them on, no one was.

They were an army of blood-crazed megalomaniacs, with strength and numbers. They enforced the laws, and anyone who threatened them was extinguished.

I'd angered Emory de Monsos for a long time, pushing my luck with my evasion of his demands.

How he would fucking love to see me fail. To have me crawl to them, to break, to submit and join the Bael...

"We need to get Jess off the island. *Now*." My shallow heart stirred into a frenzy. "We need to run."

BOOKS BY NICOLA ROSE

ALPHA ATTRACTION NOVELLAS

Breaking the Gladiator

EWLOOD LEGACY TRILOGY

Taste the Dark

Burn the Dark

Free the Dark

Are you ready to find out what Alex has in store for Jess?

What happens when the good guy goes bad, and the bad guy swoops in to save the day?

Read Burn the Dark now to find out! There's magic, and darkness, and angst galore!

ABOUT THE AUTHOR

Nicola Rose is from the UK, where she lives with her husband and two boys.

When she's not writing or reading, she can probably be found walking and cycling in the countryside, or playing boardgames in her pjs!

Find me on social media, I'd love to connect with you!

Even better, join my Facebook reader group and come at me with your views on the hottest badboys and anti-heroes of all time!

Nicola Rose's Romance Rebels

www.nicolarose-author.com
Nicola@nicolarose-author.com

ACKNOWLEDGMENTS

Thank you for reading Taste the Dark! I hope you enjoyed the Elwood Brothers as much as I enjoyed writing them!

This book was a long time in the making. It began in 2009 when I wrote half a story and then put it aside to focus on other things. It took the unwavering support of my family and friends for me to pull those files out and finish what I started all those years ago.

In particular, I'd like to thank Chelle, Sarah and Karen - who not only pushed me to get the book finished, but have also become fantastic beta readers and endured several rewrites in the process! You ladies are my rocks, I couldn't have done this without your encouragement (and cake, and games days)!

A massive thank you to the Bookstagram community - to the ARC readers, the bloggers and reviewers, the other authors who offer support and help each other to stand stronger... you guys are all amazing and I'm proud to be amongst you.

I must also thank my editor Mat, for giving it to me straight with the red pen and helping me sculpt the story into something far better than those original words.

Thank you to my husband for believing in me, for helping me to achieve this dream, and for patiently waiting a looong time before I let him read a single word! For being a brilliant Daddy to our boys, and an amazing husband, too.

Lastly, but by no means least, thank you to my mother-in-law, and apologies that I refused to let you read this. I guess I can't stop you now!

54587926R00278

Made in the USA
San Bernardino,
CA